THE VEVELLIS CHRONICLES

THE VEVELLIS CHRONICLES

THE CRESCENT AND THE CROSS

ZACK VARKARIS

For Munchando and Wackomolio
My greatest loves

AUTHOR'S NOTE

In writing this book, I tried, wherever possible, to use words, phrases, titles, military ranks, and units of measurement that were current during the fifteenth century.

For dates, I use the modern calendar, numbering from the birth of Christ not the Byzantine Creation Era calendar that starts from the supposed date of creation 5509 BC. So, 1440AD would have been recorded as the year 6949.

To the people of the late middle ages, Italy was a geographical area incorporating a collection of various city-states, not a political entity; Venice, Genoa, Milan, and the Papal States. The Greeks would have called all western Europeans by the generic name of Latins, as they thought of themselves as Roman. The Latins called the Byzantines, Greeks. The term Byzantine did not come into use until the eighteenth century.

The Ottomans were known simply as the Turk or Moslems. The Ottomans in turn, viewed the Christians as either the Catholics or the Greeks.

For the modern reader, I have differentiated calling them by the modern names of Byzantine, Italians, Ottomans, or from their respective Cities, depending on the situation.

CONTENTS

SAMARIA 1440 AD

*V*ergotis rested both hands on his knees as his aged body gave way under the relentless pace Nicola and Antonis had set. Taking in a deep breath, he felt the oppressive August heat fill his lungs, and shook his head as he glanced up to see the sun had not yet risen to its mid-morning height.

Resigning himself to his weakness in letting the boys persuade him against his better judgment to do this trip, he tugged the rein, and the stationary mule obediently followed along the path. The smell of heated rocks mingled with a hint of pine persistently assaulted his senses as he strove vainly to catch up with the boys. "Don't go too far ahead, wait for me," he shouted.

Their father had asked him to take the boys to see one of their 'estates', for soon, they would be men and it was time for them to know about the family holdings. It was on one of his regular trips and he saw no harm in it. Besides, how could he refuse his benevolent master such a mundane request? A quick sail from Chania and back; what was the harm in that?

All had gone according to plan until the journey back from Frangokastello. The boys, full of youthful exuberance, asked if they could quickly visit the narrow gates in the Samaria Gorge. The fastidious old man instantly refused, with a litany of reasons as to why they couldn't. Undeterred, they continued and in tandem, flipped effortlessly between Nicola's persistent energy and Antonis' reasoned logic, until he consented.

Now, he found himself under the searing Cretan sun, walking along a near-dry riverbed with sheer rock faces either side as they narrowed to the width of three men. Looking up to take in the natural splendour, he shook his head and chortled to himself. At least it wouldn't be long until they reached their destination and turned back. It was the first time in his sixty-plus years that he had ventured into the gorge and grudgingly admitted that it was wildly beautiful. Though, he always felt more at home in the safety of a farm or fortified house; adventure did not appeal to him.

Nicola excitedly bounced along the path, jumping from rock to rock that lay strewn on the ancient gorge floor. He always felt at his most happy when on some sort of quest, especially with his younger brother Antonis in tow. "Vergotis," he called, "We are going to climb up the rock-face here and walk down to the village on the higher path."

The groom eyed the clear footway some thirty feet above and gulped at the sight of the sheer face, but before he could protest, the boys were already climbing. Frozen with his outstretched hand, he watched as the two adroitly navigated their way through the tree-peppered outcrops towards the path overhead.

"You see, it's fine," shouted Nicola.

Vergotis' bland smile was lost in the distance.

"We will see you down in the village. Bet we get there before you do," said Antonis.

Realising the futility of giving them further instruction, he turned his mule around and started the trek back to the fishing village at the bottom of the gorge.

Looking down from their vantage point, Nicola placed his hands on his hips and theatrically breathed in a deep lungful of the thyme-infused air.

Standing calmly next to his brother, Antonis noticed how the kri-kri effortlessly clung to the sheer rock-face above him.

"If those old goats can do it, so can we," Nicola pointed out, "Let's climb up and walk down the ridge of the mountain."

Antonis looked up and a murmur of trepidation entered his throat. Though not as extrovert as his brother, he was no less brave and admitted that it would be fun to walk down along the ridge. He saw his brother wasting no time, take off his shirt, and begin to scale the perilously smooth rock-face.

Nicola's wavy dark blond hair flopped on his shoulders as he pulled himself up onto the small outcrop of rock. As the elder, it was natural to take charge. His shoulders began to glisten in the sun from the exertion of the climb. His torso was muscular, like a full-grown man's, not a boy's, one month off his fifteenth birthday. A heart-shaped birthmark the only blemish on an otherwise perfect physique.

Antonis inhaled deeply then took his first steps, following his brother up the slope. The boyish physique and wavy black hair in stark contrast to his brother's, even though less than ten months separated them. His slender limbs however, belied the fact that he could keep pace in speed and stamina, if not in strength.

Nicola paused halfway up the climb and looked up to the top of the ridge then turning to look down, saw his brother nimbly following. "We had better pick up the pace, Vergotis will start to panic if we take too long."

Antonis laughed, "So considerate, Nicola. But he is such a fussy old woman."

Nicola murmured agreement and turned back towards the ascent then felt the slap on his left calf, announcing that his brother had caught up. "Come on, you big lump." And with effortless ease, he surged up the cliff face.

Antonis paused on the small outcrop to draw breath and peer up the gorge. Beauty spread before him, leaving him speechless. He focused on the old fig tree, standing as it had for centuries; a number almost too great for his fourteen years of life to comprehend. His gaze followed above the line of the trees as the gorge narrowed to a point, the smooth rock faces reflecting the azure sky through its light sprinkling of quartz. He could feel the sun bearing down on him and started climbing once more.

Craning his head upward, Antonis saw his brother reach the summit and quickly disappear. Letting out a snort of defiance, he was not going to let him think he could not keep up, and promptly picked up his pace to join him. As he reached the crest, he padded his fingers around to find a good grip. Locating one, he braced himself for the final exertion. He yelped as a sharp pain seared his scalp and felt himself hauled bodily up by two rough hands that scooped him under the armpits and yanked him fully onto the top.

The sight that greeted him made his heart leap into his mouth. His brother stood sullenly in the shadow of a spectral-looking bandit. Antonis nervously sucked in every detail as he tried to process this new development and looked around to see who had grabbed him. Large bellies pulled in by wide leather belts, filthy beards, and lined puffy faces told the boy they were threatening but not frightening. Antonis gagged from the foul stench of a breath, when one laughed loudly in his face.

"Well, well, well, what do we have here? A couple of lost little boys? I wonder if anyone is looking for you right now?" said the leader whilst looking at the latest arrival.

Antonis' mind raced. *Does he know who we are? Who are these people? Can they be reasoned with?* The last thought had a calming effect on him, and he again took further stock of his surroundings in detailed precision. His larger brother stood morosely in the shadow of the tall thin leader, whose dark beard framed his hawk-like face with large, black, malevolent eyes. Their captors' unkempt worn boots were in stark contrast to the polished supple leather of the boys'. The situation seemed almost comical to him.

"What is your name? How dare you do this! Let us go at once," said Antonis. Surprised at his own clarity and firmness.

The bandit chuckled. "You are a feisty one. Very well, my name is Michalis. Now, tell me your father's name and for your sakes it better be worth it."

Antonis swallowed hard and the sound reverberated. Fear began to grip him as it dawned on him this outlaw was not bluffing. Now, he regretted persuading Vergotis so effectively. His eyes relented as he reasoned that brains would outwit brawn. "There is no reason to be angry with us. Our father is wealthy, Andreas Vevellis of Chania. If you don't harm us, I am sure he will be willing to pay handsomely for our safe release. You can send one of your men down to the village with a ransom note, where our groom is waiting for us. I can sign my name to it so that he knows it is genuine."

Emotionless, the bandit listened to the young boy and as he absorbed the words, his grip slowly began to relax on Nicola's shoulder.

Following his brother's voice intently, full of impotent rage at the situation, Nicola sensed an opportunity. Cautiously, he fixed his eyes on his brother, to convey a signal, while being careful not to arouse suspicion in the men flanking him, to whom he appeared broken, as he sagged under the brigand's hand. His gaze connected with Antonis' for a second, and taking that as the sign, he sank his shoulders lower as he implemented his hastily thought out plan. Slowly and very carefully, he reached down and pulled the small dagger from his boot, the one he used to peel figs with, and with lightning speed and all the force he could muster, stabbed the two-inch blade into the side of the leader's knee, who hollered in pain and fell writhing to the ground.

"Run!" yelled Nicola.

Quick as a flash, the two boys sprinted down the high mountain path towards the end of the gorge. Fear making them alert and agile as they leapt on the loose rock with a nimbleness that would have made the watching goats envious.

"After them, you idiots, and make sure you keep them alive, especially the big one," bellowed the stricken leader.

The boys were already out of sight, but the brigands knew there was only one place they could go, the village at the bottom of the gorge, and unless they grabbed a boat, they were stuck there, as no roads led out of it.

The path was relatively straight, without too many branches, or loose rocks in the way and before long, they crested the peak and ventured down towards the village; their legs aching and their lungs beginning to burn. The path widened and the trees became sparser as the mountain ridge flattened towards the water.

"What have you done, Nicola?" screamed Antonis, as they ran into the village.

"What had to be done, brother. There is a time for talk and a time for action, and it's better than finding out if he was going to keep his word," replied Nicola.

Agia Roumelli was really a collection of white-daubed one-storey homes more than a formal village. There were two shepherd huts at the end of the gorge on the flat plain that sprang into a pebble beach and splayed its way into the crystal-clear Libyan Sea.

Vergotis was wide-eyed with concern as he saw the children run towards him, instantly regretting his decision to let them go alone. Panting as they arrived, they couldn't relay what had happened fast enough.

"We had a little incident," said Antonis, recovering quicker than his brother. His tone measured, belying the enormity of what had just occurred.

"What kind of incident?" responded the worried groom.

Before Antonis could reply, Nicola blurted out the events without pausing to draw breath.

Vergotis listened to the deluge of information pouring out then looked around nervously, knowing they needed to leave at once. It took all his self-control not to show panic. "Quickly, get your horses, we need to get on our boat now." He hurried the boys, who dashed upstairs in focused silence to grab their knapsacks.

The tavern was a low-slung building, the eating area on the ground floor arranged around an open-hearth fire. To the left, was a staircase that led up to the second floor, where there were five rooms for guests; basic, but functional. It was deathly quiet. The innkeeper and his wife were present but apart from them, the place seemed devoid of life. This worried Vergotis, for he knew it wouldn't be long before the bandits found them.

"Hurry," he yelled. Seeing the boys come out of their room, he then turned to the door, where he was presented with the two fat bandits in the doorway. He tensed yet kept a calm composure and nodded tentatively. "Afternoon, gentlemen."

"You with them?" barked the one on the left.

Vergotis raised a weak eyebrow of incomprehension and turned to the boys—by this time at the bottom of the stairs—the panic now palpable in his eyes.

As the boys stood there, they saw their groom's face turn from fear to a surprised grimace as he looked down and saw the point of a sword sticking out through his stomach. Over his left shoulder, the smiling bandit twisted the blade. Antonis let out a scream of terror as Vergotis' hands splayed across his body then crumpled to the floor, while Nicola, ashen faced, pulled his brother, and ran through the door at the back of the room.

They entered a luscious walled-in garden, from which there was no escape. In desperation, they ran to the orange tree growing in the corner, their only chance of clearing the wall, and started to climb it. The other bandit rushed after them and grabbed them both off the branches and threw them unceremoniously to the ground, winding them both.

With a grunt and a shuffle, the leader appeared; blood running down his left leg and his face even paler than before from all the exertion. "You fucking brats. There isn't going to be any ransom. I'm just going to stick you both, and very slowly." Michalis bared his teeth like a wolf closing in on the kill.

The boys backed fearfully up on the ground as the three men stepped closer.

"Excuse me. Don't you know it's the height of bad manners to disturb a gentleman whilst he is bathing?" spoke a deep gravelly voice.

The three men spun around to see a man in a huge granite bath in the shaded corner of the garden under the vine trellis.

Michalis noted that he was a warrior; his armour and sword resting against the stone wall, but out of reach. He gave a thin smile as he scanned for any other threats then looked back at the man, only his head and shoulders rising above the soapy water. He had large, almost feminine brown eyes. The rest of his face was angular and defined, a roman nose over a square jaw with a full mouth. His dark hair was cropped short in the Genoese style, yet his accent was Greek. He had the outward appearance of someone you didn't trifle with even though he had a slight mocking look to him, which infuriated the leader. Anyway, what did it matter? they were three he was one, and unarmed.

"Mind your own business, I have no quarrel with you," rasped Michalis.

"Aye, that is true, and I should mind my own business; however, it does strike me as rather unjust to see that it takes three grown men to kill two little boys. You see, my sense of fair play just will not tolerate it."

The three bandits guffawed in unison.

"What are you going to do about it then, splash us with your bath water?" challenged one of the fat brigands.

The warrior calmly rose, stepped out of the bath, and kept rising to full height. A good head taller than the largest bandit, he was a bull of a man and his measured movements made him even more imposing. His right hand was holding a wet wash towel, the only visible weapon apart from the impressive one nature had given him. "Ready for your splash now?" he mocked.

With speed that surprised the boys, the two fat brigands rushed at the bather, swords raised for killer blows on either side. It seemed an eternity to the youngsters.

The warrior did not move, keeping his arms firmly to his side. The left sword aimed for a disembowelment and the right to cleave his head from his shoulders. As the left blade closed for the killing blow, he reacted. The speed was mesmerising, despite his size. Stepping to his right, he gripped the bandit by his wrist and with a deft touch, used the attacker's force against him and threw him onto the side of the huge stone vessel, knocking him unconscious. The other attacker swished his sword in the now vacant space and landed in a heap next to his comrade. Before either could react, he dispatched them with two perfunctory slashes to their throats.

"Well, looks like we have evened up the odds," he said to the remaining man.

Michalis knew he was beaten, and tried to kneel, begging for his life.

The warrior released his pose for a second but before he could do anything, Nicola sprang behind the kneeling man and stabbed him with full force in the throat. The bandit crumpled to the ground, gurgling in his own blood.

"That's for Vergotis," snarled Nicola.

The venom and composure of the boy surprised the naked warrior, who walked over to his pile of clothes and armour resting in the corner and rapidly dressed, being more than curious to discover what this was all about. "It's over now," the huge man said. "So, tell me, whose boys are you and who is this Vergotis?"

"We are the sons of Andreas Vevellis, and Vergotis was our father's groom, whom those bastards just murdered," Nicola spat out.

"Who are you?" enquired Antonis.

"Alexis Sartis and I think it is time I took you two home"

2

____

HOME

They sat silently on the deck of the boat as it cut through the rolling waves on its homeward journey. Alexis cast his watchful eye over them and shook his head at how fate had brought them together.

Taking stock of the situation, events had turned out as best as could be hoped for. The tavern keeper was very accommodating; probably due to a combination of how efficiently he dispatched the bandits plus the full leather pouch of gold. Together, they wrapped the aged groom's body whilst the boys looked on. They had not seen death before and he was at pains to show respect due to a loved one, carefully straightening the limbs and closing Vergotis' eyelids. The faintest wrinkle touched his nose as he murmured a prayer, his only tell-tale sign of the stench of split bowels as they wrapped the body in a linen shroud, offered by the handsomely paid tavern keeper.

Alexis had made way as soon as possible. Bandits invariably had friends and willing accomplices to exact revenge and the idea of standing guard all night waiting for a reprisal did not appeal. He had instructed the other boat to make its way to Chania, to deliver the amphorae of olive oil.

Springing back to the present, he walked across the deck to the boys and rested his huge hands on each of their shoulders in a sympathetic and genuine offering of consolation. Death was never easy but to experience the senseless killing of one so close was even harder.

"Why were you in that village?" asked Antonis.

The big man smiled. "I was on my way from Cyprus to visit an old friend in Chania, and decided I wanted to see the renowned Gorge. I was relaxing after my journey when you two happened along."

"Thank you for saving our lives."

Alexis nodded, "I regret not being there earlier." He gazed at Nicola, staring mutely into the deck, who had taken a big step to adulthood. "How is my young Achilles?"

Nicola did not respond.

Alexis paid it no heed for his heart went out to the lad, who would soon be home in the safety of his family.

Disembarked at the port of Chania, Alexis drank in the bustle of the Venetian-built harbour, the strong smell of fish piled high in baskets filling his nostrils. He smiled as he saw the fishwives shouting out to their customers, who, once engaged, duly haggled the price with a suitably aghast look on their faces.

Vergotis' bound body was loaded onto a mule and both followed the warrior as he trundled off towards Tavronitis. Knowing they would reach home before noon and sensing the proximity of their goal, the boys began to relax, and their steps synchronised exactly at double the speed of their newfound chaperone in worshipful obedience.

Maria's diminutive svelte frame had been shuffling around all morning, constantly peering towards the horizon for any approaching figures.

"Andreas, something is not right. Please send one of the men to find them."

"Don't worry, dear, everything will be fine. I'm sure Vergotis has just indulged the boys in one of their little adventures." The pinched brows were the only giveaway of an otherwise perfect lie. Then he turned to one of the staff. "Yiannis, get a couple of horses ready, will you? But keep it quiet," he whispered.

In hope, he looked towards the hills that separated his estate from the city of Chania. Seemingly, his prayers were answered as over the brow of the knoll, three specks appeared. He cursed at his aged sight and waited for them to get closer.

Noticing the strange figure and the clear absence of Vergotis warned him there was bad news in store as the boys began to rush towards the house.

Maria cooed happily as her son rushed towards her outstretched arms. Welcoming Antonis into her bosom, clutching him tightly and garrulously, voicing her pleasure at his return.

Nicola stopped short of running into his father's arms as he saw the stern look on his face.

"Where have you boys been? And where is Vergotis?"

The mention of their groom's name brought blank stares from the boys.

Andreas had seen it with his men on campaign many times, so now it was to find out the how. His composure softened and he asked them again where his old friend was.

The boys spilled out all that had transpired to their parents.

Andreas had all but forgotten the distant figure, his mind racing in a mixture of shock and relief at the extraordinary tale he was hearing. Maria wanted to reprimand them for suggesting such a foolish journey in the first place but thought better of it.

Leaving the mule tethered at the gate, Alexis entered into the courtyard as the duo started to recount the final part of the tale.

"Yiassas," the huge stranger said.

Andreas' shoulders tensed. The voice was gravellier but the pitch he recognised, yet the man who stood before him couldn't have been more different than the memory he attached it to. "Alexis? Is that you?"

"None other, Strategos. Have I changed that much?"

"Well, it's been eighteen years and a lot can happen, no?"

As they clasped each other like father and son rather than long lost friends, the boys and their mother looked on perplexed. Then it occurred to Antonis that this might be the friend he was coming to visit.

"So, you were the man in the bath who saved my boys? I hope they did not dishonour me too much and we will see how true their story is when I hear it from you."

"It will be. Of that, I am sure."

Andreas believed his old friend and their unexpected reunion filled him with joy. He wanted to drink and be merry, to recollect the old days, but his heart was heavy at the loss, and his first instinct was to attend to that. "Did you bring Vergotis' body?"

"Yes, Strategos, he rests outside upon the mule."

Alexis followed as the old general wandered out to see the linen-bound cadaver.

Carefully, Andreas came upon his groom and rested a hand on the lifeless form, his face grimly controlling his emotions. "Go in peace my old friend," he whispered then stood by the corpse for a few moments, talking to it in such hushed tones that Alexis could not make out what he spoke. Having said his goodbyes, he called one of the servants to remove the body to a storage room and to fetch a priest for burial the following day. Satisfied, he turned back to Alexis. "He shall be buried in the family plot," A sad smile cracked across his face. It was a bitter-sweet reunion, he mused. "Come, tonight we shall reminisce."

Cradling a cup of wine Alexis listened to the symphony of

Cicadas at their high point of the day whilst the sweet smell of geraniums washed over the atrium of the house, lulling him into a sense of calm.

"So, tell me my long-lost friend, what has happened to you during these past years?"

3

THE JOURNEY BEGINS, 1441

Antonis turned from his Mother's fussing and glanced at his Father. The look of pride on Andreas' face as he clasped his adopted son to his bosom, shot bolts of jealousy through him. He saw the difference in Nicola, his shoulders seemed broader and his back straighter, appearing more fully-grown than before. A glow emanated about him that made Antonis shrink. Yet, it was the unspoken gestures that hurt the most, the warm glances, the outward show of pride, and worst of all, the paternal approval that his brother had shown such extreme courage in attacking the bandits. He also noticed for the first time how similar they looked, not facially or in colouring, but in physique and poise.

"W-w-w-we did good, did good, didn't we, Father?" he chimed in nervously.

Andreas paused enough for his son to notice. "Yes, you both did well," he responded kindly.

Maria's heart went out to her boy, seeing how her husband favoured Nicola. She felt that Andreas being such a physical man, would of course be unduly harsh on Antonis because his own flesh and blood did not live up to his high martial standards. He had never come to terms with Antonis' physical weakness and it clouded his view of his other qualities; an alert mind and clear vision of situations.

She had no such misgivings and knew he was destined for great things. Antonis had that air of deep confidence, which came with great men. Though hidden right now under adolescent flaws, she sensed his time was yet to come.

After retiring to their chamber together for the first time since Alexis had returned with the boys, Maria lay cradled in her husband's arms. The aroma of geraniums mingling with their bodies filled their senses and lulled them into a calm serene state.

"Is everything all right, my darling?" she intoned.

"Yes."

"I mean between you and Alexis?"

"All is just fine, my dear."

"Is there something you're not telling me? This is about Antonis, isn't it?"

"Not just him, it's about both."

There was a surge of fear in her breast as she looked neutrally into his eyes.

"Well, they are of an age when they need to begin learning the ways of the wider world."

"But they are not even fifteen yet, they are still children," she countered.

"The Spartans sent their boys at seven to the Agoge," Andreas replied.

"That was two thousand years ago and a more barbaric time."

"It was certainly more ancient but no less barbaric. We are wracked with war, the Turk is constantly knocking at our door, and the freedom of the Greeks is in serious jeopardy for the first time in our long history. And because of it, they don't have the luxury to be children anymore."

Maria listened in silence; her maternal instincts anxious for her son. His stammer would make him an object of ridicule in the outside world, needing the protection of his bigger brother. Andreas had adopted Nicola after Zenon's untimely death, his compatriot in arms, treating him as one of his own, and she loved him dearly for that. She loved Nicola too, but he was not of her blood, and naturally favoured Antonis.

Andreas didn't share the same fear, asserting the boys would look after each other. Alexis would be like a father to them, protecting and nurturing them. "Maria, do not worry, they will only be gone for two to three years."

"Three years? Will I even recognise them when they return?"

"They will be men by then, my love."

Maria suppressed her dread at the thought of losing her children. "I know you go back a long way, but who is this Alexis, that you trust him so?"

Andreas sighed deeply and clutched his wife a little tighter. "He was the son I didn't have back then. He joined the Laconians as a boy, not much older than ours are now. At the siege of '22 he saved the city and protected the Emperor from the assassin's blade. Which set me free to return to Crete to start a family of my own with you. A man of proven courage and loyalty, he was the only man I trusted to command the Laconians then, and is the only man I trust with my sons' lives now." He caressed his wife, feeling her tension ebb but knew that some trying times lay ahead.

STANDING in the courtyard of the house at dawn, the boys listened intently as Andreas told them they would be leaving with Alexis and going to Mistras in the Peloponnese to begin their instruction in becoming gentlemen. He trusted him with his sons' lives, but still felt the need to give guidance about how to deal with them. They discussed at length their plans for the boys, from philosophers and clerics to the musicians and poets they would meet. Of course, their martial training was not going to be neglected, but under Alexis, no better teacher could they wish for. The following few days were abuzz with activity.

Maria noticed how excited the boys were on their last day, though each expressed it very differently. Her son was quiet and pensive, observing the commotion around him, his demeanour almost catatonic. Nicola was robust in his actions, helping carry the heavy packs to load on the mules, and running around at a frenetic pace.

As they drew out of sight, Alexis looked upon the boys and felt daunted at the depth of trust placed in him. Silently he said a prayer, vowing to protect them from all danger to his dying breath.

4

INTRODUCTION TO PHILOSOPHY,
1441-1443

The journey via Methone flipped between fizzing energy and morose silence. A twinge of envy entered Alexis' thoughts, these boys had led a sheltered and charmed life in Chania. At their age, he had been full of hurt and anger caused by abuse at the hands of his alcoholic father. It had made him strong, but at a price.

He started planning what training the boys were to be given at Mistras; they would receive tutelage from Gemistos Plethon, the finest mind in all of Byzantium, in fact, all of Christendom. He thought it ironic that a Frankish-built castle would become the cultural seat of the remnants of the free Greek-speaking people.

The Vale of Sparta was especially rich for this time of year, the slopes on the mountains green and lush, the river burgeoning upon its banks; its movement sending out cooling airs and calming noises. The refreshing smell of thyme permeated the whole valley.

Antonis let out a long sigh, as the road coiled with many blind turns, making a mile feel like five. Reaching the final bend, a town presented itself nestled at the foot of the mountain. The

20

boys looked up the escarpment, at the buildings that had been built upon it over centuries, and as their heads moved up, they saw the fortress set atop like an eagle's eyrie.

"It looks like Samaria, but with more buildings," enthused Nicola, as he picked up the horse's pace, taking the lead ahead of Alexis.

The procession continued up the spiral-winding path that clung to the mountainside and just as in the valley below, every turn presented itself with a new vista or building that had been constructed with ancient precision. Halfway up to the castle, the view broke and the red-tiled domes of the Panatanassa Convent came into view.

Sensing they were close, Nicola turned, looked over the haunches of his steed, and saw the Spartan Plain arrayed before him. For the first time it really felt that he had left the safety of home. Then the road became bereft of dwellings again, as the mountain slope steepened before the final leg to the stronghold.

"Ah-ha, Alexis, where have you been?" bellowed an old man.

His voice, whilst loud, was measured and forceful and it took both boys by surprise. They turned to stare at the man who had spoken.

Of middling height and slight build, his thick white hair was combed back into a ponytail. The long beard was curled in the antique Persian manner. His face was ancient and weathered except for his eyes, which burned with fire and bored through the visitors. The old man moved with alacrity to embrace Alexis, the sight only making him appear frailer compared to the hulk of their mentor.

"Mastre, I see that you have lost none of your energy; you must be one hundred years old," the smile made Alexis look boyish.

"Not quite, my pupil, but I will still be a match for you at the lectern."

Alexis laughed; it was always a pleasure to see him.

"Who are these young men?" *Had Alexis decided to adopt a couple of strays?*

Both boys pulled their shoulders back, standing to attention.

The old man eyed them up and down as if they were on a parade ground, enjoying the theatrics. Going first to Nicola, he gave a loud dismissive snort. As he turned his head to stare at Antonis, shuffling along, he bore at a point between his jaw and neck, making the young man feel very uncomfortable. "What is your name, boy?"

"An… An… Antonis Vevellis."

"And you?"

"Nicola Vevellis."

"What is your name?" asked Antonis.

The old man turned his head and concentrated his gaze on him, who didn't flinch, though he desperately wanted to. "I am Gemistos, and in time, you will get to know me a lot better."

"W… wh… who was that?" asked Antonis, stammer back, defiance gone.

"That is Plethon. There has not been so keen a mind for centuries and it is he who will be teaching you."

The boys looked at each other and nervously laughed, not understanding quite why.

"Come, let us go to the barracks and I will show you where you are staying," continued Alexis and as was happening more often, the boys trotted along behind their mentor.

MANY DAYS PASSED and the boys began to get restless. Alexis had left them in their billet, leaving them to their own devices whilst he had been talking and meeting with a great many people in the city, only occasionally popping in to tell them to collect firewood or do an errand.

"I… I thought we were going to learn something. Why are we just sitting around?" said Antonis.

Nicola did not mind the wait, as he tuned out of his brother's droning. They had seen Plethon wandering around, yet, the old man never acknowledged them. It did not matter; he was just enjoying the different flavours that people and the hustle and bustle of the city presented. There was none of the Venetian influence, here it was purely Greek. "Relax, Antonis, I'm sure Alexis is just busy. He will get around to us."

Antonis let out an exasperated sigh, that spurred his brother into action. Grabbing him by the shoulder, Nicola led him out of the billet to go exploring.

Surreptitiously, they crossed the square and found a door ajar in the castle wall. Hastily, they entered and followed the long corridor studded with doors. They tried one and finding it unlocked, sneaked through into a dark room with voices talking at the far end. Nicola carried on whilst his brother gripped his arm firmly.

"We had better get back," hissed Antonis.

Nicola shook his head and pulled his arm free of his brother's grip. Antonis lost his footing and landed with a thud.

The voices at the far end of the darkened room stopped abruptly and both knew they had been discovered. Quickly, they hurried out as fast as they could and rushed back down the corridor to the exit and into the square. As they entered the light, their smiles of relief dissolved as they saw an awaiting Plethon, who looked at them sternly.

"You know why you boys are here?" he asked.

Both shook their heads, then Nicola offered, "To receive an education, sir."

"Correct."

"But we have sat in our billets for two weeks, doing nothing. Why are we here? I thought we were supposed to be learning something." said Antonis.

Plethon chuckled. "Education comes in many guises. There is more to learning than swordplay and books."

The boys looked quizzical.

"Patience is a virtue that must be respected and understood, and that has been your lesson. Inquisitiveness is another such virtue and in both, you have done quite well so far."

The boys puffed out their chests in pride.

He walked them back to their room and when they entered, they saw a small pile of books, sheets of paper, and writing implements wrapped in leather set out on their beds.

"Bring these with you tomorrow to the Church of St. Dimitri. I will see you there at dawn."

The boys sat down and looked at what was left for them. Thumbing through the books of philosophy, law, and mathematics they also noticed books from the East, which meant nothing to them presently. Nicola cast them on the bed, picked up his dagger and started to sharpen the blade. Antonis began to thumb through the first book. They spoke no more and each concentrated on his own task.

They awoke before dawn replete with excitement, Nicola eagerly opened the shutters and looked out to the clear pale blue dawn sky. They dressed silently, and with anticipation, took their leather writing sets.

Making the short journey to the church, Antonis noticed how simple it was, but welcomed the cool air as they entered.

Plethon greeted them and led them into an antechamber that was filled with books and had a large old wooden table with benches on each side. "Take a seat, boys."

They duly obeyed.

"The books in front of you will constitute your lives for the next few months. You will learn about our history and culture as well as those of our rivals and friends. You will also come to understand mathematics and why it is so important to our daily lives. Finally, you will learn about politics and the law, and why these are the codes we live by. These things separate us from the barbarians and make us civilised men. Now, you both can read, can you not?"

The boys nodded in silence, unsure of what they were supposed to do.

Plethon smiled. *A good start. Now, let's see what they've got.* And the next few weeks were spent in deep study of all these texts.

He was a hard taskmaster, driving them forward, starting with the Greek philosophers, followed with the Roman historians, and finally Byzantine law, drumming into them the two and a half millennia of their history. Weeks turned into months and summer gave way to autumn then winter. Both learned all their tasks with great ease and he was impressed with their ability to absorb information and negotiate it with clarity.

Antonis showed a great deal of interest in the radical teachings of the ancient philosophers, especially Plato—his view of an equal society where the individual answered for his actions to the body politic, seemed so logical and clear to him. In contrast, Nicola marvelled at the Heroes, such as Lysander and Odysseus and their exploits. However, what Plethon remembered most was an interesting moment when they were discussing Alexander the Great and all his achievements. Neither would agree with the other; in the end they agreed to disagree, though it carried on between them in low intensity for weeks.

Their only respite from learning was the gymnasium, where they practised athletics, riding, wrestling, and swordplay under the tutelage of Alexis and a tough lochias called Gouzaris. Nicola excelled in all. The only time his brother matched him was in archery and knife fighting; his greater concentration and patience better suited for the bow and his slighter frame allowing more rapid moves, though, only just. The boys enjoyed their time at the agoge and looked forward to their daily practice.

On a particularly chilly January morning, Plethon went

along to see them at training, the crisp air numbing the end of his antique nose. In silence, he watched with Alexis as Gouzaris instructed them in close quarter wrestling.

"Mastre, I've noticed you have not taught them much of the Christian faith," Alexis said.

"That pastiche of religions melded into an incoherent pile of horse manure," snorted Plethon.

"That may be so, but they still need to know and make up their own minds. I want them to be fully versed and understand the faith aspects of our culture before I take them to Court in Constantinople. You know that the Blachernae is a dogmatic nest of vipers and they need to be able to conduct themselves in those matters."

"Alexis, I have lived a long time and my way has stood that test."

"Understood, Mastre, but we must work with what we have today. I am but a simple soldier, I can teach them the art of war, but I need your help, or at least a competent priest to help me teach them the importance of Christ."

Plethon stuck out his bottom lip in puerile disdain. "Very well, though, it will not be me. I have a good friend who is an intellectual sparring partner of mine, The Bishop of Patras, Gregorios. Though a true believer, he will give them a balanced view."

"Fine. When can he come here?"

"I will write to him. He will probably be able to come next spring."

"Hmm, a long time, but if he is as good as you say, then we shall wait."

Plethon chuckled to himself at the younger man's attempt at control.

Alexis looked over at the boys' stick-fighting. Antonis had measured footwork, more cautious in his approach, waiting for the attack then sidestepping with a counter-attacking move.

Nicola's aggression was focused and structured though he relied on his mesmerising speed and skill, not thought, to get himself out of attacks and lunges.

THE BOYS GREW in mind and body, matching the blooms of spring. Antonis still raged against the world as he saw it, siding with the radical thoughts of his mentor, discounting the deep traditions the empire had created over the last millennium. Nicola found solace in his peoples' history, the art, and codification of law that enabled a civilised society to govern itself.

"We have much to be proud of," said Nicola one day after a particularly interesting recount of the repulsion of the second Arab invasion in 717 AD.

"Pah," replied Antonis, "fat lot of good it's got us now. Enemies surround us, Christian and Muslim alike. We need help to defend ourselves, and the Emperor must pay tribute to the Sultan. What are we doing about it?"

Plethon listened intently. They truly were gifted, but with wildly differing views. He felt sadness, knowing these divisions would only increase as they grew and forlornly asked the universe to spare them that torment.

Alexis, frustrated at the non-arrival of Plethon's friend, insisted they start learning the teachings of Christ and made the boys attend church. Neither enjoyed it very much, finding it boring and tedious.

They were not the religious type, something that amused Plethon immensely, who decided to announce. "I received a letter from the Bishop. He will be here before the summer solstice, a couple of months late, but better late than never."

"Well, I want them ready before the winter sets in," replied Alexis.

. . .

HEAVY GREY CLOUDS spewed bullets of water onto the roof of the veranda the men were using as protection. "I have never known weather like this before," said Alexis.

"I have. It was the year the Tartars at Ankara annihilated the Turks. Perhaps it is an ominous portent," reminisced Plethon, something he was prone to do. How could Alexis blame him? He had already been in his fifties when that event occurred forty years ago.

Flanked by two outriders, a plush carriage pulled by four fine greys clattered into view. Golden double-headed eagle insignia popped on the plain black livery. The vehicle screeched to a halt in front of them.

The window pulled down and a portly bald man with a bloom on his nose stuck his head out. "Plethon, you old goat! You haven't aged a day! Tho good to thee you," lisped the high-pitched voice.

"You, on the other hand, have a much bigger bloom since the last time we met, Gregorios," replied Plethon mockingly while stroking his nose.

The man smiled and waited for the carriage driver to open the door for him. He was as wide as he was tall, with pock-marked sallow skin, which even his thick cleric's beard could not hide. His priest's clothing was plain, a long black frock and a cap simply adorned with a wooden cross. The men embraced. Although the bishop was much younger, they both looked of a similar ancient age.

"Gregorios, I would like you to meet Alexis Sartis."

"An honour, your grace," replied Alexis and, unusually for him, leant down to kiss the bishop's hand in the reverent fashion, an action that surprised Plethon.

"I read your letter, Gemithtoth, and wath intrigued, tho have dethided to come and thee how I can help you."

The three men went inside and started their discussion on the way forward.

In the months that followed, Gregorios instructed the boys in the way of the Lord. However, he did not just stick to the teaching of the Nicene Creed. He also taught them other religions—Islam, Judaism, Buddhism, Hinduism, Confucianism, even the pagan Greco-Roman gods. He saw how the boys absorbed all he said with gusto and their perception changed almost overnight, as they now saw the purpose of the power of belief and spent hours discussing the merits of different religions.

"The true sword of Allah shall smash your infidel shield, my brother," chirped Antonis as he lunged towards his brother.

"The wall of Christ will smash the brittleness of your heathen blade," responded Nicola and blocked his brother's slashing movement.

These repartees carried on incessantly in anything they did. Sometimes, Nicola was a Hindu battling his Greek god brother. Other times, Antonis was a Confucian arguing against his Buddhist opponent. Strangely, Gregorios noted, neither took to the Zoroastrian faith as a role model, which he regarded as a shame for there was something magical about the fire and light of that most original of religions.

Plethon chuckled to himself as he turned to Alexis. "I knew Gregorios would inspire them. See how they now apply those principles of faith in their everyday lives?"

"Yes, you were right. Though, it's strange how they seem to favour different ones, but they choose the faith that suits their personality," replied Alexis as they continued watching the boys stick-fighting, each calling upon their personal deity.

"This is what religion is, gentlemen, a framework around which a man can construct his reality," said Gregorios as he shuffled up to them. "Although, these boys need to be careful in the way they speak, as it could be construed as heresy from on all sides. Such flexibility and vision of mind makes ordinary men fearful. Alexis, you must teach them this lesson before they reach court and the outside world. They are no longer children but fast becoming men, who will not be forgiven such transgressions as easily."

THE LONG SULTRY summer passed into the welcome cooler haze of autumn, which heralded the first unwelcome and abundant snows of winter that fell early that year. The Taygus Mountains were majestically capped in white, well before the end of November, with a cold wind that constantly blew, chilling everyone to the bone.

"Marvellous, another miserable winter to endure and we are still not through December," quipped Alexis.

"Wait until you get to my age," replied Gregorios.

At that, they saw Plethon walking across the square with his usual spritely step.

"It doesn't seem to affect him."

"He is a freak of nature. I have no idea how he does it," replied the portly priest.

"It has been nearly six months now and I think the boys are ready to move on to court with me," Alexis said.

"They have absorbed all I can teach them. At their young age, their knowledge is far greater than a great many supposed wise men that I know. But remember of what I warned you, they must control their radical thoughts, especially in the company of powerful, weak-willed, avaricious men."

"I have. It will be hard for anyone to teach them these things in the presence of both yours and Plethon's subversive views. I understand he is an open philosopher and is expected to be that way, but you are a man of the cloth and I never imagined that of you," replied Alexis.

"It takes all sorts to make up a world," said Gregorios.

"And that is why he is my friend," added Plethon, who joined them. He stood for a moment before continuing, "Alexis, I know you have not been paying attention to the events that are going on in the outside world for some time, but I think you need to speak with the Governor."

Alexis was surprised at the suggestion. But it was true he had neglected politics during the last few months, only concentrating on the boys' training. This period had been very relaxing, and he had had a chance to forget all the intrigues of the outside world, not even giving it a single moment of thought.

But as requested by Plethon, he visited the quarters of Theodore II, who, as usual, was dressed in his ubiquitous plain black doublet and leggings of the finest quality money could buy.

"My Lord, you sent for me?"

Theodore sat behind his large oak table piled high on either side with books and parchments, his head in the middle as if he were poking his cranium between the crenulations of academia. He did not pause in his writing, merely nodded for the man to sit. "Do you know why we have summoned you?"

"No, my Lord," Alexis responded.

"We have been speaking with our brothers and have decided that it is in the best interest of the family that we exchange our dominions in the Morea for Selymbria.

Alexis looked perplexed. "But… my Lord, surely this is a far more powerful territory in which you have created such serenity and prosperity."

"Agreed, but our brother Constantine is a more energetic man and would be better suited to rule here. We, on the other hand, have to prepare ourselves to become the emperor at Constantinople, and so would be better to be located nearer to it."

Who am I to argue with the next Emperor of the Eastern Empire?

"Therefore, because of this, I would like you to be my emissary and travel to Selymbria to parley with our brother."

Alexis sat there impassively, trying to take in the enormity of what had just been said.

"Furthermore, I wish for you to remain in the city as I think sane heads will be required there in the coming months. I get a sense that the long truce we have with the Turk is soon to be shattered and we will need well-trained and practiced men of war such as you, to be at hand."

"I understand, my Lord. However, the Laconians are stationed here, under my command, and I must follow orders."

Theodore stroked his chin, admiring the man's dedication to his duty, but his presence was needed in the capital at this sensitive juncture. "Leave your second in command to lead the brigade until your return. It is imperative that you undertake this mission."

So, it is settled, I will be going to Constantinople, and the boys with me. Much earlier than expected.

Alexis wandered over to the agoge where the boys were deep in training with Gouzaris. The sergeant was a good man, very stern, but fair. A competent swordsman with many years of training under his belt, he had taught them all the underhanded tricks one would need to survive in battle.

He studied the squat body with short legs and long arms, much like an island fisherman, balding slightly with grey hair, and a wide-open earnest face. His strength was legendary amongst the brigade as well as his stamina and tolerance to pain, which had been tested on many occasions.

"Do you think the boys are ready?"

The sergeant rubbed his head and paused for a moment. "Nicola is gifted, probably the most gifted pupil I have ever had. His speed, power, agility, and instinct are second to none. However, he is of an open heart, a dreamer, and that will be a problem, as he trusts people too readily, but has great loyalty."

"And Antonis?"

"Whilst not as natural an athlete as his brother, he has steel inside of him, and a cruel streak too. He has picked up all the dirty tricks and will use them ruthlessly. His focus is superb, which makes him great with the bow and his killer instinct makes him deadly with the dagger."

Alexis nodded, fair assessments. "Gouzaris, it is time we moved on," he said sharply, pulling himself away from his reverie. "We will be going to the capital, as there is work to be done in the Queen of cities."

"Permission to speak freely, sir?" replied the sergeant.

"Always."

"May I suggest that you give the boys a weapon of their own, as a rite of passage."

Alexis pondered momentarily on the notion. It was now over two years, and both had studied hard and excelled with no complaints, whining, nor any outward sign of homesickness. "What a good idea. However, they should have something that is suited to each of them and their individual personality."

Gouzaris agreed and they continued the discussion to find a suitable reward.

It was an ordinary day for the boys and as usual, they had completed their daily run and were about to commence their afternoon of studying, only this time, there were no books or quills, only Alexis, Plethon, Gregorios, and Gouzaris standing behind the now familiar long oak table.

Nicola looked at his brother with alarm in his eyes. Antonis didn't show any emotion, yet both knew something serious was about to happen.

Alexis stood in the centre, a clear head-and-shoulders taller than the rest, with Plethon to his right and Gouzaris to his left. Gregorios sat, as he couldn't stand for too long due to the excess weight he carried. It wasn't the fact that they were all there that concerned the boys, it was that all carried serious sombre faces.

"Sit down," gestured Alexis.

The boys obeyed.

"You have been training here at Mistras for over two years and in that time, you have learned and excelled in every task and lesson set before you."

The boys smiled though their eyes were still wide, betraying their apprehension.

"However, you are now no longer boys but rather young men, and as such, must be treated accordingly." Alexis looked at Gouzaris and nodded for him to continue.

The sergeant stepped forward to the front of the table. "You boys have studied hard with me and earned my respect. Antonis, you are an exceptional bowman with a keen eye and calm pulse, and so I give you this compound bow made in the eastern fashion." He turned, picked up the bow and quiver and gave it to the young man.

Antonis marvelled when he saw it. It was of perfect proportions, made of animal horn with layers of ivory and ebony, and bound with resin. It had not been strung, as that was for him to do, after all, it was his bow now. The quiver was a functional leather case, sturdy, with a cap to prevent the arrows falling out, with a quick release catch. "Thank you, sir." Saying no more as he lovingly stroked his new prize possession.

The lochias turned, "Nicola, you have displayed excellent speed, footwork, and strength, so I give you a sword as your weapon."

Nicola smiled and took the hilt. When he withdrew it from the scabbard, he saw that it was no ordinary blade. True, it had the classic handle and hilt and the blade was broad, but it had a curve at the tip, like a scimitar. The blacksmith had moulded the balance and precision of the Eastern blade with the weight and power of Christian steel. It was truly a marvellous weapon and this fine tool was also housed in a plain, functional scabbard of waxed leather.

Gouzaris stepped back and Plethon came forward, theatrically shuffling a little more than usual, and gave one of the two leather bound books he was holding to each of them.

The boys looked and saw that they each had different books.

"Antonis, I give you 'The Republic', so you may hone your views on how a society must run. You have shown a great deal of interest in that great philosopher's opinions and I want you to keep this so it will always remind you of man's responsibility to his City."

Antonis nodded in thanks as he cradled the book.

"Nicola, to you I give Xenophon's writings, a hero in the truest sense, a man of honour who had glory thrust upon him when he did not seek it, and saw it through to success, protecting his people without compromise. This is how you should live your life and this book will remind you of that."

Nicola smiled proudly, clasping the precious object to his heart.

Plethon looked at both brothers. Now they were young men, not the boys who had arrived in earnest uncertainty two years ago.

The Bishop did not rise from where he sat but slid two books swiftly across the table, which made the boys move quickly to catch them before they fell to the floor. "You have to share these," he told them.

They took the books off the table and looked to see that one was the Bible and the other, the Holy Qur'an. They looked quizzically at Gregorios. Even by his standards this was unusual.

"Always know thine enemy, and what better way than their rule book."

Finally, Alexis came to the fore. His hands clasped behind his back, he paced around the table to look more closely at his wards.

"Your father would be proud of how you have progressed.

He entrusted me with your care and as this is a rite of passage, where you have gone from being boys to young men, I thought of something that will remind you of our meeting, the fact that you are brothers, and so must stay together always." With that, he pulled out from the folds of his cloak two sfakions—the traditional fearsome Cretan dagger—that looked more like a short sword than a knife. On the hilts, one was engraved with an A, the other with an N, and Alexis handed them over. "Your bravery in the gorge was tremendous that day, so keep these close forever to remind you of home, and probably will save your lives on more than one occasion," he added the last bit with a wry smile.

The boys were overwhelmed with the recognition and gifts that had been bestowed on them and instantly began comparing the relative merits of their newfound possessions.

"Ha-ha, you could never reach me with that sword because I would have you with my bow before you came within striking distance," said Antonis, in a rare moment of braggadocio.

"Hmm, well, you better hit a killer strike otherwise I will have you," replied Nicola.

Seeing them playing like children annoyed Alexis and he moved swiftly to intervene. But a spidery ancient hand clasped his forearm.

"Leave them be. You were young once, don't you remember? It is the last time they will get to be this way." Plethon interjected gently, as he noticed the look of angered concern on Alexis' face.

The big man relented for sadly he knew the philosopher was right.

5

THE EMPEROR

High on the deck Alexis pondered the effects that the swapping of territories would have to the chain of power; Theodore's messages concerned him. If he was correct in his predictions, the future was certainly bleak. The first stop was to be Selymbria, then, after a parley with Constantine, to the capital.

The captain of the Carrack, a gruff Rhodian, who went by the name of Nico, sailed close to the shore so the boys could see the fluttering red crescent pennants of the Turkish coastal towns. The brothers gawped at the brightly coloured palette slowly unfurling before them. Their knowledge of the Ottomans had been solely at the study lectern but now they were witnessing the reality.

"Are the Janissary as good as they say?" asked Nicola.

"Better," replied Alexis.

"Why are they better?"

"Because they are fanatics, and believe their faith is stronger than any sword."

"The power of an idea is stronger than any army," Antonis quoted one of Plethon's favourite sayings.

Alexis let the phrase hang in the ether, thankful the sea was calm as the maritime air spritzed across his face, and all gazed in meditative silence upon the coastline as they passed it by.

A ruined city appeared on the left bank, whose walls were collapsed and derelict. Once, it must have been the proud home to many but now was reduced to rubble.

"Did the Turks do this?" asked Nicola.

"No, this was nature," replied Alexis. "A large earthquake collapsed the walls nearly a century ago and that is when the Ottomans first stepped foot in Europe. The city has never been rebuilt as the Turks took it as a sign from Allah that they would take up the mantle of Jihad and conquer the infidel."

Nicola instinctively placed his sword hand on the scabbarded hilt, feeling the welling of patriotism inside, whilst Antonis stroked his jaw in contemplation at the inexorable advance of the Turk. Their minds reeled with unanswered questions. After the ruined city, the strait opened into a turquoise and calm body of water and they sailed uneventfully onward towards Selymbria.

Once the captain was paid with Venetian ducats, Alexis and the brothers disembarked, leaving their few belongings on board. "You will wait here until we return," Alexis told him, "no matter how long."

The captain nodded in obedience, not questioning the giant Greek, partly in respect and partly in fear.

Noticing the confused response, Alexis tossed him another coin as he left the boat.

APPROACHING THE GOVERNOR'S RESIDENCE, everything appeared dilapidated. Moss grew on the walls, a dullness imbued everything from soldier and civilian to building and monument.

"We have an audience with the governor."

"Your name?" asked a suspicious herald.

"General Alexis Sartis," came the terse response.

The herald raised an eyebrow, the only display of recognition the man was capable of.

Hurry up, you useless piece of blubber

The half-man turned, raised his hand, and beckoned a younger version of himself who, after curt instruction, disappeared through a doorway. Within a moment, the door opened and the three were shown in. A lot of pomp and ceremony for such a tin-pot province.

"General, we are pleased you have come," said the governor.

"You are welcome, sire."

"What news have you from my brother?"

"I have a letter for you, as well as a speech that I have memorised, and is only for your ears. This was the strict instruction of Theodore."

"My brother and his scheming," smiled Constantine. "The letter?"

Alexis handed the scroll to the governor's outstretched hand, who, with a practiced theatrical flourish, opened the seal and began reading. It was the first opportunity Alexis had to study the man. In his mid-forties, he carried himself with an abundance of energy. Handsome, with an aquiline profile, and intelligent grey eyes. The theme common with this family—tall, imposing, and regal, though far more athletic than his scholarly brother.

Once he had read the letter, he passed it over a candle next to him. Casually, he placed the lit parchment in a stand bowl and watched it being consumed to a small pile of white ash. "Nothing spectacular in that. Now, let's hear what this speech is about," he turned to his attendants and commanded, "Leave us."

The room emptied of the three florally fragranced eunuchs present. Nicola and Antonis looked at Alexis, who nodded for them to follow.

Once they had all left, the demeanour of the governor

instantly changed. "Thank god. I am practicing at being emperor and so have all this ceremony, but I tell you, it's frightfully dull. All I really wish for is an honest campfire."

Alexis let out an audible sigh of relief.

"Now, tell me what this message is."

Alexis took a few steps closer to the governor and repeated the speech word for word. It was not long but at the end of it, Constantine was pale with shock, and speechless.

It took some moments to recover his regal composure. "Do you believe it?"

"I don't know, sire, but I do know that your brother has a great deal of foresight and that it does make sense."

"You must be on your way to the capital as soon as possible. I will have horses and a small escort prepared."

After they left Constantine, Alexis had a greater sense of urgency about him. He instructed Nicola to go down to the port and collect the chest they had left on the boat and release the captain of his services then he told Antonis to make sure the pack animals were fully loaded. Both went speedily about their tasks.

Once their duties were completed, the three sat to enjoy their well-earned meal before departing. Nothing fancy, just a spicy chicken stew with some fresh bread.

Their mentor brought out a bottle of wine. "The first part is complete, now, we go to the capital, so I think we should have a little toast," he said, while pulling out three small cups and carefully pouring the red liquid into them. Always controlled with his excesses having learned moderation with the passing years, he wanted to imbue this into the boys.

"Yammas," said the three as they raised their clay cups and drank.

Alexis noted how they drank the ruby red wine, Antonis the more controlled. Nicola lived through his emotions, something he understood well. Though they were great friends, there was a foreboding in Alexis' heart. As if the two were like a tinderbox, which just needed a spark to make it explode.

"Why did the governor appear so ashen-faced after you relayed the message to him?" asked Antonis.

"It was a message for his ears only."

"Is that why we are rushing to Constantinople, to tell the Emperor the news, too?" asked Nicola earnestly.

"Yes." answered Alexis.

"What could be so bad that we have to rush to the capital?" Antonis continued to dig.

Alexis gave his best avuncular smile and finished his wine. "Time to rest, we have an early start. I want to reach the city before sundown."

THEY LEFT in the damp pre-dawn air that held little hint of the heat that was to come. The boys expected to see the capital over each crest and their disappointed impatience grew.

But at the fifth peak, the city came into view. The hill sloped down to a flat plain and the brothers' eyes followed the topography until massive walls abruptly cleaved it, with huge square towers placed at regular intervals and bands of red stripes cut horizontally into the gleaming white face. The sun had begun its daily descent and the rays bounced off the shiny brick, giving a dazzling display; like beacons into the sky, she truly was the queen of cities.

Alexis smiled. *Everyone is amazed at the first sight of her, reactions differ but the effect is for life.*

The brothers were mute as their horses carried them onward, passing through the outer palisade and into the inner curtain, the structure radiated power and continuity.

Nicola turned his head to look down the peribolos and all he saw was a killing zone for any would-be attacker. "The books do not convey the majesty of this construction."

"Nothing like first-hand experience," replied Alexis.

But as Antonis looked closer, he could see cracked lines of brick running throughout with wooden supports behind them to maintain its integrity. Inside the walls, whole swathes of the city had succumbed to nature; goats and sheep grazed amongst the abandoned houses.

It was Alexis' first visit in over a decade and it saddened him to see his beloved capital had sunk even further into disrepair. They had to travel nearly a mile into the city before urbanisation once again took a complete hold.

The party went across the Lycus River and under the Aqueduct of Valens toward the Twelfth District. The houses became more salubrious as they entered the northern part of the city. The signs of trade gave way to displays of familial wealth, larger windows, the balconies broader and the pleasant scent of herb gardens.

As they approached one of the houses past the Christ Pantokrator Church, Alexis slowed and with a deft move, dismounted and strode up to large oak double-doors and pulled the bell chain.

Instantaneously, the door flap opened, and two black beady eyes looked out, "Yes?"

"I am here to see Thanos."

"Take your horses around the back," and the flap shut.

They rode down the alley, where a heavy old door opened. The man with the coal black eyes stood there replete with lank thinning hair, and his potbelly propped up with a tooled-hide belt.

Dusk was falling rapidly, blanketing the courtyard in mystic shadows.

"See to the horses," Alexis ordered the brothers as he followed the man inside.

The house was well-appointed, no doubt due to all the booty acquired.

"Alexis, you old goat! Good to see you again. It has been ten years, no?"

Alexis grinned as he embraced the speaker, dwarfing the man. "Thanos, some things remain constant in the universe and you are one of those things."

"Just like cream rising to the top."

"Or shit sticking to your boot," countered Alexis.

Both laughed, happy to see each other again.

"So, tell me what is so important that brings you here after all this time? Leaving your beloved Laconians in Mistras."

"I am here on business. Theodore sent me with messages and letters for the Emperor. In fact, I have an audience with him tomorrow."

Thanos stroked his reddish-brown beard in thought. "Well, you are most welcome to stay here as long as you need."

"I am not alone. I have two wards with me."

"When did you become a father?" Thanos' green eyes sparkled in amusement.

"They are the sons of Andreas Vevellis and I have been training them at Mistras for the past two years. I thought it was time for them to come to the capital."

"Where are they?"

"Taking care of the horses. Remember your animal husbandry, or have you grown lazy in your old age?"

"Oh, I think I remember. Perhaps, those wards of yours can remind me how to do it, as long as you didn't teach them!" came the swift response.

Both burst into laughter, as only old friends can, and with that, they went to the stables.

The saddles were off, the horses fed, and rubbed down. The two wooden trunks and other accoutrements had already been offloaded and placed by the side.

Alexis grinned as he saw they had worked quickly and

completed their chores. "Boys, this is Thanos, an old friend of mine, and we will be staying with him for a while."

"Hello, sir," they said in unison.

"The sons of Andreas Vevellis, huh? Well, you have his colouring," Thanos said to Antonis. "But you certainly have his build," directing the last comment at Nicola. "These are his sons, alright."

"Sir, actually, I am adopted," replied Nicola.

"Could have fooled me. You even have his movements."

"My father was Zenon, a compatriot of my stepfather."

"Zenon! I knew him. But… whatever you say, I still stick to the fact that Andreas was a naughty boy and Zenon helped him out."

The brothers tightened at his comments and their fists clenched.

Alexis moved speedily to defuse the situation. "Thanos has a filthy mind, and no tact to boot. These are not the product of camp whores. I would have thought a few years of civilised living in the Capital would have rubbed off on you." He placed his giant arm around Thanos' shoulders. "Now, apologise to the boys, otherwise, they might unleash all my training on you."

Thanos turned to look Alexis in the eye and it was evident that he truly believed what he was saying. A look exchanged between the two men and the host relented. "I apologise. I forget that not everyone thinks as basely as I do. Zenon was a fine warrior and an honourable man. You should be proud to count him as your Father."

The boys relaxed.

"I meant no offence; it was merely soldiers' rough talk. Welcome to my home. Mia casa è tu casa," said Thanos in impeccably accented Italian.

"Come on, boys, you will have to get used to soldiers' talk."

The brothers finally relented as Thanos held out his hand.

The rest of the evening passed without further incident and

after a light snack, the boys meticulously rubbed oil into their leather breastplates and honed their weapons.

The pre-dawn noises of the city jolted the boys into consciousness. The general bustle a cacophony they were not used to. They descended to the courtyard to find Alexis taking a bath. For all his bluster, he took his cleanliness very seriously, thought Nicola. However, his strict regimen had rubbed off on them and both had also become fastidious with their hygiene.

"Finest clothes today, boys. We are seeing the Emperor."

Later, Alexis looked approvingly at the brothers. Nicola was in dark blue and Antonis in maroon. The tailor had done an excellent job, they looked every inch the young gentlemen.

The November morning was crisp and clear as they travelled the short distance to the Blachernae Palace, a section of the city that was still proud and thriving.

Alexis took the lead with the two boys flanking him but a pace behind. The court guards pushed open the large bronze doors. The room was rectangular with a series of small domes across the vaulted ceiling, each with a small opening at the apex that let in the light. Its effect was to crisscross the hall in red and yellow stripes of light, an ephemeral barrier between the audience and its Emperor.

Nicola saw John VIII on his throne overseeing the entire room. To his right, stood three members of his council, all men in their early fifties, short, and pudgy. Dressed in sombre finery, their shoulders hunched in smug self-serving earnestness and their hands clasped in front of them like wise men thinking. Flanking either side of the pathway, there were small crowds, gathered lords of the Senate, and their ladies. The room appeared impossibly long to the boys, every step taking an eon under the intense gaze upon them.

Nicola caught a glimpse of their small group in one of the mirrors. *How impressive we look.* They approached the dais and bowed deeply to the seated Emperor.

"Sebastokrator," said Alexis.

"General Sartis, it is our pleasure that you have come to see us," replied the Emperor, his voice deep and measured. "You have news from our brother in Mistras?"

"Yes, sire, a letter and a message that is for your ears only," replied Alexis. He handed the letter to a courtier, who then passed it to the Emperor.

He read it, betraying no emotion, just as his brother had. "We shall hear our message in our private chambers later. Now, tell me news about the Morea. Are your Laconians still in fine condition? And how is dear old Plethon?"

"My men are always on alert, the best thousand soldiers in Christendom. Plethon is well, still full of energy, and his writing has not yet slowed down."

A smile stole across the Emperor's face. "Good to hear. Tell me, how have you been? We last met at the first Council of Florence, if I remember correctly."

"I have been training my two wards here," Alexis gestured to the brothers with his hand. "I present Antonis and Nicola Vevellis, sons of Andreas Vevellis."

"Yes, our general from the siege of 1422. These are his sons?" his eyes turned upon them. "Welcome to Our city."

"Thank you, sire," came their nervous reply and they duly moved to their allotted place.

Once away from the spotlight, Nicola began to scan the room. Amongst the throng of courtiers, wives, dignitaries and all the finery, his eyes halted opposite a deep emerald gaze, shaded with exquisite long dark lashes that took his breath away. His neck stiffened to slow his turning head and his eyes looked upon her. Around her feline eyes formed a predator's face—high cheekbones, a defined jaw, full sensuous lips, and the smoothest pale skin, all framed in luscious curling Mediterranean auburn hair. Sensing he had stopped too long, he hurriedly continued turning.

Antonis' eyes caught the foreign embassies. The Italians dressed in short over-gowns with doublets underneath in different shades of blues and reds, each man trying to outdo the other with their outlandish hats. Contrastingly, the Ottomans wore uniforms in silver and purple brocade, with sashes of various metallic colours, caftans lined in contrasting bold hues, and bobbing turbans resembling fruit on top of a sea of rainbow sticks. The precise and ornate style fascinated him; the subtle intricacies adorning the beardless men drawing him further in.

The three men took their place at court and watched the rest of the events unfold.

Antonis noticed a man who was constantly organising the proceedings; short and rotund with a full mean face and sallow skin. "Who is that?" He asked.

"That is Lord Planedes, one of the senior officials of the chancery," replied Alexis.

Planedes' eyes popped wide and looked at Nicola as Alexis said his name.

The young man caught his look, which sent shivers down his spine.

Antonis saw the stare and it puzzled him. A fleck of auburn hair caught his attention, the angular face staring at Lord Planedes. The creature followed his gaze to its destination. Antonis instinctively turned away. In what felt an eternity, he summoned the courage and pulled up to see these feline eyes staring in his direction, mesmerizingly fathomless. He could only gasp at the wondrous beauty. Crestfallen, he saw they were not looking at him but at Nicola, who was duly reciprocating. An unknown sensation instantly welled in his breast, a confusing mixture of anger, jealousy, and helplessness as he saw the two drown in each other's eyes. His lip pursed into a thin line as he bit the inside of his cheek to stifle his emotions.

As the proceedings ended, one of the courtiers came up to Alexis and asked him to join the Emperor in his quarters. All three followed the courtier to the private chambers. The boys waited outside in the antechamber as Alexis entered the last room to find the Emperor in discussion with Lord Planedes.

The oily man offered a curt glance. "Protospatharios."

The formal title irritated Alexis as to him, it had little meaning. "Kankileos," responded Alexis, equally formally.

A satisfied smile came across the palace official's face as the giant Greek responded with the more senior ranking title.

The baubles that men live by. No wonder the empire is in ruins with fools such as this in charge.

"You have changed little, General. Still keeping in shape, I see."

"Thank you. How are affairs of state coming along?" replied Alexis.

The Emperor interjected before the palace official could respond, "Lord Planedes, please leave us."

Controlling his look of surprise, the official duly obliged, and now it was Alexis' turn to smile.

John VIII turned to his remaining guest. "Now, tell me this message that my brother has need to send in private."

"Sire, the Hungarians are about to invade Ottoman territory with a large force of mercenaries and conscripts. Their aim is to expel the Turk from Serbia and push them further out of Europe. They are going to try and drive a wedge through to us in Constantinople."

A resigned look came across the recipient's face. "We knew this would happen, though, somewhat ambitious in attempting to reach our city," replied the Emperor. He had reigned too long to believe in these wild dreams of re-conquest.

Unperturbed, Alexis continued, "The Pope and the Catholics want us to join with them by attacking their southern flank using all the forces at our disposal—our men here in the city and the Laconians from the Morea. However, Theodore thinks that if we do that we are doomed as the Turk will turn all his forces on us once they win and that our best hope is to stay neutral to see the outcome."

The Emperor nodded in agreement.

"He urges that we must do two things: One, stay out of the fray with the Latins and see how the events unfold. Two, contact the Pope and use his influence to get French and Genoese help. If we do not do this, the Empire has at most ten years left before we are conquered," finished Alexis.

The last phrase turned the Emperor grey. He knew his brother would not make such a statement, unless he had clear proof to show it, and for the next fifteen minutes, he sat there ashen faced as Alexis recounted Theodore's evidence.

In the stuffy antechamber, Planedes cast a glance over to the boys, who were shuffling in adolescent indecisiveness. The wily politician had noticed them at the Court, where they stood out but here in this small room, they felt uncomfortable in their finery.

Enjoying this moment, he scrutinised them further, adding to their discomfort. His gaze initially rested on Nicola, too tall and good-looking by half. Remembering where his eyes were focused at Court, a shudder of revulsion went down his neck and into his shoulders. The other boy, with the alert eyes that gave him a brooding look, intrigued him. He had been more interested in the foreign dignitaries.

His mind turned to the conversation in the other room. He felt his hands tense, becoming claw-like as he deduced that he would have to get closer to Alexis to discover what this intrigue was. The very thought irritated him, having always disliked the open-hearted bluff soldier ever since they were young men, but as the consummate politician, he would wheedle it out of him.

The door opened and Alexis strode out into the antechamber, purposefully and clearly relieved at whatever had occurred inside.

Planedes glided towards him, "General, it has been a long

time since we have broken bread. Why don't you come to my house for dinner?"

Alexis contained his dislike. The purpose of the invitation was clear but however distasteful he found Planedes, this could be a good opportunity for the boys to see a political snake at close quarter. He smiled broadly at the request. "That will be a pleasure. I shall bring my wards with me."

Planedes' lips pursed but likewise, knew he couldn't refuse. "With pleasure," lied the courtier. "Does tomorrow suit you? We are having a few guests and it would be good for you to meet some new people."

"Excellent. See you then," replied Alexis and they parted company.

The brothers were happy to get home and take off their stiff clothes. It had been a long day, some of it overwhelming, and they now looked forward to some welcome relaxation.

Alexis saw them crumple in tiredness and for a moment was about to let them be. "No rest for you two, there is still a couple of hours of sunlight left. We will be doing some hand-to-hand combat," he told them.

Nicola and Antonis looked at each other and rolled their eyes in tortured disbelief. They knew this would be a bruising and exhausting session but thought better than to argue, as the edge in Alexis' voice told them that.

The mentor, still in his finery, drew his dagger and stood in front of them with his legs slightly apart, casually tossing his blade between his outstretched hands. "Pick up your sfakions and attack me, and you boys better make it good, or else!"

Resigned to their fate, the boys went to the table and picked up their weapons, the blades freshly oiled. A silent nod of understanding went between them and with feline speed turned to face their teacher and began to circle.

The giant Greek let out a contemptuous snort but inside

knew that his days of doing this with ease with them were numbered.

Lord Planedes' house was close to Thanos', near the Golden Horn, well-proportioned, with fine masonry, and maintained to exacting standards.

The boys felt like trussed birds, as again, Alexis insisted they wear their finest clothes. They still had not become accustomed to wearing formal dress, much preferring military or loose attire. Antonis bristled even more than his brother in the restrictive garb and wished he were wearing what the Turks had displayed yesterday in Court, mentally deciding to try some on one day to see how it felt.

Their host was in the atrium to greet the trio as they entered. "Strategos, welcome to my humble abode, and welcome to you two, as well," and turned to look at the brothers.

They duly bowed in response then followed the older men into the main hall. Standing there in conversation were two nobles, whom Antonis recognised from the previous day. Clearly, part of the inner circle; both had that air of arrogance about them. Their host introduced them and quickly the two heavily scented courtiers engaged Alexis in deep conversation of a political nature. Nicola grew bored listening to their monotonic hum and his eyes began to wander around the room.

"You must be Nicola," said a voice behind him.

He turned to see a tall, slim woman standing before him. The accent was foreign, but he couldn't quite place it.

"Yes, I am, ma'am."

"I am your hostess, Lady Planedes," she replied with a disarming smile.

Unconsciously, he stared at her in such a way that had he been older would have been regarded as rude. She had an understated beauty with high cheekbones, a full mouth, and an elegant neck, all highlighted by having her hair swept up and back into an unusual shape which defined her features even more. Her round eyes were warm, welcoming, and large, her irises a deep iridescent emerald. There was something familiar about her.

Nicola felt himself relax and quickly found his tongue again. "It is a wonderful house you have Lady Planedes, and thank you for your hospitality."

"So kind," she replied, turning her head slightly.

Antonis saw his brother speak to the woman and his attention of the political debate that had been raging was broken.

"And you must be Antonis, I am Lady Planedes."

Her warmth instantly relaxed Antonis.

"I knew your father from the siege of '22, I was only a child then, but he was instrumental in saving our glorious city."

"Thank you, ma'am," replied Antonis.

"So, which one of you is the elder?" she inquired.

"I am ten months the elder," replied Nicola.

Noticing the tenseness in his voice. "I hear you are both good in the martial arts."

Lady Planedes focused her disarming gaze on Antonis.

"I am good with the bow and the sfakion." He said, while puffing up his chest in pride.

Nicola nodded in half agreement. "He's pretty good with the dagger, but not quite as good as me. The sword is my best."

Antonis shot Nicola a look of annoyance.

Lady Planedes realised there was something that irritated the younger one with his sibling. Nicola didn't even notice; he was only jesting.

"Well, it takes calm and patience to use the bow with any decency," retorted Antonis, whilst looking at his hostess.

She indulged the adolescent with another of her most serene smiles.

She reminded Antonis of his mother. Tension that had

rapidly built-up in his shoulders eased and his bottom lip receded just as quickly.

"I can see that you are both keen sportsmen and it's good to know that you have such passion for it."

The rustling of a dress and soft footfall of silk slippers emanated from behind the boys. Lady Planedes' face creased into even more warmth at the sound. "Katerina, let me introduce you to these charming young men."

The boys turned in unison to see whom she addressed and froze with astonishment at the vision of beauty before them. Tall and slender with square shoulders, her thick auburn hair was up, exposing the nape of her neck, exquisite in its perfection.

"This is Antonis and Nicola Vevellis, and this, is my daughter, Katerina," said the mother with great love in her voice.

Both brothers stood transfixed.

She smiled serenely but her curiosity was piqued. *These are not the usual wet fops that frequent my father's terminally dull dinners.* They were both robust, with open honest faces, and strong hands. An unexpected thrill of excitement shot through her, unused to the presence of such handsome and physical boys.

"How do you do?" said Nicola.

Katerina's gaze now glowed as she rested it on the taller brother, his eyes infinite dreamy pools and his voice deep and melodic.

"Preatna svami pavnakomitsa," interjected Antonis, before she could reply.

Katerina shot him a look of surprise, his intense blue gaze boring through her; beautiful, but cold, she decided in that instant. "How did you know I spoke Russian?"

"As your mother is Russian, I assumed that you would speak it, too," he replied, with a hint of triumph in his voice.

"You spotted the Russian in my accent? Very observant of

you, Antonis," said Lady Planedes.

Planedes' reptilian eyes had been watching the interaction with interest. Seeing his daughter's response to the taller of the brothers, he disengaged from his conversation and snaked across the room, avoiding any possible distractions. The short man obliquely inserted himself into their sphere of discussion, strategically positioned between his daughter and the two perceived threats. She was a most valuable asset, that he would not sell cheaply.

"Spiros, did you know that young Antonis here speaks some Russian? He recognised my accent."

"No, I didn't, Sophia. It seems young Vevellis has a keen ear for languages."

The protective father turned to Antonis and shot him an approving glance. He always admired strong intellect. "Can you speak Russian as well?" he asked casually, looking at Nicola.

"No, sir, I do not," came the curt reply.

Something in his response reminded him of Alexis; he disliked the young man even more. "So, what can you do?"

Lady Planedes was surprised by the tone of his voice and smiled warmly at her guests, deciding that he was only being the protective father.

"I am good with the sword," responded Nicola calmly.

Planedes' lip curled, letting out a thinly veiled sneer, as he questioned whether Nicola's lion eyes saw through him. Inexplicably, he felt intimidated by this boy. "Well, we must all be good at something. Come, Katerina, let us sit down to eat," replied the host and taking his daughter by the elbow, he led her through to the dining room with the others following behind.

The Guests were shown to their places, the brothers interspersed amongst the other dignitaries, and Alexis was given the privilege of a place to the right of Planedes himself. It was not hard to deduce the whole dinner was being given for him to provide the wily politician with the information he so desperately wanted but he was going to enjoy playing the ignorant bluff soldier.

Antonis looked around the room and involuntarily, cast a glance over to Katerina. He willed her to look in his direction but to no avail, she was engaged in conversation with one of the courtiers. The fat man was trying his damnedest to be his most charming, no doubt talking about the latest fashions to come out of Venice. Katerina, at least, had the grace to smile and feign interest. He liked that. His brother was entertaining one of the matrons, her porcine eyes and thin lips pursed in her best efforts at flirtation. It annoyed him intensely that his brother showed so little self-awareness, because the more Nicola indulged her with smiles, the more she shrilled in conversation.

"What do you think of our fair city, Antonis?"

He turned to see the serene face of his hostess, noticing how her mannerisms and skin were so similar to that of her daughter's.

"I haven't had much time to explore yet, as we have only just arrived."

"You must see Agia Sophia, it is most beautiful. In fact, I think you should join us the next time we attend." She paused while she calculated something in her head. "Yes, that will be All Souls Day, in two weeks."

Antonis smiled as the first of many delicacies was placed before him, for he knew that would give him another opportunity to speak with Katerina. He stole another glance in her direction.

"How is it being back in the city, General?" asked Planedes.

"It is bittersweet, my Lord. I have good memories, but I see there has been no improvement in our situation. There seems to be even less people than a few years ago."

"Yes, we have been hard pressed by both the Italian cities and the Ottomans, and it seems that the power of gold usurps any beliefs nowadays."

"What can you expect from the Catholics and the Muslims? They have always coveted what we have."

"And what is it we have left that they want so badly, do you think?"

"The city itself is all we have. We have always known the Turk's desire for the Red Apple. They are just taking up the mantle as Mohammed's representatives on this earth."

The use of the Islamic name for the city set Planedes' mind racing again. "How is it being the mentor to the boys? It is a big responsibility General Vevellis afforded you."

His guest's eyes softened, and his smile had more warmth. "They are very good students and the honour is mine to teach the sons of my mentor."

Planedes looked over to the boys. "Which one is the elder?"

"The big one, Nicola, by ten months," replied Alexis.

"Funny, they do not look very alike. Perhaps the elder looks like his mother." His distant memory of Vevellis telling him the younger was more akin to his father.

"Nicola is an adopted son. His father was killed in battle and his mother died in childbirth, so Vevellis brought him up as his own."

"So, his is not of the noted bloodline, then?"

Alexis intensely disliked the judging of a human by their lineage. "He is an extraordinary young man who has had the good fortune of high patronage."

Planedes smiled and berated himself for not having thought of this before; self-made men such as Alexis detested nepotism. He had finally found a chink in that confident bastard's armour and he wasn't going to let go. "Yes, but the other son will inherit all of the Vevellis lands and wealth, will he not?"

"Almost certainly, though, I am sure that Nicola will receive a stipend."

An imperceptible grunt came out of the host's mouth.

Alexis could see the man's mind at work, and he was trying his hardest to not show his disgust.

"His real father, I assume, had nothing?"

"He was a captain in the brigade, a career soldier, so not too much."

His attachment to the boys was how he would get close to him. Satisfied, Planedes changed course yet again, before Alexis grew suspicious.

The dinner carried on later than anticipated, with course after course being served. Venison stuffed with goose, which was stuffed with partridge—a veritable Italian delicacy, being the crowning finale to an excellent feast. The wine flowed, and the courtiers and their wives indulged fully in the hosts' generosity.

The postprandial drinks were served in the atrium of the house, the guests split into the sexes, going their separate directions, and Antonis clenched his jaw as he saw Nicola and Katerina steal another of their half-dozen glances of the evening.

Before they parted to their allotted areas, Lady Planedes gracefully went up to her husband. "Dear, we must bring these young men with us on our next visit to Agia Sophia. They have never attended a service there and it would be good for them."

Planedes could have kissed his wife then and there, but his cunning was too ingrained for him to show it. "Well, if you insist, Sophia, when are we next going?" He feigned an indifferent voice.

"The end of the month for the orthodox festival."

"Why, that is only the end of next week," said Planedes, "I think you should bring your wards with us, Alexis. What do you think?"

"With pleasure," he replied, noting the use of the familiar and wondered whether that was the drink or another subtle play.

The brothers stood by Alexis and both smiled as they knew what this meant. Sophia Planedes smiled too, as she knew her husband was up to some scheme but had learned over the years to ignore it.

It was the early hours before Alexis and the boys left the company of Lord and Lady Planedes and the courtiers. The brothers wanted to walk back and Alexis happily obliged. As they wandered down the deserted cobbled street in the fresh early morning it was balmy and mild, especially for the time of year but it could have been freezing and the boys would not have noticed. Nicola had an unusual spring in his step and Alexis noticed the boy's eyes were shining brighter than usual. Even Antonis had an energy about him that he rarely exuded.

"I've never seen such beauty," enthused the elder brother. "I couldn't keep my eyes off her. It was so difficult with that old windbag I had to entertain, yet we did manage for our eyes to meet on more than one occasion." There was a pause. "I think she liked me, too," he added, a matter of fact tone at the last.

It only served to infuriate Antonis more, the certainty of the statement leaving him no room to respond. "Well, she looked at me too, you know." The retort sounded weak in his own ears. He knew his brother had him beaten in the looks and charisma departments, but he had intellect and persistence.

Nicola ignored him, enthusing again, "She has the most beautiful eyes, like a cat, impossible to read."

Antonis, knowing he wouldn't get his point across, joined in on the same line. "Her neck and mouth are exquisite," he countered.

"Yes, yes," agreed Nicola and they carried on, analysing every detail of Katerina and their opinions of her, all of which were, of course, totally flattering.

Alexis looked on in amusement and certainly agreed with them—she was undoubtedly a beauty—as they continued in this vein all the way back to the house. Which made him relive his first flush of love from all those years ago, and he chuckled softly to himself.

6

COUNCIL OF FLORENCE

The fine dust of the agoge filled Thanos' nostrils and clouded his vision, yet, he was relishing another of his 'real fighting' lessons. He had taken it upon himself to teach the boys this most ungentlemanly form of combat. As he cleared his eyes, he remembered the disapproving comments from Alexis when he suggested the idea a few days prior and relished pointing out to his friend that for all his bluster it had saved his life on numerous occasions.

Nicola was feeling sluggish as he joined the group for their morning session. The last two weeks had been a blur and this new discipline they were learning was clouded by the all-consuming thoughts of Katerina, her scent, her movements, her green eyes, and her melodic voice. Across the quad, he saw his brother's brooding eyes boring through him. A more regular occurrence since the dinner at Lord Planedes, he noted, and returned the stare.

A thin smile stretched across Antonis' face in response, relishing today's training. He found the unorthodox strategy and sudden switches of tempo liberating. Instinctively coming up with lethal counter-attacking moves that nullified Nicola's greater power against him.

"Right boys, sparring this morning," said Thanos.

They squared up with the sfakion. Both set in a crouching position with their legs slightly apart, the grip on their knives relaxed, yet firm.

"Always use the fingers," Alexis offered. He had noticed how Antonis' confidence had grown, which in and of itself didn't bother him, but the hardened look in his eyes was unsettling. Simmering resentment bubbled beneath the surface and he couldn't fathom exactly why. Nicola felt no aggression, the overriding emotion for him was one of cocooning warmth.

"Begin!" barked Thanos.

Nicola snapped back to attention a fraction too slow. His brother kicked up the sand of the agoge into his face, filling his mouth with dust, and he instinctively turned to his right, to avoid the predicted blow to the side. However, Antonis foresaw the move and twisted the blade inside for a slashing blow across the abdomen. Although he pulled the edge, both knew that it would have been a fatal blow if it were real, yet the tweak was not enough, and the tip of the weapon sliced across Nicola's belly.

"What the fuck are you doing, Antonis?" he yelled.

The brother smiled but there was no humour in his face. "Why, what's wrong? Can't keep up? Dreaming of sweet scents, are you?"

An uncontrollable rage abruptly welled inside Nicola and his right leg kicked out, hitting his brother full on his side and throwing him cleanly to the ground. Antonis' face screwed up in pain as his body hit the dirt. Nicola's blood was up, and he didn't stop as he prepared to stomp on his grounded brother. Antonis anticipated the move and prepared to defend with his knife.

"Stop, both of you!" shouted Thanos.

They ignored him and Nicola's boot came full down onto his brother. In desperation, Antonis stabbed with his blade but this time his move had been predicted and was parried clear.

Standing on the side-lines, Alexis saw with horror how the events would unfold, hastily rushed at the standing sibling, and dived into him full tilt, taking him clean over and rolling him to the ground.

Thanos quickly grabbed Antonis by the right wrist before he could react.

Their mentor was furious as he jolted Nicola up by the throat, his eyes burning with fury. "What the hell do you think you are doing? You're not animals! Control is always paramount, lose that and you are dead."

The castigated brothers looked downward.

"Dead, do you hear me?" repeated Alexis.

"Yes, mastre," they replied in unison.

Antonis felt a strange satisfying sense of calm.

Nicola, though, felt confused as his instinct was for self-preservation; it wasn't pleasure he felt, more necessity and these emotions towards his brother disturbed him.

Alexis saw the conflict in the elder and joy in the younger. *So, it begins.*

The incident at the training grounds profoundly disturbed him and he concluded that they should focus on their academic studies as it avoided physical contact between them. Leaving them in Thanos' care with strict instructions that if there were any more incidents, they were to receive a thrashing to within an inch of their lives.

The brothers knew better than to speak out against that and set about their studies with renewed vigour.

A MESSAGE HAD ARRIVED for Alexis to attend to the Emperor in his private quarters that evening.

So much more can be achieved in an informal setting. He shivered in the chill evening wind as he approached the palace, which seemed strange considering how warm September was. Perhaps, his ruler had been brooding for the past few days, trying to figure out a solution to the problem before him. Somehow, he felt he would be part of the solution and, though he would carry out the order, something inside said it didn't portend well.

The Emperor's private quarters were modest in comparison to the rest of the palace, as he preferred the calming view across the Golden Horn. Alexis nodded as he walked past the sentries and upon entering the rooms, saw there was a table set for two, with an assortment of fruits and cold meats arrayed most artistically upon it. A flagon of wine was resting on a stand beside the fireplace, which had been lit but with only half the usual amount of wood. Candelabra were placed to excess, blazing with dancing light in the warm autumnal breeze from the open window, and sporadically positioned scented oil lamps gave a faint hint of geranium and rose.

More like a boudoir than a meeting place. In fact, I've done some of my best work in boudoirs.

"Strategos, welcome."

John VIII appeared resplendent in dark red damask with refined gold and blue embroidery, which spread like eagle wings across his chest, flowing outward to his shoulders with the tail following down the robe to his legs. It made the man appear broader across the torso and slimmer in the trunk, which, given his natural stature, made him look most regal. He wore his beloved silk slippers of a matching colour. Yet, he had none of the trappings of kingship.

"Your Majesty," replied Alexis, with the slightest of bows.

John looked favourably at the Laconian, a man of no nonsense and perfect for the task at hand. Remembering him from twenty years earlier, he marvelled at how he hadn't aged, with only the slightest hint of the ravages of time, moulded in the cast of the great Byzantine generals, way back to the days of Belisarius. *A dying breed.*

"We have given a lot of thought to our last conversation and think that we have a plan to counter this predicament we find ourselves in. We have two choices—either supplication to the Turk or raising support from the West. As you know, we have close relations with Halil Pasha, the Grand Vizier. He has served the old Sultan well and I hear is a clear guiding force for the new one, Mehmet."

"What do we know about this boy king?" interjected Alexis.

"Not much, just that Murad has made him his heir and wants to retire to let him rule."

"But he is just a boy of thirteen!"

"Twelve, actually, and will be guided by the Vizier. This is why the Hungarians and Poles have invaded, thinking they can steal a quick victory before Murad can mobilise from Anatolia. Both my Father and I have had close relations with Halil, and therefore will maintain that relationship. He will represent our interests as well as placate the Sultan directly."

Alexis nodded. Who was he to argue with that logic?

"The problem we have, is the Latins. They are the only ones who can help us in the long term. We need full military support from them. However, the Venetians are more concerned with their trade agreements than supporting their fellow Christians. Without doubt they will help if they think their trade routes could be threatened by rampant Turkish expansion and so I think we should use the forum of the Council of Florence to voice our concerns to the Pope, and in lieu to the Italian city states that will be present."

Alexis raised his eyebrows in surprise. "But, sire, these councils have just been a platform for the Catholics to enslave us. We have only made concessions without meaningful return."

The Emperor appreciated the frankness. "Yes, General, but

we have no choice. They are our only hope. Not until we regain the lands of central and northern Greece will we have the significant manpower to defend ourselves. Secondly, if Constantinople were to fall, there would be nothing to stop the Sultan from turning his full attention to the rest of Europe, so we must impress upon the Pope that he must keep us secure whilst my brother in the Morea builds up his forces to retake Greece."

Alexis agreed with his reasoning, although, events would have to unfold perfectly for success to be achieved. "When is the next council due to convene?"

"The latest council starts in a few weeks and has now moved to Rome, under the stricter guidance of the Pope. We have had our delegates move there, in an effort to conclude something substantial. Alexis, we would like you to attend as well. You will travel via the Morea and collect Plethon. There is no one more eloquent to put our case forward, both clergy and rulers alike respect him. Between the two of you, we think it is our best chance to secure real aid. A courier has already been despatched some four days past in preparation for this, so don't worry too much. He awaits your arrival."

He is leaving nothing to chance.

Alexis decided to walk the short journey back to give his mind time to process what had been said. His first concern was the boys and what to do with them. When he got back to Thanos, he told his old friend that he was being sent as an envoy to Rome on behalf of the Emperor.

"Why is he sending you to deal with those duplicitous Catholic pederasts? What can you hope to achieve in that nest of vipers?"

"For now, I am leaving the boys in your care as there is much to do until I leave."

"Are you taking them with you?"

"That remains to be seen. I want you to keep them occupied

for a couple of days as I have some business to attend to. I will return two days hence, in time for the visit to Agia Sophia with Planedes and his family."

"Understood, my friend, are you sure you do not need help?"

"Thank you, Thanos, but this is something I need to do alone."

ALEXIS CROSSED THE CITY, intent on carrying out his plan, and went to a building closer to the land walls, where the streets became narrow. The large windowed edifices gave way to lower roofs and crumbled stone that had been daubed with cheap whitewash to smooth over the cracks. The giant Greek strode through the streets with purpose and memories of long ago. The aura emanating from him kept any would-be troublemaker clear of his path in the run-down neighbourhood. It had been a few years but eventually, he found the place he was looking for. The doors were of solid oak, newly made, and set into a simple ingress with a plain stone arch above. Inset over the semicircle was the sign of Christ, the Xi and the Ro. There were no other markings and not even a bell to ring.

Alexis rapped on the door loudly, the doorway so low, his eyes were staring directly at the Christ sign. He heard a shuffle behind the door.

"Who is there?"

"I am here to see Sister Irene."

"Who shall I say is calling?"

"Alexis Sartis."

There was a pause and the voice asked him to wait. After more shuffling, the door opened, and a tiny nun stood there. Except for her weather-beaten face, she could have been mistaken for a child in both size and zest of movement.

"Please wait here," she said, gesturing for Alexis to take a seat on the stone bench.

The building was without the usual icons adorning the walls. Whitewashed stone with a solitary ancient wooden cross set above well-kept but understated plants.

The nun came back into view with a figure beside her.

Even after all these years and the plain attire, she still glowed with fresh health, gesturing to her fellow bride of God to leave them. "It has been a long time, Alexis."

"Yes, it has, Sister Irene."

"I am the Mother Superior now."

"Well, it's incredible how quickly twelve years pass." Alexis' surprise was evident.

Irene's face broke into the smile he remembered so well. "So, why do I have the pleasure of your company after all this time?" Her voice carried with it a berating tone, but her eyes glowed with joy at seeing him again.

"I have a favour to ask. It is rumoured that there is a nun in Constantinople who has a network of informants from as far east as Georgia all the way to the land of the Franks in the west. You wouldn't know anything about that, would you?"

She feigned mock innocence, her face showing a youthful conspiratorial look, where the large brown eyes had lost none of their passion, and the fires burned brighter than ever in her soul.

Alexis laughed at the theatrics then proceeded to tell her of his concerns and the plan he had formulated. He had never had a wife, yet the bond he shared with this nun was deeper than anything he had experienced with any other woman. His heart felt a twinge of regret that he never carried it further with Irene. Tonight, he would find a tavern and become inebriated into a state full of happiness and hope. She was the only person who could do that to him.

He left in the dead of night, but they had agreed to meet again the next day once she had contemplated his request seriously.

Sister Irene sighed as he left, knowing where the general was headed, as she pondered on how in another life things might have been so very different. Pushing those unrealised dreams aside, she quickly turned her mind to his conundrum that needed to be solved. Whilst difficult, it was within her power to grant, and for him she would use any and all the tools at her disposal to assist.

Alexis returned as he said he would at dawn on the Sunday of the Feast of the Eighty Martyrs, with dishevelled hair and his beard needing a trim. The eyes, though, shone brighter than ever.

"Had a good time, did you?" asked Thanos with a wink and a sly look.

"I achieved what I needed to."

"I'm sure you did," smiled his old friend.

"How have the boys been?"

"Diligent. I think they are shitting themselves in case they step out of line."

"Good. Let's keep it that way. Now, I need a bath."

ALEXIS, Nicola, and Antonis arrived at Agia Sophia promptly. Waiting on the steps was Planedes with his family. The oily politician stepped forward, greeting them with open arms as if they were long lost friends, with the customary kiss on either cheek. The brothers formally greeted the family as well, yet their eyes were fixed expectantly in the direction of Katerina, whose plain figure-hugging turquoise silk dress highlighted her blossoming femininity. Her chestnut hair was curled and worn up to display her swanlike neck.

She smiled politely at the brothers, betraying no preference, merely exuding serene beauty, though inside a welling of excitement brewed at the appearance of these interesting boys.

Planedes noticed the interaction; his daughter's tranquillity did not fool him, but he chose to ignore it. "You have arrived in good time," he said and gestured for the group to follow him inside.

The cathedral was buzzing with people—old friends catching up, business being subtly conducted, and rivals losing each other amongst the throng. The architecture of the building effectively muted the noise so that it carried around the room at a low level. The brothers were astonished at the size of the dome and the way the light shone through at the base, giving it the sense that it was a lid hovering above its huge square container.

"Our church of the Holy Wisdom is beautiful, is it not?" Lady Planedes said.

Antonis spoke first, as Nicola was still lost in the splendour of the Church. "It is as if God Himself built this. The outside does not do justice to the majesty that resides within," he replied.

"Yes, our ancestors must have had the breath of Christ inside them when they constructed this. You know, it was completed in less than six years," replied Lady Planedes.

Antonis' eyes widened in disbelief.

Planedes carefully placed all the members of the party into the family pew. Antonis to the far left with Katerina next to him, followed by himself then Alexis, with Lady Planedes and Nicola to the right.

Briefly, Katerina stole a look at Nicola, who was feeling forlorn and left out in the cold.

Planedes coldly smiled to himself.

The brothers were excited as the service started promptly with the Patriarch conducting the proceedings, against a backdrop of a slight murmur amongst the great and the good that the Emperor was not present.

"Strange that the Emperor is not in attendance, you wouldn't know why that is, would you, Alexis?"

"Haven't a clue. I suppose it must be a lot of work running an empire, even one as small as ours."

The unctuous politician knew better than to press the point.

"This is a wonderful festival full of pomp and splendour. It is the largest in terms of remembering saints," said Lady Planedes.

Already too engrossed in the ceremony, Nicola barely nodded his response.

The Patriarch stood through the iconostasis over the altar, the gold cross resting on the table next to the small plate of bread, and to the right was the gold cup filled with wine. In the gallery above, the madrigal choir began their rhythmic chanting of the eighty martyred priests' names. Slowly, from the side entrances, the clerics entered, each carrying in either hand an icon of the saints. Twenty entered from the left and twenty from the right, walking down the centre to the echoing of the choir's low melodic hum. The congregation closest to the aisle reached out in frantic faith to touch the icons in veneration, furiously crossing themselves with the other hand. Its effect sending some of them into a trancelike state as they prayed and came closer to God.

The slow metrical procession of the priests combined with the bass tones of the chanting now had the whole congregation swaying in unison. Nicola was unconsciously caught up with the rest of the crowd and became lost in the depth of the service venerating priests that had died in the name of Christ over a thousand years earlier. The young man's chest filled with pride, his jaw set, and his shoulders straightened so that he came to stop swaying as his imagination wandered into the lives of those saints and how they had stood up for their beliefs.

Antonis looked at the clawing hands in disdain, as if by touching some painted wood it gave them access to redemption. Obliquely looking to his right, he saw that Katerina was fully into the proceedings and deciding it was his moment. "You know that Christ is a prophet for the Moslems, too?"

"No, I did not. I thought they believed in only one God."

"They do and it is the same God as ours. They also believe that Christ and all the prophets of the Old Testament are part of a long line that ends with Mohammed, the final prophet."

"But they do not believe that Christ is the Son of God."

"No, they don't. However, their teachings in the Qur'an are very similar to ours."

"Strange, but for a few points they believe the same things as Christians?"

"Yes, they do."

"How do you know about the Islamic ways?" Katerina asked intrigued in the knowledge behind those cold blue eyes.

"Because I have been taught them," he replied.

Nicola stole a glance in Katerina's direction and saw her body language showing interest in the words his brother had to say. His heart grew heavy. At that moment, Antonis looked up and caught his eye. The malevolent look chilled Nicola.

Planedes, realising that these children could spiral into a noisy embarrassment for him, looked over sternly instantly halting their chatter.

The Patriarch stepped forward, raised his hands, and the choir trailed off. The grey bearded cleric stood there in supplication for a few breaths until he was satisfied he had the congregation's full attention. "Today, we celebrate the feast of the Eighty Holy Martyrs, the priests who died for their belief in the Holy Trinity." His voice was high and shrill, not really becoming of the mood, and the trance was broken.

Nicola switched off and let his mind wander to the beautiful girl at the other end of his pew as the sermon droned on.

Finally, with the piercing falsetto ended, the deacons brought out the gold chalices filled with sweet red wine and the junior priests held baskets full of freshly cut bread. Communion had arrived.

The best bit, thought Nicola, looking forward to inhaling the smell of that most delicious of loaves. Being near the front, they didn't have to do much waiting for their piece of Christ.

Planedes and Alexis elected not to take communion, feeling it was really for the young and the women; on that point at least, they agreed. Besides, they hadn't done the three-day abstinence from all things animal, a necessary requirement before taking the wine and bread.

Alexis looked at the two brothers either side of Katerina. Oblivious to their attentions, she was solely focused on the chalice in front. As she bent down to receive her spoon of wine, he saw both brothers tense and hold until her mouth had been wiped by the attendant priest. *If I leave these two here, there is going to be war. Perhaps a month or two away will calm their primal urges.*

"Will you be joining us now with the Emperor at his next council?" asked Planedes.

"Unfortunately, I will not be able to attend as I am traveling to Rome to represent our interest at the Council of Florence."

"Who else is in your retinue?"

"I will be going with Plethon," replied Alexis. Reasoning that withholding such information would only further sour his relationship with the politician.

"You will be in good hands, he is very experienced in these matters."

WITHIN A DAY, they were on a boat bound for Mistras. However, after they passed the Island of Evia, the vessel took a more southerly passage instead of hugging the coastline.

"Why did we change course?" asked Antonis.

"We have made good time so I decided we shall visit your parents for a few days."

The brothers leapt for joy. It had been a long while and for the first time in weeks they looked at each other as friend.

Together they stood at the gunwale and looked longingly south.

As the carrack pulled into the port of Chania, the boys were impatient to disembark.

"Just take enough gear for three days. We will leave the rest on the boat," said Alexis.

The ride was a hurried one through the winding road that clung to the hills along the coast. They snaked with all the speed they could muster across the olive groves, taking every shortcut they knew to reach the beloved stone house nestling on the hillside.

Sadness overcame Andreas as he watched Maria carefully pruning the stems of her rose bushes, paying particular attention to their shape and form. He had no regrets, as it was the passage of life that the boys left to find their own way, but he had not imagined what a toll it would take on her.

Maria smiled to herself as her husband withdrew, ignorant that she had noticed him all this time. He was the one constant in her life that she so relied upon and loved him ever more so for it. The sweet scent of the flowers filled her senses with their calming properties as once again she heard the sound of rapid heavy footsteps approaching towards her. In curiosity, she turned, to see two men with broad smiles striding through the archway. Concern gripped her before she let out a squeal of delight as it dawned on her that these warriors were her sons. She threw her arms wide open as they rushed towards her and smothered her in kisses.

"How you've grown! Let me have a look at you both," said Maria, as she broke free of their enveloping hugs.

The boys looked at her, beaming with huge smiles.

"Well, mama, they have put us through a lot of training," said Antonis.

Maria cocked her head slightly as she heard the confidence in his voice. Her son was soon to be a man and it seemed that his stammer had disappeared. The worries of the last three years were instantly washed away.

The smell of roasted lamb filled the courtyard. Andreas, full of vibrant energy at the unexpected return of his sons, had ordered a feast in celebration and an energetic fizz emanated around the house as the staff went about busily preparing the repast.

After the initial surprise of the children's return, Maria mothered them as she had before. Her surprise at how they had become so self-assured evident when she saw Nicola tending to the coals and casting an expert eye on the slow cooking meat on the spit. She conceded that he had grown into a handsome young man and whilst he focused on his task, he seemed so much more mature than his eighteen years.

"Mama, where would you like these loaves?" asked Antonis.

"Darling, you shouldn't be doing that. Let the staff handle it."

"That's fine, I can manage," he replied with a smile.

"Put them over there," she said, relenting as he walked away to complete his task.

It was still a shock to her to see her little boy so grown up. His sinewy body moved with deliberate precision and he openly wore his dagger in his belt. She had so many questions but knew it was best to wait until they sat down to eat to get her answers. It was only then that she realised her husband and Alexis had been away for most of the day, possibly in deep discussion about the state of the Empire. She let out a sigh, he was probably also getting a full breakdown of his sons' performances. Not a conversation they could have in front of the boys, or her for that matter, she reflected.

. . .

ANDREAS SAT at his favourite round table with his sons placed on either side. Maria sat next to Antonis with Alexis next to Nicola making up the circle. The patriarch glowed with happiness at the reunion of his family. He had made sure all the goblets were filled and raised his to the gathering.

"Yammas. Welcome home my boys, and to you, my friend Alexis."

"Yammas!" they replied in unison.

Andreas nodded in thanks before he drank then the men drained their goblets before the brothers eagerly tucked into the delicious roasted meats that had been place on the table.

Maria gave a maternal smile; as she saw her not so little boys voraciously devour the food. Though, she noticed with a small sense of satisfaction that Antonis was far more controlled than Nicola. "Andreas, I cannot believe how handsome our boys have become."

"Yes, my dear, but there is more to them than just good looks, you know."

Ignoring her husband's curmudgeonly words with a wave of her hand she carried on. "Oh, you must have the girls fluttering about at court. Have either of you boys found anyone special?" She cooed.

"No, mama, no one special, we are too busy studying," said Antonis.

Something about the look in his eye gave her a sense of foreboding and she thought better of pressing the matter further. "Then tell me, what studies do you like best?"

Antonis paused in reflection for a moment.

"Pah! Enough, Maria! Alexis tells me Thanos has been teaching you some of his real fighting. Do you know who taught him? I did!" The wine was beginning to take hold of him.

The Boys perked up at that.

"Really, Papa?" said Nicola.

"Yes, and tomorrow I will see how well he has taught you both."

"We are better than you think," added Antonis.

"I'm looking forward to it," replied the father as he polished off another goblet of wine.

Alexis contained a little smile and contemplated the interesting morning ahead.

ANDREAS AWOKE WELL AFTER DAWN, feeling groggy. Stepping off the bed pallet, his aged body creaked when trying to spring into life after the alcoholic punishment of the night before. He quickly splashed some water on his face and getting dressed, wandered out to see what the rest of the household was doing. Entering into the morning glare, he instinctively covered his eyes and from the shade of his fingers, he saw his two sons returning from their morning ride.

Antonis let out a low whistle as he spotted his father standing in the courtyard and quickly digging into the horse's flank, sped the last part, leaping off its back and athletically landing next to him. "Good morning, papa, we are looking forward to your lesson today."

Andreas scratched his white beard in contemplation, whilst waiting for Nicola to dismount.

Antonis, full of eagerness, pulled out his sfakion, and tested its point in anticipation. "Where is your blade, papa?"

"All in due time. So I don't appear to have favourites, we shall do this traditionally and the eldest goes first. Nicola, you're up."

Antonis' shoulders slumped a little whilst his brother adjusted his belt and drew his knife in preparation.

"Where is your sfakion, papa?" asked Nicola.

On cue, Andreas pulled out the blade that had been tucked away in the small of his back.

Nicola smiled nervously as he began to circle. Suddenly, the old patriarch became a predatory cat; scarier than he had ever imagined.

Eventually, Nicola made his move and with his customary lightning speed, lunged at his father, who deftly read his thrust and easily parried it, sending his son stumbling off balance into the dust. Picking himself up, Nicola smiled incredulously, patted himself down and began again.

Antonis watched calmly in anticipation, whilst the two sparred for a few rounds more.

"Not bad, boy, not bad at all, you're getting there. Soon, you will be as good as your old man." He patted his eldest on the shoulder and turned his head to Antonis. "You're up now, my lad."

A hard glint shone in Antonis' eye as he squared up to his father and slowly, they began. He felt a cold calmness run through him, remembering the last time they were all together, and how his father had heaped praise on Nicola. Now, it was to be his turn.

Andreas saw the steely look in his son's eyes and knew he had something to prove. *Good, it's about time.* Unhurriedly they turned, before, eventually, Antonis lunged at him. As expected, he dodged it, only to find to his astonishment that it was a feint and he was now off-balance.

Antonis swiped with a slash and drew blood on his father's forearm, who let out a soft grunt. He smiled cruelly.

More cautious now, the old man waited for an opportunity. Knowing he couldn't match his son for speed, he settled on guile. He could feel Antonis' pent-up aggression and decided to use it against him, tempting the boy to counter-attack again. After a few thrusts to entice him, Antonis obliged with a lightning onslaught. This time, Andreas stepped into the blade and punched his son full in the face, knocking him down, a pained surprise clear on his face. "You have more weapons than just a blade when you fight, boy. I see the steel in there now, the training has done you well."

Antonis smiled at the high praise and got up feeling vindicated. Moreover, he had to sheath his knife before his father relaxed, which made him feel even better.

"Come, let us rest now, for tomorrow you leave, and I am sure that your mother will want to spoil you boys some more before then."

The brothers duly obliged and spent the rest of the day lounging around the house. All was peaceful, except Nicola had the nagging thought of a task he had to complete before he left.

It was late afternoon before he took the short walk up the hill to the small walled site that rested there, and hurried, as he did not want to be discovered. Reaching the crest, he saw the top of the dull grey stone on the other side and made his way to the entrance of the square block. Unsure what he was looking for at first, his eyes rested on the cut stone cross that lay atop the simple sarcophagus. He smiled at the fact that his father had spared no expense in housing his lifelong friend and servant. He read the inscription out loud, "Emmanuel Vergotis, born February 1374, died June 1440." *So, he was sixty-six years old.*

"It's a pleasant view you have here. You know, I never knew your true age until today. I have grown a lot; you wouldn't recognise me now. Constantinople is an interesting city; you would like it. It's certainly more interesting than Crete. I miss you." He crossed himself three times before making his way down the hill. This time though, he took the other path down and back into the compound from a different route. To his surprise, he found his father standing in the courtyard.

Andreas noticed his son check his step as he spotted him and instinctively knew where he had been. Silently, he nodded in approval.

The following morning the entire family congregated in the courtyard. Maria fussed emotionally over her sons, making sure they had packed their provisions. Seeing the boys say goodbye to their mother, Andreas got the sense this was the last time they would all be as one. Maria had a glow in her eyes, but he could see how these last three years had aged her. She fought back the tears as her sons rode off with Alexis towards their waiting ship.

TIME SPED on the journey from Chania. Stopping off at Methoni, they collected Plethon, and without delay made their way to Rome. The brothers basked in the warm afterglow of returning home, whilst the men had deep discourse on how to present their cause to the Pope and his allies.

"Who will be present with the Pontiff?" asked Alexis.

"Difficult to say. Certainly, some of the Cardinals, representatives of the Genoese, and Venetian senates," replied Plethon.

"What are they going to demand in order to help us?"

Plethon's face broke into a humourless smile. "Union of the churches of course; that will be from the Pope. The Venetians and Genoese will want further trade rights, under the guise of the church union."

"So, slavery in all but name?" Interjected Alexis.

Plethon said nothing and looked away, imbibing the salty sea air.

As the boat pulled into the small dock at the foot of the Necropolis, three men stood there, awaiting their arrival. Plethon gave a snort of contempt as he eyed them up and down. Alexis turned in surprise to the old Greek.

"John Argyropoulos and his acolytes, self-professed expounder of Greek philosophy to the Italians," said Plethon, answering the Laconian's unspoken question.

The edge in his voice made Alexis smile inside, it wasn't often that Plethon felt threatened.

"Gemistos Plethon, it is an honour to have you here to represent our interests."

"A dubious honour at best."

The boys looked at the three men standing there, all dressed as prosperous Florentines. Cropped beards, felt caps, and long tunics. Clones both in dress and physicality.

As Alexis approached, he towered above the short frail-framed men, their hands so slight, he felt as if digits were missing when he shook them.

"You are the last of the delegates to arrive. First session is due the day after tomorrow in the Vatican," said John Argyropoulos.

"What will be the main topic of conversation?" asked Plethon.

"The Filloque clause," John replied.

"We are going to dispute the Council of Nicaea's ruling?" asked Nicola incredulously.

"That is over a thousand years old," added Antonis.

The frail philosopher shot a surprised look at the boys.

"Still judging books by their cover, I see," chuckled Plethon. "We shall rest this evening and convene in the morning to finalise our plan of action."

"So, it shall be," replied Argyropoulos.

The Byzantine embassy was on the western bank of the Tiber, conveniently located next to the Vatican, so it could be covered by a short walk. The delegates took two full carriages to make the five-minute journey.

Alexis, ever the bluff soldier, said they could just walk over; for once, both Plethon and John agreed; that would not be possible as the loss of face would be too great.

The Vatican was a separate walled entity outside the borders of mediaeval Rome. The carriages pulled up to the gate that faced the Basilica of St. Peter and was ushered through toward the Holy See of the popes. The brothers looked on in curiosity at the building that presented itself before them, nothing like the churches they were used to in Greece. Low-slung steps led up towards three Romanesque arches. To the right of the ramshackle façade, additional porticoes had been added with a bell tower sprung up behind them. To the left, were two tiers of different arches, all bound together by red brick walls. Its imposing size and unadorned exterior gave it the effect of being a large barn with the pointed gabled roof completing its imprint of friability.

Not as awe-inspiring as Aghia Sophia, thought Nicola.

In the main hall, a group of cardinals were deep in conversation. The hundred red-clad clerics opened like a flower as the Greeks entered and one of them came up to Plethon, a smile across his face.

"Cessarini! You heretic," bellowed Plethon.

The rest of the Greeks shrank at his blatant insult.

The cardinal didn't miss a step and bellowed back. "Plethon, you old atheist dog. I didn't think you would be here."

Now it was the turn of the cardinals to shrink at one of their own's rudeness.

They embraced like brothers. After some time chatting, Plethon turned to introduce Alexis and the boys to the Italian. "Cardinal Cessarini, this is General Sartis."

"A pleasure, Cardinal."

"No, the pleasure is all mine, your reputation precedes you," replied Cessarini as he shook hands, the strength of his grip surprising the Greek. "Some of us Cardinals do more than communion in the service of Christ. I am the commander of the papal forces."

Alexis studied the man under the cloth, small but wiry and gaunt in the face, but intelligent eyes and an unusually large Roman nose. The Greek took an instant liking to him, understanding why Plethon and he were friends and the discovery put Alexis more at ease.

The brothers stood mutely scrutinising the hall as each image seared into their brain.

"Where is the Pope?" enquired Plethon.

"He will be joining us soon, or rather, we will be joining him," said Cessarini, pointing to the large double doors at the far end of the hall.

Nicola followed his finger toward the doors. Whatever was behind them felt ominous.

"A pleasure, old friend, and I look forward to getting to know you, general," said Cessarini, before striding off to re-join his conclave.

"That was interesting," said Nicola.

"Don't think too much, Nicola. You will only tire yourself out," quipped Antonis.

"Why? Are you thinking for both of us now?" countered Nicola.

"You two snap out of it and concentrate. We have work to do. Save your petty squabbles for later," barked Alexis.

A formally dressed priest approached them. "The Pope will see you now," he said, gesturing them to go through the forbidding doors.

"And so, Daniel enters the Lion's den," muttered Antonis under his breath.

THE POPE SAT upon his throne at the end of the long hall, appearing more king than the humble shepherd of God's flock. The Cardinals stood to the right in obsequious obedience. To the left, stood the Genoese and Venetian delegates along with some other Latins, most probably French, judging by the fleur-de-lis on their tabard. Arrogant pomp and splendour abounded.

"It feels like we are in an Emperor's hall," said Nicola.

"Where do you think they got it from?" replied Plethon.

The irony was not lost on Antonis.

"His Holiness, Pope Eugenius IV," announced the well-dressed priest.

"Plethon, it is good to see you again," said the Pope.

His voice was too young for the pockmarked face and the large wart on the end of his prodigious nose. He was truly an ugly man. Bulbous watery brown eyes protruded from his skull, his simian jaw and cheekbones salted with stubble, framed his thin-lipped, mouth. The cap on his head only magnified the unpleasantness of his features.

"Your Holiness, it seems our paths have crossed again."

"Yes, it does, and we wish to hear more of your philosophies before our time is finished."

Plethon smiled and introduced the rest of the delegation.

The papal herald came forward and guided the delegates to their assigned places. Antonis noticed the subtle differences to the Emperor's court. There were no proclamations, just a gentle ringing of a bell and as the majority of the participants were clerics, there was a more subdued tone. Even the Austrians, notorious for their crassness, behaved more respectfully in the presence of the Pope.

Eugenius IV had decided on a more informal, egalitarian setting. The main representatives sat in an allotted place with their assistants ensconced behind them. The white cloth-covered tables had been laid in a rectangle with one or two representatives at each. The Pope was at one end, with the Greeks mirrored at the other. Along the sides were three smaller stalls, each with their representatives, Genoese and Venetians flanked the pope, a sign of their influence with the French and the Holy Roman Empire next. Either side of the Greeks were the Coptics and the Florentines.

"Now, for the boring parts. They will read out all that occurred at the last four councils then state the objectives of this one. A good time for a snooze," said Plethon.

Alexis smiled as he looked at the old Greek's agonized

expression. But he was not wrong; it became a full three hours of monotonic droning before they finished.

As the priest ended, the representatives sprung back into consciousness. The agenda was announced for this council, promptly followed by a recess for lunch.

"And now, for the interesting parts. This is where we get the real work done, over food and wine," said Plethon.

They had their prearranged plan of attack. The Venetians and Genoese were Alexis' remit. The Pope and his Cardinals, Plethon's. The French and other Latin states rested with John Argyropoulos. The three men fanned out across the crowd. Alexis, with his predator's gait and aided by his two young cubs, approached the richly dressed Genoese. The excitement was palpable in Nicola and Antonis as they followed their mentor.

After such a dreary session, the brothers returned to their residence drawn together in a common cause from the boredom and lack of stimulus.

"This is a fucking waste of time," said Antonis angrily.

"But it is our best hope of buying the time we need to get our house in order."

Antonis continued. "Every recess we speak to these Italians, we get nowhere. Anyway, why would they help us? The Turk can pay them more. I wouldn't be surprised if they are arranging to transport the Sultan's army right now from Anatolia, no doubt for a handsome fee."

Nicola couldn't argue with the reasoning. "It's funny how the incense burners don't crush the smell of all those unwashed Italian bodies"

Antonis looked at his brother and laughed. "True. I wonder if the Ottoman court smells so foul?"

"Fancy practicing some of Thanos' lessons? But not too crazy, all right?" said Nicola, sensing a change of mood.

"All right."

After almost two months of deliberation, the clerics on both sides agreed to some of the key issues. The council was drawing to a close and the Greeks knew their time was up. The boys could not have been more relieved when the foolhardy approach of Skouras to the Genoese nearly ended the council a week early.

ANTONIS SPIED their host in unusually fine fettle as he approached the dock. He rubbed his eyes to dismiss the tiredness, his mind venturing back to the heated conversation with Nicola the previous night. These arguments were becoming more frequent as they differed on fundamentals regarding the direction the empire was taking. He sighed, his brain ticked over in the early morning, and he consoled himself that soon, they would be back in the city and there would be no more pretence.

The endless rounds of diplomacy had started to weigh heavily upon Alexis and although agreements had been reached, he held out no hope of them being honoured. Resigned to their fate, the big man turned to bid farewell to his hosts and once more assumed his pleasant mask.

A dull grey blanket smothered the dawn sky but to John Argyropoulos, it felt like a blazing sunny day. The emperor's delegates were returning home. A smile broke across his face. *Things can get back to normal, without that meddling old man and his entourage.*

Nicola was still in a daydream; a casual poke from Antonis brought him to and he fell into line with the others to bid their formal goodbyes. However, his mind went to the latent tension from another of their heated debates. Already forgotten was the reason how it started, all that seemed to him was the increasing regularity and energy put into them. Antonis had excelled in the cauldron of diplomatic intrigue whilst he felt adrift in conversations where there were meanings hidden within meanings. To him, it was a simple, help your Christian brothers or not. Antonis thought him foolish and vain to think this way. That's when he remembered why the argument started. He wondered what Katerina's opinion would be as he stared into John Argyropoulos' bland eyes and bade him farewell, surprised at the ease with which the false smile broke across his own face.

Before long, all were on board and the carrack threaded its way southwards out of the port of Ostia towards Napoli. The wind picked up and filled the canvas sails, driving the vessel through the calm azure water.

Alexis stood by the captain. "We should be home by Christmas, if we don't delay," then turned to see the shuffling figure of Plethon approaching him.

"Winds depending, I think you are right."

His heart soared at the prospect. Looking along the deck, he noticed the boys were unusually pensive. Snorting out a gust of salty sea air, he thought those monikers were fast becoming obsolete, as they were on the cusp of manhood. The sobering realisation that they had been his wards nearly four years, started him thinking.

"Have you considered sending them to Pandekterion? They would be with others of their own age, and meeting new contemporaries might take the heat out of them both."

Alexis raised an eyebrow in surprise. The twinkle in Plethon's voice was not lost on him. His plan of taking them to Rome had not had the desired effect. He pondered on the appealing suggestion and decided to explore that possibility on their return to the city.

THE SQUAWK of swirling birds irritated Planedes as he waited impatiently at the harbour's edge for the carrack to dock. He was under strict instructions to take the returnees immediately to a private audience with the Emperor. Spying Plethon on the deck, he used all his skills of diplomacy to hide the annoyance he felt at being the errand boy for that old man and his hulk of a sidekick. "Welcome home, Gemiston," said the unctuous Planedes.

"Thank you," grunted the old man, as he shuffled off the gangplank.

"The Emperor requests that you meet with him presently with news from the council."

Plethon opened his hands and smiled, as he gestured for Planedes to show them the way. Following close behind, Alexis steadied himself as he stepped unevenly onto dry land. The politician noting with pleasure that he was fallible after all.

The news of the delegation's return from the west spread rapidly and there was a sense of hopeful anticipation. Constantinople had a buzzing energy about it, the likes of which Alexis had not seen in years. It was in stark contrast to the muted silence inside the carriage.

The tension was palpable as a conflicted Planedes, desperate to hear the news, held his tongue as his years of diplomatic training decreed. It was with a mixture of eagerness and relief when they eventually arrived at the Blachernae Palace and he finally led them to the Emperor's chambers.

"Tell me what has transpired," said John VIII, dispensing with pleasantries.

"We achieved our overall aims on paper, though, I doubt we will be able to hold all the Genoese to the bargain."

"Orsini agreed not to use his ships to transport the Turk?"

Alexis nodded.

"And the Pope?"

"He has committed to continue paying for the crusade."

John VIII's brow furrowed in thought. It was the other Genoese merchants that concerned him. "I fear the yellow sheen of gold is too beguiling."

Alexis nodded in agreement.

Planedes looked on, a fascinated spectator.

Plethon sighed as a resigned sadness came over him, and that no matter how bad, it was his duty to give his understanding of their predicament. "Your Majesty, the stark reality is that we are appealing to the Latins' sense of Christian unity. When in fact, what drives them is the acquisition of wealth and power. There is nothing that we can truly offer them that will compete with the Turk. Our goodwill and heritage is all but exhausted with them. Only the Pope views this as we do but, he has no standing army."

"He can pay for one, which he is doing,"

"Agreed, but, that on its own is not enough," said Alexis.

"It's a start and better than nothing," was the royal reply.

The finality in his voice put an end to any further discussions and taking their cue, the philosopher and the soldier bade their leave.

Planedes turned to leave with them but to his surprise, the Emperor beckoned him to stay.

"I want you to contact Halil Pasha and arrange a meeting with him."

"Yes, Your Majesty."

Walking along the stone corridor from the Emperor's apartments later, his mind raced at the turn of events. Strangely, he did not agree with the dire situation that the others seemed to see. Maybe that was due to his lack of knowledge of the situation. Perhaps another more private visit to Sartis would help clarify things. Survival was key, resources were limited, and his one trump card would have to be played carefully.

His thoughts were broken as the last sentry noisily pulled his spear aside and he walked out into the palace courtyard. The afternoon sun beat down on his balding pate as he stopped to mull over an idea, then, it occurred to him. Carefully, he pulled out a linen cloth from his waistband and patted the sheen on his forehead in satisfaction, and with a spring in his step, began to play his pieces in his head.

"It looks as though you have gained a little weight, Lexon," jested Thanos.

"You haven't changed." Came the reply.

Thanos beamed back at his friend, stepped towards him, and gave him a big hug. "Well, boys, how did you like Italy? Meet any nice Roman girls?" His twinkle and tone were infectious and both broke into an embarrassed grin. "As I thought, Alexis has been neglecting an important aspect of your studies. Not to worry, Uncle Thanos here, will take care of that," he added, topped with a theatrical huff of mock exasperation.

"Thank you, Thanos," replied Nicola.

One of the house servants appeared and Alexis used that as his cue to stop that line of conversation. "All right, enough of this, it's time to eat."

With immediate obedience, all obliged and filed through towards the dining room. Thanos changing topic towards their trip as deftly as any diplomat, noted Antonis.

The smell of coriander and stewed meat wafted towards them as they sat down to a table weighed with dishes. The boys' stomachs rumbled as the familiar scents of home cooking ignited their taste buds. Antonis eagerly eyed the mishmishya. He had found the food in Rome so bland and uninteresting that the sight of the Byzantine delicacies almost made him lose control. Without ceremony, the boys lunged forward and piled their plates with the foods they had missed so much. Lucanian sausages and olive stuffed chicken sat with fresh salad and stuffed vine leaves. Silence descended as the men savoured the homely flavours.

Thanos smiled as he gazed upon his family being home. *There will be time enough to catch up on events later.*

. . .

NICOLA WAS in a mood to match the gloomy morning. It was close to three weeks since their return and all they had done was more training, in-between sitting around. He wondered what Katerina was doing. Surely, she knew they had returned. Alexis was busy with the Emperor, no doubt dissecting every aspect of the council of Florence's deliberation, so they had been left in Thanos' care. He looked up as three swallows swooped over the crenellations of the sea wall, complimenting Thanos' sounds as he trained with Antonis on the agoge sands.

"Boy, pay attention!"

Nicola turned and saw a dried lump of red soil hurtling in his direction. With catlike reflexes, he tipped his head to the side and the projectile missed its intended target. "Got to do better than that."

Thanos smiled and turned back to his other pupil.

ALEXIS TRIED DESPERATELY to hide his frustration at the bloated bureaucrats wanting their opinions heard, no matter how inane and uninformed. The last few days had been an endless repetition of what should be planned regarding the agreement rendered in Rome. John VIII did not help matters by letting everyone have their moment in the sun.

Perhaps, he thinks it will unite everyone. His thoughts turned to the boys; he had been more than happy to let Thanos take over but that could last only so long. Plethon's suggestion of sending them to the Pandekterion did not seem such a bad idea now.

On the far side of the hall, Planedes' reptilian eyes spied the general in his daydream and decided this was the moment to approach. Weaving around the throng of standing ministers, he sidled up to Alexis. "They do like the sound of their voices, don't they?"

Alexis smiled humourlessly in a rare moment of agreement with him.

"Tell me, how old are the boys now?"

"Seventeen."

Planedes nodded sagely. "Their education is nearly complete, no?"

The hairs on the back of Alexis' neck tingled, unsure of where this conversation was going. "Yes."

"Perhaps if they spent one year at the Pandekterion it would finish off their studies well. Don't you think?"

Alexis almost choked.

Unaware at the pertinence of his statement, Planedes carried on. "I am one of the directors at the institute and could have them enrolled within a week."

Surely this cannot be a coincidence? He turned to face the politician and gazed directly into his eyes. The world moved in mysterious ways so who was he to question such providence? Alexis nodded graciously. "Yes, that would be most appreciated."

"Good, I shall make the arrangements," Planedes smiled back.

"Thank you and please come to dinner, will a week from today work for you?"

"Yes, see you then," replied Planedes, who promptly turned back into the baying crowd of senators.

7

GRAND VIZIER

The carriage clattered along the cobbled road. Inside the sweltering cabin, its occupant let out sighs of exasperation, as the wheels seemed to find every rut in the infernally ancient highway. He noted that as the fortunes of the empire dwindled so did its thoroughfares. A wry smile sprung to his face in a rare moment of relief as he entertained the thought of asking his ruler to use the tribute he gained from this vassal state to improve the quality of the highways, perhaps to even add a good lodging house or two along the way.

Pulling the curtains apart, he gazed at the undulating countryside, allowing himself more of his fantastical daydream. For the briefest of moments, he stared along the Via Diagonalis and saw gleaming fresh cut stone paving the street. Another jaw-rattling pothole jolted him back to reality. Still one more day of this torture, he grumbled, sinking back into the plush cushions in resignation to his lot.

The stench of civilisation brought him out of his fitful slumber. Usually, he would be disgusted with this assault on his senses, today however, it filled him with joy.

"How much farther?"

"We have approached the outlying villages and should arrive at the city walls before sunset, My Lord."

He could barely contain his relief that at least he would be able to bathe in comfort that evening. If he were efficient, he planned to be gone from the city within the week, for he habitually found this place depressing, never quite knowing why. The carriage rumbled on and by the setting of the winter sun, arrived at the regular abode of his country's ambassador. Stepping out of the claustrophobic cabin, the immaculately dressed dignitary greeted him.

"Welcome to the Red Apple, my Pasha."

"Thank you, Kerim. Have the arrangements been made?"

"Yes, my Lord. This missive arrived for you." Kerim clutched the scroll tighter in his left hand. The arrival of someone so important had made his naturally fragile disposition even more nervous. With a slight tremble, he handed over the document he had received earlier that day.

Arching one of his elegant eyebrows and extending one of his impossibly long fingers, the Pasha gracefully took the thick vellum scroll and without ceremony broke the wax seal and blankly read the contents.

Kerim looked on perplexed as the visitor tucked the communiqué into the folds of his doublet.

Perhaps this trip won't be such a waste of time after all.

NICOLA AWOKE before dawn full of excitement. Lying on his bed, he inhaled the damp morning air. They would be going to court for the first time in months, out at last from the confines of the house. He glanced over to his brother, the rhythmic breathing confirming that Antonis still slept. With a nonchalant huff, he flipped onto his back, waiting for daylight to arrive.

The winter sun hung low in the sky, its weakened rays

providing scant warmth on this crisp morning. Antonis felt the chill in his ears as they walked. Even by his standards, he was unusually sullen, putting it down to a fitful night's sleep. He felt no anticipation about going to court. Boredom had begun to creep into his being, not just of the day but a general malaise of his existence. During the last three weeks, he had processed over and over the events of the Council of Florence and arrived at the inescapable conclusion that the Greeks were doomed. Undoubtedly, Plethon and to a degree, Alexis, were highly respected by the Latins, but that was not enough to change the eventual outcome.

The palace was its usual morning bustle and it was with surprise that Antonis found himself greeting ministers and other bureaucrats in a manner that had now become second nature. Many, curious to find out about Rome. Replying with impeccable courtesy, inside, he seethed with contempt at their superficiality. Most only wanting to be seen talking with him rather than paying attention to what was actually said.

A horn sounded, signifying the Emperor's arrival and the assembled throng took their places. Glancing to the foreign quarter, he noticed that the Ottoman presence was unusually bloated. Tall colourfully dressed Turks stood next to the usual envoys and diplomats who resided in the city. His curiosity was piqued at these new arrivals and as silence descended upon the gathering, the announcement of the first visitor to be granted an audience that day was proclaimed.

"Halil Pasha, Grand Vizier of the House of Osman," said the herald.

The slender Turk stood alone, attired in a sober blue and white coat, his clasped hands hidden within the generous sleeves, making him appear like a silk-clad monk. The huge white turban, his only concession to vanity. All eyes were upon him as he calmly walked towards the throne, betraying no hint of awe in the presence of the emperor. Arriving at the foot of the dais, the vizier inclined his head in the slightest of deference.

"Welcome to our court, Halil Pasha."

"I thank Your Majesty, and bring the yearly greetings from my ruler, Sultan Murad."

Antonis noticed the lack of deference in the visitor's tone. Instead of feeling umbrage, a grudging respect grew for his confidence.

Carefully, the Pasha pulled out the scroll from within his cloak, and walked to the throne to hand it to the Emperor.

With a subtle glance to his left, one of the equerries hurried across and smoothly accepted the missive, who then deliberately placed it on the arm of his throne.

John VIII seethed inside at his impotence in the face of such open insolence but resigned himself to a fate out of his control. "We look forward to reading the Sultan's greetings at our leisure."

Halil smiled.

Antonis decided he wanted to meet the man. Glancing to his side, he noticed the tightly-pursed lips and knew Nicola did not share his sentiment. As his eyes moved back to centre stage, they locked onto the staring gaze of Planedes. The young Greek raised his lids, exposing the roundness of bright blue irises, and saw the faintest of smiles creased across the wily politician's face. Perplexed, he focused attention back on the proceedings and wondered when he would get the chance to meet this elegant Vizier.

With the brief but meaningful exchange concluded, Halil exited from the Emperor's presence, and the once silent room began a low hum of chatter. The volume rose accordingly as courtiers extolled, expounded, and then exaggerated what had just occurred.

Alexis, having no desire to be part of this, told the brothers to make their way to the training ground. Reluctant to be leaving as finally there was something interesting, the disappointed boys slowly turned to follow the now all too familiar path to the agoge.

There must have been good reason for Katerina's absence at court because that old goat never missed an opportunity to parade his finest possession. Then he wondered if his brother had given her any thought. Glancing over, he saw Antonis mumbling to himself in frustration.

"What's the problem now?"

"Back to the agoge for more training. I mean, how much swordplay must we do? We had a great opportunity to meet the grand vizier and instead we practice like fucking grunts."

"Know thine enemy," replied Nicola.

His brother's head spun round in surprise.

"It's what Bishop Gregorios told us, remember?"

"Yes, I do, and how are we going to do that in this place?"

"Alexis will be here soon, let's get this done, there will always be another time."

"That's just it. There may never be another opportunity like that again," hissed Antonis in reply.

Nicola shrugged resignedly and wished Katerina had been there today.

THE JASMINE-IMBUED INCENSE swirled around his head as he sat and waited for his host, stuffing the clarity he had arrived with. Being an errand boy, no matter for whom, was not his style. Planedes felt his left shoulder twitch uncontrollably as the irritating thought played on his mind. Glancing across the atrium towards the fine pair of sculptures, the politician conceded that his host did indeed have exquisite taste. Sighing at his own relative penury, irritation was replaced with envy.

"Kankileos. Welcome."

"Thank you, Halil Pasha."

The immaculately dressed host observed his guest, who had grown more rotund since their last encounter, and the ravages of time were also beginning to make their mark. Although maintaining his perfect diplomatic mask, he knew this meeting was futile. Another back-channel communiqué from an emperor with nothing to offer.

Planedes returned the welcoming smile; though did not miss the briefest of contempt in his host's eyes.

All the Vizier could think of was leaving the city as soon as humanly possible. "What is it you have come to see me about?"

The directness caught Planedes unawares. "My Emperor brings you greeting and wishes you to know that he will send no troops to join with the invading crusade from the north, honouring the agreement that has been in place between our two nations."

What troops does he have anyway? "Thank you, and I shall relate that to my Sultan." Halil felt a pang of pity for this man. Undoubtedly intelligent and cunning, he was handicapped by living in a dying state. "We have never spoken much before, have we?"

Planedes opened his hands upwards and pulled his chin down, swelling his already stout neck.

"You know, I have always admired the dignity with which you carry yourself, but it must be difficult with all the obstacles in your way."

He could have shouted with relief; his host had opened the gambit. "It has its moments, Vizier."

Halil smiled. Not at what was said but at what remained unspoken. He enjoyed such mental sparring and though on the defensive, his guest would be a worthy opponent. Such a rarity had to be savoured. "Men like us serve our masters, always loyal, even during those moments we know we could do better."

Planedes' face remained neutral.

Halil let the silence hang a little longer, confident in the knowledge that his guest would seize the opportunity once presented. "It is at these times that it's useful to have friends and allies."

Planedes smiled in acknowledgement.

Halil could see the cogs turning in his guest's expression and casually raised a finger towards a servant who lurked in the dark corner of the room.

Out from the shadows appeared a man carrying a small rosewood box and placed it in front of the visitor.

"And I always look after my friends."

Without further instruction, the servant opened the box to show a small collection of jewels.

The Greek's eyes narrowed conspiratorially. "I see that you do." Glancing inside, he spotted a small leather pouch next to his gift and pulling it out withdrew what appeared to be a small gold ingot. Upon closer inspection, he saw it bore the markings of a crescent moon with a small cross next to it.

"Whenever you wish to make contact, always use that seal and deliver it to this house."

Admiring the cleverness of using a Christian symbol to hide its true meaning, he tucked the ingot inside one of the secret pockets within the folds of his doublet.

Another of Halil's seemingly endless supply of servants appeared, this time with a tray, upon which rested a gold flask and two matching goblets. Meticulously, the domestic filled the drinking vessels and served them to his master and guest.

"I thought fermented drinks were not allowed in Islam," said Planedes.

"May Allah save me from the temptations of the infidel."

Planedes laughed and raised his hand. "To friendship."

Both men enjoyed the wine almost as much as their conversation.

Planedes stroked his beard in contemplation during the journey home. The gift tucked in his clothing weighed heavily on his body, a fresh reminder of the recently concluded meeting. He had done his master's bidding, and in return had been given another path to safety from an unforeseen benefactor. Though this required a different service, the outcome was more in his control than the other. He caught himself unconsciously scoffing at the thought. It was not the morality of treachery that was of concern, more the practicality of which path served him best. After all, wasn't that what politicians did? He smiled.

THANOS RETURNED to the house late afternoon to a cornucopia of delicious smells. Intrigued, he strode into the kitchen to find his full complement of staff hard at work preparing a small feast. "Eleni, what is all this?"

The housekeeper paused from rolling vine leaves and mopped her soaked brow. "Kyrie Alexis asked us to prepare this for a guest you are having this evening."

Thanos raised his eyebrows; it was not Alexis' usual practice to have guests. Curious to discover what his friend was up to, he went in search of him. "I didn't know you could read."

Alexis ignored him.

Put out, his friend reached down and tipped the leather-clad tome upwards.

The general let out a frustrated breath.

"The poems of Al-Tifashi. My, aren't we feeling romantic. Reminiscing on some Syrian lovely?"

Alexis slammed the book shut and stared at his friend. "Thanos, sometimes you are very irritating."

A great smile broke across the smaller man. There was a certain satisfaction in getting under that clever giant's skin. "So, what's all this preparation for tonight?"

"We have the Kankileos as our guest."

Thanos momentarily creased his brow in confusion until he pieced it together. "Planedes? Why him?"

Alexis smiled enigmatically. "You will see. Now, go check that the boys are doing what they were told."

Too bewildered to argue, Thanos went off in search of Nicola and Antonis.

Alexis stifled his chuckle and sank back in the chair, satisfied that he would have another hour's peace, and eagerly returned to his reading. He was still deep into his tome when Thanos returned to tell him his guest would soon be arriving. Reluctantly, he placed the weathered thin leather strap to mark his place. Leaving the cool stonewalled library, the sticky evening air sprung on him. How appropriate to have unpleasant humidity this evening. After a quick check that all was going to plan in the kitchen, he prepared for his guest's arrival.

The last glimmers of light finally squeezed below the horizon before Planedes eventually made his appearance. Full of anticipation since they had discovered from Thanos who their guest was, the boys could not hide their disappointment when they saw that he was alone.

"Welcome, Kankileos, to my humble abode."

Thanos thought better of making a witty quip.

"Please, General, let us not stand on ceremony this evening," replied the guest with a broad beaming smile.

The snake-like charm made the hairs on the back of Alexis' neck prickle. "As you wish, Lord Planedes. This is my friend, Thanos Mavroides."

Planedes inclined his head in greeting, assessing that this was a man of no consequence. Probably a retired soldier who now lived off his plunder, judging by his boots. Giving it no more thought, he turned to face the boys, flashing another of his false smiles, "You two have grown since I last saw you," and he effusively shook their hands.

Perplexed, they returned the greeting with silent grins. Antonis' mind flashed back to the previous day. *Perhaps, this dinner has more relevance than I initially thought.*

As the meal progressed, Planedes began to really enjoy holding court. At first enquiring about their trip to Rome, focusing his attention on the boys. Initially, they were reticent but the politician wove his questions with such skill that by the main course they were into deep discussions about politics, religion, and philosophy. Alexis offered little by way of opinion, instead having moments of panicked worry as the boys started giving their unguarded views to an outsider.

Planedes was impressed with the boys' knowledge and grudgingly even gave credit to Nicola for his reasoning, though, his views were too simple and honourable. Antonis though had politician written all over him and more importantly, as the blood son, he would inherit. Satisfied that he had heard enough, he scooped in another mouthful of meat and washed it down with the surprisingly good wine. Licking his lips like a wolf after the kill, he leaned back in his chair, interlocking his fingers over his ever more prodigious belly. "Your knowledge and reasoning is most impressive. A credit to your teaching and guidance," he said, turning to his host.

Alexis inclined his head in reciprocation.

"You're also a credit to your father," added Planedes, turning to face the boys. His gaze however only rested on Antonis, a subtle slight that was only noticed by Alexis. "You two would be a fine addition to the Pandekterion. One year at our empire's finest institute of learning will polish off your studies just perfectly."

Nicola and Antonis' eyes widened in pleasant shock.

"As one of the directors of the university I have it in my power to grant you immediate admission, after an interview," Planedes paused for effect. "In which, I may say, you both did splendidly. So, when would you like to start?"

Now, both broke into boyish grins.

With mock deference, Planedes turned to his host. "With your permission, of course."

Seeing the expectant look on the boys' faces, he knew there was only one answer. Luckily on this, they all agreed. "I grant my permission."

"Very well, it's ten days till the end of the month. Shall we say they enrol in time for the next period?"

Antonis' heart leapt, for this meant no more agoge. He looked at a beaming Nicola and for the first time in months, they agreed.

8

____

PANDEKTERION

Katerina sat at the mirror in her room. Agatha, the maid, was brushing her luscious auburn hair, the streaks of dark red shining through ever more strongly with every stroke. Rightly, she was proud of her thick locks and how they framed her face, highlighting her cheekbones. As her green eyes met in the mirror she smiled in satisfaction at the reflection. Stifling it, as her mother's words of 'take care of your looks but do not revel in them' flooded her thoughts. Most of her mother's advice she did not fully grasp. She sighed in consolation that perhaps in time, the full meanings would become apparent.

She was still in disbelief with the turn of events. Over the months, she had grown bored of her tutoring and began to dream in the forlorn hope that she could attend the University of Constantinople to further her studies. In the depths of her doldrums, she had played out scenes of attending the renowned school of philosophy. Imagining walking through the centuries-old colonnaded buildings laced with the ever-present scent of rose discussing with her fellow students the classes they had attended.

Eventually plucking up the courage, she tentatively asked her mother if it would be possible for her to enrol. Unsurprised, Sophia Planedes said that she would discuss it with her father. For a month, there was no glimmer of a response, and her hopes began to fade.

Then one cloudy grey afternoon Planedes returned home earlier than usual and summoned his daughter. Nervously, she entered his private writing room to find him poring over one of his countless letters.

"Your mother tells me that you wish to enter the university."

"Yes, papa."

"And why should I allow it?"

Katerina paused, unsure how to respond, noticing her father's pursed lips as he awaited her answer.

"Is this the sort of thing that a young high-born woman such as you should be doing?"

At that moment Katerina's heart leapt, as she now knew how to answer; citing the many famous women who had attended over the centuries. Planedes relented and gave permission to attend, on condition that rhetoric would be one of her classes. Nodding agreement at such a small price to pay, she leapt over to her father, hugged him and showered him with kisses of profuse thanks.

Agatha opened the window, allowing the invigorating dawn air to rush in. "Shall I prepare your paper and quills?"

"No, thank you. I want to do that myself."

The maid smiled, thinking it best she left her young mistress some solitude for preparation.

Once alone, Katerina excitedly skipped over to her favourite wooden chest. Carefully opening it, the smell of ink and leather assaulted her senses. She reached in and took out two hide rolls, the softness of the calfskin melding with her hands as she clasped them.

Gingerly, she placed the items on the bed and unfurled each

one to reveal her most precious of possessions, her writing tools. She pulled out one of the four ebony sticks, neatly tucked in the soft brown leather. Holding it between her thumb and forefinger, she gazed upon it whilst rolling it in her hand reminiscent of miniature javelins. These were her weapons of war, as she theatrically swished it in the air. Replacing the wooden dart, she checked that all was in order, carefully wrapping them again, her heart full of hopeful anticipation.

THE PALANQUIN WOUND its way between the third and fourth hill, towards the Mesa. It made the journey as level as possible, a skill the transporters had by necessity become adept in. *At least it's a lithe young girl, instead of some bloated dignitary,* thought one of the perspiring porters.

The passenger peered out from behind the curtains as she felt the downward trend of travel. Gazing up, she saw the great Valens Aqueduct throw its shadow from above. "This will be fine here."

"But mistress, the university is still another two streets away, and we are under strict instructions."

Ignoring his pleas, Katerina unlatched the door and stepped out of the still moving carriage. "I will be fine," she replied, flashing her most charming smile.

The transporters watched helplessly as their cargo glided away.

Katerina let out a nervous sigh of relief as she walked the last two streets. The previous night, she dreaded turning up in the Kankileos' carriage, anonymity destroyed, labelled before she could prove herself. Throngs of humanity assaulted her senses, crowds of young people hurriedly seeking their destinations. Now, she regretted her show of independence and momentarily froze as she tried to work out where to go.

"Are you lost?" came a voice.

Katerina turned, to see a fresh-faced boy not much older than her, his ruddy cheeks still with the remnants of pubescent acne. "I am looking for the School of Rhetoric."

The boy smiled and pointed over her shoulder. "It's the third building on the left. There are no signs here, but you will get used to it soon."

His accent was peculiar. She couldn't quite place it but thanked him.

"What's your name?" enquired the boy.

"Katerina."

"I'm Giovanni Tezzo. Welcome to the Pandekterion."

Katerina smiled and feeling in a buoyant mood made her way to the hall. Within minutes the morass of students magically dissipated to a few stragglers. Anxiously hurrying towards her destination, counting under her breath as she passed each building. "One... two... three."

Arriving at a low-slung wooden door, she drew sharp breath at the uninviting entrance, and entered. The six-foot thick walls created a small passageway through which she reached a splendid amphitheatre. A long wooden table sat in the middle, flanking it were two smaller desks, with chairs. Rows of benches rose up in a semi-circle around the stage. The room was devoid of people. Insecurity gripped her again, *did I mishear what he said?* Frantically, she scanned the room once more. Far up in the rows, she noticed a sleeping student propped against the wall. "Excuse me."

The student did not respond.

Gingerly, she climbed, counting the rows as she went. At fourteen, she stopped and turned toward the slumbering figure. "Excuse me," this time shaking the body.

The figure stirred groggily. "Have classes started?"

"There is no one here."

"Don't worry, there will be," replied the sleeper, without opening his eyes, and began to doze off again.

"Is this rhetoric?"

The sleeper opened one eye. "First day?"

"Yes."

"Take a seat and wait," he replied and promptly turned back towards the wall into instant slumber.

The confidence in his voice was strangely calming and taking his advice, she took a pew and waited.

In ones and twos, students filtered through the two entrances, and as the room filled so did her excitement grow. Most of them were scruffily dressed, the boys showing their newfound manliness with their varied attempts at growing a beard. More sporadically, girls entered in pairs, sometimes small groups, or with a maid, but none alone, yet none chose to sit beside her. It was her first day, but it gave Katerina confidence that no one had accompanied her. The low hum of conversation, steadily grew louder.

Through the main entrance entered the boy she had spoken to earlier, looking a little more dishevelled than before. Looking up, he espied Katerina, and flashed a boyish grin whilst making his way towards her. "May I sit next to you, Katerina?"

"Of course."

"It's Giovanni!"

"I remember. You know, I wasn't sure when you sent me to that door, it looked so uninviting."

Giovanni nodded. "Yes, but to direct you to the main entrance was a lot harder, most likely you would have got lost through the passageways."

Katerina looked at him wide eyed.

"Anyway, you looked like the type of girl who wouldn't be afraid of a small stone passage."

Now she broke into a full smile and her feline eyes sparkled. The transformation transfixed him.

"Hey, Spanos, trying it on with the new girl?" came a shout from behind.

Giovanni reddened and slouched at the insult to his masculinity.

The callousness incensed Katerina's sensibilities. "Ignore them, they are probably just jealous of you," sparkling at him again.

Perking up with the show of solidarity, he straightened his shoulders once more, and looked at this new student with genuine curiosity.

Katerina saw his puppy dog look and knew she had won an acolyte. Not her intention but certainly could do no harm. The lecture hall was brimming with youthful energy and idly, she wondered where this famed teacher could be. Most likely, an overweight geriatric who liked the sound of his own voice. After all, wasn't that rhetoric?

"Determining how to present your invention. What is that called?"

The loudness of the voice jolted Katerina, however, it was the proximity that confused her. Turning, she saw the earlier sleeping student uncoil languidly and stand up with a full command of the now hushed room.

"Anybody?" he asked again.

To her left, Giovanni's hand shot up, grabbing the teacher's attention. "Style," he answered.

"Very good."

"Spanos," hissed out the previous voice at the back.

"Heckling comes under delivery, Simeon," interrupted the teacher. "And you have a long way to go before you can do that."

To a backdrop of sniggers, the admonished wag was silenced with impunity and Katerina, instantly warmed to the young dynamic professor. With the room under his spell, the thin bookish tutor meandered through the rows to make his way down to the stage, all the while expounding to his class.

. . .

"Quick," snapped Antonis, "we are going to be late again." Annoyed that he had allowed his brother yet again to side-track him on some tomfoolery.

Nicola picked up his pace and they hurried to the class. He found Rhetoric deathly boring, requiring all his self-will to attend. Mostly, he did it for his brother, who excelled in it. The last two months at the Pandekterion had been magical. As if they were children once more in Crete. The new horizons had cooled their rivalry and brought them together again. Ahead, he saw Antonis slip into the class and quietly loped up to the doorway.

Thankful it was still ajar, he tried to squeeze past; his nose filled with the metallic smell of the iron bands as it rubbed against the door. But it was just too narrow, and a piercing creak emanated from the hinges as it opened. Relieved to hear no break in the lecture, he looked up to see the teacher's back and slunk into the nearest pew.

"Glad you could make time for us, Vevellis," boomed out the professor without breaking his stride.

"He never misses a trick, that's why they call him Leo the Great," said an excitable Giovanni to Katerina.

His newfound friend nodded dumbly whilst staring at the back of the latest entrant, and a flutter filled her breast.

Excitable students congregated in the courtyard, brimming with energy, some standing around in discussion, others sat on the low-slung stone walls gossiping in pairs or observing alone. Katerina's finger twirled a strand of hair behind one ear as she soaked up the atmosphere. The last month had been a whirl. Meeting new people had given her a sense of freedom from the tight leash of home. Now she knew why her father had insisted on her attending rhetoric, as it was after all the foundation of politics; perhaps, he was more progressive than she had given him credit.

Observing these young intellectuals prompted a twinge of envy. For her, all this was a phase, after which she would be married to a stranger, spending the rest of her life as a pampered nobleman's wife. Idly, she wondered if that was crueller than ignorance, then decided it was better to have at least known this feeling for a while than never to have tasted it at all.

Across the courtyard, the piercing blue eyes focused on his prey. For once, she was alone, and he had vowed to take the first opportunity when it presented itself. They had exchanged a few pleasantries but nothing meaningful. It was usual for her to be surrounded by her followers, a motley crew of foreigners and oddballs whom she genuinely appeared to like. He found it strange for a high-born to want to associate with those medi-ocrities, as he saw them. Even his brother, with his already vaunted charisma, had not managed more than a few nods with her. Chastising in self-reproach, he caught himself overthinking yet again.

Plucking up the courage, he strode purposefully towards the seated girl and blurted. "How do you like being at The Pandekterion?"

Katerina looked up into the penetrating gaze. "Yes, it's fun."

The closed response made the insecurities creep in as he thought of a reply. "We met before at your father's house a few months back. I'm Antonis Vevellis." He felt the skin tingle at the back of his head in foolishness.

"Yes, I remember, Mama introduced us. You came with the big general. I'm Katerina."

The enigmatic smile confused him. Was she just being polite? But it did not matter as he had her undivided attention now.

Katerina gestured for him to sit beside her, which he took without hesitation. "Aren't you usually with your brother?"

Antonis raised his brows. "I think he is off doing some fencing practice, he never seems to get enough of it."

Katerina laughed at the exasperated tone.

The response piqued him, and he seized upon her interest in his predicament. "You don't seem to say much in rhetoric."

"Unlike you, who are always in some form of debate. Leo seems to love it when you get involved."

Antonis self-deprecatingly shrugged, whilst inside he burst with pride that she had noticed. "Well, I suppose it's just that I always have something to say." He held up his hands in a mocking admission of guilt.

"What you say is good and your responses are definitely the quickest in class."

Acknowledging the compliment, he decided on a change of tack not to labour the point. "Where is your Italian friend?"

"Giovanni?"

"Is that his name?"

"Another class most probably, he should be out soon." Katerina looked up into the clear blue eyes and became intrigued to know more about him. Perhaps her initial impression that he was cold was misplaced and instead she should have seen it as intelligence. "You are not from the Polis, are you?"

"No, from Crete."

"How long have you been in the capital?"

"Eighteen months, and before that nearly two years in Mistras."

"That's a long time to be away from home. Have you been back to see your parents at all?"

"Yes, we returned to Chania a few months ago on our way to Rome."

Katerina saw the momentary glimpse of sadness in his face as he spoke and felt for him. "Don't you miss home?"

Antonis shrugged, though in truth, he didn't anymore. The things he had witnessed would never have happened if he had stayed in Chania and the prospect of more adventure was preferable over the life of a landowner's son in Crete. Looking at Katerina, he knew that was not the answer she was expecting. "Sometimes," he lied.

The sympathetic smile in response confirmed he had made the right decision. "What were you doing in Rome?"

"I was part of a delegation who went to see the Pope."

"Really?"

"Yes."

"What was it for?"

"To discuss the union of the churches and the formation of alliances with the Genoese and Venetians."

Katerina let out a slow whistle; now, she was truly impressed. How did a seventeen-year-old boy happen to move in these circles? Perhaps his arrogance in class was not so misplaced. The bell sounded in one of the towers above, signifying the passing of noon.

"Oh! I must attend a class in logic," she politely excused herself.

Antonis, sensing he had caught her attention, smiled, and bade her farewell, watching the elegant young woman as she walked across the courtyard. Knowing that the next time they met in class she would not be so distant.

Turning away, he espied his brother at the far end of the octagon, holding court after another of his undoubtedly magnificent fencing displays. Envy-laced pride overcame him as he saw the adoring students surrounding Nicola. He chuckled to himself, conceding, albeit of a different variety, Nicola collected followers just as Katerina did. The laugh turned into a satisfied smile as he made his way towards him.

"If you hold the handle lightly in the fringes it allows for more fluid defence. Grip too tightly and speed is sacrificed."

With a nod, Nicola instructed his opponent to attack. Effort-lessly, he parried the blade then patted the flat of his weapon on his challengers' buttocks. "You see, and with that, your adversary is off-balance."

The surrounding boys murmured their approval.

"Antonis, where have you been hiding?" said an ebullient Nicola, who revelled in the sharing of his knowledge.

"Oh, just chatting to some people."

Nicola shrugged, the draw of the classroom was no match for the thrill of the training ground and his brother had become a bit of a lone wolf whilst he had collected a sizable group of followers. It did not matter, as to him they would always be brothers; even as they grew with each new beginning to find their own path.

The congregation began to dissipate as each pupil reluctantly left to attend class.

"You never join us, Antonis. You should, I need a challenging duelling partner."

Antonis proffered a wan smile at his brother's egotism. "If I never train on the sand again it won't be too soon," he replied. "Come, we have a logic class to attend."

Now, it was Nicola's turn to show disappointment. Carefully, he wrapped his swords in the blankets and tied them together with one of his leather straps, fashioning the excess length into a shoulder strap, and slung it across his back. At least logic was preferable to other classes and he jadedly followed for another afternoon of dullness.

Katerina paid little attention in class that afternoon, her mind intrigued by the conversation with Antonis. Now she understood why he was so good at public speaking having been exposed to such vaunted company so young. It certainly explained the aura of quiet superiority he displayed. Grudgingly, she knew it was justified. Yet, his brother was so different, the boyish enthusiasm he had for play over studies. He affected no airs but was always surrounded by a crowd. Occasionally, she overheard some of the other girls gushing over his dashing looks and winning smile. She had felt that when she first saw him at court all those months ago. Surely, he was not so cock-sure with all those dignitaries in Rome. She vowed to see what this fencing was all about when the next opportunity arose. Satisfied she had decided, she focussed on her studies for the rest of the day.

PLANEDES PRIDED himself in always having the best available knowledge on hand and he balked at the facts presented before him. The meeting with Halil Pasha some months before had proven most useful. Ostensibly, he was his emperor's messenger, but he had access to the true might that was arrayed before them. Whatever magic Plethon and Sartis conjured with the Latins was no match for this. Undoubtedly, he had to continue the pursuit of his other plans for his safety. A grim smile crossed his face at the realisation of what Halil had achieved. With merely a few missives of credible information, he had set one of the leading ministers onto a clear path of desertion.

Perhaps he was better suited serving masters such as these, because at least then, he would be close to the power, something he would not readily have in the Latin states. Only Crete would offer that option. Planedes' mind turned to his daughter, wondering how she was faring at the Pandekterion, and decided that he would speak with her at the next available opportunity. The palace felt claustrophobic and the desire to leave for the comfort of his home was compelling. Politely, he excused himself from the other windy old men with a case of 'chilled humeurs'.

Stepping into his carriage, he mentally calculated the different tasks he had to complete over the next lunar cycle and was still lost in thought when the transport rattled into his courtyard. He stepped inside to see his daughter chatting animatedly with his wife.

"What are you two ladies talking about?"

"Nothing much, Spiros, my dear. Mother daughter things that do not concern you," replied Lady Sophia, her smile disarming any possible riposte.

"Very well, I will make myself scarce." Leaving the girls, Planedes made his way to the seclusion of his library, ordering one of his servants along the way to bring him some lemon water and honey cakes.

Sophia placed a hand on her daughter's arm. "Katerina, please go speak with your father after we finish. You know how he likes to hear about what you are doing."

"Yes, mama." She had been meaning to chat with him, both to tell him what she had learned and in gratitude for his permission to let her study.

THE PAPER STARED BLANKLY BACK at Planedes as he contemplated what to write; bizarrely the prose was not flowing this afternoon. Idly, he wondered if he was being too subjective, as his daughter was the subject of this communication. Searching for inspiration, he had devoured almost a full plate of honey cakes before deciding to revert to type and be pragmatic.

Once decided, the words began to flow and before long he had penned a missive to the Conte di Valmerana in Venice. Sitting back, he reread the message and was pleased with its contents, succinct and to the point; extolling his daughter's virtue and heritage and stating the suitability of a possible union. Reaching into the thick leather box on his desk, he pulled out a flat square piece of wood and stared at the painting upon it.

Satisfied that it showed Katerina in her true likeness, he carefully wrapped it in a linen cloth and tied it up. Placing it together with the sealed letter, he was confident that the dribbling old count would be overjoyed to receive such an offer. Beauty and breeding always worked well with such men. Perhaps the Greeks were a waning power, but they had the one thing the Latins coveted, lineage from the ancients, giving their wealth the legitimacy they so craved.

"Hello, Papa, how are you?"

Planedes looked up and instinctively gave his warmest smile. Katerina was the only thing, apart from himself that he cared anything for. Returning his smile, the politician wondered if his daughter had the same manipulative ruthlessness. He was not sure, it might develop over time, then thought that maybe it was best if she did not have it, as she would be easier to control.

"I am good, my darling. How are your studies?"

"They are going well, papa."

Sensing his daughter wanted to speak, he decided to give her some time. "So, what is your favourite class? I hope it's rhetoric. Have you met good people?"

Katerina inclined her head and smiled shyly as she sat next to her father. 'No, papa, it's Philosophy. I find rhetoric too extrovert for me."

With a tenderness that surprised even himself, Planedes put an arm around his daughter. "Well, we are not all destined to be public speakers. Philosophy is commendable and requires an erudite ordered mind."

Katerina nuzzled her shoulder into her father's chest, enjoying this rare moment of intimacy. "But our teacher in rhetoric is brilliant. Everyone loves him," she replied seeking approval.

"Who is your teacher?"

"Leo Chartemenos."

A moment passed before Planedes registered who that was. "Ah, the son of John Chartemenos, who was my teacher and one of the greatest ever to expound in our hallowed halls. I have never heard his son, so I wonder if he is as good as his father?" Making a mental note to visit sometime in his capacity as director. "Are there any good exponents in your class?" he enquired more from professional curiosity at upcoming talent than a desire to empathise with his daughter.

"My friend Giovanni is pretty good."

The quizzical look on her father's face prompted her on.

"Giovanni Tezzo, he is a Genoese from Galata."

Planedes pursed his lips and nodded, hoping that the best was not some foreigner, in a rare moment of patriotism.

"But the best is Antonis Vevellis, who is brilliant, and far outclasses everyone. Maybe you remember him, papa, he came with the big general once to our house."

"Vaguely," he lied.

"Did you know that he was in Rome as part of a diplomatic mission visiting the pope? Incredible, don't you think? That's why he is so good at public speaking."

The admiration in her tone for the lad buoyed his spirits; always good to have options.

"Though, surprisingly, his brother is not so good, he prefers fencing."

Planedes huffed contemptuously, his assessment of the two boys correct and to his pleasure it appeared his daughter preferred brains over brawn as well. He could sense the pieces he had placed inexorable moving in the direction he had planned; perhaps another gentle caress to keep these ships sailing in the right direction. "I remember the boy now. From an old distinguished family in Crete and the sole heir if I recall." The lack of subtlety grated in his own ears.

Cuddling up against him, the message of approval was not lost on Katerina. At least he was giving her some choices.

. . .

ANTONIS WAS full of anticipation for the coming week, especially looking forward to shine in rhetoric for his newfound audience. However, his excitement was cruelly cut short, as Alexis decided they needed to spend a few days refreshing their martial skills. In his darkened mood, he berated his mentor, saying there was no need for it. After all, they had been training for years and now was time to exercise their minds.

Alexis ignored the outburst and smiling enigmatically, told them to get dressed for the training ground.

Unaware of the true reason for his brother's outburst, Nicola happily obliged. Anything was better than the boredom of the lecture hall. "Come on, let's see if you've got rusty after all those classes," he said, following with a firm pat of solidarity on Antonis' shoulder.

The younger brother's head slumped in admission of defeat and followed sullenly behind.

WITH A TAP on her left shoulder, Giovanni startled Katerina, who was lost in thought. The impish grin the first view as she abruptly entered the present.

"Where were you just now?"

"Nowhere, just daydreaming."

The young Genoese narrowed his eyes in disbelief.

Katerina returned a firm stare to prevent any further questions. In truth she wondered why the Vevellis brothers had been absent the last few days.

Thinking better of upsetting his only true friend, he relented. "It's the competition today. Are you prepared for it?"

This meant a lot to him and Katerina was overcome with guilt that she had totally forgotten. "Yes." Grateful that at least this debate was about logic, and secretly hoped she would not be chosen.

Leo bounded in, silencing the murmuring room, his dark green hose and doublet unusually sumptuous. Pursing his lips and staring up into the expectant crowd, he casually brought his hand to the simple felt hat that rested upon his head. "Today is debate," boomed the thin man, theatrically removing his hat, and doffing it to his pupils. The crowd electrified in anticipation of what was next.

Sitting unusually far back from the front, Antonis wrung his hands, relieved Alexis had decided that three days 'refresher' was enough. Now, he just hoped his name was picked and clutched his folded piece of paper ever tighter.

Still holding out his cap, Leo Chartemenos started to walk up the aisle between the rows, offering it to his students to put their pieces of paper in.

"I hope all of you are ready," he said as the hat passed around, like a church collection.

Katerina watched with interest as it slowly made its way towards her, and from the corner of her vision, she noticed Antonis' penetrating gaze, who nodded a greeting across the room. His brother sitting next to him seemed lost in his own world. One by one the teams deposited their papers until it reached her. Carefully, she placed the paper in the hat, surprised at its softness; her fingers lingering a fraction longer than normal, appreciating the quality of the cloth.

Eventually, the vessel returned to its owner, replete with the entries. Deliberately, the teacher put his hand in and pulled out the first entrant. Opening the fold, he blankly viewed the names. "Antonis and Nicola Vevellis."

A hush came across the hall, as everyone knew how good Antonis was, who surreptitiously clenched his fist with relief. Nicola sighed in resignation. But Leo lived for these dramatic moments in class, the anticipation of what would happen next and greedily savoured it with another scan around the lecture hall before putting his hand back in the hat. Pulling out the second paper, he opened it again in the same manner. Only this time, upon reading it, a smirk came across his face. "The second team is Giovanni Tezzo and Katerina Planedes."

A collective hum descended over the room. Leo was overjoyed; the result could not have been better, the two best debaters duelling it out. Though unlikely the Genoese would beat the Greek, he was the only one who could give him a contest. He paused for a moment, before deciding the subject on which they were to present their arguments. "The topic is, a woman's place in church and state politics. There you have it. Will the two teams please go prepare, and we shall start after lunch."

Without pause, Antonis tapped his brother and led him out to one of the study rooms to prepare. "This is going to be easy, those two don't stand a chance. He's too scared and she is just a woman."

Nicola grunted in response and was still coming to terms with the fact that he had to do some work, instead of dozing off as others debated.

Antonis could barely contain his excitement, already confident in his abilities; it was the fact he would be directly against Katerina. Her earlier nod before the draw, still seared in his memory. Probably though, the Genoese, being the better of the two, would state their argument. But it was good enough, he reasoned. Ignoring Nicola's moodiness, he sat down at the desk and quickly began piecing together his argument. Though not his speciality subject, he soon had a clear reasoned case and began to present it to his still sulking brother. Halfway through, he looked up to see the blank stare in front of him. "Pay attention, will you," he barked.

Nicola rolled his eyes. "It doesn't really matter; you will win the argument. The Italian hasn't got a chance."

"Yes, but there is your part too. The rebuttal can win or lose it for us."

"Sure, sure. All right, you have my attention." Nicola dragged his feet around loudly to face his sibling.

Finally satisfied, Antonis started from the beginning to his singular audience.

Giovanni was too nervous to eat and merely pushed the food around his plate. He had no illusions that he could beat Antonis, and creeping doubt grew as he imagined a renewed round of ribbing from that horrible Simeon and his cronies. Turning the fork up, he stared at it, wondering who the unnamed Greek was who invented it some seven hundred years earlier. Maybe it was a woman. He let out a chuckle at the thought.

Katerina put a hand on his resting arm to quell his nerves. "It's a good argument, don't worry. We will just do the best we can." Her mother's advice rang in her ears, 'be careful what you wish for'. This time she understood. "Come, let's go to the hall and get ready." Reasoning that activity might take his mind off worry and calm him down somewhat.

The empty lecture hall seemed vast as Katerina entered, grateful to Giovanni as he unintentionally focused her on keeping him relaxed. Deciding to take the lectern on the left side of the main table, both plumped down heavily on the two chairs set out for them. Giovanni busied himself organising his papers then began to read his piece, muttering inflexions at what he considered crucial points.

Strangely, Katerina felt a sense of calm and wondered if this was what her father experienced before one of his speeches amongst the council of nobles. Perhaps it was that she had already accepted they would not win, so felt liberated. Either way, it did not matter and she turned to see the first of the chattering students enter. In what seemed an instant, the whole class returned, but still no sign of their opponents. Smirking to herself, she fantasised they had decided to forfeit; a forlorn hope.

Nicola fidgeted impatiently in the study room. "Why are we still waiting?"

Antonis ignored him as he peeped through the cracked open door, waiting for the right moment.

"Antonis?"

"Wait, I will tell you when," he hissed as his concentration broke.

Peering out through the crack again, the sign Antonis had been waiting for presented itself. Mentally, he began the countdown. For it was as much theatrics as content that won a crowd. "Right, let's go," he said, prodding his brother into action.

Giovanni's nerves began to get the better of him when the green-clad teacher entered the lecture hall.

Calmly, Leo sat down at his adjudicating desk, and waited, soaking up the atmosphere.

"Where could they be?" flustered the Genoese.

Katerina shrugged. "Who knows? Maybe they're too scared to show."

The joke had no effect on him, instead, his eyes widened even more at something behind her. Turning, she saw the two boys enter, like conquering heroes, dwarfing the room with their presence.

Antonis led lightly, holding a scroll, his gaze focused on his opponents. Behind, Nicola looked more like a warrior than debater with his dusty boots and weather-beaten baldric. They made an impressive duo.

"I feel like a young girl about to fight some northern knights," whispered Katerina.

The words jolted a memory in Giovanni as he recalled something his father had spoken of some years before during his visit home to Genoa.

Katerina saw the spark of inspiration fill her friend's face, replacing the worried look with one of surety.

"You're a genius, Katerina," he replied as he picked up a quill and busied himself again with his papers, drawing lines through text and adding words.

"What are you doing?"

"Don't worry, I have an idea." The confidence in his voice preventing any further questions.

Leo elected that the Vevellis brothers were to open and Antonis rose to address the crowd.

He cut an elegant figure as he began to present his case and Katerina could not help but admire the skill with which he blended his argument and delivered it to the now captive audience. Her heart began to sink as piece by piece he laid out his reason and knew that their effort was no match for this.

Sitting to thunderous applause, Antonis turned to see his opponent rise to make their case.

Giovanni felt unusually calm. The shaking he usually felt in his hands replaced by a steady grip. "Thanks to my esteemed colleague for his most reasoned view. He lays out woman's role clearly and I agree with everything he says." He paused for effect. "Except for one thing. A woman can decide the course of history directly on the battlefield as capably as any man."

Katerina was filled with alarm. This was not what they had written down and clutched her hands together, hoping he did not make a fool of himself.

Antonis smiled to himself, this was going to be fun, then sat back in his chair and crossed his arms against his lithe body.

"In my argument, I will show you how a simple farm girl led her nation to victory against an invading oppressor. Finally ended a war that had raged for over one-hundred years. And in the process, became their greatest talisman on the battlefield. Her name was Jeanne d'Arc."

A hush settled across the audience, no one really knowing who she was, or what she had achieved, but now waited with anticipation as to what the little Italian would say.

Sensing the shift in momentum, Giovanni became emboldened even more, going on to expand his structure.

Antonis' confident mask began to slip with every word his opponent uttered.

Katerina looked on impressed and wondered what the brother could do in response.

Riveted to his seat, Nicola listened intently, knowing he had to pull something out of the hat to give them any chance. He could sense his brother's temper begin to boil and this was now a matter of family honour. He hung on every word, waiting for the hook onto which he could latch himself. The more Antonis fidgeted, the more clarity Nicola gained. With a patience that surprised even himself, he waited for his opponent's mistake, suppressing every morsel of doubt as Giovanni began to wind up his argument.

The Genoese finished and sat down amid a deathly silence. Initially, he thought he had misjudged his effort but a quick glance at the sea of stunned faces soon rectified that, causing him to bite the inside of his cheek to stop his smile of satisfaction.

A sense of liberation accompanied Nicola as he rose amongst the mute crowd for the rebuttal. The Genoese had presented a near flawless argument and Katerina followed with a competent rebuttal to Antonis' argument. There was nothing he could say that would win the contest for them. For once, he was grateful that no one expected anything from him. Glancing at his brother's stony face, he knew he had to at least try; his sense of loyalty demanded it. Scanning the audience whilst mentally going over his response one last time, Nicola steeled himself for the retort. Clutching at everything he could to win the crowd, he turned to face Giovanni, using every ounce of his charisma to dominate the room. Once the momentary blankness came, he knew he was ready.

"'No man is an island.' I can't remember who coined that

phrase, but it is true, and the same applies to woman. Clearly, Jeanne d'Arc was an exceptional leader as my esteemed colleague reasoned most well. Yet, without the support of her experienced and able lieutenants, who not only saved her life but provided invaluable war craft knowledge, The Maid could never have achieved what she did."

Antonis' dark mood perked up, surprised at his brother's tack, and a glance over to his opponents, saw that it seemed to be working.

Katerina looked on in utter amazement. She had no idea that a keen mind lurked beneath that athletic exterior. This day had already been full of surprises and she wondered what would happen next.

Summing up, Nicola sat down to hearty applause, and felt pleased with his efforts, though doubting he had done enough to win, he had at least acquitted himself well.

Leo Chartemenos was momentarily stunned, "Excellent efforts all-round, with some unexpected results. Congratulations to the participants."

The class acknowledged the two teams' efforts without hesitation.

"Now for the fun part," boomed Leo. "Voting."

A sharp intake of breath emanated from the audience.

"We shall do this the traditional way. Loudest applause wins. First, Antonis Vevellis."

Huge applause burst out for Antonis, but he knew it did not have that force, and he sat back to await what they thought.

His fears were confirmed as Leo signalled for Giovanni. Thunderous applause accompanied by cheers made him the clear victor.

Nicola felt for his brother.

"Now, for the rebuttals. Katerina Planedes."

Solid applause followed her name.

Nicola saw her smile graciously and knew that however well he did, it would not be enough to win the day.

"And finally, Nicola Vevellis."

To the surprise of all, there was a strong showing for his effort.

A smirk crossed Leo's face. The result was totally unexpected and because of that even more appreciated. The final decision came down to him and without hesitation he declared the Tezzo/Planedes team the victors.

Nicola consoled his brother with a pat on his forearm and walked to the other side of the adjudicator's table to congratulate his opponents. Flashing his most winning smile, he proffered his hand. "Well done. That was excellent, and a good contest."

Giovanni nodded with a beaming smile.

"Let me try to win back some dignity. Would you like to come and join us for some fencing practice?"

Giovanni stood there wide-eyed in shock, whilst Katerina gasped.

"You are most welcome too," added Nicola, turning towards her.

Antonis had walked up behind his brother, determined to turn this defeat into a victory. Grateful for once for his brother's open-hearted charm, he forced himself to smile as he offered his hand to Giovanni; the feeling false to him, as losing was never an option. The only consolation was that his practice at the Council of Florence had perfected his political mask.

Nicola, clasping one of his huge hands onto the little Genoese's arm, guided the group out of the classroom and headed for his usual training place. As they left the hall, he veered into the left corridor and walked purposefully towards what looked like a pile of rags.

"Isn't the quad over on the other side?" asked Giovanni.

"It is, but we need to collect my weapons first. Wouldn't be much fun without them, would it?"

Giovanni nodded mutely as they came upon the heaps of different coloured cloth.

Nicola leant down, quickly took two rolls, and handed them to the little Italian, who gulped at their weight. Noticing the noise, confirmed a different blade was needed and reaching down into the pile again he searched for a suitable one. A growl of satisfaction emanated from him as he found what he was looking for. "These should do it," and led the four of them to his favourite place on campus.

The fizz in Giovanni's gait as they walked towards the grassy slope started to rub off on Katerina. Her curiosity was aroused, and she felt a spring in her step, wanting to find out what all the fuss was about.

Walking beside her, Antonis noticed her anticipation and edged closer towards her, offering his arm.

Without thinking, she looped her hand into the crook of his elbow.

Antonis stiffened slightly then asked. "Have you ever tried fencing before?"

"No, I've not seen fencing close up."

Antonis smiled. "Well, you will today."

"I've heard your brother is really good, everyone talks about it," she said and looked ahead, towards the hulking figure of Nicola setting the pace, one arm full of weapons, the other draped around Giovanni, dwarfing him. Snippets of their conversation filtering back to them.

"Yes, he is."

"Do you fence too? I never see you doing it."

Antonis nodded. "Yes, we were trained by the same master since fourteen."

"But Nicola is better than you?"

Antonis let out a relaxed laugh. Nothing could put him in

a bad mood whilst he walked arm in arm with this auburn-haired beauty. "Not necessarily, he just loves it more than me."

Katerina giggled and Antonis offered a mock questioning look.

His brother's booming voice broke his romantic concentration. "Antonis, we are here to fence, we have our honour to salvage."

An impish grin crossed his face. "Of course."

Without ceremony, Nicola tossed one of the weapons towards him.

Deftly, Antonis caught the handle of the straight sword and gave an uncharacteristic swirl then bit the inside of his cheek to prevent himself smiling at their guests' surprise.

The elder brother carefully weighed up the two remaining blades in each hand. "You're both right-handed?"

They nodded, confirming his choice.

"Right, who wants to go first?"

Before either of them could answer, Antonis spoke. "I think we should duel a little bit to begin with. So, they can get an idea."

Nicola shot back a look, at least he would have a worthy sparring partner for once. Without another word, he brought up his blade to signify commencement.

Languidly, Antonis followed suit with a straight back springing on relaxed legs.

Katerina looked on intrigued as the brothers padded around each other in a soft yet deliberate motion. Presently, her concentration began to wane, then saw a flash of movement from Antonis as he lunged with lightning speed towards his brother. A gasp emanated from her, sure that Nicola would be struck.

With equal adroitness, Nicola beat the attacking blade aside and using the slightest of foot movement stepped out of harm's way. He let out a joyous booming laugh. "Good to see you haven't become too rusty."

Antonis smiled back. Surreptitiously, he glimpsed a transfixed Katerina. Time for a show, and again went on the offensive.

Giovanni started to bounce up and down and gripped Katerina's arm in focused, silent excitement. They watched as the two carried on their martial dance, their speed and agility dazzling the onlookers. Katerina knew of Nicola's skill, everyone did, but was surprised to see how well the intellectual Antonis fared. To her untrained eye, she could not separate them. A few reciprocal lunges later, the boys slowed down, saluted, and came together in a fraternal embrace. Unable to hear what passed between them, Katerina waited as they turned towards her and the now less bouncy Giovanni.

An unspoken look passed between the brothers and Nicola turned to their guests. "Who's going to start?"

"I think Ladies should go first," said Giovanni, much to everyone's surprise, except his, as he was still worried about looking the fool.

Placing the flat of the blade on his forearm, Nicola handed the rapier, pommel first, to Katerina.

Tentatively, she reached out to clasp it whilst being shown a gripping motion with his free hand. The leather-bound handle initially felt strange as her fingers clasped around it, but as Nicola released the blade, the sensation started to feel surprisingly natural.

"All fencing is based in two areas, the forearm and the feet," said Nicola, glancing at her grip. "Place your feet further apart and keep the front foot pointing forward. Relax your arm in a level position, like this," he instructed. Observing a little misplacement and without pause, he edged up behind to get her into the right posture.

The move was so smooth, Katerina did not notice until he

had clasped his arm around hers to straighten the blade and froze as his body enveloped hers. A bolt shot through her arm and into a tight knot deep in the pit of her stomach; a unique sensation she had never felt before and could not comprehend.

"There, that should do it," Nicola stepped back to admire his work.

Katerina, however, did not hear the comment. All she could think of was the thrill of his touch.

He had felt the electrical charge too, much to his surprise, and turned away to hide his confusion, displaying no sign of his reaction to those present.

Antonis squared up against Katerina with Nicola mirroring her to show a parry followed by a lunge. The inscrutable blue eyes of Antonis gazed through her, whilst he held up his blade for her to practice on.

"Good," said Nicola after her first parry and thrust. "Lead with the arm, then the feet. And again," he commanded. "Do it ten times."

Katerina began to giggle by the fifth time at the joy of it; she had never felt so alive. The thrill of the clashing blades sent the blood throbbing around her body, and now she understood why boys, like Nicola, liked it so.

Antonis smiled back, thinking the laughs were directed towards him.

Giovanni had been mimicking Nicola's stance but seeing how quickly Katerina grasped it, leant down and picked up Nicola's large sword that lay on the ground and began again to copy, only this time, holding the blade. Feeling his confidence grow after a few attempts, he nonchalantly swished the weapon; its weight made him lose his footing and he lurched towards Nicola's back with a yell of alarm.

The high pitch broke their concentration and Nicola turned to feel the searing pain slice across his midriff. He looked down, as the creeping crimson stained his shirt.

Katerina shrieked and rushed over to tend to his wound.

"I will be fine. It's a minor flesh wound. I would be more worried about Giovanni."

Antonis knew his brother was going to survive, though, would probably be a bit sore for a few days. He turned to see the fear-stricken ashen face of the Genoese and in a rare moment of empathy, went over and put his arm around his former adversary to console him. Looking up, he saw Katerina fussing over his brother and smiled at the frailties of the fairer sex. Worrying over such trivial things was not something a Vevellis, or his women did. A sardonic smile crossed his face, at least, she had the intelligence to adapt to his way, he reasoned.

"A little bit lower with your nick and my brother may never have been a father."

Giovanni gulped in fear.

Antonis laughed. "Don't worry, it was never meant to be."

9

———

VARNA

"That settles it, General Sartis, you will take a small detachment and join with the Crusaders as they invade southwards. It is imperative we have our troops on the ground to observe first-hand how our Christian brothers are faring against the heathen."

"Yes, Your Majesty."

The mumbling of dissent did not go unnoticed by Alexis. He shouldered the appointment with his usual humility though secretly overjoyed that he had been chosen. It would give him a close-up view of their allies' capabilities and moreover validate the ambitious plan of Theodore.

"How long will it take you to prepare?"

"I can have the first and second lochias of my Laconians ready to move out in a week, sire."

The Emperor meticulously stroked his beard, "Very well, make it so."

Sartis nodded obediently.

Adrift amongst the courtiers, Planedes inwardly seethed at that big oaf's display of humility as he accepted his orders and realized now he had been utterly excluded from the emperor's inner circle. Stifling his anguish, he vowed to pursue his own routes to safety.

THANOS DRAINED another goblet of wine and was beginning to feel lightheaded. "You know, Alexis, mid-morning drinking is the pinnacle of decadence, too late to be a carryover from the night before and too early for a fresh day. Only hardened debauchers such as me have the pedigree for it."

Ignoring the comment, he couldn't help but agree that Thanos did indeed live a carefree life. He pressed his hands in worry.

"Look, you were their age when you first had battle ."

Alexis pursed his cupid bow mouth into a slit as he contemplated. "Yes, but it was thrust upon me. Here, I am knowingly taking them to war."

"That my friend is the joy of Command. Knowledge is a heavy burden to bear."

Alexis nodded in agreement.

"They have to be blooded sometime. This is as good a time as any."

"But they are still so young. I mean, look at that incident that Nicola had a few years ago."

"Boys will be boys and you worry too much. Have another cup of wine," said Thanos as he unsteadily reached over to fill Alexis' goblet. "That should help you see things plainly."

"Sometimes I envy how simply you view life. It gives you clarity."

Thanos let out a knowing chuckle. "It's all the years of whoring and drinking that has led me to this state of lucidity. Enjoy it while you can, as nothing lasts forever."

His friend was nothing but consistent, and conceivably, he did have it right. "Perhaps this season is as good as any." Alexis relaxed and drained his goblet.

. . .

NICOLA DAWDLED IN A DAYDREAM, as Laconians bustled around him unloading equipment and provisions. The last ten days had been chaotic. One day, returning from classes, Alexis told them with a solemn face that they would be accompanying the Greek Contingent joining the Crusaders in the north. A peculiar mixture of excitement and sadness smothered him. One month earlier, he would have jumped for joy at such news but since that debate his focus was elsewhere. Subconsciously, his fingers felt the scab under the bandage, he hoped it would not slow him down too much in the forthcoming battle.

"Stop daydreaming, boy," boomed the voice of Themis, the Senior Sergeant.

He snapped to and turned towards the boats. His brother beamed a smile as their paths crossed on the supply line. Antonis had been unusually quiet; not in his usual sullen way but in obedient calmness, following instructions without complaint, as instead, it was he who was grumbling about their predicament. A burley Laconian handed him a cloth-covered bale. Ominously, he felt a twinge shoot through his left side as he reached out to receive it. How different it felt to the soft fabric of Katerina's gown. Whenever he let his mind wander, inevitably it related to her on that day.

"Careful, you are going to drop it," said the unnamed Laconian.

Nicola clutched his cargo tighter and steadied himself. Things were different since that day at the university. But resigned to his current fate, he hauled the parcel towards the camp.

Antonis unloaded the latest bundle of supplies and wiped the moisture from his brow. Using this moment of respite, he surveyed the area. Familial coats of arms floated upon a sea of equine easels draped with canvases of red and silver eagles sprinkled with blue and yellow stars. Though initially the numbers seemed modest, the smallness of the Plain of Varna magnified it, making the army appear vast. He felt a sense of detachment as he scrutinised the unfamiliar throng. Only two weeks before, he had been cajoling his brother to help him win a debating contest and now he was preparing to do battle with the Turk. His first no less.

At least Nicola had killed before. Doubt crept in, training on the agoge was one thing, live action something else. Hopefully, the Laconians were seconded to the papal forces, well behind the front line. A posting in the command tent would suit him just fine. The thud of arrow bundles being dropped on the ground brought him to from a pang of guilt as he pondered on his thoughts.

"Hard work, huh?"

Antonis looked up to see his brother's linen smock drenched in perspiration, his usually vibrant hair stuck to the contours of his skull, making him appear a mad fool. He laughed, full of nerves and fear.

Nicola paused for a moment before joining in the revelry.

"I am glad you boys are enjoying yourselves. Perhaps, Themis is not working you hard enough. That can be rectified." The brothers became silent and stood to attention as their General addressed them. Alexis looked them up and down, nodding his head, satisfied they had been properly at work. "Clean yourselves up and meet me at my tent before noon."

"Yes, Strategos," they replied in unison. Nicola wondered again at yet another change. They carried an officer's rank but were nothing more than drudges being enrolled in every piece of back-breaking sweaty work. Alexis clearly making the point of no favouritism to his wards. Confused, the brothers watched as he carried on walking through the camp.

With wet hair and feeling refreshed, they hesitantly arrived at their commander's tent. Alexis stood outside, issuing orders to his two captains. He looked at the boys and nodded in satisfaction. "You two come with me. Keep your mouths shut and your ears open, understood?"

He made way before they could respond, giving them no choice but to follow; weaving through the surprisingly well-ordered row of tents towards the command post perched on the highest point the flat plain had to offer.

The oversized white canvas structure was adorned with the King's pennant. Two giant Polish guards nearly a head taller than Alexis, barred entry to any unwelcome guests. But without prompting, they stood to and allowed the Greek General with his two companions to enter. Inside, all the allied commanders were present.

Antonis recognised Cessarini from their visit to Rome a few months earlier, who had swapped his priestly robes for full plate amour. Only the red skullcap remained, as a clue to his calling. The Cardinal, along with two other warrior priests, acknowledged Alexis' entry. His reputation made him an integral part of the proceedings even though he only brought two hundred of his Laconians for support.

"We have those tee-totalling bastards by their tiny little balls," bellowed the King, slamming one hand on the table.

The Generals laughed with their leader. Confidence was high; the campaign earlier in the year had been hailed a success and the Sultan, in seeking a ten-year truce, had emboldened them even further. Alexis flinched at their hubris.

At the centre of this group stood a slight man with a weak chin and large bulging eyes that fanatically bored through his audience. Wladysaw had been king since a boy and wore the crown as if born with it. Despite his strange look, his courage was legendary and was never one to back away from a fight. This bothered Alexis, because knowing when to retreat was as important as knowing when to attack.

"Sire, the Ottomans are approaching fast from the West and

will be here in three days at the outside. We must move our troops to better ground."

The King fixed his bulbous stare on the Cardinal, whilst he was supreme commander, he had to show his allies some respect; even old women such as Cessarini. Something in the Italian cardinal's imploring look got the better of him. "Pah. Our cavalry is a match for anything those Turkish pederasts can throw at us. Even outnumbered two to one."

The Generals growled their approval.

"What about three to one and throw some bowmen in for good measure."

The Slav generals let out a low hum of condemnation as the King started to shudder in an apoplectic fit at the cardinal's insolence.

Cessarini shifted uncomfortably in his armour, not from fear but at this ignorance. He had years of fighting the Turk and did not share the man's confidence. Their much-vaunted successes of last year had in truth barely slowed the Ottoman juggernaut. As the papal representative, he had to show willing-ness, but his soldier's instinct cried out for a retreat to better ground.

"Are the scouts back? Do we have any idea of their size and disposition?" The deep voice of the Greek cooled the King's rising temperature into a puerile scowl.

Cessarini inclined his head in acknowledgement to a kindred cautious spirit.

Sensing a rift, Hunyadi the Hungarian and co-commander-in-chief interjected. "Our reconnaissance has not yet returned but we know the enemy is not more than two days away. Also, Murad himself is leading their forces."

Shouts erupted again from the gathered commanders.

Antonis observed the buoyant emotions, with the exception of Alexis and Cessarini counselling caution, there was not one cool head among them. Kouzaris' mantra constantly echoing inside, 'The man that stays calm stays alive'. The tug on his sleeve alerted him that Nicola was bored with the proceedings. He nodded in the direction of the exit, Antonis opened his palms to suggest patience.

Nicola creased his forehead and slipped out into the sunny afternoon. With hands on hips, he sucked in the crisp winter air, to clear the tent's stench from his nostrils, and surveyed the field from his vantage point, oblivious to the on-looking amused guards. A lake sat atop a cliff bordered by sea washing up against a brooding fortress, now understanding why Alexis and Cessarini wanted to withdraw.

"It's a killing zone, isn't it?" said Antonis, joining his brother outside.

Nicola nodded. "Looks like it, if the Turk approaches from the West."

"Which they will."

The brothers watched in silence as the Yeomen constructed the wagon laagers and wooden spike defences.

"Is Alexis still in there?"

Antonis nodded. "He is suggesting we relocate to better ground, but the King is having none of it and with Hunyadi supporting him, the rest of the Slav generals will too."

Nicola remained silent, focused on the activity in front of them, then said, pointing to the men putting in the defensive stakes. "They should be closer together. You could sail a dromon through there."

Antonis gripped his arm. "Come on, let's go back to our camp."

Nicola relented at the softness in his brother's tone. As they passed through the compound, groups of Moldavian and Wallachian knights prepared their armour whilst their squires tended the horses. Though the sounds were familiar; the whetstone and hammer of the blacksmith, the continual bleating of goats mingled with conversations of camaraderie, it was the conflagration of these activities in this small area with such purpose that was new to them. Sniffing at fresh opportunity, the local whores had already ventured out to ply their trade.

They arrived at the Laconian's camp, attached to Cessarini's papal troops, as agreed in Rome earlier that year. There was genuine camaraderie between them as the brothers saw Catholic and Orthodox mingle around their various campfires sharing food and exchanging experiences.

Yet it was the little differences that they noticed. The Greek banners were not heraldic, instead they displayed a simple lambda, echoing the ancients from millennia past. Their beards were longer and less groomed than the Latins' and many wore silk vestments, more reminiscent of Turkish garb than of Christian knight. Some carried broadswords, others the scimitar. Alexis and the commanders before him had developed an eclectic style. If a man showed promise in a certain method, it was developed and integrated into their system. The smell of roasted goat filled their nostrils as they came closer to one of the Laconians' fires.

"Hey, boys, have some food. You're going to need it," chuckled Themis, the experienced Laconian sergeant.

Surprisingly, they found they were hungry. Both took a hunk of meat and sat down, lost in its taste. "Look how different we all are. We dress differently, have different beliefs, and have different leaders, each with their own agenda to pursue."

"Yes, it's great that we can all come together in a common cause," replied Nicola.

"Maybe, but the glue that binds us all is very weak. This is a fragile alliance and it is facing a united, strong, and motivated enemy." Antonis remarked.

His brother nodded agreement, "It's just pre-battle nerves, we can succeed in this."

"Don't get me wrong, it's not that I don't think our men, be they Greek, Latin, or Slav are not a match for the Ottoman.

Man, for man, we are probably better, it's just that we do not have unified leadership and their strength of organisation. Just look at the arrogance of where we have located the camp and the dissention amongst our leaders. Cessarini and Alexis want to withdraw. The King and Hunyadi want to attack, and the others don't know what they want."

"Well, we just have to make sure we stay alive and acquit ourselves well."

SPEECH WAS HEATED in the King's tent, not in disagreement but in unison of victory. Alexis, bored with such arrogance, noticed that the boys had left, he hoped they were in preparation and not sitting by, idly chatting.

"Sire, the scouts are back."

"Excellent, show them in," said the King.

A short bow-legged man ducked hurriedly under the halberd blocking the doorway. The mud-splattered rider paused for breath as the expectant eyes of the King and generals rested upon him. "Sire, we have located the Ottomans and they are marching towards our position. Some of their Arab light cavalry spotted us and gave chase. We lost all but three of our troop."

Alexis looked out of the tent and saw the scout's horse drenched in white frothy sweat. A sense of dread overcame him.

"What distance?" questioned the King.

"Sire, less than half a day. They will be within sight before sundown."

"The advance guard?"

"No, Sire, the full army."

The generals began their murmuring again.

"How large is their force?" interjected Hunyadi.

The scout audibly gulped. "Difficult to tell, sir, with all the dust, and the terrain hindered our view. But I would estimate at least forty thousand."

Alexis thought the King's eyes would pop out of his head.

Shouts of disbelief sprang up from the generals, their thin veneer of confidence dissipating. Two of the more seasoned commanders swiftly left to send word to their men.

"So, those heathen bastards are impatient to die. Very well, time to get our men ready," commanded the King.

Nicola was absentmindedly sharpening his blade, enjoying the satisfied feeling of a full belly when he noticed heightened voices emanating throughout the camp. He looked up to see Themis approaching.

Clutching a hunk of meat in one hand, and holding his cudgel in the other, Themis told them. "Looks like you will be popping your cherries tomorrow," then wandered off to speak to some of the other men.

The brothers blankly looked at each other and set about checking their equipment to keep themselves occupied. Wiping the moisture from his palms. a tinge of envy overcame Antonis, as he watched his brother calm and focussed as he inspected the edge of his blade.

Alexis approached his men, glad to be out of that circus, and wondered what the boys were doing. His concern was soon assuaged as he observed supreme focus in their preparation. Perhaps their time in Mistras had worked well. Unnoticed, he walked up to them, leaned down, and picked up one of Antonis' elbow guards. A little squeak emanated as he moved it. "Make sure you oil all your armour joints; you don't want them sticking in the heat of battle."

The boys looked up wide-eyed.

Alexis smiled calmly, picked up the oily rag, and began to wipe the joint. After a few strokes, he moved the metal in a noiseless motion. Satisfied, he handed it back to the seated Antonis. "It's a shitter when that happens."

Antonis did not question and began to work on the rest of his steel plate.

Nicola wondered how many scenes like this of commanders speaking to their men, calming their nerves, and preparing them for battle were happening. For a moment, he was about to calculate the number then thought better of it.

The sun had begun its descent on the horizon, when the Ottomans came into view. Their light cavalry, archers from Anatolia, and Arabs from Syria quickly taking up position on the Franga Plateau. The speed at which the army appeared shocked the Christians. Before the light finally dipped, a full forty thousand men had appeared.

In admiration, Alexis watched them seamlessly spill onto the field of battle. Sipahis, ethnic Turkish cavalry, took up the right wing. Judging from their banners, Rumelian Turks. Finally, the beating drums and clashing cymbals of the Janissary were heard taking up the centre between the two Thracian burial mounds on the plain. By the time darkness arrived, the two sides faced each other in the Bulgarian cauldron.

Alexis returned to Wladyslaw's tent later than most, in no rush to revisit what he knew would be a shouting match and breast-beating contest. The King stood at the table with oil lamps burning furiously, whilst the other commanders gathered around.

Janos Hunyadi stood up and raised his hands and looked around the room into the eyes of every commander, letting the silence build. "Cessarini councils that we escape at once, as we are trapped by the landscape and their army is superior in number." He paused. "To escape is impossible, to surrender unthinkable. Let's fight with bravery and honour."

The commanders cheered.

And so, the decision is made. Time to make peace and prepare. The likelihood that most of his two hundred Laconians would survive was slim.

"General Sartis, I would like your men to be stationed

between my command and Cardinal Cessarini's men," said Hunyadi.

He nodded in reply. Usually, he would have been offended to be placed in such a non-frontline position, however, this was a fight for survival not victory.

Hunyadi immediately set about shaping the battle formation of the smaller Christian army. It wasn't until the early hours that the plan was finalised. The commanders went out to their men to have an hour or two of fitful rest before the sun arose.

ALEXIS RUBBED the sleep from his eyes, to be greeted by a blanket of heavy mist, capped with moody impenetrable clouds. He felt like the universe only existed in this shallow bowl between the plateau, the marsh, and the lake. Shaking his head, he turned to more pragmatic concerns and scanned how Hunyadi had arranged the army.

He had laid out the troops in an arc between the lake and the plateau. The King's bodyguard and the Second Banner mercenaries under Hunyadi's command held the centre. The right was a mix of papal forces and German mercenaries and to the left the remainder of the Hungarians. His small group was with the reserve Hungarian force whilst there was another full standby force of Wallachians under Mercea. He pursed his lips in respect and got up to see to his men before the dawn fully broke. Along the lines, priests were zealously leading the troops in prayer for salvation and victory. The religious fervour much more acute given it was a sanctioned crusade.

Antonis lined up with the rest of the Laconians; his armour felt heavy, pulling on his shoulders, and driving him into the saddle. He glanced at his brother next to him before his gaze wandered over to the Turkish lines. Murad's oversized pennant fluttered showily in the centre.

Banner commanders rode up and down the lines making

sure their troops were in the correct order, their fussing calming the men. *The Turks are saying the same things to their men just a thousand paces away from here,* he thought.

Nicola looked at the horde arrayed before him; the flanks were cavalry and in the centre the Janissary, the Turks' famed infantry, and the levy-men from Anatolia.

As the day began to heat up, the mist lifted, and the armies could see each other across the shallow bowl. There was an eerie silence that was occasionally broken by a snuffling horse or clanking armour. The dark and brooding clouds were ready to burst and unload their malevolence onto the waiting throng below.

Hunyadi at the centre, rode across his troops towards Alexis and asked. "What the fuck are they waiting for?"

"That," he said, pointing above.

On cue, droplets started to ping on metal. At first it was a light drizzle, then, the moodiest of clouds appeared over the Franga Plateau. The sky oozed forward and as it reached over the right flank of the crusader army, tore open in a loud crack and sheets of water landed on the hapless Hungarians. Horses shied at the thunder and a lightning bolt shot to the ground, splitting the main battle standard. The army looked on horrified; it was if the Sultan had ordered the weather to attack on his behalf. Hunyadi rode towards the storm, ordering his men to stand firm. Then just as abruptly, the rain stopped, and the clouds passed overhead.

That was the moment the Sultan ordered his Arabs into the fray. With lightning speed, the hollering light cavalry smashed into the side of the German mercenaries, still recovering from the weather's onslaught, firing arrows with deadly accuracy; and as they closed, slicing and dicing the pin-cushioned soldiers.

Cessarini had seen enough and ordered a retreat behind the laager wagons for his men. In unison, they turned tail, and panicked horses stumbled into each other as the entire right wing crumbled before the Muslim onslaught.

In disbelief at such an easy success, the attackers threw caution to the wind and carried on to the waiting men in their wagons. Torrents of flames spewed from all sides of the wagons as bombards and arquebus scythed down the lightly armoured enemy. The cardinal looked on, satisfied at his decision.

Back in the centre, Hunyadi, sensed a shift in momentum and detached two of his banners to drive away the attackers, as clipping the Turks' wings was essential. "Keep your men stationed here. We have them bloodied and I will crash into their left flank. Wait for my return and together we will drive straight through the middle with our combined forces," said the Hungarian general to the King then added. "Alexis, bring half your men with me."

Though few in number, the Greeks' presence would be invaluable.

The boys looked on, knowing they were being called into action. Alexis though, decided to take three squadrons with him, leaving Themis in charge of the one remaining with the King. "You boys stay with your sergeant until I return."

"But we want to fight," blurted Nicola.

"There will be plenty of time for that," growled Alexis and rode off.

As Hunyadi predicted the Turks on the left turned and fled, giving control in the crusaders' favour.

"Ha, those dickless bastards!" screeched the King, jumping animatedly in his saddle. "What do you think of that, Greek?" he added, as he turned.

Antonis looked on bewildered at all the chaos and sudden change. The smoke from the bombards had obscured the centre of the Turkish lines and as it began to breeze across, the red pennants of Murad's position, revealed themselves again. He was surprised how close the Sultan was and the thin white line of Janissaries seemed such frail protection. He felt nervous in the presence of this young ruler. "Looks like the Sultan is there ready for the taking," he blurted out, caught up in the King's bellicose mood.

"Ha, a Greek who is not afraid to fight. That's a rarity," replied the King in admiration, his eyes bulging even more fanatically. "Let's finish this now. Our knights can smash through," and with a flourish of his sword, charged headlong into the heart of the five thousand janissaries guarding their Sultan.

Themis, to his horror, knew Antonis' comment had spurred the Polish King. He could have throttled the lad.

"Come on, Laconian, what are you waiting for?" Said a polish knight and slapped the hindquarters of Nicola's horse with the flat of his sword, making him bolt for the lines.

"Nicola! Wait!" yelled Antonis, but his voice was lost as the shouts went up, and the fifty Greeks charged headlong into the abyss alongside the King's five hundred.

Time slowed for Nicola, seeing the knights in front of him smash through the line, the cries strangely muted by his own muffled breathing rattling inside his helmet. He spotted a tall janissary rushing towards him with a pike levelled at his mare's breast. There was no fear in the man's eyes, just a murderous look of contempt. Nicola's vision tunnelled, fixing on the point of the Turk's weapon, and brought down his sword along its length. The man's surprise froze permanently, as his head was severed clear-off in one slash. Ahead, he saw the King had nearly reached Murad's pennant. The lines of their famed infantry had broken, it now seemed so quick.

Antonis watched in horror, as he followed his brother. He slashed uselessly at a Turk who had been knocked aside by the horse in front. In his frustration, he failed to notice a soldier charge him, impaling his horse; the mare's legs buckled and he was thrown clear over her head.

Instinctively, he went into a roll, and looked up, stunned, to see the same man charging with his drawn sword. Baring his teeth, he waited for the attack, and as the blade came crashing down, stepped into the blow, simultaneously catching the Turk's forearm, and driving his sfakion into the man's groin.

As the death scream jarred through him, he entered a state of violent euphoria. Picking up a small round shield, he attacked the Turks who had surrounded him. Relieved of the rulebook, time slowed with acute clarity and the fear in his opponents spurred him onwards.

Nicola lost his bearings, only taking on what was in front of him. He heard a shout and looked left, to see the King surrounded by janissary. One jabbed his pike forward, knocking him off his horse as the Turks swarmed over him, chopping and hacking, and the deep bellowing cheer confirmed his fate. Their numbers seemed pathetic, as all the knights were now surrounded by the white and red-capped soldiers. He saw Themis still on his horse, beating the swarm away with his broadsword.

A Hungarian, standing a full head-and-shoulders above those around him was slowing the Muslim onslaught. His eye caught the unmistakable blue plumed helmet of Antonis, back to back with the giant, his knife and shield whirling at a frantic pace but it was only a matter of time until he was overrun. Nicola turned and cut a path to his brother; his only thought now to save him. A janissary's pike struck the knight and the remaining white-capped troops pounced on him, opening a gap in the circle that surrounded them.

Nicola pushed through. "Antonis, give me your hand!" he shouted.

Lost in the fury of killing, Antonis could not hear.

Nicola reached down with his free hand and pulled his brother upwards.

Antonis turned, ready for the kill and for a split second there was no recognition. Only Nicola's imploring brown eyes bringing him back to the present.

Using his prodigious strength, Nicola hauled his brother onto the back of the horse. "We have to go," he said urgently then seeing a gap, spurred his steed through the surrounding enemy towards the rear of the Turkish lines. Breaking free, they rode furiously to the plateau above, the bay struggling under their combined weight as she galloped up the slope. There were no enemy soldiers ahead and Nicola blinked his eyes in thanks for the lucky escape.

Antonis' thighs squeezed onto the bare flanks of the horse with his arms clutched around his brother to keep himself from slipping off. As they reached flatter ground, he spun his head around, letting out a grunt in relief at the emptiness behind them.

"You all right?" shouted Nicola, fearing an arrow had found its mark.

"Yes, I'm fine," came the curt response.

Satisfied he was uninjured, Nicola pushed the horse onward, propelling them to the safety of the plateau.

As they scrambled up the slope every jolt shot through Antonis, fuelling his sense of euphoria; he wanted to carry on fighting. In frustration, he turned to survey the battle below. All he could see was a thick mob of white-capped janissaries covering the plain. The acrid smell of war filled his nostrils and coated his throat. Resisting the urge to cough, he instead used the discomfort to remind himself of the thrill he had just experienced.

Nicola felt his horse failing under him as she took her final steps towards the flat high ground. The eerie quiet was in stark contrast to the battle they had just left, his ears ringing from the clash of steel and the shouts of the men killing or being killed, but the smell of fresh pine told him they were out of the immediate combat zone. His legs trembled as they landed on firm ground and he vomited profusely as the welling of relief surged through him.

Antonis calmly looked on in surprise then observed Hunyadi's banners as they tried to break through the Turkish lines to retrieve the King's body.

Freshly purged, Nicola joined his brother in watching the final throes of the battle unfold, seeing the Laconian banners fluttering amongst the Hungarians as the sound of retreat wafted towards them.

"Finally, the first sensible move of the day."

The contemptuous tone rankled Nicola. Laconians dying for no good reason, did not sit well with him. The Papal troops were pathetically scattered through the marshes, hotly pursued by the Ottoman cavalry. "Do you think the Cardinal made it?"

Antonis curled his thin lips as he surveyed the carnage. "Unlikely, judging by the fiasco down there."

Nicola grunted, "If a few things had gone our way, we could have won the day."

Antonis spun to face his brother. "Like what?"

"For a start, if that stupid fool King hadn't charged but held his ground, as he was meant to…"

Antonis laughed coldly. "You think that would have changed the outcome?" He surveyed the scene below. The Turks had total command of the plain and were in the final stages of slaughtering any remnants of the crusader force. "You think this was close? We broke through their lines and still they came back, never wavering. You live in a dream world."

There was a difference in Antonis' voice; a harder, more deliberate edge. He had seen the look in the blue eyes when he rescued him on the battlefield. The savage joy was chilling but the tone piqued him. "Yes, well, this dreamer saved your life."

Antonis bristled. Though he would have eventually been brought down, at least he would have been fighting. He didn't need to owe his brother anything. "I was doing just fine, you're lucky I didn't kill you when you grabbed me!"

"Sure, whatever you say," Nicola's tone hardened slightly.

The mocking inflection irritated Antonis. "I don't need any favours from you," he snapped.

The murderous look was back and Nicolas felt as if he had become the enemy. "Then sorry I saved your life, next time I might not bother." He couldn't comprehend why tension was rising but wasn't going to back down either.

A welling of contempt sprung up inside, as Antonis studied at his sibling; the large brown eyes were insipid rather than dazzling and the defined face had become a shallow mannequin. He wondered how they would fare in a real knife fight.

Seeing the lips tense into a thin slit, his instincts feared the worst, but his head told him to calm down and meet his gaze.

"Yes, next time don't bother," came the calm reply.

"I won't."

They stared at each other for what seemed an eternity, saying nothing.

Antonis broke the silence. "You just don't see, do you? We Greeks are finished. Today should show you this. We needed the help of foreign kings and mercenaries, and all we could muster were a few hundred of our native troops. We were destroyed out there, and for what? It is only a matter of time until we fall."

Nicola shook his head in denial. "What are you saying? We must fight for our city, our culture, our beliefs."

"You are pathetic. There is only one way, to align ourselves with the Turks. It is the logical choice." He was surprised by the clarity of his thoughts and calmness that rose from within.

Anger broiled in Nicola. "Our family has been part of this empire for centuries. You don't turn your back on that," his voice grew louder.

"My family, not yours. You're just the bastard son of a career soldier." A veil of malevolence descended across his crystal blue eyes as the barb struck home. "I am tired of you using my family's name to get what you don't deserve. Do you think a girl like Katerina would go for a poor common man like you?"

"Better a man true of heart than a boy with a full purse."

Antonis' lips pressed into a thin slit at the retort as he recalled the fencing lesson. Slowly, he withdrew his sfakion and held it low, facing his brother, the realisation that she preferred him spurring his cold fury. "Maybe it's time for your heart to bleed, bastard brother."

Nicola clutched his head in disbelief.

Seizing the opportunity, Antonis lunged at his elder sibling; this was one fight he would not let him win.

The sun glinting off the blade's edge alerted Nicola, who spun away from the lightning strike, his instincts taking over, and withdrew his own weapon.

Antonis bared his teeth in response and padded away slowly towards his opponent whilst Nicola circled warily just out of striking distance. Like a predator looking for a weakness, the younger matched the elder, the jealous vitriol inside focusing his mind. "You think you could get her?"

Nicola stayed silent, concentrating on the threat before him, his thoughts in confusion.

"Her father doesn't approve of you. So, you know what I'll do when I return? I will ask her father for her hand in marriage. He will agree, as it is I who will inherit." A cruel smile crossed his face as he stopped circling and stood up straighter. "And you can watch helplessly as I take her again, and again, and again."

Nicola let out a roar and charged his brother, his blade coming down in a murderous swipe.

Antonis felt the cold pleasure course through his body seeing his brother lose his composure and waited till the blade almost struck before turning out of harm's way. Anger boiled as blades clashed in a sequence of attack and defence.

. . .

"Salu, what is that over there?" said a Turk to his fellow outrider.

"Looks like two men fighting."

"Obviously, but why and who are they?"

The Turk notched an arrow to his bow and spurred his horse forward to investigate. Having nothing better to do and curious, his companion followed. Even from a distance, they could appreciate the quality of the combat. Going closer, they saw it was two of the crusaders.

"They seem to worry more about fighting themselves. No wonder they lost," said the amused rider.

Keeping a safe distance, they decided to watch the sport and began to lay odds on who would win. They were evenly split, one choosing the smaller more agile combatant and the other the big hulking one. The fight raged on with neither giving ground.

Ignorant of the audience, all hesitation left Nicola, knowing he had a life and death struggle on his hands. He looked for the wounding blow so he could subdue Antonis.

Circling again for the countless time, the two riders came into his view, and for a moment, Nicola's concentration broke.

Seeing doubt creep into his opponent, Antonis lunged forward and the blade sliced across the hip. A shout of pain confirming he had hit the mark.

Another rider came to join the spectacle, his curiosity aroused as he saw who they were. "Don't let them kill each other, you fools. Look at the way they are dressed, they have ransom value," he screeched.

Antonis, sensing he had gained the upper hand went for a killer blow to the neck of the now limping Nicola.

Using his instincts, Nicola managed to pull his head back enough to miss his throat being slit but the blade still managed to slice across his face. In agony, he fell to the ground as he saw his brother's murderous look closing in for the kill.

The third Turk, fearful that he would lose at least half his bounty, spurred his horse forward and withdrawing a club from his saddle, swiped the back of Antonis' head, knocking him out cold. "Let's hope he isn't dead," he said, before ordering the others to subdue his bounty.

10

CAPTIVE

*A*ntonis awoke with a pounding head and clouded vision. He dug his nails into his arm, the pain centring his mind and ridding the panic that gripped him when he realised he was trapped in a dark stone room. Fragments of memory started to flow as he regained control of his breathing.

His last recollections were of Nicola wounded on the ground as he prepared to dispatch him, then, blackness. Idly, he wondered where his brother was. Wailing sounds filtered through the thin slit in the door, which he recognised as the Islamic call to prayer. He screwed his face up; in his fury, he had allowed himself to be captured. He nodded his head forward in frustration, drawing a sharp intake of breath at the mad pain from the back of his head. Carefully, he ran his hand the length of his skull and felt the large swollen lump.

Realising the futility of anger, he gingerly sat back on the wooden pallet and took stock of the situation. The stone cell meant a permanent camp; likely, the castle near Varna. Clearly, they must have assumed he was wealthy so kept him alive for ransom. Probably, Nicola was somewhere nearby, unless they had killed him, which was unlikely as that would be a wasted purse. The tops of his shoulders felt knotted and tense.

Antonis assumed a crossed-legged pose on the threadbare mattress and began one of the Eastern mediation rituals Alexis had taught him. Blocking out his thoughts, he focused on his breathing, confident that before long, one of the captors would be along to check on his status.

Nicola lay on the bed, feigning sleep. Conversations drifted in and he cursed himself that he had not paid more attention in his tutorials at Mistras. Antonis would understand. Surreptitiously, he reached up to his face and felt the soft covering of a taut bandage. Satisfied it had been tended to, he began to replay the tumultuous events of the past day. His thoughts were filled with the murderous blue eyes of his brother closing in for the kill, knocked to the ground by a Turkish club. The dull thud had such an air of finality about it, he wondered if he still lived. Powerless, he resigned himself to be as comfortable as possible, silently hoping the wound was not too disfiguring.

Selim pondered what to do with the two knights. Visibly wealthy, he was sure they could fetch a healthy ransom. The Captain stroked his beard as he imagined buying his wife a small farm with the coin he would receive. His concentration was broken by a loud knock on the door. "Enter."

"One of the prisoners has woken up, sir."

Lazily he raised an eyebrow. "Which one?"

"The Crusader you knocked out."

"Very well, give him some food, and let me know when the other wakes." He was surprised, as for a moment, he thought he had killed the man. He might still die, knocks to the head were notoriously fickle. For the moment he was grateful that he happened to be on patrol; perhaps these idiot crusaders could make him rich.

The metal gate at the bottom of the door scraped open and a plate was shoved through but Antonis did not break from his meditative pose. He waited until he completed his eighth cycle of breathing before opening his eyes to the putrid meat assaulting his senses. He was not in dire need and was sure it would not be long before one of his captors paid him a visit and a proper meal would be afforded him.

Nicola stirred from his fitful sleep again and this time the ache was firmly on his hip. His body shuddered at the recurring vision of his brother's venomous actions. Unwittingly, he let out a groan, instantly regretting it as a Turk attended at once. Through squinted eyes, he saw the corpulent nurse, carefully observing him, before he waddled down the grey stone corridor.

"The other one has woken up?"

The mute nod was enough for the slender Captain to leap out of his chair and march purposely towards the infirmary, ignoring the quizzical look of the nurse. Why would that fool understand his motives? Since he witnessed the two Christian knights fighting, he knew his course of action, deciding it was best to deal with the injured one first. His instincts dictating that he would get more from him.

Nicola heard two pairs of feet approaching. The nurse let out a satisfactory cluck as the Crusader came into view. All pretence of sleep had gone, and he stared at them both.

"My name is Selim, the commander here, what is your name?"

The softness and clear elocution of the man's voice eased his tension. "My name is Nicola Vevellis," he replied.

"You are Greek?"

Nicola nodded and for the second time that day regretted not being more fluent in Turkish.

Selim was confused. The dress was too fine for a mercenary but there was no report of a Byzantine force being present at the battle. "Mercenary?" He asked in Turkish.

Nicola shook his head.

"Then what are you?" The round-eyed, pursed-lip response confirmed to Selim that his prisoner spoke limited Turkish, and his Greek was hardly any better. He turned to the nurse. "Is there anyone here who speaks Greek?"

"I am not sure, sir, we are mostly from eastern Anatolia here."

It would be just his luck to have a bunch of rustic eastern peasants under his command, which gave him no choice. "Abo bou eise?" Selim asked in heavily accented Greek.

"Constantinople."

"Yati eise etho?" asked Selim again.

Why am I here? The answer is pretty fucking obvious. Already he knew this conversation was going to be a waste of time. He wished Antonis were here, but was also too aware why he was lying in this Turkish prison. However, there was no chance that any sort of negotiation could be made without a translator. "Bou eine o alos?" He asked.

The Turk screwed up his brow in confusion before realising he was asking after his fellow Christian. "He is fine, he lives," he replied in his native tongue.

"Milai Turkika," replied Nicola.

A relieved smile broke across the Turk's face. "What is his name?"

"Antonis Vevellis."

Selim's confusion was apparent.

"We are brothers," added Nicola.

Now, truly bewildered, he turned to his orderly and ordered him to take care of the bandages and feed him a proper meal. Then promptly left to speak to the other crusader buoyant that he would get some answers but more importantly, the possibility of ransom.

Judging by the tightness in his stomach, Antonis knew he had been in this jail for about a day and a half. An edge of concern began to creep into his otherwise calm state. Looking up towards the slit in the wall, he saw the light was coming in. Someone should visit him by tomorrow, he reasoned. Until then, he had a half a cup of water to survive on. His thoughts were broken as he heard the heavy metal bolt slide open on the thick wooden cell door that creaked open.

"Welcome to my jail, Antonis Vevellis, your brother says hello."

"He is well, I hope."

"We have patched him up as best we could."

Antonis returned a steady gaze.

Selim was surprised by his faultless accent and even more impressed with his calm demeanour. "Your Turkish is excellent."

"I paid attention in school."

Selim smiled, deciding that he liked this Greek. "Expensive education, was it?"

"Yes, but probably not as expensive as it will be for me to get out of this place."

Selim laughed. "You don't waste any time, do you?"

"Time is the one thing I cannot afford to waste." Antonis saw the avarice register in his jailer's eyes.

The Turk could not have chosen better, a captive such as this one would be his golden fleece. However, he knew he had to play this cleverly.

"Why don't you give me a figure, for me... and my brother, and we can go from there."

"Very well, but one thing puzzles me. Why were you fighting your brother to the death after being in battle together?"

"We had a difference of opinion and were discussing it."

Selim paused for a moment, too long for Antonis' liking, before bursting into laughter and shaking his hand. "You Greeks are crazy."

"I am Cretan."

"Ah, the most insane in the asylum."

Satisfied, Antonis exhaled heavily as his cell door slammed

shut then smiled when the bolt slid home. The trumped-up Turk bit on every bone he threw at him and he was now sure they could come to an arrangement. All that was required, was to have his brother back on his side. His neck stiffened at the thought of Nicola, but he forced himself to relax. Taking the meditation pose of earlier, he channelled his energy into forming a persuasive argument.

Selim had a spring in his step all the way back to his quarters. Undoubtedly, these two brothers were wealthy and he wondered which was the elder. Still, he was intrigued as to what caused the quarrel and vowed that he would find out. Putting that thought aside, he started calculating what he would need to buy his farm and find the wife he so dearly coveted. The piece of land he wanted bordered his mother's village, that nestled in the hills overlooking the Black Sea. The wife was not so clear, there were two whom he liked. If he had enough, he could buy them both. Muhammad in his infinite wisdom, chuckled Selim to himself, those foolish Christians only had one wife.

Slowly, he estimated the upper and lower limits that he would need, assessing what their father might be worth. He slapped his forehead; what if there was another son at home and he would not pay? What did it matter? he had nothing to lose. He called in one of his men and ordered him to send a proper meal with wine to the Greeks in the cells. Warning him that if he were told it was not satisfactory, he would be flogged. The nervous guard gulped as he acknowledged the instructions and scurried off, leaving the commander dreaming of his new luxurious life.

The smell of delicious food wafted as the cell door opened but Antonis did not stir, even though his stomach tightened painfully in anticipation.

"With the complements of Commander Selim."

The Greek opened his lids, his eyes following as the guard apprehensively laid the tray on a small table that the other guard had brought along with a small chair. He waited until the entire meal had been placed on the compact wooden top and the guards stood there expectantly. Languidly, he uncrossed his legs, stood up and placed himself upon the chair. A hunk of roasted lamb lay next to some boiled greens. In the basket rested a small loaf of bread and a small clay bottle of Olive oil. On a smaller plate, half a lemon, a cucumber, and a tomato completed the offering. The guard clumsily poured some wine and stood back anxiously.

Realisation dawned. Antonis cut a sliver and ate. The meat was grilled to perfection, even had he not been so famished, he would have acknowledged the cook's skill. "Please pass my thanks to your commander and compliments to the chef."

The guard beamed a relieved smile and hurried back to report his good news.

Nicola awoke to see Captain Selim and two guards standing over him. Startled, his first thought was that they were there to execute him but the idea was quickly dispelled as the Turk smiled warmly.

"I have spoken with your brother and we have come to an arrangement for both your releases."

Nicola winced as his face grimaced in suspicion.

Selim saw his guest's—as he now called them—confusion and pointed to one of his guards, who promptly opened the door.

Antonis strode in and stifled a smile as he saw the thick bandage covering the left side of Nicola's face. The time for gloating was later, first, they had to plan their escape. "Hello, Brother."

The neutrality in his voice surprised Nicola. Cleary, that was for their captors' benefit. His breath skipped a beat as he tried to make sense of this new development.

Antonis turned to Selim and asked if they could have some privacy.

The Turk duly obliged, ushered his men out, and with that, himself. It was time for the brothers to make amends, if only so he could get double his ransom.

Once alone in the alms room, Antonis pulled up a chair next to the bed and sat down. Resting his piercing blue gaze upon his brother, he waited for a moment before he began. "How are the injuries?"

"How do you think? You've sliced my face and gouged my hip," came the terse response.

Antonis nodded his head in understanding, his face the best mask of remorse he could muster. "Please forgive me. I wish I could take back what I have done."

"But you can't," snapped Nicola.

The blank stare in his brother's brown eyes confirmed that he would not be able to easily persuade him. "I don't expect you to, but the reality is, we are prisoners of the Turk."

"Thanks to you."

"…and we have a limited period for us to arrange our release. Their patience and their greed will only carry us for so long. One of us needs to go and get the ransom for both."

"Don't tell me you will volunteer to do it," snarled back Nicola.

The response was a delight to Antonis' ears. He adjusted himself on the seat and leaned forward as carefully as he could. "I thought we could let the fates decide, remember the game we played as children?"

"Stone, cloth, knife?"

"Yes."

Nicola did not trust his brother, that had been shattered these past few days. Yet, what choice did he have? If they could not get a ransom soon, they would be killed, and this game seemed a pretty fair way to decide. Carefully, Nicola sat upright on the bed and slowly swung his legs around and out over the edge. Surprisingly, his hip was not as stiff as he thought it would be. "Very well, how many rounds do you want to do?"

"Best out of three?"

Nicola nodded in agreement.

Antonis put his clenched fist out.

"Same rules, on three?" said Nicola.

Antonis grunted in reply as his brother put his fist opposite. Still surprised how small his hand looked next to his. The fists pumped... one... two... three...

Antonis watched intently. On the third rise, their hands set and his finger cut the cloth.

"One to you," said Nicola, catching his thumbs and fingers, and rubbing the curves of his mouth, putting his fist out again.

"Ena, dio, tria..."

"Stone blunts knife. One apiece," Nicola nodded in satisfaction as he looked towards his opponent. He stuck his clenched fist out. "This is the decider."

Antonis returned with a blank stare then slowly, brought up his fist for the final roll. "Ena, dio, tria..."

Nicola looked down to see his clenched fist covered and knew he had lost. "It seems the fates have decided," he said.

11

RETURN

Giovanni felt helpless as he sat next to his friend on their usual stone wall that overlooked the university square. Gone was her usual energy, replaced with a listlessness that cut him to the core. When word had reached the city of the disaster at Varna, Katerina feared the worst. Each day that went by without news ate away at her innate gaiety, making her more withdrawn and silent. He looked up to see the other students playing and chatting without a care in the world; resentment welling up at his powerlessness in the situation.

"Don't worry, they will be fine. General Sartis would have made sure they were not in the front line." He regretted saying the words as soon as they left his mouth.

Katerina stopped rubbing her hands together and began to twirl the hair at the back of her neck. Something she had been doing more regularly these last few days and was in danger of it becoming a nervous tick. "The king and his personal body-guards were wiped out. I don't think there was a safe place for them anywhere on that field." Her calm voice betrayed none of the turmoil she felt inside. "It's been ten days and not even one Laconian has returned yet." Her voice trailed off as she rested her hand on her forearm, subconsciously reliving the electricity she had felt during her fencing lesson.

Giovanni sat in silence beside her, vowing that he would ask his father to find out through his merchant contacts any news of the survivors from Varna. The bell sounded for the end of break and the students began to file back into their classrooms. He gripped his friend's arm to move but with surprising strength she remained firmly on the wall and waited until the area cleared.

PLANEDES SAT amongst the shouting throng of nobles straining to have their voices heard. Raised comments of how exposed the city was and few of how the Turks would wreak vengeance upon them. Steadily, the words became infectious and doubt began to creep in with fear. But he used his logic to quickly shut out any indecision, confident that he had a clear grasp of his predicament. His missive had been sent weeks previously and even with the best intentions there was no possibility of an Ottoman siege before next year. Secure in his fate, he started to contemplate what would become of his fellow grandees.

Sphrantzes, the old fool had finally had his voice heard and a bemused Planedes looked on. What could these anachronisms offer anyway? It would be better for this world if they were consigned to history. The wily politician rubbed his hands in satisfaction, at his cleverness in getting his plans of future safety in motion. Yet, the news that the fate of the Laconians present at Varna was still unknown brought mixed feelings. On the one hand, if Sartis had been killed that would be joyous, but on the other, he had noticed how withdrawn his daughter had become in the last few days.

It seemed his plan of getting the children closer had worked, but not how he had intended. He wondered which of the boys she was sad for. But it was of no purpose wasting time on the subject, and he allowed his mind to drift onto more pleasant things. Eventually, news would filter back and only then with the facts, could he gloat, or not. Sphrantzes' febrile voice cut into his thoughts like a baby's wail just as he allowed himself the pleasant daydream of a mortally wounded Sartis with the crumpled slain body of Nicola at his feet surrounded by the sultan's fanatical janissary. His lips thinned into a slit of disappointment at the broken train of thought. Just being left with the emotional echo as to why he hated that boy so much.

ALEXIS COUNTED THE REMAINING MEN, falling back on his military training to block out his feelings at the loss of so many troops. The second sergeant called out the roster. The lack of responses as just two or three names were read out, stung like needles jabbing into his shoulders. Missi, the only remaining officer noticed how his superior flinched at the periods of silence during the rollcall. Finally, with the list complete, he rode over to his commander to solemnly deliver it.

Reluctantly, the General perused the paper, nearly two-thirds of his men had perished, and he took scant solace in the fact it could have been worse had he brought a larger force. Inwardly, he cursed the headstrong King for his foolish actions. The boys' names sprung out at him and dread filled his heart as to how he would break the news to their father. He had failed his mentor at his first true test of trust.

Seeing the sadness in his General's eyes, the sergeant offered, "Sir, there was nothing you could have done."

Alexis returned a humourless smile at the words, but it would never assuage his guilt that he should have made different choices. "Have the men provisioned and ready. Rest the horses. We leave for the city at dawn." *There is no point lingering on this field of death.* Moreover, there was likely panic welling in the capital and his presence would help calm things down.

The sergeant nodded and proceeded to carry out his orders.

"General, should we not wait another day or two as we could have wounded men still left on the field?" Missi interjected.

Sartis paused for a moment. "Very well, one more day, but no more. So, you had better busy yourself in finding any survivors."

Without pause, Missi detained four men to follow him in search of living comrades at any of the numerous field hospitals that had sprung up.

The general appreciated his junior officer's industrious faith but held out no hope. Deciding to bid farewell to Hunyadi before his troops left, he instinctively searched for Themis, to accompany him, before he realised that even he was lost. In a flush of frustration, he spurred his horse toward the remaining crusaders' encampment. The moon had risen fully in the cloudless night sky before he returned to his men.

He was greeted by an excited Missi. "Sir, we found a survivor," he said triumphantly and led his commander to a tent nearby.

Entering, Alexis saw the huge prostrate figure lying unconscious on the wooden pallet. Bandages seeped in various shades of aged crimson covered the left arm, chest, and middle. "Themis," he exclaimed.

"He is sleeping, sir."

"Where did you find him?"

"He was amongst a pile of dead in the middle of the field. Somehow, the local scavengers overlooked him. Any other man would have died from his wounds."

"Did you find any others?"

"We identified about thirty Laconians."

"The boys?"

Missi shook his head.

For a moment, Alexis allowed himself some vestige of hope, but they had probably been the first stripped by the robbers of the dead, due to the richness of their uniforms. "Well done, keep following your instincts."

"Thank you, sir," Missi bristled with pride.

"Will Sergeant Themis be able to travel tomorrow?"

"Unlikely, sir, the next few days will be critical."

Alexis nodded sagely. "Very well, then stay here with him until he is well enough to be moved. I want to know what happened and he is the only one who can tell us." The general walked over to his trusted sergeant and laid a hand gently on the uninjured shoulder. "Recover soon, my friend," he murmured under his breath before walking out to attend to other pressing matters.

ANTONIS FELT MILDLY uncomfortable in his Turkish garb as he walked with Selim towards the stables.

Selim was in good spirits since it seemed the brothers had made peace. But even in the buoyant mood, he saw the concern on the young Greek's face. "Don't worry, you can lose the outfit once you pass south of the lake. With your good grasp of Turkish and this conduct order, you will be fine going through any checkpoints to the south. Besides, our victory at Varna was so complete they are not looking for survivors."

Antonis nodded in comprehension and the logical choice. But the reality of wearing the enemy's uniform still felt alien to him. "Remember what we discussed?"

"Yes."

"I will keep to my bargain, and you will be half as rich again."

Selim responded with his most avaricious grin, still in surprise at the deal the young Greek offered him. At first unsure, it very quickly made perfect sense.

Antonis stifled a smile, clearly, the tale he wove was believable to the Turk. He mounted the horse and one of the prison guards handed him a sword and a small knapsack with some provisions.

Selim looked upon his prize as the Greek attached the weapon to the saddle and rode southwards out of the fort towards home. "Remember, after the lake, take the left fork as that will hide you from any onlookers. May Allah be with you."

"Thank you, and I shall return before the rise of the second moon."

As soon as he was out of sight of the citadel, Antonis relaxed into a steady pace. Still amazed that he had so easily escaped the clutches of an Ottoman jail, he chuckled out loud as he saw how greed blinded a man's judgment and wondered how long it would take the foolish Turk to grasp what had transpired. Perhaps, he would execute his brother in a fit of rage.

He laughed again at his cleverness then looking up, saw the marshes of Varna come into view in the distance. He scourged himself for not paying attention sooner, as in a moment of hubris he let the horse meander into the right fork. The luxury of basking in self-congratulations had to wait, as the flat plain offered little protection and he knew he had to have his wits about him, avoiding both Turk and Crusader until close to the city.

Decision made, he focussed all his energy into achieving his aim, spurred the horse southward, and scouting around the back of the plateau, avoided the remnants of the Turkish forces that were on the battlefield. Thankfully, they would pay him no heed, as there were far greater prizes to be had off the fallen Christian Knights. Gold coins, weapons, and armour always sold well. Trinkets were given to wives and sweethearts. Cleaning up the dead was profitable business.

He made sure not to make any sudden movements so as not to draw attention to himself as he skirted the area. Once through the field of death, he navigated due south through the marshes, toward the fortress of Galata, where the remnants of the Crusader army were holed-up licking their wounds. In the marsh, mail-clad bodies lay in grotesque positions, their eyes picked clean and mouths gaped open, frozen in the final moment of life.

There was an eerie silence in the wetland marsh, save for the noise the busy carrion feeders made. It unnerved Antonis and he spurred his horse on. The bay picked up on the mood of its rider, whinnying at each corpse and he patted her neck to calm her down. The sun was setting, and he wanted to get through the hellhole before bedding down for the night. Ahead, he saw a road to higher ground with some trees and a ruined shepherd's hut. His senses snapped to, in case there were unwanted fellows around. It felt like an aeon until he broke free of the marsh and moved towards the cabin. There was no sign of anyone as he approached, and he was relieved, as there had been enough killing.

The open part of the hut's wall faced towards the trees, providing perfect shelter for him and the horse against any passer-by. It was starting to cool but Antonis wasn't about to light a fire. Taking the blanket from under the saddle for warmth, he fell into a deep dreamless sleep, the excesses of the day finally taking their effect.

THE STENCH of death permeated through the fort in Galata, where knights of different races lay side by side waiting to recover, but with some, hoping that death would take them. Missi had sat next to the huge sergeant throughout the afternoon, praying for the man to pull through. Looking upon the peaceful sleeping soldier, his craggy face vividly showed the years of hard living. A legend in the brigade it was difficult to see a man such as he so weakened. The young officer sighed, and the room began to feel claustrophobic. Deciding he needed to stretch his legs and breathe fresh air, he rose from his comrade's bedside and walked along the rows of the infirm and dying to the exit at the end.

The fresh dusk air swirled around him as he drank in its refreshing vigour. Still needing more, he walked up the narrow stone steps inside the stone wall to have the canopy of the sky as his own. Resting on the crenulations, he looked onto the marshes below, the site of utter devastation for the fleeing crusader army. Even after these many days there were still scavengers knee-deep in mud picking through the remains. In disgust, he looked away to the plain on the other side.

A glint of metal caught his eye on the horizon. He squinted, to see a horseman skirting the edge of the marsh. A full white plume on his head easily identified him as a Turk, yet there was something familiar about the way he moved even at this distance. He shook his head at the thought. Still, he avidly watched the rider as he trailed his way through before disappearing into a hidden gully, briefly reappeared again then disappeared totally. That distinct riding style stuck in his head as he patiently waited for the last vestige of light to vanish before the moon rose in the east. Finally feeling relaxed, Missi wandered down to have a meal, before checking on his patient and some well-earned rest.

ALEXIS PULLED up at the house in the Phanar district. It was the first time in weeks that he felt he could relax.

Thanos greeted him warmly as only an old comrade could. "My friend, it has been a long time."

Alexis said nothing and hugged his old companion.

"The news has been all over the city about the disaster."

"What have you heard?"

Thanos raised his eyebrows, his eyes widening. "Well… That you received a royal thumping and the Polish King was killed along with his bodyguard. The other knights turned and fled in panic, followed by a slaughter in the marshes."

Alexis pursed his lips together and nodded. "Yes, that was pretty much it."

"How many did you lose?"

"Over half."

Thanos let out a low whistle.

"Including the boys," added Alexis.

Thanos' shoulders slumped. "Oh, Lexon, I am so sorry. I know how much they meant to you," he sighed. "And me too," then he added, "Is this the first place you have visited since arriving in the city?"

"Yes, I left the remainder of my men outside the walls at a lodging house to recuperate, whilst I wait for the most injured of my force to join up with us."

The bitterness grated on Thanos. "Do they have any nurses to help them recover? I know that after any campaign I was always grateful for medical attention." He saw Alexis couldn't help but smile at his irrepressible behaviour. Gently, he reached up and put his arm around his old friend's shoulder and they walked into the house. He knew Alexis needed to collect his thoughts before reporting to the powers-that-be. "How many men are there, and where exactly is the lodging house?"

"Forty-six, half of them with minor injuries, and in the guest house on the Selymbra road, three stadion outside of the Golden Gate."

Thanos smiled in recognition. He walked to his writing desk in the salon, took a quill, and after quickly inspecting the nib, began to write a note. "Yes, I know the place. I think two dozen should do the trick." Hastily, he called out to one of his servants, and a slight young man instantly appeared. Carefully dripping wax on the vellum scroll, he pressed his seal into the still soft blob. Satisfied at his work, he handed it to the courier. "Take this to the red painted house by Santa Maria of the Mongols and hand it to the doorman. Understood?"

"Yes, sir," replied the domestic.

Pleased with himself, he turned back to pay attention to his friend.

Alexis had a bemused look on his face. "The red house by Maria of the Mongols? There is no hospital there."

Thanos feigned an innocent look. "No, but it is the finest whorehouse in the city and the girls would welcome being bedded by some real men, instead of those feeble old senators, as much as your men will enjoy their sweet pleasures."

Alexis boomed one of his big laughs and put his head into hands. "My men will happily oblige, but it's going to cost you a small fortune."

Thanos waved away any further thought on the matter. "It's worth it to just have those old fools without their honey for a few days."

"You never cease to amaze me."

"Now we've dealt with the housekeeping, let's talk about other issues." Thanos turned and gestured for his old friend to sit.

Alexis slumped down with uncharacteristic laziness, as another servant magically appeared with a goblet full of wine. "It's too early to drink."

"It's never too early to drink, Lexon. Anyway, it will help you relax."

Considering that his host would not take no for an answer, he raised the goblet.

"To the boys," said Thanos.

Alexis nodded in response and drank.

A HEAVY BLANKET of cloud covered the dawn sky, and Alexis couldn't have been more grateful for the lack of sun. The chill in the morning air aided his rapid pace through the vaulted palace chambers and cleared the fog in his head. It was much needed, as he was now in the presence of the full council of nobles, and the Emperor, who came forward to welcome him.

John VIII's nostrils curled slightly as he greeted his General.

Surprised at his rare lack of discipline, Alexis turned to more pressing matters.

Gently, the Emperor put out his hands, palm down to stop any of the nobles speaking.

The portly middle-aged men gazed expectantly upon their celebrated general.

Alexis knew this was his cue and braced himself as he began to repeat the events, as he had witnessed them at Varna, with the occasional murmur the only disturbance in an otherwise hushed room. Muted silence followed for some time before it was shattered with a barrage of questions.

"Why would the King be so stupid as to order the charge like that?" queried Sphrantzes.

"Something must have convinced him to do it."

"Or someone," shouted another concerned noble.

"He was young," said another.

"And foolish."

"Now, we have no army between our walls and the Turk."

"This is the work of Turkish spies," came a shout from the back of the group.

Gabbles of agreement gathered volume.

"A king doesn't sacrifice himself like that."

"Even a Polish one," shouted another wag.

Through his disdain of the nobles' bravery to speak from a group, Alexis conceded there was a strong possibility of sabotage, as he found it strange that Wladyslaw had been so reckless. He hoped Themis recovered and from there learn more of the truth.

"Did any of the Laconians survive from the charge?" asked the Emperor.

Finally, a sensible question. "Yes, Your Majesty, we have a heavily wounded sergeant who is slowly recovering."

"Can he speak?"

"Not yet, sire, he will take longer to return to the city due to the nature of his injuries."

John VIII nodded. "Very well. I wish to be informed immediately upon his arrival in the city and he is to be brought here, where my personal physicians will take care of him. Then we shall discover what happened."

"Yes, sire," replied Alexis. At least Themis would get the best medical care possible and frankly that was all he cared for. Understanding this debacle was a moot point, he also accepted the fact that people always needed to blame someone.

"In your opinion, general, how likely is a Turkish attack on the city?" asked Lucas Notaras, one of the more level-headed nobles.

Alexis stroked his chin in contemplation. "Unlikely, my Lord, as the Ottomans suffered a great many casualties in their victory, from which they will need to recover. Furthermore, there is always their fear of further crusader armies being raised from the German or Italian states."

The Emperor listened avidly. It seemed that his brother Theodore's 'Megali Idea' could still work.

"Saying that, I cannot guarantee what the Sultan will do. But this is my opinion," replied Alexis.

The Emperor was pleased with the General, his cool-headed report had calmed the nerves of his fragile nobles, and, hopefully, their gossiping wives, along with their servants, would spread the news that there was no need to panic.

Alexis watched as the official meeting concluded. The informal chats would now begin amongst themselves and it was these more than anything else, that determined the mood this senatorial rumour-mill would produce.

ONCE PAST the field of death, Antonis headed southward towards Constantinople. Satisfied he had passed far enough from the fort of Galata, reasoning that he would simply be viewed as a random Turkish outrider from afar. However, he vowed to be more careful with the rest of the journey as lady luck might not shine on him again.

Gouzaris' calm monotone voice echoed in his head. "Prepare and plan, always prepare and plan."

Bringing the horse to a dawdle, he came to a fork in the road and he planned the best route. Undoubtedly, the quickest would be to press to the right, towards the Ottoman capital at Edirne and take the Via Ignata to the city. He shook his head at the thought, knowing there was too much risk of discovery by an overzealous border guard.

The left road was to the coast, with a myriad of small coves that were frequented by smugglers, which would afford him the anonymity he required, and without further hesitation, he spurred his horse towards the Black Sea.

It was dull farming country, flat plains filled with fields, and the occasional wooded copse, not the inspiring scenery of his own island, but then nothing he had seen to date matched the stark majesty of the Lefka mountains of home. Instinctively, he patted the purse that was strapped to his inside thigh—the ten gold coins still there—surprised his former captors had not discovered them. He let out a gentle sigh, these would be useful now, smugglers were not in the habit of giving free boat rides. Reaching inside the knapsack provided by Selim, he pulled out a dried oat cake and slowly ate it, the bland flavour offering no pleasure, merely sustenance. It would suffice and he kept a keen lookout for any passers-by.

The stone road ended abruptly, and the clipped sounds of the horse's hooves became dull thuds, the added quiet freeing his thoughts. Perhaps the Turks were good warriors, but they had a lot to learn about road maintenance. Hills began to appear on the right and the track narrowed more, and he noticed the ruts in the road got deeper. No doubt, smugglers rode in line, so as to hide their numbers. Again, the monotone of Gouzaris echoed in his head. Another simple, but pertinent mantra, registering subconsciously. He lay his hand on the hilt of his sword, as he felt close to his destination.

The track twisted and went through two small tors before sloping downwards. A smell of thick salty air confronted him, and he knew that by sundown he would find a transport to take him to his objective. Turning the last twist, he finally laid eyes upon the sea and as expected three caravels were dragged onto the yellow sand beach. Two small plumes of smoke drifted up to the sky in the windless bay before twirling together as they cleared the top of the surrounding hills. A small group of men huddled around the camp, ignorant of his approach.

He knew this was the most dangerous moment, before he had a chance to introduce himself, as they could easily fire arrows at the lone rider and steal his horse. Hesitation gripped him. Then with a final resolve, he pushed himself forward through his doubts. Careful to make no sudden movements, he rode slowly towards the men, who had now noticed the approaching rider.

"Who goes there?" shouted one of the bearded men.

To Antonis' surprise they spoke Greek. "I'm a traveller in search of transport," he shouted back.

His Greek accent confused them, as he was in Turkish garb. They talked amongst themselves for a moment before one shouted back. "You may advance, but do it slowly, Greek."

Carefully obeying, he rode towards them, swiftly dismounting to walk the last few yards on foot. Tightness welled up inside him, instinctively resting his left palm on his sfakion. Soaking up every detail of the unsavoury characters; three squat mariners stood their wide stance emphasising their bowlegs. They unfolded their arms as he approached, and in unison, all rested their hands on the hilts of their weapons.

The young Greek strained his peripheral vision to look for any movement that would give away hiding men. "Good afternoon, gentlemen."

The faintest of nods confirmed their reply.

Unperturbed, Antonis continued. "I'm looking for a transport to Constantinople. Do any of you travel there?"

The one on the left sniffed, spat on the ground, and walked back to tend to the campfire, leaving a bewildered Antonis.

"A Greek dressed as a Turk seeking transport. Ivan doesn't trust you, and frankly, neither do I." The smuggler's eyes hardened as he finished his explanation.

"I have money to pay for the trip."

"I doubt enough, as passage for you will be very expensive."

"You seem to me to be a man who wants to stay hidden," said the other remaining smuggler.

His sardonic look irritated Antonis and he felt a cold fury build up inside him. "Then I've come to the right place, haven't I?" Pulling out his right hand, he casually opened his palm to reveal four gold coins.

Both nodded their appreciation at the sight of the shiny metal.

"That might get you half the way."

Antonis cursed beneath his breath at showing too much, too quickly, and knew that by the time his haggling had finished, he would be lucky to have the shirt left on his back. Instinct told him to quickly dispatch the filthy brutes and take the small boat himself, before logic took over. "That's an expensive journey," he replied and began nonchalantly looking around for any other boats beached on the shore.

He noticed a slightly built man in a hooded cloak walking towards them with a limping, grey dog. As they drew closer, he saw the hound was missing a leg and the man appeared exceptionally old. They ambled straight towards him.

"Ah, Penelope, my beauty, what are you sniffing at?" rasped the old man, as he pulled his hood off.

Antonis drew a sharp intake of breath as he laid eyes on the withered head. Tufts of white hair sprouted from the heavily tanned crown; his face leathered like a dried raisin. But it was his eyes that unsettled him the most. Round, brown, and staring with more than a hint of madness. By this time, Penelope was sniffing intently at Antonis' feet.

"You like him, do you?" said the old man without even introducing himself. "What do you think? What do you think?"

The dog's tail began to wag more and gave a decrepit bark.

"Very well, if you say so, my dear. We shall take him."

Penelope barked again in confirmation.

Finally, after finishing the conversation with his pet, the maniacal eyes rested upon Antonis. "Where are you going, boy?"

"Constantinople."

"How many coins do you have?"

Antonis flashed the four in his palm.

The old man walked towards him and picked one of the coins out of his hand, taking it up to his eye to inspect it, before hiding it in the folds of his cloak. "Keep the others, you will need them when you arrive."

The two smugglers grumbled their disapproval at the old man's meddling and stepped forward to be met by a growling dog.

"You missed your chance. Now, he is with me," he said without even looking up.

Muttering again, they paused, before turning to join their comrade at the campfire.

Antonis could not believe his luck at the turn of events and overcome with boyish enthusiasm, stuck out his hand in greeting. "I'm Antonis Vevellis."

The old man curled up his nose. "Good for you. I hope you are hungry as my fire is nearly ready. It's of no consequence if you aren't, Penelope eats everything anyway." Clicking his fingers, the dog limped to his side, and both turned towards the shore without another sound.

Confused but thankful, Antonis followed in silence.

The small skiff offered little shelter from the elements, but it did not seem to bother the old man at all. Once out on the open water, he stripped to a white loincloth covered with a small woollen tunic. His tanned sinewy legs showed perfect balance as he economically scurried around the small deck adjusting the sails for maximum speed. There was something strange about this man, who still had not proffered his name, yet he knew all about Penelope.

The blend of quirkiness and the gentle motion of the sea, contrived to relax Antonis, allowing him to take stock of the situation. He began to plan his movements once arriving in the city. *What story must I present to Alexis? Is he even back in the city yet?*

Certainly, Thanos would be, and that was his first port of call. Once that was straight, he would call on Katerina and tell her the sad news of his brother's demise. His head shook at the thought of Nicola at the Ottoman fort and for a moment felt a pang of guilt. What would his father think of his actions?

"Regretting your decisions, boy?"

Startled, Antonis saw the old man was fixing one of the sail ropes. "What decisions?" came the weak response.

The old man chuckled knowingly. "Well, whatever you've done, you have to see it through now." The old man finished the last adjustment before resting his unsettling eyes on his passenger. "Know why I took you?"

Antonis shook his head.

The old man smiled. "I didn't want you to kill those men, which, if I hadn't turned up, would most probably have happened. You, my boy, have killer written all over you."

He took that as a compliment but thought it might not have been meant as one.

"And, life is precious, even those three on the shore," the old man added.

This man was strange with his odd dress, mangy dog, and weird logic. Deciding that his nature was merely benign, he thought no more of his temporary companion and turned his mind to the future. Playing out different scenarios in his head until he was satisfied with his plan.

Time must have flown by, as the looming cliffs that heralded the mouth of the Bosphorus were in plain view on the horizon and he became impatient as the boat drew closer to the city. As it eventually docked in one of the smaller northern shore harbours, a now visibly agitated Antonis, bade a swift farewell, and leapt onto the stone-sided dock.

The old man screwed up his face at the parting. "Boy," he shouted. "I will wait a while for you here, I think you have need of me." For a brief instance, madness left his eyes as he spoke.

Antonis nodded, more in obedience than thanks, doubting that he would ever see this old man again and made his way briskly to his first destination.

DECEPTION

He was thankful they had arrived from the north, which meant he did not have to travel far to reach Thanos' house. Even so, he took care to avoid anyone who might know him, as it would be best not to have any mishaps before he had relayed his story.

The heavy ornate door had a welcome air of familiarity about it and knocking loudly on the burnished wood, he stood expectantly for it to be opened.

One of the many nameless servants answered. The shock on his face clearly indicating the news was out that he was presumed dead. "Welcome, sir, the master is present, along with General Sartis." The man pulled the door wide for Antonis to stride in.

"Where are they?"

"In the garden, sir."

Hurriedly, the young Greek went off to greet them in the private green space. Once out of sight of the servants and before entering the garden, he paused and ran the palm of his left hand over his face whilst thinking sad, remorseful thoughts, tilling the soil of his personality, leaving no trace of any impurities within his consciousness. Finally prepared, he entered into the sweet-smelling atrium of Thanos' house.

His heart skipped a beat upon spying the two men seated in what appeared to be casual conversation. Unnoticed, he walked towards them. "Hello."

In unison, the seated men spun around as if hearing a ghost speak.

"Antonis? Is that you?" exclaimed Alexis.

"Dear God, it is," added Thanos.

In shock, both men stood and clasped the boy marvelling at his return.

"How did you survive the slaughter?" "Where did you go?" "Were you injured?" "When did you arrive in the city?"

The young Greek hunched his shoulders and dipped his head at all the attention he received. He could not get an answer in before the next question bombarded him.

"What happened to Nicola?"

Antonis froze at the query and silence descended upon the two men. He had practiced his reaction many times on the journey but did not imagine it being such a success. "The last time I saw him was on the battlefield. He was surrounded and I tried to reach him..." he trailed off.

The two men stood in silence, looking down at the ground in contemplation, steadily patting the boy on the shoulder.

Alexis was grateful one of his mentor's sons had survived. At least he had not totally let Andreas down. A pang of guilt overcame him at his selfish thoughts.

"You are the only survivor of that fiasco. So, tell me what happened. How did you escape?" said Thanos.

Antonis pursed his lips and frowned in his practiced mock recollection. "It all happened so fast. One moment we were standing in line on the battlefield. The next, the King and his knights charged. Before I could collect my thoughts, my horse was speared from under me and I was left standing, with a giant

Pole by my side, as the janissary surrounded us. I lost count of how many but thank you for teaching me 'real fighting', Thanos, because that is what kept me alive. There was a brief respite when I saw Nicola still upon his horse, and then in a flash he was down. Surrounded by the janissaries, I let out a scream and rushed to his aid only to be blocked by another wall of Turks and was forced back. At some point, I saw a rider-less horse and seeing a gap in the lines, seized the opportunity and mounted the horse to dash through the lines to what I thought was the safety of our position." Antonis paused for breath.

The two listened on intently as his piercing blue eyes looked upon them.

Swallowing, he continued. "It was only once I broke free that I realised it was the other side of the Turks that I had escaped to. Understandably, there was no way back, so I charged as quickly as I could up to the plateau and to what I thought was safety."

"Then what happened?" asked Thanos.

This, Antonis knew, was the crucial part. The delivery had to be perfect. "Once I discovered the Turkish army was between me and safety I decided to hide and evade any patrols. I saw the battle unfold down below. When you, Alexis, tried to relieve us, but all I could do was watch helplessly from the vantage point above."

"Were there no Turks there?"

"No, I presume they thought it was a safe area."

Alexis nodded his agreement, remembering the topography of the land.

Antonis looked down in feigned shame before he spoke again. "As I saw our forces retreat, I just hid from any passing patrols, making my way back to the city as best I could, taking care to avoid any enemy forces."

A silence befell the room and for a moment, Antonis was filled with dread that he was not believed.

Alexis let out a deep sigh. "You did well, my boy, given the circumstances."

"Amazingly well, if you ask me," added Thanos.

Relief washed over Antonis, knowing that with Alexis' support everything would be fine now. "Am I the only one who survived?"

"For the moment, yes. But we have some of the men checking the hospitals," replied Alexis. He did not want to raise the boy's hopes by telling him about Themis. Instead, it would be a pleasant surprise for him if he pulled through.

For the first time since meeting the smuggler, Antonis smiled.

NICOLA SCRATCHED his head furiously in frustration, time had slowed to a snail's pace. The gash on his hip was still weeping after six weeks and he dreaded to think how his face looked, though in truth, he had little to complain about. The accommodation was clean and functional, and his bandages were checked and changed daily by the corpulent Turkish nurse. Clearly, he was of value to Selim and briefly, he felt a warm pang for his brother. The period since Antonis' departure had allowed him time to think. He still could not fathom why he had turned on him that way, refusing to believe Katerina was the cause, and instead, assured himself that the stress of battle was the reason. His eyes fixed onto the corner of the stone frame that surrounded the window.

By now, he knew all the chips and cracks in the carved rock and created stories for each of them. The big chip in the centre left was from a wayward axe blow from a jealous wife who missed its target. That was his favourite. At the bottom, the crack was from a fallen candelabra. He also judged how long ago they had occurred, devising a grading system that included discolouration and smoothness of imperfection. Glancing again at the window, he could not find any new marks for a further story. Looking down, he saw his clenched fist and a stupid idea sprung to mind. He raised his hand three times before forming it into a shape.

"Best three out of five," he said out loud to himself and proceeded to do it one more time.

Holding a swathe of bandages in one hand and a small scalpel in the other, the nurse made his now regular walk to check upon his only patient in the infirmary. He had grown to like the big Greek he tended to with the sad brown eyes. Which he noted was an added bonus, as he was under strict orders to care for him. It was to his surprise he found the large frame of his prisoner patient sitting on the side of the bed moving his fist up and down three times before making a shape with it. "Good morning," he said in heavily accented Greek.

Nicola turned his head and responded.

The nurse waddled over to the patient and placed the bandages on the bedside table. "What is that you are doing?"

Nicola creased his forehead for a moment before registering. "It's a game. Let me show you," he reached out and took the nurse's hand and pressed it into a fist. "You have three choices. Cloth." He held out his hand flat. "Stone," keeping his fist clenched. "Knife," sticking out one finger. "Cloth covers stone, stone blunts knife and knife cuts cloth." He let that sink in for a second. "You understand?"

The nurse nodded and indicated he wanted to play. They began raising their hands in unison and on the third count the nurse stuck out his finger. Blunted to Nicola's stone.

"Again?" said the Greek.

The nurse nodded and they repeated it. This time, the Turk won, and he let out a squeal of laughter. Enjoying the interaction, Nicola repeated it again and again until he started to lose count. Then the strangest thing began to happen; every time he made a move it was defeated.

At first, he thought it was chance but after losing ten in a row he stopped and stared at the now smiling nurse.

The nurse looked at the Greek and showed him his fist whilst frowning. Then the cloth symbol and raised his eyebrows. Finally, the knife and pursed his lips.

It took a moment to dawn then the horror of what he was seeing hit him. His body wobbled, almost fainting at the shock.

The nurse snapped out of his playful mood and jumped up to steady his patient.

Nicola raised his hand to signify he was fine and forgetting the game, busied himself with the bandages.

It was over a week since Antonis returned to the city and still he had not been able to visit the person he most wanted to. A sense of urgency began to creep into his psyche, why, he could not fathom. Nicola was trapped in a Turkish jail, with no possibility of escape and once Selim discerned he had been duped, would most likely execute him. Yet, that nagging doubt remained. Alexis had told him to remain at Thanos' until the arrival of the remaining Laconians in the city, which would not be for a few more days.

Casually, he held his sfakion, still surprised that Selim had returned it to him before he left, sharpening, and polishing the blade with excessive diligence. The house was deserted, and the lugubrious surroundings only made him stew even more in his own thoughts. He had been playing over in his mind how to approach the 'Katerina conundrum' as he had begun to call it. Logic and custom dictated he approach her father, his ego demanded he see the girl first. Fiddling with the dagger, whilst he pondered his next move, the blade slipped, and the razor-sharp edge sliced one of his fingers.

He flinched in pain and annoyed began sucking his finger to staunch the blood. The metallic taste flooded his mouth, reminding him of how Katerina had rushed to Nicola's side when Tezzo accidentally wounded him. That settled it, if he couldn't decide with logic, he would let the portents have their say. Briskly, he walked to the kitchen to find a linen cloth. Tearing it into a small strip, he quickly tied it around his finger and once satisfied, hurriedly left to follow the augur.

The students bustled around the Pandekterion in their usual display of intellectual self-importance. Antonis felt a strange sense of detached superiority, recognising how the events of the last few weeks had changed him. Now, the pointless rounds of rhetoric did not carry the gravitas he once assumed. Strength was acquired and kept from the point of an arrow or the edge of a blade. The young Greek exhaled as he mulled over his newfound thinking.

Putting his hand to the dark felt cap that he wore, the disguise was working. He wondered where she would be. Deciding against going to class, he reckoned he would find her at the usual place in the quad by the low-slung stone wall. Hearing the bell sound, he felt tightness in his chest as he watched the flowing chestnut locks glide out of the doorway towards her preferred spot. His jaw clenched in satisfaction, as she was alone, watching her carefully for a moment as she sat down. Quickly, he decided on a frontal approach in the possibility she would see him arriving. Ironic, his brother would have deliberated, vacillated, and then gone with his heart. Taking the first of his purposeful steps, for a second, he thought that runt Tezzo was going to join her, before seeing it was someone else.

He needed to speak with her alone and as he drew close, quietly spoke. "Hello, Katerina."

Her feline eyes shot a surprised emerald look up at the voice above. "Antonis?" She replied in disbelief.

He silently acknowledged her.

"You're alive? You're here?" She stood up to face him. "You survived? We heard you were dead. What happened?"

With his now well-practiced grim face he let the silence hang in the air. "It all happened so fast, one moment we had lined up for battle, then the King ordered the charge. Before I knew what was happening the Turks had encircled us."

"And Nicola?"

"I saw him knocked off his horse surrounded by the white-capped spearmen."

Katerina's eyes froze into round orbs, her torso quivered in shock, and she stood there in silence. Her reaction stung him in the arcane reaches of his mind.

"I saw a rider-less horse and seeing all was lost, tried to break through to our lines but ended up in the confusion behind the enemy positions. To my eternal shame, I watched helplessly as the remnants of our forces were annihilated." He looked down in his practiced way.

Katerina reached out her hand and clasped his arms. Tears brimmed in her eyes as she looked at him, "I'm sorry, I know how much you meant to each other," and rested her head on his chest.

Slowly, he cautiously put his hand on her resting face, and they stood there in silence, ignored by the throng of students around them. But that nagging doubt in the recesses of his mind persisted, telling him to withhold revealing his true intentions for the moment, and decided in that instant to follow the traditional path. Proven, bloodied, and with family provenance, he knew he would be accepted by her father when he made the offer. He pulled back slightly, wanting to leave before any other student recognised him. "I have to report back to the Laconians."

"I understand."

"I will come and visit you in a few days at your house."

Katerina looked blankly at him.

"If you like?" he added.

She smiled. "That would be nice," she replied.

He smarted at the blandness of her response, confirming the certainty of his chosen path.

Doubt crept back into Alexis' thoughts as the hot bath relaxed his aching body. He had pushed himself very hard at the training ground, in an effort to exorcise the events of the past few days, but his gut told him Antonis was not revealing the full picture. *Possibly feels shame he fled the field.* Whatever was the truth, he would probably never know it. Leaning his head back against the granite lip, he wondered what he would have done at his age and in that situation. Wiping the sweat from the tops of his eyelids, he turned his mind to more pressing matters.

Word had reached him that Themis was going to live, though, he would require a long convalescence. True to his emperor's order, he placed the trusted sergeant in the care of the royal doctors. A relaxed smile crossed his face as he remembered the look of fear on the surgeon's face when he gave them strict instructions that he was not to be disturbed at any cost. He could act with the best of them, he mused, but as his commander, he wanted to speak with him first and another week or two before the Emperor found his answers would not make a difference.

Finally feeling cleansed and relaxed, he stepped out of the bath, grabbing one of the towels laid out for him. Thanos always found it funny how he liked to have his space and not be washed by one of the servants. But Alexis relished his private time. Holding the crisp white cloth, he patted his face then his body dry before wrapping the towel around his waist and walking to the bedchamber. Doubt still needling his now relaxed being.

Fully refreshed, he made his way downstairs to find a sullen Antonis sitting in the kitchen. His heart went out to the boy. To lose one's brother was tough for anyone, something as an only child, he thankfully would never have to face. He would give him time to grieve before getting him back to tasks, though, honestly, he was not sure what to do with him. Sending him back to the Pandekterion might not suit him now. Perhaps it was time for him to fully join the Laconians. He silently berated himself for being such a worrier of these boys. "How are you doing, Antonis?"

"I'm fine, thank you."

"You don't sound it to me."

Antonis let out a sigh, not from guilt but instead at the understanding of how Katerina really felt. "I was just thinking, Alexis."

The general sat down next to him and placed a hand on his shoulder.

"What was the point of it all? Why were we, the Greeks, even there? As observers?"

Alexis swallowed hard, hearing the boy's frustration.

"My parents have lost a son and I a brother. I must inform them of that news. There must be a way to soften the blow." Frustrated anguish seeped from the young man's every pore.

"Boy, I hold myself responsible for leaving you there."

"But you were right, I was in the safest place. If only that idiot King had not been so hot-headed."

"We can never control all aspects of our lives," replied Alexis. His response sounded so fatuous. Having given his word to their father to protect them, he had failed at that test. And even though Andreas would understand, he could never forgive himself. He also wished he could find a way to make it right, but death was final. His body let out an involuntary shudder.

Antonis could sense the guilt that consumed his mentor. He had never seen this emotional softness before and only now realised the depth of feelings Alexis had for them both. He turned purposefully to his teacher and fixed his piecing blue eyes on him. "Do you trust me, Alexis?" he asked.

The general's eyes squinted in confusion. "Of course," he replied.

"I mean, do you trust I know how to do the right thing?"

"Yes."

A pragmatic smile crossed Antonis' face. "We cannot bring him back, that is true, but we can honour his name."

Alexis silently agreed but was in a state of confusion about what he was driving at.

"I know how we can do this, but you have to let me do it my way."

"Very well, do what you think you must."

His azure orbs flickered respect at his mentor's response. Satisfied, his thoughts went to the next phase.

THANOS' carriage made its way to its destination. Inside the ornate wood cabin, Antonis felt the stifling heat under the weight of formal clothes that he wore. He had decided to opt for a traditional blue and gold braided tunic of finest quality weave; with matching hose. Although his instinct was for the youthful look, he knew that tradition would be more persuasive on the person he was about to visit. The only concession he made was a large ostrich feather in the deep red felt hat atop his head. He adjusted his sfakion to rest better against his leg. Another carefully constructed symbol, this time to show the location of his origins.

Taking off the cap, he let the cool December air run through his hair, bringing a welcome respite. On the leather seat next to him, lay the note of acceptance for his visit. He breathed in deeply, closed his eyes, calming himself, focusing on the task ahead. Though in his mind he was sure of the response, there was always that element of doubt and he wanted to leave nothing to chance.

The carriage pulled gently up to its destination, the

coachman hollered for the houseboy to open, and forthwith the studded oak door swung wide. Slowly, the visitors entered.

Carefully, Antonis put his hat back on, grateful it shielded a sheen of perspiration on his brow and waited for the carriage door to be opened.

The host watched interestedly at the formality of the young cub's arrival; his curiosity piqued at what favour he was about to ask.

Antonis nimbly exited the carriages and presented himself to his portly host. "Good afternoon, Lord Planedes."

"Good afternoon, young Vevellis. Thank you for your letter. What brings you to my home with such formality?" he gestured to his guest to follow him inside as he made a clear note of how the boy had grown in stature and confidence.

Servants arrived with cooled lemon-scented water and Planedes proffered one to his guest. They both drank healthily.

"You know, I find the lemon takes away that stony taste we sometimes have in our water here. It's all those ancient reservoirs; God only knows what lives down there."

Antonis cleared his throat and nodded agreement as he primed himself for his prepared speech. Shuffling his feet and showing just the right amount of nervousness before standing fully upright, he faced his host. "Sir, I would formally like to ask for your daughter's hand in marriage."

"What can you offer my daughter?" came the instant response.

"I am from an ancient and noble family with excellent provenance."

Planedes silently nodded.

"I hold good rank in the Imperial Laconian Guard."

"Hmm."

"I am the only issue that will inherit my family's estates in Crete," he paused. "Now."

"Very well," Planedes was enjoying himself immensely. This

was fantastic news as he now had his safety net all but assured and a boy such as he would be easy to control. Certainly, it would be more pleasurable than dealing with that old Ventian count. He looked at the young man's intense face and saw something he liked. He always had. Perhaps teaching a son-in-law such as he could be interesting, he mused. "Have you spoken of this with my daughter?"

"No, sir." Antonis could feel his stammer returning. "I wanted to ask your permission before I would even consider it."

"Very well. I give my permission," replied Planedes.

Antonis broke into a wide grin. "Thank you, sir."

"Perhaps you should go ask my daughter first before you get too excited. I believe she is in the house today, in her usual spot." Planedes gave him a warm smile.

"Yes, sir." With martial precision, he left to go and claim his prize.

He was full of excitement as he walked through the politician's house to find Katerina. True to form she was resting in the day room and thankfully, alone. He paused for a moment to gaze upon her before making his presence known.

"Antonis, what are you doing here? And... why are you dressed so formally?"

"I came here to ask your father for something very important."

"And what happened?"

"He told me I had to ask the person that mattered most."

Katerina returned a blank stare.

Antonis stepped forward towards her, clasped his hands on her slender arms, and took a deep breath. "Katerina Planedes, will you marry me?" It felt surprisingly easy once he said it.

She looked at him in surprise, speechless, genuinely not seeing this coming. Her feelings were not as strong for Antonis, but Nicola was dead. Something she still did not fully believe. Yet if she must be married, at least she knew Antonis. Clearly, papa approved, though, in truth, she had not discussed it or even contemplated that step fully.

Panic began to grip him at her lengthy silence. "We have both lost someone we love and deserve happiness," he said.

"Antonis, I like you very much, but I cannot give you an answer right now. I want to speak with my parents first."

His gaze broke and he looked down, unable to hide his disappointment. "Your father gave his blessing."

"I understand, but can we take it slow? I want to finish my studies at the Pandekterion. It's not seemly for a married woman to be studying." She smiled and clasped his hands before looking imploringly at him. "I'm not saying no. I just want to speak with mama first. You understand, don't you?"

"Yes, I do. Take your time," he replied, seething inside, and it took all his self-control to give her a genuine smile.

THE portly nurse let out a shrill laugh at the story he was listening to. Nicola had grown to like this gentle soul with his peculiar ways. The daily routine had allowed him to grasp a few more Turkish words, and all for one purpose; escape. His nights became besieged with sleeplessness as he pondered over the discovery that he had been betrayed. At first, he refused to believe it, looking for excuses for his brother's behaviour. But as each avenue of argument was processed, he knew he had indeed been deceived by the very person he was closest to. Anger followed the devastating sadness, eventually to be replaced by a desire to balance the scales, and inspiration on how to redress this injustice came to him in a series of waves. The first was to think more like his brother, strategic and logical. Second, was to get a full grasp of the situation with which he was faced. Third, plan his escape.

Taking stock of his surroundings, he found that the situation was not as dire as one would imagine; his prison was more a secure living quarters. Once his injuries had begun to heal and mobility returned, Selim had him moved to a different part of the fort, neither under lock nor with a guard permanently present. He, however, was at pains to exaggerate the extent of his injuries, feigning a more pronounced limp, because as long as his captors thought him lame, they would be less worried about his movements.

Touching his hip, he could feel it was healing nicely. His face however was a different story altogether. When Jezra, the nurse, first took the dressing off to have it changed, Nicola was too scared to see what his face had become.

Jezra told him it did not look bad, that in fact it added character. Not believing the nurse, who was insistent that it was the truth, he refused to look in the mirror to see for himself. It was vanity, as well as fear that made him refuse, but the persisting jolly nurse ground him down. Each time the dressing was changed, he would bring along a polished metal mirror for Nicola 'to see'. With each refusal, it became increasingly difficult to say no. Curiosity finally got the better of him on the fifth bandage change.

Once Jezra took out the stitching and cooed with satisfaction at his handiwork, Nicola gritted his teeth and reached down to the mirror that was placed on the bed. Swiftly, before he could change his mind, he brought it up to his face. An angry red ridge presented itself running from the top of his cheekbone down his face into his neck, the initial sight drawing an intake of breath. He was lucky the slash did not kill him, because somehow, the blade had missed vital arteries and organs. Inspecting more closely, he realised the surgeon who patched him up had done a splendid job; there was no sign of the stitching that had been performed. Forcing a painful smile, he saw it only pulled slightly on his left eye.

"You see. Good, yes?" said Jezra.

"Hmm, it seems that you were right." Tentatively, he lifted his finger to touch the wound.

"Don't do that, your hands unclean. Give you infection."

"How long before the redness goes away?"

Jezra pursed his lips. "Three weeks. Put this ointment, in two moons all will be good."

Nicola looked at the nurse questioningly.

"I prepare it for you after next change."

Nicola shook his head, having come through his first battle unscathed and saving his brother, it was the very person he saved who disfigured him. Now, the looks he so prided himself on had been permanently marred. In anger, he punched his clenched fist into the palm of his hand with such venom the nurse jumped in shock. "When do the bandages come off?"

"End of the week."

Nicola smiled and stood up slowly, taking great care to emphasise his non-existent limp. Painstakingly, he shuffled to the open window and breathed in the fresh morning air. "If only my hip would heal as fast, then I would be able to walk out of here," he said in a light tone.

Jezra laughed nervously, not quite sure how to answer. At least though he could report back to Selim that his guest would not be able to leave of his own accord anytime soon. "It will heal eventually; the blade must have cut one of the connecting sinews. Good rest and food, you will heal in few weeks."

Nicola smiled wanly at him.

"Come, let me put the dressing back on your face and then I must leave you to attend to other duties."

Obediently, he limped back, vowing that once the bandage was removed, he would make good his departure.

In the secret gallery above, Selim watched as his captive spoke with Jezra. He did not trust this Greek and was in no doubt he would attempt to escape at the first opportunity.

However, satisfied that this was not happening soon, the greedy snob relaxed.

The brother had said he would send a note regarding the ransom within two moons, that was fast approaching. A twinge of concern gripped him, wondering if he was good for his word. Looking down at his prisoner below, he hoped so, for the death he would receive would not be quick or pleasant. His thin lips stretched across his teeth as he mulled over a vindictive consolation.

13

ACCUSED

Sophia brushed her daughter's hair with maternal pride as she admired the thick luscious locks. Katerina fidgeted in the chair like she did as a young girl, always rough and tumble, never liking to dress up in the girlish things she had wanted her to wear. She sighed as memories of the past seventeen years flooded back. This moment had come too soon. Now, she was looking at her reflection in the mirror, weighing up the biggest decision in her life.

Katerina always loved the smell of her mother's bedchamber; it relaxed and comforted her. Something she was in dire need presently. Antonis' offer had caught her off guard, but she was grateful, as it forced her to think deeply and honestly about her emotions. In her heart, she did not believe Nicola was dead but when his brother made the proposal, only then, did she truly understand the depth of her sentiments for the elder. That hollow-stomach sensation had become a constant whenever she thought of him. It was strange that something as innocuous as a fencing lesson had been the trigger to exposing that depth of feeling. The news of his death had cut deep and now she had to contend with this offer from a man she liked but did not love.

"What do you think of the proposal of marriage from Antonis, Mama?"

Sophia raised her eyebrows as she composed her reply. "Well, he is a nice boy, from a good family and seems to have his priorities set straight. I don't think he is the type of person to do things rashly, so I would say he has given this a lot of thought."

Katerina smiled wanly. "Yes, Mama."

Sophia stopped brushing her daughter's hair and looked at Katerina's reflection in the mirror. "What is worrying you, my dear?"

Katerina wrung her hands in indecision.

Her mother was confused, wanting to know why her daughter fretted so, noticing her breathing becoming faster, and shallow.

"I'm not sure I love him."

"You can grow to love someone, my darling. It's not so bad. At least he's not some horrible fat old man."

"You don't understand, Mama. I love another and have for some time now."

Sophia could not mask her surprise. "Who is it?"

Katerina bit her lip hesitantly then replied. "His brother, Nicola."

Sophia let out a low murmur. Katerina's behaviour of the last couple of days began to make sense. "Does Antonis know?"

"I don't think so. I have been thinking about how he behaved towards me at the Pandekterion and I'm sure he doesn't."

The mother came around and sat on the chair beside her daughter, reaching out to clasp the nervous hands that lay in her lap. Betraying no surprise at their clammy coldness, empathising instead. Silently, she stayed there until the fidgeting stopped. "You are in a pickle, my dear."

Katerina nodded silently.

"What do you want to do?"

"I don't know, mama. It's not as if I thought of marriage with

Nicola but I felt this charge when I was around him. It was a shock when I heard he was dead." She turned her conflicted tear-filled eyes towards her mother. "Any girl would be happy to have a man such as Antonis propose, but it was then I truly knew what I felt for his brother. That unspoken sentiment just isn't the same."

"Oh, my poor darling, but all is not lost. Love comes in many guises. Perhaps he is the better choice for you."

Katerina smiled at her mother's platitudes, but that was all they were. There was no possibility she would feel the same intensity with anyone, but Nicola.

Sophia gently stroked the young hands in understanding. Soon, Planedes would want her married off, most likely to some decrepit Venetian noble. At least with Antonis, she would find youthful vigour if not the throes of ecstasy. "It is sad that Nicola has left us. But perhaps by accepting the proposal, you will do him the most honour and you would also make another handsome young man happy."

Katerina's fingers clenched her mother's in thankful acknowledgement. "I love you, Mama." Then she marched forward to embrace her, gripping tightly.

ALEXIS' thick nails had been subconsciously scratching the constant itch on the side of his neck all morning, leaving a bright red welt. He huffed in uncharacteristic frustration and decided he wanted to walk through the city this morning to clear his cloudy mood. He breathed in deeply the crisp air as he left Thanos' house on the way to the palace. It was the best time of year for a brisk stroll, the coldness reduced the civic stench, and the weaker sun prevented those stifling heat pockets developing in the narrow alleys. The only worry he had was from a stray pickpocket, but scoffed at the thought, pitying the fool who would try.

Part of the enjoyment for him was helping people he did not know. Today, despite his troubled nature, was no different. Spying an elderly woman struggling with a basket of loaves, he crossed into the alley and offered his aid. The weary old lady thankfully accepted, eulogising how she wished she had a granddaughter to marry him off to. Alexis smiled and replied that he was not the marrying kind. Undeterred, she rattled on how she wished more men were like him as he carried the basket the half stadion to its destination. He bade the woman a wonderful morning and walked the last part to the palace with a spring in his step; good deeds benefited the giver as much as the receiver.

He entered the Blachernae Palace through one of its minor entrances that were close to the infirmary. He did not want to risk being seen by anyone important until he had a chance to speak with his sergeant alone. Turning off the main approach road and walking down the side alleys, whole buildings lay unoccupied and dilapidated. He vowed to explore the other parts of the city he did not usually frequent. Perchance they were not as dire as here. Either way, it was a good gauge of the health of the capital.

Weaving between the pale stone buildings, he soon found himself at the entrance, close to the part where the sea wall met the land walls. The guards stood-to, in surprised attention as they saw the general entering the little-used gate. He acknowledged them briefly, before turning his mind to becoming inconspicuous. It was typical for the infirmary to be near the emperor's chambers, so he needed luck for no one to be present as he crossed the main corridor.

Carefully, he ascended the stairs that approached the second floor. The cool air made him shiver as he carefully took increasingly quiet steps until he reached the door leading to the main passageway. Pulling it slightly open, he waited a few moments to see if anyone was there. Satisfied, he swiftly pulled the door ajar and nimbly darted his bulk into the corridor, hurrying the fifteen paces to the connecting door leading to the infirmary.

"General Sartis."

Alexis' shoulders slumped as the withered old voice called out to him along the corridor. Turning back, he saw the smiling face of a council member.

"Where are you off to? I have just seen the Emperor."

He cursed his luck. What was Sphrantzes doing here so early? The elderly noble's bushy white eyebrows raised a notch as he realised where he was heading. "I will go fetch the Emperor presently."

Alexis raised his hand to stop him, but the old man had spun with surprising speed and waddled back to fetch his ruler. Resigning himself to the inevitability of company, he entered the infirmary to see the sergeant. Resting on a rigid wooden pallet, he lay alone in the oversized Royal Ward. He scuffed his boot on the floor to announce his arrival.

Themis, awake, turned to see his commander enter. Pushing himself up, he prepared as best he could.

Alexis sped to assist the soldier to a sitting position. "How are you doing, Sergeant?"

"I am recovering well enough, sir," he replied. His weather-beaten face beaming a proud smile.

"You look strong enough to wrestle a bear."

"Thank you, sir."

Looking upon his sergeant, he thanked the lord that at least he was spared. "I wanted you to recover before I came to speak with you and hoped that we would get the chance to speak alone together first, however, we have company. When the Emperor and his council arrive, just relate to us all that happened as best you can."

The joy on Themis' face was replaced with concern as a bustling noise came from the distance.

Alexis placed his hand on Themis' shoulder and smiled reassuringly. "There is nothing to worry about."

"General. I see you've decided to speak with your man." The disapproving tone was clear.

Alexis looked around slowly to see the Emperor along with five council members in tow. "Good morning, Your Majesty. I was coming to see my sergeant first."

The council members pursed their lips in indignation at his unapologetic behaviour.

"Very well, have you had a chance to speak with him?"

"No, sire, I was preparing him to speak with you first."

Honour satisfied the Emperor as he gazed upon the hapless patient. "What is your name, soldier?"

"Themis of Rhodes, sire."

"Tell us what happened at the battle."

"Sergeant, take us step by step from when I and the rest of the Laconians left you." Alexis instructed.

Themis gulped as he began to recollect the events from a few weeks past. Overawed by the presence of the Emperor, he focused his sight on Alexis. "Well, sir. After you left with the Hungarian General, we all waited alongside the Polish King and his knights whilst the main force attacked on the right. The Laconians were interspersed amongst the other crusaders. I was slightly behind the front line when I heard one of the Greeks say that the Sultan was too close and unprotected. Then, the next thing I heard, was the King sound the charge." Themis paused to gather his thoughts.

"Which Greek said it? Do you remember?" asked the Emperor.

"It was Antonis Vevellis."

A murmur came from the gathered nobles.

The Emperor frowned. "Are you sure?"

"Yes, sir, because I remember thinking what a foolish thing he had said."

"Or, very clever," said one of the nobles.

"Did you not say that Vevellis survived the massacre, General?"

"Yes, he did."

"Antonis is alive?" exclaimed Themis.

"Where is he now?" asked the Emperor.

"At my house in the city."

"We will need to speak to him."

Alexis nodded calmly, though inside, he was confused.

The nobles started chatting amongst themselves, their tone turning alarmingly negative.

"Have you spoken with anybody else about this?" Asked Alexis.

Themis shook his head in response.

Alexis turned to see a concerned Missi standing a few paces away.

"Apologies, sir, but I was coming to check on sergeant Themis' progress." he offered.

"Wait for me outside."

"Yes, sir."

The Emperor ordered the gathered nobles back to his chamber. Obediently, they shuffled out.

John VIII placed a hand on Alexis' shoulder and leaned towards him. "Get me the boy, I do not like what I just heard."

"Yes, sir."

Promptly, the Emperor left, leaving his general unsure of what to do next.

"General, did I say something wrong?" enquired Themis.

Alexis shook his head. "No, you did fine. It's just that when there is a disaster the powers-that-be need someone to blame." He signalled for the attendant to bring Missi in and rubbing the pads of his fingers deliberately on his crown, went back to planning his next move.

· · ·

ANTONIS HELD the parchment with trepidation at the formality of it all, shaking his head at his decision to be traditional. Tearing open the seal, he read its contents. Crumpling up the letter, he marched out to the courtyard and told them to get the carriage ready.

At the Planedes' house breakfast was a silent affair. Sophia ate, quietly confident that her talk with Katerina had been useful, Planedes sat expectantly, waiting to hear of his daughter's decision. The absence of conversation was too much for the man and he slammed the palm of his hand on the table, rattling plates, and persons alike. "Well, what have you decided?"

Katerina calmly finished chewing her food before facing her father. No one, not even him would force her to do something she did not want or for that matter how to do it. Slowly, she dabbed her mouth with the napkin before placing it firmly back on her lap. "I have decided; however, I feel that Antonis should be the first to hear it."

Planedes pursed his lips at his daughter's impudence, yet grudgingly admired her strength of character.

Prepared for an argument, Katerina was thrown off balance by his calm demeanour. "Don't worry, Papa."

"Let's hope." He replied.

Katerina smiled back, she had made her decision and would now stick to it. That was her way, but it had taken sleepless nights of deliberation and justification to do it.

"When is young Vevellis returning to hear your answer?"

"He should be here by mid-morning. Assuming he received my letter, that is."

Planedes put one of his lank strands back on his head before returning to his morning repast. Deciding that he would stay a while longer today, to find out the result. She was after all his only child. Having not quite finished his meal, Planedes' daily routine was disturbed yet again by the announcement of a visitor for Miss Katerina. "Seems like the boy is as eager to find out as I am."

Katerina looked blankly at her father.

"Well? What are you waiting for? Go out and see the boy. Just don't bring him in here and disturb what's left of my breakfast."

Obediently, she rose from the table and went to give her eagerly anticipated answer, finding a nervous Antonis waiting in the hall. "I see you are not so formally dressed this morning," she said, flashing a big welcoming smile.

Antonis shifted awkwardly in his duds, grateful at least she liked this outfit. "I thought I would leave the formalities to you today."

Katerina stifled a giggle before her face turned serious. Fixing her gaze on him, she noticed for the first time how beautifully clear his eyes were, the long dark lashes bordering his large light blue orbs. *Perhaps Mama's advice was not so far off the mark after all.* "First, I would like to thank you for having the consideration to let me decide in my own time."

He lowered his eyelids in reply. *I want an answer, not banalities.*

"I have given your proposal a lot of thought, and I do agree to marry you."

Antonis laughed, more out relief than joy, and stepped forward to hug her. "That is wonderful news. Have you told your parents?"

Katerina shook her head. "NO, I wanted you to hear my answer first."

He leaned down and brought his mouth close to hers.

She froze as he lunged forward, unconvincingly offering her lips to his. The feeling as they made contact a pale imitation of the experience with Nicola. There was something else too, a guilty shame in what she was doing. But it was too late, she had made her decision.

A smile spread across his face as thoughts of his brother imprisoned alone, and no doubt soon dealing with a wrathful jailer entered his mind.

"I am glad you are happy," said Katerina, misreading his emotion.

Sensing no time to lose, Antonis hooked his betrothed to his arm and walked them both through to her parents, who waited with anticipation. The relieved excited faces said it all and Planedes uncharacteristically stood up and exclaimed his pleasure at 'this union'.

Sophia Planedes hugged her daughter and congratulated her future son-in-law before becoming a little flustered at all the plans that would have to be made. Her voice becoming shriller every time she thought of something that now needed to be done.

Planedes clasped Antonis' hand. "Welcome to the family, my boy. I expect a promising future for you."

"Thank you, sir, I will do my best," he replied.

"I look forward to seeing your father again."

"You know my father?"

"Of course. He was the Commander of the Laconians when I was a young man, very respected for his service to the empire."

It made sense when he thought about it, though he had never considered it before. "I will be sending word to them of this marriage immediately, and hopefully they will come."

Planedes looked over to his excited wife. "Depends whether they will have enough time to get here," he replied before letting out a deep belly laugh. "All right, I shall leave you with the ladies, no doubt there is a plethora of instructions for you."

Antonis shrugged and turned towards the rest of his future family, wondering how Planedes excused himself with such consummate ease.

Sometime later that morning, the wily politician entered the palace slightly behind schedule with a surprising spring in his step. The guards exchanged a questioning glance as they watched the usually surly politician with interest. Ignoring them, he strode straight towards the ministers' chamber and the daily briefing, feeling optimistic for the first time in years.

"Twenty-two, twenty-three, twenty-four, twenty-five," grunted Nicola as he counted out the last of his exercises.

Every day since deciding escape was the only solution, he had surreptitiously been strengthening and nursing his hip back to health. His routine was always the same. Rise in the dead of night, train till just before sun-up, then plan the requirements needed for escape before returning to bed and being 'woken' by one of Selim's attendants.

Lying in bed waiting for his morning reveille, he took stock of his situation to date. Though his jailer had kept his distance, he had learned a great deal from Jezra. He knew the location of his confinement as well as the number of guards in the fort, and satisfied that he had correctly estimated their strength, had given him more confidence in his plan. His hip, though not fully fit, would be well enough to make good his escape. The big issue would be stealing a horse unnoticed. If he could achieve that, he would have half a day's lead on any would-be pursuers.

He caught himself running his fingers down the now exposed scar on his face. It was a habit he acquired while deep in thought, perhaps through the routine of applying salve. Flicking his head to snap himself back to task, he tried to recollect how long he had been in this place. Reaching down, he counted the marks he had scored on the wooden pallet every morning before breakfast arrived. Finally tallying up the gouges, nearly two moons had passed. The sound of a turning door handle brought him out of his reflections, and he lay silently on his bed waiting to be roused.

With his usual noiseless regularity, Jezra entered and softly announced his presence.

Nicola responded with a theatrical yawn and bade his jailer good morning. However, there was a concerned look on kindly nurse. "Did you have a bad night's sleep, Jezra?"

"No, sir, I did not," he replied.

Nicola found it strange how he remained formal and deferential, after all, it was he who was the prisoner. "Then what is the matter?"

"Nothing, just been busy." Jezra glanced around furtively before setting his eyes on Nicola. "I think it's time you leave this place."

"What?" replied Nicola, feigning surprise.

"I know your hip is good, you pretend so bad." The Turk's mastery of Greek was nominal, but his understanding of physiology excellent.

Nicola shrugged his shoulders and put the palms of his hands in the air.

Jezra smiled knowingly at him. "I have known for a while, and I know your brother betrayed you."

Nicola inclined his head intently.

"Who is Katerina?"

His big brown eyes enlarged and rounded even more.

"I hear you call out at night, her name."

It dawned on him then that he had been spied on even when he thought he was alone. Involuntarily, he glanced up as his eyes followed his suspicions. The lattice above could easily hide a gallery in there. He berated himself for not being more cautious. "She is… a friend."

"You will need a horse."

Nicola was confused. Why was this man helping him? Perhaps this was a carefully laid trap? but that did not make sense either.

The nurse grabbed Nicola's solid arm and led him to the

window. Silently, he pointed to the far corner of the courtyard where the wall bordered the river. "There will be a horse and provisions from dawn, the day after tomorrow."

"Why are you doing this?"

"I understand what it is to be betrayed by the one you love."

Though he wanted to believe him, every fibre in his being was on alert. What he would do with this offer, he would decide later. Only one thing was sure; time was no longer on his side. Heavy footsteps entering the room broke his concentration.

"Kyrie Vevellis, I see you are up and about this morning. You seem to be getting fitter every day." A smiling Selim walked towards him without a care in the world. "I have good news for you. Today, I have received a letter from your brother. He shall soon be returning with the ransom and you will be free to go."

Nicola offered a wan smile.

"I would like you to dine with me this evening. So we can celebrate each of us getting what we want."

"I look forward to it," Nicola replied, turmoil raging inside, as he knew what his brother truly intended.

"Jezra will come fetch you when it is time," added Selim, before promptly leaving.

Nicola waited until Selim had fully left the room before putting his hand on his unexpected Samaritan. "Perhaps you should have the horse ready for tomorrow morning, and make sure you get my sfakion too."

The calm tone unsettled Jezra slightly, but he acknowledged the request without question.

Nicola spent the rest of the day preparing himself for what was to come, even taking an extended walk around the parts of the fort he was allowed to visit, while making sure he never lost his limp, and carefully inspected the masonry that would require him walking on it in the dead of night. There was only one part he could not get a close look at but was confident he could hold his footing. The guards who wandered around, watched him with curiosity, and he made sure to speak with as many as he could, obliquely finding out who would be around later. Gouzaris' mantra repeated in his head, 'Prepare and plan, prepare and plan'. Satisfied he had done all he could, he hobbled back to his quarters to bathe, and ready himself for dinner.

The cool evening air wafted through Selim's quarters as they sat and talked through the evening. Nicola's mind was elsewhere, but thankfully, his host was in such good spirits that it went unnoticed; more interested in discussing the house designs he was going to build with the ransom money.

He smiled, how easy it must have been for Antonis to fool the man. Greed and snobbery, such easy vices to manipulate. Deciding to take a leaf out of his brother's book, he spent the rest of the evening indulging his jailer with stories of the emperor who resided in the golden city of Constantinople. It was the dead of night before they finished, and he was escorted back to his chambers. His mind was made up, he just hoped Jezra was good as his word, otherwise this was going to be a very short trip.

Lying silently in bed, every sense strained to make sure there was no one watching from above. Satisfied after a period that he was alone, he arose, quickly dressed, and took his makeshift escape equipment before walking to the window and the first part of his getaway.

It was a cloudy night, and that suited him fine. The moon peeked out from behind the dark cover and he judged it to be about two hours before dawn. That should give him enough time if he was lucky, thinking how little of that he had of late.

Without delay, he stepped out of the opening onto the thin ledge that ran across the face of the fort and towards the curtain wall. With his back flat against stone, he inched steadily towards the edge of the building, where he climbed down onto the houses that nestled inside the fort. Beads of nervous perspiration swamped his hairline as this was the most exposed part, and placed his feet cautiously, checking the surety of the tiles that covered the roof. Any noise would alert the sentries on the walls a few feet above. The moon made an unheralded appearance, which gave him better vision as he navigated on the strongest beams and his heart skipped a beat at every creak that emanated from his foot placement.

He lost track of time, solely concentrating on the next step until he finally reached the outer wall. Luckily, there was some scaffolding, as the Turks were restoring this part of the fort. Quickly, he climbed up onto the wall to dash the final part to the corner of the castle. Noiselessly, he reached the end, looked over the wall with bated breath, and saw a horse saddled and ready to go. Silently thanking Jezra, he took the rolled sheets off his shoulder, tied one end around the crenulations, and released the other over the side. Hurriedly, he clambered over and made his way down, jumping the last part, and landing with a dull thud as he ran out of sheet. The horse whinnied softly, and Nicola soothed the bay as he quickly inspected the saddle and provisions pouch. He smiled with thankful relief to find that, good to his word, the nurse had placed his sfakion along with a small loaf of bread, and a lump of cheese in the cloth bag.

Without delay, he mounted and rode off as quickly and quietly as possible into the night, silently thanking his benefactor.

14

TRIAL

*A*lexis returned home that evening with a heavy heart, bitter in the knowledge that when wolves circled, an innocent was always sacrificed. "Where is the boy?"

"I don't know. Most probably with the Planedes girl."

"Those old bastards are trying to find a scapegoat for the failure at Varna."

Thanos frowned. "Why? It wasn't even our battle. We were there just as observers."

"How the fuck do I know, probably some political wrangling behind the scenes. We offer a sacrificial lamb and in return they attack the Turk again." Alexis knew exactly what this was, opportunism at its most base. But he would be damned if he let this foolishness get out of hand.

"Who are they trying to blame?"

"Antonis."

"What? That's absurd."

"I know, but when the herd mentality starts it only needs one to call for a head on a stake, and the others follow."

Thanos grunted in agreement. "Is there any proof?"

"Only circumstantial."

"That's all they need."

"Not if I have anything to say about it."

"And, my friend, you do have a lot to say."

Alexis let out a humourless laugh.

"So, what will you do?"

"All I can. Which is making sure this idiocy dies a swift death when we all meet again in the palace tomorrow."

Thanos growled an approval as Alexis went to change into something more relaxing.

It was the dead of night before Antonis, still in an exuberant mood, arrived back at Thanos' house. He was not sure where all the time had gone after he and Katerina had declared the news to her parents and it had swiftly descended into the minutiae of guest lists, wedding feast, and finery.

As it was her only daughter to be married, Sophia Planedes' maternal instincts went into overdrive, fussing over her with an equal mixture of tears and laughter. Clasping her future son-in-law's hand every time she wanted to emphasise a point. Repeating endlessly about the excitement in meeting his parents. It soon became claustrophobic and Antonis was relieved to finally be home. Hoping that this was a brief phase and not his future life. Consoling himself that at least the mothers would get along.

The light fluffy mood disappeared in a puff as he spied his mentor and friend sitting amongst the blazing candlelight of the formal reception room. "Why the long faces? Did someone die?" He asked.

"No. Not yet anyway," replied Thanos.

Antonis ignored the quip. "Well, I have some good news. I am getting married to Katerina Planedes." Deftly, he planted himself onto the remaining free sofa with a big boyish smile.

Alexis forced a smile. "Congratulations, that is wonderful news."

"Yes. I asked, and today she accepted. I have spent the whole day with Katerina and her mother planning the wedding."

"Did the father approve?" asked Thanos.

"Actually, he was the easiest."

The older men failed to hide their astonishment.

"It was Katerina who took a while to decide. She was surprised by my proposal and needed time to think it over." Antonis twirled his fingers together in contented satisfaction.

"When is the wedding planned for?"

"The family want to have it in the early part of next year. I need to contact my parents with the good news, and they will make preparation to come over to the capital."

"Are they planning a big wedding?" asked Thanos.

"Yes, looks like it."

"At least the news will soften the blow of Nicola's death."

Antonis stopped his boyish fidgeting at the mention of his brother's name. "Poor consolation, but it is the best I could do. I will write both pieces of news in the letter to mama and papa."

Alexis sat silently, waiting for the right moment to tell his ward of the other news, but this unexpected turn of events threw his clarity into confusion. Deciding it was best to spring it on the boy in the morning, he stood to his full height, congratulated Antonis again, and made his way to sleep.

Thanos looked on as his friend departed, knowing he must have his reasons for the silence at this hour, and took up the reigns of conversation with the excited boy. Letting him savour his moment.

THE EMPEROR'S room was palpable with tension as the full council of nobles gathered to hear the witnesses from Varna. Alexis looked upon these men with a mixture of disdain and trepidation. More unnerving than any battle as the enemy's threat could spring from anywhere. He had vacillated throughout the morning about what to tell Antonis, then choosing discretion as the best course of action. He knew the boy had nothing to hide and was confident this would be over quickly.

Antonis sat patiently in the antechamber that led to the imperial council hall. Nervousness pervaded as he waited, playing over in his mind the conversation he had had with Alexis earlier that morning. It was not what his mentor said, more the way he said things. There was sadness in Alexis' eyes, which he could not quite fathom. This morning was an official inquiry into what occurred at the battle and as a survivor of the ill-fated charge, he was required to testify.

Confidence soon replaced the fleeting moment of concern, as it was only him who could relate events, and thinking nothing more of it went back to dreaming about his impending marriage. Trawling over in his mind all the tasks he had set out for himself. Pleased that he had written the letter to his parents. Slowly and deliberately, he began to mull over all the demands his future mother-in-law was imposing, when he was called in to see the council.

Rising calmly, he followed the attendant into the great hall to be greeted by two dozen sets of eyes glaring wide-eyed at him. Unconsciously, he checked his step as he walked towards an inscrutable Emperor, who sat upon his throne. He caught sight of Alexis standing to the side, grim-faced and serious. Initially thinking it was just for the occasion, deep-down misgivings started to form. Finally, he came to rest in front of the questioning grey eyes of John VIII.

"Do you know why you have been summoned today?"

"Yes, Your Majesty. It is to hear my report of the Battle of Varna."

The Emperor inclined his head a fraction and raised his hand for the young Greek to commence.

Antonis stood there mutely unsure what to do next before

he slowly began to recount his experiences exactly as he had before to Alexis and Thanos days earlier. The room was deathly silent, except for his voice as each of the onlookers avidly listened to his recollection.

The Emperor nodded sagely as Antonis finished his tale then casually brought both his hands back to rest on his throne and asked. "That is everything?"

"Yes, as I remember it, Your Majesty."

"Do you have a memory of speaking with the Polish King?"

"I think so, but I don't recall what was said. I was too nervous on the eve of my first battle," Antonis replied truthfully.

The doors to the other waiting room opened and Antonis turned to see the bed-ridden figure being carried into the audience chamber. *Themis is alive? Why did no one tell me?* Frantically, he searched his memories for anything incriminating, but nothing came to mind. It felt like an age until the palanquin was brought fully into the room, its passenger looked nervous and avoided eye contact with him.

"Sergeant, I hope my physicians are giving you adequate care."

"Yes, Your Majesty, they are," replied the simple soldier. The nervous gulp at the end drawing a couple of condescending sighs from the gathered nobles.

"Tell my full council that is gathered here what you told me you heard on that fateful day at Varna."

Themis paused for breath then related the story as he had previously for the Emperor.

Cries of foul play began to emanate throughout the room.

A stately gesture quelled the rising noise. "Are you sure that is what you heard?"

Themis nodded. "Yes, Your Majesty."

"What do you say about this, Vevellis?" Demanded the Emperor.

Antonis was in total confusion and could not believe his

ears. "Sire, I don't remember saying those words." In truth, he had virtually no recollection of that day prior to being knocked off his horse. Thereafter, it was seared into his brain.

The Emperor signalled again, and Themis was slowly transported out and another Laconian took his place in the hall. It was the slender frame of lieutenant Missi who now had to testify.

Standing close to the throne, one of the old council members, Lukas Notaras began to conduct the proceedings. "Lieutenant, please, can you repeat what you told me the other day for the benefit of the gathered nobles?"

Missi nodded hesitantly. "Yes, my Lord. Whilst I was tending to the wounds of sergeant Themis at the crusader fort in Galata, I took a break and went up to the battlements to get fresh air. It was there that I spied a rider on the edge of the marshes. At first I thought I recognised the rider but then dismissed it as I saw clearly that he wore the uniform of a Turkish cavalryman."

"Are you sure it was Turkish?"

"Yes, sir, the white turban was distinctly visible from that distance."

"Who do you think it was?"

"Antonis Vevellis."

Gasps emanated throughout the chamber.

"Are you sure?" asked Notaras.

"Yes, sire."

"How can you be so sure?"

"He has a distinct riding style. Something you notice when you train with someone."

Alexis was reeling at this turn of events. Where did this come from, and when did Notaras get this information from Missi? Looking at his young officer, there was no doubt in his mind that he was telling the truth, his discomfort plain to see; conflicted that his testimony might condemn a fellow Laconian.

He knew him to be an honest man and as such did not expect any distortion of what he saw as the truth.

"How is his style so distinct?"

"Well, sir. Vevellis has a habit of cocking his right leg across the saddle when he is riding long distances. A habit that is most unusual."

"Amongst Greek riders perhaps, but it's not unusual with the Eastern Anatolian tribes." interjected the Emperor.

"Yes, your Majesty, that is true, however, the rider was not wearing an eastern Anatolian uniform but that of the European Turkish army, which rarely has nomads in its ranks."

Alexis looked over to see Antonis fidgeting at this. He hoped the boy did not lose his cool. Hearing the jarring voice of Notaras puncture the room again, he feared this was turning into an impromptu trial.

"What do you have to say about these pieces of evidence?"

Antonis' mind spun, he could kick himself for missing that left fork. A sense of dread overcame him and he looked around the room, catching his future father-in-law's eye. To his surprise, he proffered the slightest nod of encouragement. Emboldened, he straightened his back and augured his full power towards Notaras. A cold fury grew inside him, he was not going to be accused of something he did not do. This was rhetoric and this old fool would be his whipping boy. "Evidence, my Lord? Evidence of what?"

The pugilistic reply caught the old noble off guard and sensing a shift in momentum, Antonis continued. "You have two pieces of observation from my fellow Laconians, neither of which constitute any wrong-doing on my part. First, I may have spoken to the King, however, why would the word of a junior officer and a foreign one at that, carry any weight in his decision? Second, whilst I don't doubt that Missi thought he saw me riding, how could he be sure at that distance who it was? Furthermore, if I was anywhere near the fort at Galata, I would have headed straight to the safety of the crusader encampment."

"So, you were nowhere near the camp at that time?"

"No, I was not." Antonis clenched his jaw as he told the lie.

"Then, where were you?"

"My Lord, this questioning is unreasonable, and for what purpose? Should we not be grateful that one of our own survived?" interjected Alexis.

"General, you will refrain from interrupting again," said the Emperor firmly.

"Your Majesty, this is outrageous."

"General, you will be silent, or you will remove yourself."

Admonished, Alexis nodded and kept his council.

"I respect General Sartis' loyalty to his men. However, it has come to our attention that sabotage was at play and we are investigating all avenues along with our allies," said Notaras.

Alexis gritted his teeth; all his fears were coming true. These fools were looking for a scapegoat and they would find one even if the evidence didn't stack up.

Notaras turned back to Antonis with a victorious smirk. "You will please answer the question."

"I made my way northeast towards the coast to find a passage back to the city."

"Why did you do that?"

"Because the entire Turkish army was between me and my fellow Christians and it appeared to be the safest route."

A few wags sniggered at the boy's defiance.

Notaras detected the faintest shift in momentum and looked towards the emperor briefly. He wanted this to be a clean case and suddenly felt he was in danger of losing it. "Your Majesty, I request that we break for sustenance and resume this afternoon."

The Emperor nodded. "Very well, we shall reconvene when the sands run down."

In the corner, a servant turned a large sand clock to signify the countdown had begun.

Antonis stood unsure what to do next, half expecting to be led away in chains.

Notaras noticed the indecision and spoke up. "Vevellis, you are still at liberty, we are a civilised nation and persons under trial are innocent until found guilty."

The young man acknowledged gratefully and turned to join Alexis but was under no illusion as to the predicament he was in.

A SENSE of urgency enveloped Nicola as soon as he broke free of the fort. Acting on his instincts, he pushed the horse as fast as it would go. At the previous weigh-station, he had stolen what was apparently a fine steed, reasoning the owner would not be too put out as he had switched saddles. Now on the home stretch, he cursed as the trotting gelding buckled under the exertion. He should have stolen a better animal. Thankfully, the cloudless night had allowed him to ride unchecked towards the city.

Determining that he was not being hunted as a horse thief, it would be wise to rest the animal until dawn. Spying a small wooded copse near the road, he turned off, to utilise the remaining few hours of night for a welcome rest. Entering the small clump of densely packed trees, he swiftly unhitched the saddle, placed it by one of the thick trunks, and wiped the horse down as best he could. With his maintenance completed, he sat and pondered, unaware until that moment, what a toll the two days of continual trotting had done to his weary back.

Using the techniques taught by Alexis, he lay on the ground and relaxed his sore muscles and joints so the pain would abate, strangely, finding the breathing exercises the most useful. Once satisfied, he turned to see the gelding sleeping. He sighed in sympathy and reached into the bag to pull out the remaining piece of bread and cheese. A sharp pain hit under his fingernail as he rummaged. His curiosity piqued, he pulled something out to find it was a piece of folded parchment. The night was too dark for him to see clearly so reading was left for the morning.

Nicola awoke just as the low winter sun began to break on the horizon. Groggily, he cleared the sleep from his eyes and swiftly readied for the final leg. Then opening the folded paper, he discovered it was written in Turkish, and although he could not fully understand the alien script, the penmanship was definitely his brother's. Folding it carefully, he placed it inside his tunic.

Though feeling rested, he was at pains not to push his steed too hard for the final part of the journey and judging the distance covered, Constantinople would come into view before noon. He mulled over whom he could find to translate the letter. For Jezra to have placed it in the knapsack, it must carry significant importance. A wry smile crossed his face at the unconditional help he received from this peculiar man, wondering what had happened in his life that he felt the necessity to assist him.

Knowing the futility of dwelling on a question he could never know the answer to, he turned his thoughts to what he would do upon arrival in the city. He was sure Antonis would be there, most likely at Thanos', maybe even Katerina's. His jaw clenched in anger at what his brother had done, vowing he would have his revenge, though gazing at the rising sun, he was not quite sure how.

THANOS BIT into the perfectly grilled chicken, the juicy flavours coating his taste buds. He reached over the plate, grabbing his goblet of watered-down wine to wash it down. Alexis and the boy had not yet returned. Worriedly, he looked up at his favourite piece of art. The workmanship of the icon was exquisite and though not a religious man, the courage of St. Stephen struck a chord with the former soldier. He let out a chuckle at how those bastards in the church continuously got you. Selling an afterlife that no one could prove existed, but everyone was too scared to discount. Absolute genius. Either way, he liked the painting and with his mood perked up, took another chunk of the tasty meat, almost choking as he heard a pounding on the main entrance. "Spiros, go check which idiot is at the door, and get rid of him quickly," he said.

The servant acknowledged and hurried off to do his master's bidding.

Without further thought, he had another swig of wine to calm the disruption. With the cup to his lips, he heard an upheaval, followed by the appearance of a ravaged man. It took a moment before he choked on his wine. "I must be fucking dreaming. Is that you, Nicola?"

In the low archway that separated the dining room from the Atrium, the hulk of Nicola stood. "Yes."

Thanos rose from his chair in shock and gazed upon the man before him. The bright red scar the first thing that caught his attention before fixing his gaze on the wild-looking brown eyes. "This is amazing, fantastic, incredible. I can't believe it. You're alive." He walked over to the young lad and clasped him in joy. "My boy, you're alive," he repeated, to convince himself this was no hallucination. "This is cause for celebration. Spiros. Wine!" he shouted. "Wait until your brother and Alexis find out. They will be overjoyed."

"Where are they?"

"At the palace. There is a review of what happened at the battle." Thanos pointed to the ruddy gash on his face, "Varna?"

Tight-lipped, Nicola nodded.

"Very well, you can tell me about it later. Gives you character though, my boy."

The young warrior looked around just as the servant returned with a full goblet and another for his master. Hurriedly, he put the wine to his lips and drained it in one gulp. "Do you have any servants who read Turkish?"

"One of the cooks served at the Ottoman embassy a few years ago. Perhaps she does."

"Good, fetch her as we will need her services."

Thanos obeyed at once and asked for her to be brought to them. Something was different about the boy. He seemed bigger, more menacing, even frightening. Battle had a way of doing that, he reflected, though this was somehow different.

"What are my brother and Alexis doing at a review?"

"They are trying to find out who is to blame for the disaster at Varna and it looks as though they are trying to pin it on Antonis."

Nicola sneered a cruel smile. "Where is that cook? We shall see about that," he barked, whilst going over and filling his goblet to the brim again.

Thanos was desperate to find out what had transpired but understood that now was not the time, deciding to go and look for the cook personally. The young lad was clearly on a mission, no doubt to exonerate his brother.

Nicola drank more measuredly and before he had finished, the matronly cook appeared. Taking the cup from his lips, he looked upon the diminutive servant. "Your master tells me that you read Turkish. Is that so?"

"Yes, sir."

"Good, I want you to read this letter and translate its contents for me."

After twice reading it, she relayed the information to an impatient Nicola.

"You tell no one of this, even your master, do I make myself clear?"

The woman nodded fearfully as Thanos joined them.

"Ah, I see Phaedra has arrived."

"Yes, nothing of importance. However, I must go to the Palace now to be at my brother's side. It is imperative to see that justice is done. We shall speak later."

Thanos thought it a strange use of words but before he could reply, Nicola ran out of the house, leaving him thinking it would have been better if he had changed into some clean clothes.

Nicola dashed towards the Blachernae. Arriving at the palace gate, the guards ushered him in as soon as he declared he had come to give important documents to General Sartis. On entering the long stone corridor, he paused, wiped the sweat from his brow and took a few deep breaths to calm his anger, before walking purposefully towards the Ancient Oak door where groups of nobles were filing into the council chamber. Making the final few steps, his instincts told him to enter through one of the minor doors on the side. Deftly, he raised his hand to the guard to prevent the main door being opened and walked around to one of the side entrances on the upper level. As he had hoped, there was no one present, and cautiously crept in. He stood by the wall to see what was occurring in the political pit below. His body tensed as he spied Antonis standing alongside Alexis, as the full council and their entourage poured into the hall. He simply watched the proceedings, using all his will to restrain the urge to shout out.

A sense of pride inveigling Planedes as he stood amongst the gathered nobles and gazed upon his future son-in-law. Under normal circumstances, he would have sent word to his wife to cancel everything, yet, he was happy, for the boy's bearing under such scrutiny had been that of a man of far greater experience than one his age. Years of politicking told him this was mere panic reaction to the renewed Ottoman danger to the city.

He was sure the boy was innocent and furthermore, he had Sartis' support, who, wisely, was biding his time. He switched view to Notaras, who was winding up his antiquated brain for the afternoon session, it was unlikely Antonis needed help.

"Welcome back, my Lords, to the reconvening of the inquiry at Varna," proclaimed Notaras with a flourishing swirl of his hands. Turning to face the young Laconian, he haughtily suggested he resume his position as before.

Without acknowledging his questioner, Antonis took up his previous spot. During the break for lunch, Alexis had invigorated his confidence even further, noting the total faith his mentor had in him.

"To refresh our gathered esteemed Colleagues. We were discussing the whereabouts of Antonis Vevellis after the debacle at Varna. So, if you would be so kind, Topoteretes Vevellis, as to tell us your whereabouts after the battle?"

"As I said before, I broke through the enemy lines and then looped back towards the safety of our city."

"Then how do you explain that after you spoke to the King, he made a crazy charge which resulted in the loss of everyone except a heavily wounded sergeant Themis, and a surprisingly unscathed you?"

"The King was an idiot!"

A few laughed.

"Is it not strange how only you broke through the lines and no one else? I put it to you that you deliberately persuaded the King to charge at that moment, causing the battle to be lost. And, as under pay of the Turk, were allowed to escape through their lines, whereupon you were given an enemy uniform, which allowed you to safely return to the city."

Antonis stifled a laugh at the ridiculousness of the premise.

"You find all this funny?" said Notaras.

Something in the old man's tone struck a nerve deep inside and incredulity turned to cold fury. "No, I do not, my Lord. I find it unbelievable that I must justify myself to you. Was it you who volunteered to join the Crusade? No, it was me, and a heavy price I paid too, for it was I who lost a brother and best friend in the battle, not you. And you claim that I am the traitor? Where is your proof?" Antonis replied.

"Right here," said Nicola holding up the folded piece of parchment.

Antonis spun around to stare towards the gallery from where the voice came. His face ashen in shock, as he caught sight of his brother looking down, not at him but at Notaras. Dumbfounded, he lost his ability to speak.

"What is this proof you have?" asked Notaras, the triumphant pitch in his voice slicing through a paralysed Antonis.

His eyes followed his sibling as he made his way down towards the open hall, the large frame briefly disappearing behind stone pillars before striding through the open door towards the elderly Notaras and handing him the letter.

The prosecutor's eager face turned to frustration as he opened the parchment. "This is in Turkish," he hissed. Promptly regaining his composure, he nodded his head to a faceless bureaucrat in the crowd. Within a moment, a narrow-shouldered eunuch appeared with a small wooden box. "Translate this for me on paper."

The apprehensive scribe took the letter and busily set about translating the missive. Once satisfied, he handed the original along with the translated copy back to Notaras, who, with great deliberation, read the interpretation. Silently, he handed the paper to the Emperor, who read impassively.

"Do you acknowledge that this was written by your hand?"

He knew from the glint in Notaras' eye that his shock had betrayed the truth. "Yes."

"So, how do you explain the contents of this letter, the offering of money to have a fellow Greek, your brother no less, executed after you had returned to the city? And, if you are capable of this, then perhaps all the other evidence begins to make sense as well."

Antonis stood there mutely, feeling the piercing gaze of the prosecutor and his wronged brother boring into him. Before he could formulate an answer, the Emperor slammed his hand on the arm of his throne.

"I have heard enough. Take him away, until I decide what will be suitable justice."

Two palace guards stepped forward and seized the still shocked Antonis. Neither brother lanced at the other when their paths crossed as one was marched away.

15

RECKONING

lexis held his face in his hands on hearing the calls for blood. There was no doubt in his mind why Antonis did what he did, although no one there was willing to believe it, and mostly, because it did not fit their need to find a scapegoat. Looking around, he saw all the old men's faces light up at the prospect of an execution. The Emperor sat there, emotionless, casually drumming his fingers, as he listened to all his councillors advising retribution. Alexis wasn't fooled by his ruler's quiet demeanour. He knew John VIII was seething with anger at this apparent act of treachery.

The fingers stopped drumming. "Very well, it is decided. Antonis Vevellis shall be executed tomorrow at dawn. Let this be a warning to others who dare betray our Christian brothers," said the Emperor. The finality in his voice silencing any celebration.

Sage murmurings of satisfied agreement came from the gathered council.

"Your Majesty, I must protest at your course of action. I know this boy and am certain he is no traitor."

"Well, from where I'm standing, it certainly looks that he is."

Alexis knew that he had only this moment to persuade him of the reality.

"Sire, may I speak with you in private?"

The Emperor's eyelids lowered in suspicion but to refuse his greatest general would not be seemly either. "Everyone, leave us," he commanded.

Alexis waited patiently until all the council members had left. None glanced in his direction, with the notable exception of Planedes, who gave him a withering look as he departed unwillingly. The silence in the empty room weighed heavily on the big general's shoulders as he composed his thoughts, and knowing that the next few moments would decide his ward's fate.

"You now have my undivided attention, General."

Alexis sucked in a deep breath, "Thank you, your Majesty."

John VIII acknowledged his general, indicating for him to proceed.

"I understand your judgment is final in these matters and that it appears my ward has betrayed our allies. However, I have a different explanation for what happened. Whilst not redeeming him as a man, it shows that he is no traitor."

The Emperor chuckled. "This will be interesting, please proceed, General."

Ignoring the menacing tone, Alexis proceeded to tell his ruler of the boys' infatuation with Katerina and how they argued over her to such an extent that he had taken them to the council of Florence in Rome, to allow them to cool off. Finally, he completed the tale from the battle of Varna to what had happened in the jail. Though he knew the last part to be mere conjecture on his part, he was fairly sure he had it right.

The Emperor gently stroked his moustache in thought. "I appreciate your story, and although it is believable, our decision has been made."

"Sire, I beg you to find clemency in your heart," appealed

Alexis, and slowly got down on one knee. "His father was my mentor and I made a vow to protect his sons' lives. I have shown you nothing but unswerving loyalty, my King, and all I ask is that you commute the sentence from death. I implore your Majesty."

John VIII sat back in his throne, conflicted. He knew what it meant for his general to plead for the boy's life in this manner and was sure he believed what he said. "We shall ruminate on the matter, and I will give you my answer at sunrise. That is my final word!"

"Thank you, sire." Though not what he wanted, there was still hope and he bade his leave to deal with the mess that now existed.

Nicola sat alone in one of the smaller palace courtyards, a sense of emptiness mingled with a tinge of guilt. He did not think that revenge would feel this way, even though he had no doubt he had done the right thing. He worried what Alexis would say to him, especially as he appeared out of nowhere. It was strange that in all the commotion, no one had come up to speak with him, and now, he was left with his solitary thoughts. He did not return to the house, as there was still one more thing to do, although, he should look refreshed and clean. Instinctively, he patted his pocket to feel the coins, the grunt of satisfaction answering his own question. With his mind finally made up, he quietly exited the palace walls and spying a row of establishments, opted for the most respectable sign, and entered.

The slovenly proprietor eyed the scruffy warrior as he approached.

"Do you have a room available and a laundry service?"

"Three bezants and your laundry ready by dawn." Wafts of stale garlic assaulted Nicola's senses as the owner replied.

"I need my clothes cleaned before midnight."

"Ha, that will cost you an extra bezant."

"I want the clothes to be dry."

The eyes of the proprietor shone with avarice. "Coals aren't cheap, that's an extra bezant."

Nicola grudgingly nodded and handed over the five coins. "The bath water better be clean and hot."

"It will be, sir," replied the innkeeper, licking his lips at the unexpected good fortune. Then he led his guest to the finest available room.

He had slept in worse, Nicola reflected, but he hoped the laundry was better than the bedding. "This will be fine. Have your laundry woman come collect my clothes," he said, handing the man another coin.

"The hot water shall arrive soon," the proprietor replied and left to complete his tasks.

Nicola sat down heavily on the threadbare chair and let his mind drift as he waited.

KATERINA SAT in a stupor as her father relayed what had occurred earlier in the day. She had never seen him at such a loss for words and his habitually grey face was more pallid than usual. The news that his wife had begun to send out invitations for the impending nuptials did not bother him; social embarrassment seemed the least of his worries, replaced instead with a genuine feeling that his heart had been eviscerated.

Mixed emotions flowed through her. Joy that Nicola lived, sadness at her father's heavy heart, and cold fury at Antonis' actions. Revulsion enveloped her as she turned her thoughts to her former fiancé. To betray his brother and leave him to die was unforgivable and her skin crawled as she imagined how Nicola might have suffered at the hands of the Turk, quickly replaced with excited anticipation of seeing him again.

· · ·

Antonis let out a groan as he glanced around his confined space and idly compared the different virtues of a Greek and Turkish prison cell. Running his fingers along the wood that made up the bed pallet, he notched one to the Greeks. Methodically, he moved to the wall, seeing how cool the stones were, inspecting the workmanship. A second to the Greeks, he conceded. Enjoying this amusement, he gauged the ventilation and light; even money on that. A thought crossed his mind; this was the imperial palace prison and he was comparing it to a provincial jail. There was no contest. The loud rattling of keys brought him to, and the door swung open to reveal his overweight stinking jailer. He gave an involuntary smile as he notched this one for the Turks.

Unaware of his prisoner's thoughts, the jailer stepped inside and approached the manacles on the wall.

For a second, he thought of escape, before noticing the looming presence of two heavily armed guards at the door.

"You have a visitor," said the jailer, holding out the two iron cuffs.

Resigned, Antonis presented himself to be shackled. Surprised at how gently the fetters were placed on him, undoubtedly honed by years of practice.

The jailer grunted in satisfaction as he pulled the chain tight, forcing Antonis' hands behind his back, promptly leaving him alone in the cell.

The silence was excruciating, followed by curiosity as he wondered who could possibly want to visit him. The light padding of footsteps of the unknown visitor only piqued his intrigue further.

When the visitor came into view, his hands pulled tight on the chains as he gazed upon the clean and refreshed man before him, the scent of freshly laundered clothes assaulting him, worse than any putrid flesh could. "Cme to gloat over your victory?"

The cold hatred of the tone cut through Nicola and he felt a tight knot well up inside his chest. Forcing himself to be calm, he replied as coolly. "No, there is nothing to gloat over. There is no victory. I came to find out why."

Antonis let out a humourless laugh. "You really are as dumb as you look."

The elder brother suppressed the urge to punch him, knowing that was exactly what he wanted and looked earnestly at his sibling. "We are brothers, bonded by time, and you broke that, and for what? Power, love, or just to beat me?"

Antonis laughed madly again, before his jaw clenched tightly. "We… are not brothers. The blood of princes runs through my veins. What runs in yours? It is I who will inherit, I who has the brains. Not you. Yet with all of that, she loves you, not me."

Nicola reeled as he heard his brother speak. "All of this over Katerina? Are you fucking mad? Well, you're going to get what you deserve."

"Bastard. Get out!" screamed Antonis, his spittle flying out and hitting his brother square in the face. A satisfied snarl crossing his lips as Nicola wiped the fluid from his eye.

Just as he had cleared it another full blob landed on his forehead. In anger, Nicola punched him cleanly in the jaw.

Antonis buckled from the blow but remained standing.

"Good luck tomorrow, brother," said Nicola wiping the saliva from his cheek.

"I'm not done yet, bastard. I will come back for you, and your whore, and you will beg me to die," screamed Antonis at the fading footsteps.

The vitriol echoed in Nicola's ears, as he walked towards the door, grim-faced and rubbing the knuckles that had just punched his 'Brother'.

· · ·

Antonis awoke sharply before dawn, rubbing his eyes after a fitful rest. A slew of vaguely remembered dreams flooded back. His father showing his disappointment, his mother's distressed wailing, a smiling victorious Nicola standing with his hands on his hips over his executed body. He shook his head again to dispel the visions and looked up at the vent showing the stars piercing the dark night. A sense of desire to savour every moment drove him to alertness. Each detail in his confined universe took paramount importance, knowing that this was the last sunrise he would see. As the light began to thread its way to him, the frantic energy he had felt these last few days was replaced with calm acceptance, liberating his mind from the anger that had imprisoned him. He became so engrossed in his surroundings he didn't hear the jailers at his cell door.

"It is time," said the guard.

Calmly, Antonis rose and gently composed his thick black hair with the flat of his hands before turning to the attendants and nodding silently for them to proceed.

The calm aura unsettled the jailer, who deferentially led his captive to his fate.

Time slowed with each pace along the stone tunnel as the execution party made its way towards the square outside, the faint chanting of the priest as he bestowed a final blessing, accompanying their footsteps. The cool morning air hit his face as he exited into the square. A significant crowd had congregated around the wooden platform. Prison guards pushed through to make a space for the condemned soldier to be marched through. The vitriol and disgust were clear on the gathered citizens' faces with curses and insults being muttered as he passed by. A few even managed to throw rotten vegetables—he made no attempt to duck them—and one hit the side of the head to raised cheers as it slimed his hair.

He spat away a chunk that had touched his lips, stood straighter, and more determined as he was marched to the awaiting executioner. He had passed this place many times, but this was the first time he really looked at it. The ancient wood was pitted and scarred. The result of many executions and innumerable blood-lets had given the oak a dark brown patchwork across its surface. He snorted as he finally reached the top of the platform, knowing that his blood would soon join the countless others who had been before.

Replete in dark leather, the executioner stood next to the simple wooden block that rested in the centre of the dais. Behind him, stacked neatly, were the tools of his ghastly trade; swords, axes, pokers, and tongs glistening in the crisp morning sun. To the far right was a brazier being fanned by his assistant to keep the coals red-hot.

A shiver went down Antonis' spine as he briefly let his thoughts venture as to what torture awaited him. The guards placed him in front of the block and faced him towards the jeering throng. He looked over the gathering to see the tall form of Nicola staring at him grim-faced. He gritted his teeth as a trumpet sounded from the emperor's viewing box and a deathly hush instantly came over the crowd.

The Emperor stood up to address the assembly. "We are gathered here today to witness the execution of a traitor. No ordinary traitor, but one who has betrayed not only his city, but generations of his family's loyalty to the empire." He paused to let his words sink in. Furtively, he glanced towards the looming figure of Alexis standing at the edge of the crowd. "I have however, received an impassioned plea for clemency for this young man from a most venerated source, and although I hope I do not live to regret this decision, I will commute his sentence from death to exile."

Groans emanated from the crowd as their gory spectacle was denied, a few throwing rotten vegetables as a sign of displeasure.

Alexis surreptitiously clenched his fist at the news, happy at least he had achieved the sparing of his life.

Antonis stifled a smile and focused his triumphant gaze on Nicola in the crowd, whose heart filled with dread.

"But clemency does not mean that the accused shall go without punishment. Death has been commuted but he shall bear the mark of a traitor." With a wave of his hand, two of the guards held Antonis down over the execution block.

Instinctively, he resisted, but the third burly guard shoved the flat of his hand onto his chest, knocking the wind out of him.

Subdued, the guard ripped open the shirt, exposing his bare chest. A fourth joined and each of them held a limb tautly as he was splayed over the block.

The executioner signalled to his assistant, who picked up the iron rod that had been resting in the coal brazier and handed it reverently to his master. Silently, the executioner took the glowing red brand and stood over the prone figure.

Antonis stared into the blank eyes of the man and knew he felt nothing.

Holding the brand in both hands, he raised it high above his head and after a suitable pause brought the red-hot metal down onto the exposed skin at the centre of his chest.

Antonis let out a muffled cry as his flesh seared from the heat, determined not to lose whatever dignity he had left. The smell of his skin crisping assaulted the air as did the crowd's cheers whilst punishment was meted out, happy to have at least part of their bloodlust satiated.

Nicola flinched as he saw the limp body hauled off the block and dragged to the awaiting mule, to which Antonis was tied, facing backwards, then, guards led it to the road towards the Circus Gate and slapped the animal's hindquarters to get it moving.

Once clear of the guards, the mule made its way through the

short distance and to the gate, where gathered crowds shouted insults and threw rotten food, excrement, or whatever they had, at the hapless man.

Tears welled in Nicola's eyes at the shame his brother had to endure; perhaps an execution was preferable to this. His head jolted at each step the mule took, but the wooden plank tied to his back kept him upright, offering a better target for the missiles being thrown at him.

Groggily, Antonis felt the gait of the pack animal and half opened his eyes, dimly registering the jeering crowd. Haggard faces mingled with the grotesque, all displaying animalistic joy, alleviating their miserable existence with a moment of superiority over another human. His focus came into view and in the distance, he saw his brother still watching. He let out a roar of defiance. "Nicola. Nicola, I shall return," he screamed as best he could, holding his watching sibling's gaze until the mule carried him out of view.

Passing through the walls, the guards let him through unharmed and once out of the city, he again passed into unconsciousness as the animal steadily made its way on the road north.

Nicola felt hollow as the crowd dispersed from its morning entertainment. He sat heavily on one of the wooden ledges that dotted the area, resting his head in his hands, trying to make sense of what had just occurred. There was no guilt, no anger, just a sense of loss, something was now missing from his being.

"Not what you expected, is it?" came the deep voice.

Looking up to see his mentor standing over him, he shook his head in wordless agreement.

Alexis knew this was not the time for discussion but instead of containment. "Come, let's get you home," he said, patting his shoulder to encourage him.

Obediently, he rose and followed his mentor, vaguely

noticing an innocuous man in a threadbare grey cloak, as he passed from this wretched place.

Peering through his aged garment, the man took one final look at Nicola, and let out a soft chuckle as one of his mischievous thoughts sprang to mind. Savouring his imaginations, he made his way out of the city with a spring in his step.

ANTONIS CAME BACK TO CONSCIOUSNESS, accompanied by the sound of what seemed the loud chattering of busy old women. It was soon blotted out as the scorching pain returned to his chest, involuntarily letting out an agonising groan. As his eyes focussed, he saw the chattering was not old women but a gaggle of geese that had congregated around the mule as it drank from the small pond. Looking around, he had no idea where he was, only that he was north of the city.

The bonds that tied him were truly secure, preventing any movement, and to force them open was not even a possibility. Feeling around with one finger, he found the wooden plank attached to his back and in hope, searched for a rough corner or edge with which to wear through it. Sensing the faintest of splinters on the edge of the plank, he rubbed the bindings against it. Each movement was agony, as the flexing kept opening his wound. Ignoring the pain through gritted teeth, he hurried to get himself released, for he did not know how long it would be before he had visitors altogether more unsavoury than the geese that presently surrounded him.

"You have more chance of chewing off your hand, than breaking free doing it like that."

Antonis froze as he heard the voice. Recognition overcame him.

The small rescuer let out a soft cackle at seeing the young Greek's shoulders relax a fraction then stepped forward to cut the bonds and let out a groan as he caught the falling weight.

Carefully, he placed the limp body against one of the craggy boulders by the water's edge. Adjusting the legs straight out and pushing his shoulders back, he exposed the raw burnt flesh, then cut away the ragged shirt.

Reaching into his knapsack, he pulled out a roll of fine bandage, a jug, and a small brown clay pot. Breaking the wax seal on the jug, he poured the liquid liberally on the wound, accompanied by a sharp intake of breath from his patient. Wiping down the torso until he was satisfied, he cleaned all the dirt and grime away, scooped a large amount of balm from the small pot, and applied it over the wound that still burned from the earlier event in the day. Then he gently wrapped the bandage around the disfigured torso to protect the wound from the elements, pursing his wizened lips in appreciation of his work. "Leave the bandage on and in a few days that will heal nicely."

Stupefied, Antonis fixed his blue eyes on his rescuer. "Why have you done this? I still don't even know your name."

The old man let out a soft cackle, "Does it matter what my name is?"

Antonis shook his head.

"My name is Giorgos."

"Thank you, Giorgos."

"You're welcome."

THANOS SAT UNCHARACTERISTICALLY quiet as he observed the two men in conversation, this was a staggering situation even by his warped standards. He had opted not to attend the proceedings after hearing Alexis the previous night racked with guilt, remorse, and a plethora of distraught emotions, feeling that a restful morning was a better option, as a calm brain was needed in the aftermath.

But with Alexis and Nicola returning and discovering that

Antonis had been exiled, his mind had been thrown into a spin, though, he knew it paled into insignificance compared to what must be going through his old friend's head. Turning back, he could see Nicola's gesticulating as he relayed his side of the story to an aghast Alexis. All this over a girl?

Idly, he wondered how she would compare to one of his professional ladies. A wry smile cracked across his face, followed by a shaking of his head to clear his thoughts, knowing that was not a fair contest at all. He decided to leave the two to their discussions. When they were ready, he would be summoned and as the good friend he was, he would appear.

KATERINA

Katerina sat mutely in her usual spot on the courtyard wall of the university, resting her hands across her lap. She wove her fingers together, noticing how long they were. Conceding in this rare moment of quiet observation that they did indeed have the elegant form as her mother always said. It had been nearly two weeks since Antonis' banishment and yet Nicola had not come to see her. It pained her that she still had not had the chance to speak with him and now she was back at the Pandekterion as if nothing had happened. Seeing Giovanni again was the only positive to come from her return and on cue the slender Genoese parked himself next to her on the wall.

"How is my lovely Katerina today?"

Her face could not help but brighten up, and she flashed him a genuine smile. "Your lovely Katerina is doing well this morning."

Giovanni ignored his friend's mimicked reply and went straight into his discourse on the upcoming rhetoric class.

Her appetite for study had waned but she still smiled indulgently at him. Since their success in the debate, the young Genoese had attained a measure of respect from his other classmates and consequently his confidence had flourished.

"So, what is your plan of action to win this latest debate? Don't tell me you need your old teammate?" she asked.

"No, no, I have someone."

"You mean you have moved on already? You have found someone better?"

"No, no, that's not what I meant."

Katerina pouted her displeasure and sadness draped over her eyes.

Giovanni's small brown eyes widened, and his head shook slightly at the thought he had upset his friend, before noticing her smile. "Not funny," he slapped her playfully on the arm.

Katerina feigned pain and let out an exaggerated gasp.

"Is everything all right here?"

The two friends looked up, startled at the familiar voice.

Giovanni instantly stood up and hugged his friend.

Katerina felt conflicted at rushing too quickly, but to see him in the flesh after all this time filled her with longing. Yet, she could not shake the nagging thought that she had betrayed him by agreeing to Antonis' proposal. It made her feel weak and it took a moment for her to look at the two miss-sized men as they hugged. Finally, she brought her eyes to focus on his. The joy in his face, instantly dispelled any doubts she had.

"Hello, Katerina, how are you? It's good to see you again."

His dulcet tones vibrated through her, causing a momentary pause in her reply as she savoured that unique feeling. "It's good to see you too," she said and stayed rooted to her favourite stone wall, unable to move.

Nicola smiled warmly for the umpteenth time and opened his arms wide. "Aren't you going to give a hug to an old friend?"

The calmness in his voice eased her guilty tension as she took a pace towards him.

Giovanni looked away uncomfortably as they finally embraced.

The same bolt of energy shot through her as it had before, a sense of belonging enveloping her as they stood in the embrace, neither wanting to break apart from the other.

Nicola pulled away and looked deeply into her green eyes. Without further thought, he slowly and deliberately leaned forward until his lips touched hers, surprised at the frisson as they locked together. The softness captivated him, and he hungrily explored her mouth with his own.

Katerina responded willingly to his advances and without care that they could be observed.

"Err, I think you'd better stop before someone sees you," Giovanni said as he finally plucked up the courage to look again.

Both ignored him.

"Katerina, someone will pass by and the embarrassment to your family will be total."

The mention of family made her tense a little and a few seconds later she broke away from that most exquisite of kisses and looked up doe-eyed at Nicola.

The lovebirds' inaction irritated Giovanni. "Why don't you go somewhere private?"

Totally absorbed in their world, they at first smiled then broke into simultaneous laughter.

"When can I see you next?" asked Nicola.

"Whenever you want, I'm back at the Pandekterion now."

"Tomorrow, meet me by the tavern of the Boar's Head."

Katerina raised her eyebrows questioningly.

"It's outside, and to the left of the main gate of the Pandekterion. You can't miss it," he replied.

A look of concern crossed her face.

"Don't worry, it is a reputable place, and no-one will know us there."

Katerina nodded satisfied that she would not be compromised. "What time?"

"Mid-afternoon."

She inclined her head again in compliance.

Nicola leant down and kissed her briefly again, a spark of static making them jolt as their lips touched. Then, he parted with a beaming smile.

Katerina was filled with a feeling of warmth and love, as Giovanni stood, scratching his head in bewilderment.

Nicola arrived a full hour early at the Boar's Head and ensconced himself at one of the tables in the corner of the room. He was fragile with anticipation of Katerina's arrival and involuntarily let out a yawn, as he had not been able to sleep much the previous night; the élan he had felt from her embrace and kiss had played heavily on him. Strangely, when Thanos told him of the engagement, he was not fazed. He understood she had accepted under false information, yet, still, he wanted to see her face when he confronted her about it.

The innkeeper enquired what he wanted. Ordering a jug of ale, he asked if there were any free lodging rooms. Satisfied with the response, he returned to his thoughts and what he wanted to do. His mind instinctively reached to ask his brother what he would do, before depressingly admitting that he was no longer there. That emptiness washed over him again. His gut tightened painfully.

As he finished the first ale and his body relaxed again, Nicola noticed that the few customers who had decided to have luncheon began to clear out, leaving the tavern empty, except for him and another old drunkard in the corner. That suited him perfectly; he just hoped Katerina showed up as they had agreed. It took courage for a high-born young woman to enter an unknown tavern without a chaperone. He was still amazed she had even kissed him. Doubt crept in as he wondered if she would now have second thoughts, and ordered more ale to bolster his courage.

He had nearly drained the large tankard when he saw a willowy hooded figure enter and cautiously survey the room before fixing upon his location. His heart skipped a beat as the bland grey cloak arrived at his table and two slender pale hands pulled the hood down, revealing thick auburn hair. He let out a breath of joyous relief.

Katerina smiled warmly at him.

"I'm glad you came," he said as he stood to pull her a chair.

"Did you think I wouldn't?"

"I wasn't sure."

She took the seat he offered.

Doubt crept in again as she did not volunteer to embrace him, but they were in a very public place and no doubt she had spent the night in thought too.

"Well, now you are," she replied.

Nicola broke into a sheepish grin as he reached out and clasped one of her hands. She offered no resistance and they sat silently staring into each other's eyes, neither wanting to break the moment.

Eventually, Nicola plucked up the courage to speak. "Katerina, it is obvious now to me what my feelings are for you but there is something I need to hear from you first."

She raised her eyebrows and her usually feline eyes rounded. She carefully placed her other hand on top of his and fixed her gaze upon him. "What do you want to know, my love?"

Nicola paused, feeling fraudulent that he could doubt her, but still he needed to hear it from her lips. "Please tell me what happened when Antonis returned to the city after the battle."

She smiled knowingly.

"I need to know."

She stared at him intently, drew a deep breath and told him piece by piece, what occurred. That with her father's approval and after discussion with her mother, she decided to accept his offer. Through tear-filled eyes, she apologised profusely for being so weak and doubting that he lived.

He accepted it and told her not to blame herself.

The innkeeper brought a jug of water and two unpainted clay goblets and seeing the emotion in the young couple, filled their cups in a rare gesture of hospitality.

Calming herself and dabbing the flowing tears from her cheeks, she looked back at her love with newfound respect for his understanding. "What happened at Varna to come to this?"

"It had been brewing for some time, ever since we studied with Plethon. We disagreed over our people's achievements. He said it was the past and that we had to look to the future. But it worsened when we met you and he felt he was the better man."

Realising she was partially responsible made Katerina's soul heavy as she gazed upon her beloved. How could she know the kindness she showed his brother would be misinterpreted as interest?

With the colour drained from his face the long eyelashes emphasized the sadness in his eyes, his angular features making him appear as a long dead statue. Powerful feelings welled inside him, breaking his melancholy, and he leant towards her with searching lips.

She paused, unsure, worrying that someone might intrude upon them, then relented. Willingly being consumed with the masculine power of her lover she wilted into his arms as he kissed her. The sparks had returned, and she imbibed all that she could, gaining life from his potent energy.

Nicola broke away first, his lion eyes looking deeply into hers. "I love you, Katerina," he declared, his voice husky with emotion.

Her face filled with expectation. "I have been in love with you since the day I first saw you at court." Saying the words made her breast heave from within.

The young Greek broke into a smile and the sparkle returned to his eyes. "Well, what are we going to do about it then?"

"I don't know," said Katerina in feigned composure.

"Let's get married," Nicola paused and took both her hands. "Katerina Planedes, will you marry me?"

Her mouth split into such a wide smile that dimples appeared on each cheek. "Yes, I will, Nicola Vevellis."

"Great, fantastic news," he beamed, "I will have to ask your Father officially."

Katerina released herself from his grip, stating her anxiety where her father was concerned.

Nicola dismissed her doubts with a wave of his hand. "I shall come see him tomorrow, and we will make this right."

She nodded obediently.

For the first time in months, Nicola felt happy again.

LORD PLANEDES ARRIVED at the house in a fraught mood, looking forward to some relaxation. The last few days had been frantic since the disgrace and exile of Antonis. Strangely, he felt for the lad, but nothing took precedence over his own survival.

"Evening, Agatha," he greeted as the servant opened the door for him.

"Good evening, Lord Planedes, they are in the drawing room, with a guest," replied Agatha.

"Really, who?" asked the master of the house.

"I don't know, sir. A young man, a friend of Katerina's, I believe."

His porcine features screwed up in even more angst. He shuffled his portly frame towards the atrium and the drawing room then ran his chubby fingers through the remnants of his lank grey hair as he entered the room.

"Spiros, darling, how are you?" beamed his wife. "Look who we have visiting."

Nicola stood up. "Lord Planedes."

"Young Vevellis, the Laconians have returned to the city?"

"No, sir, I returned independently, as I was separated from them during the battle and ended up on the wrong side of the river."

The politician's eyes slanted even more, wondering what was to come next. "I see you received a wound during it, nothing too damaging I hope," lied the politician. The edge clear in his voice.

"Papa, did you have a good day?" asked Katerina, who even in her happy state could sense the mood darkening.

Planedes' face softened as he heard his daughter speak. "It wasn't too bad, just tiring, my dear, and I need some rest."

"Well, we have some news that will brighten it up for you," she carried on.

Somehow, he doubted that, but he was willing to humour her. "What is that?"

"Nicola asked me to marry him, and I accepted." Her face beamed with joy.

Planedes stood there transfixed, his ugly face frozen in shock, his body rigid. Only his eyes moved at first, away from his daughter and then towards the young man.

"Sir, I would like to formally ask for your daughter's hand in marriage."

Lady Planedes knew this was a shock, as this was his only daughter, yet this felt different.

"Absolutely not," replied the father. "You cannot marry my daughter."

Nicola's shoulders slumped.

Katerina's face dropped and she leapt from the couch. "But, papa…" she protested. "I love him, and he loves me."

Planedes turned to his daughter. "We will discuss this later."

Lady Planedes held fire, knowing this was not the right time to protest.

"But, sir, why not?" asked Nicola, maintaining his composure.

Planedes turned to him. "You will never marry my daughter; you are not good enough for her," he sneered.

"I am of a good family, sir, great lineage," responded Nicola defiantly.

"Perhaps, but you are not of their blood, and I have other plans for my daughter. Now, please leave my house."

Nicola could not believe what was happening and stood dumbfounded.

"I said leave," Planedes voice rose powerfully.

Nicola nodded to Lady Planedes, looked at Katerina longingly, turned out of the house, and strode into the balmy evening air.

ROAD TO EDIRNE

Antonis couldn't contain his excitement, walking through undulating hills so closely weaved they felt like rippling water; the trees urging him on like tentacles on a sea urchin to the place of its devourment. Every detail was seared into his brain; from the fat black beetle scurrying about on the path to the curved back of the old crone loaded with a stack of sticks crushing her with their weight. The balmy November air lifted his spirits, something he was grateful for as he had lost his cloak three days since.

Giorgos had told him to find the street of the swallows once in the city, and to look for the cherry wood door with white crescents painted upon it. There were many twists and turns until he found the place, where, that old mad smuggler assured him, he would be taken care of. His uncertainty increased walking down the narrow dark alley, the walls were crumbling, the plants dying, and the door belts rusted so badly it was a marvel that they still stood.

Antonis rapped on the door and was promptly shown in by a clean understated servant, to an unimpressive atrium, where he gestured for him to wait for the master.

Halil was a slight man, with a fine hooked nose. His tanned leathered skin and thin lips gave him a hawk-like appearance. Clasping his hands under the folds of his cloak, he seemed more like a Jewish moneylender than a Turkish crime lord. He slowly looked the boy over. "So, Giorgos sent you?" He opened the sealed letter with swift precision and tilting his head back, started to read.

Antonis studied every furrow and frown on Halil's brow with analytical fear. He did not know what that madman had written, and hadn't dared tamper with it for fear of angering his host upon arrival.

"Well, it seems you have a benefactor, my boy, and how lucky you are to have this one."

What is this bullshit?

"You have no idea who he is, do you?"

He shrugged in confirmation.

The old man chuckled and gestured for him to enter through the door.

Antonis gasped, the Caliphs of Cordoba would have been hard-pressed to rival the controlled botanic splendour that hailed him. The intricate details of the tiles were more Arabic than Turkish, with the many tinkling fountains completing the feel of an ordered grotto.

Halil smiled as he saw the boy's astonishment, and with a clap of his hand, servants magically appeared bearing sweetened lemon water and fruits; oranges, apples, and peaches.

"How do you have peaches in November?" marvelled Antonis.

"Some like the conquest of people, others the accumulation of power, and some the consumption of pleasure. For me, it is to enjoy fruits all year round."

"I still don't understand."

"Later. First, you must quench your thirst and then, bathe," replied Halil as he gently clapped his hands twice.

Two nubile women, one pale with dark hair and green eyes and the other a fine-boned East African, came and led him to the baths to be cleansed. Just the sort of bathing he needed. The scent of jasmine wafted over his freshly cleaned body as he made his way back to his host.

"Linen? Have you lived in poverty that long you have forgotten the joy of silk?" asked Halil.

"It is what I am used to, sir," replied Antonis, "besides, I feel the heat very easily, linen cools and silk warms."

Halil sighed, "Yes, I am but a frail old man, who even in his younger days felt the nip of the cold with ease." Then murmured approval when he looked at Antonis' feet.

He always laid out a selection of shoes for his houseguests. It was his filtering process, a test to check refinement. The Latins' never understood the fineries of correct footwear, unless it was a military boot, the Austrians, generally being the worst. Not so with this Greek, he knew; and why shouldn't he, after all, it was his ancestors who had taught Halil's. He noticed Antonis looking at the parchment he was holding and rather than explain just handed it over.

Taking the fine vellum, he read the clear and concise writing.

Halil,

My old and dear friend, it has been some time since we have spoken. Since the passing of Penelope, the juice of life has been missing for me and my body and soul are but mere husks. However, something happened to me recently that gave me belief and zest for life again. That occurrence is bringing you this letter.

He is a powerful soul but lost and needs to find his path again. I desire for him to have an audience with the Sultan, so he can be reborn as a ghazi in the service of his serene one. All I ask of you dear friend, is that you arrange this for me. I am sure that he will flourish, and I will come to check on him from time to time.

As ever,

Your Christian Brother,

Giorgos

Antonis looked at the seal, a fox; how apt, as Giorgos certainly was a sly one. Against the backdrop of the botanical atrium, his host radiated energy. He was now seeing the frail man in a different light.

"Well, we have work to do to get you ready."

"Such as?"

Halil beckoned to the boy to follow, wandered through the archway, and approached a granite screen inlaid with mother-of-pearl, ebony, lapis lazuli, and some reddish stone that Antonis couldn't discern. Intricate geometric patterns fused to create some abstract vision. It was hundreds of years old. With a deft tap, the screen opened and Halil removed a leather bag filled with coins. He pulled one out and handed it to Antonis.

He felt the weight in his hand and looked to see the stamp of Basil II, the coin was over four centuries old. He let out a low whistle of appreciation.

"Yes. The real stuff before your rulers fucked it up by debasing their currency," stated Halil.

Mustafa arrived with six wooden tubes, carefully placed a coin in each one, and sealed them with wax.

"You know where to go with these," said Halil.

"Yes, sir." And the man left forthwith.

Halil turned to the young Greek and eyed him up and down. "For you to join us, you must understand us. That is why he sent you to me."

The puzzlement on Antonis' face was clear. "Tell me about Giorgos, who is he, and why did he do this for me?"

Halil sighed and sat down next to the secret screen, his face looking strained as he paused for thought. "We go back many years. Before I became part of the brotherhood, we used to be smugglers, Giorgos, working to bring spices from the East, and me, taking Greek technology to Edirne. We met one night as our ships were stealing out of the harbour with a load of contraband. I was being chased by a rival gang. Out-numbered and out-manoeuvred, they cornered me. Clearly, he did not like the unfairness of the fight and set his crew upon them to even up the odds."

"Why were they chasing you?" asked Antonis.

"The wife of that gang's leader had a passion for me."

Antonis smiled as the old Turk's face morphed into a fond memory. Things were never what they seemed. Feeling more relaxed, he took a less hurried gulp of his drink.

Halil's eyes creased at the corner. "Let's talk. There is much I need to know if we are going to pull this off."

Antonis gave the faintest of nods in reply.

"So, tell me about how you happen to be at my door."

WITH THE PASSING DAYS, Halil came to admire his young guest. His drive, clarity of thought, and ruthlessness; it took a great deal of courage to leave his people and go to the other side. There were few men who had that strength of conviction.

Halil stood back and admired his handy work. He had given a lot of thought as to how he could maximise Antonis' impact on the Sultan.

The long dark blue silk pantaloons billowed over his thighs and came into the waist with a sash tied around of the same colour but of distressed silk. Above, was a plain white shirt topped with a Kaftan that matched the leggings with a faint silver thread pattern across the shoulders. He had decided there would be no turban as he was not yet fully a Turk. Elegant but understated, just as he had envisaged.

"How do I look?"

"Good, very good, and now I think you are ready to meet the Sultan," Halil replied.

A great big smile creased across the young Greek, as he secretly thanked his mysterious fisherman benefactor.

The breeze flowed through the carriage onto the back of his neck, chilling his skin as the moisture evaporated and Antonis realised just how nervous he was. Approaching the court, his mouth was dry and his hands sweaty at the thought of meeting the Sultan. He felt more fear now than he did at the battle.

Wafts of jasmine incense bombarded the air as he strode towards the daunting entrance. The series of small domes in the Citadel pressed down on him, making him feel much shorter than his six-foot. It took all his prodigious inner strength to keep his shoulders square, back straight, and a spring in his step.

The young Greek couldn't fathom why the door ahead seemed so scary, then noticed it had no guards. Strange how no show of arms was more ominous; he made a note of that for the future. But as they approached the door, two guards magically appeared, resplendent in baby blue and white pantaloons, embroidered waistcoat, and full turbans. They were giants of men, a good head taller than him, and dwarfing the diminutive Halil. The spears appeared like twigs in their huge hands.

Antonis looked into their eyes, dull and arrogant, and all his fear vanished. This was a challenge he understood, and it held no apprehension for him.

"We have an audience with the Sultan," said Halil.

The automatons gave way and opened the door onto the waiting ruler.

A thick wave of pungent odour slapped into them. Incense blended with sweat and fear, which had been heated into a heady aroma that invigorated the young Greek. The room felt vibrant, in stark contrast to the rigid court of Constantinople. Here, there was no distinction between Turk, Christian, or Jew. Resplendent in their showy dress, Janissary mingled with Anatolian Aristocrat, with one eye on each, and the other at the pinnacle, the Sultan.

Murad sat upon his perch like an eagle surveying his hunting ground. Surrounding him, chubby eunuchs scurried; their outlandish costumes compensating for their loss of manhood. Assured in his supremacy, he was in plain attire, which only emphasised his power.

Less is more with this man. I like that.

One of the blubbery half-men came up to them and raised a slender hand. "Wait here until you are called," came his voice, melodic and feminine.

"It's very different from the Emperor's Court," said Antonis.

"It has more life, more energy to it, no?" replied Halil.

Antonis turned in surprise to the Turk. "You have been to the court in Constantinople?"

"Yes. Here, we are a young culture, and this brings an energy and drive. We are not hidebound with tradition like the Greeks."

"That is why you will win."

"And that is why you want to join us."

Antonis smiled, relaxing in this unfamiliar environment.

The eunuch returned. "His Magnificence will deign to see you now." The floral perfume of the herald wafted heavily as he waved them through.

On entering, the crowd parted, making a direct path to the Sultan.

The middle-aged man sat cross-legged on his ornate stool, flanked by his horsetail pennants, and stared at the approaching guest with a curious look. "Whom do we have here?" He asked.

Halil bowed and inched forward with his eyes downcast, clutching the letter from Giorgos in his right hand, and his left flat against his breast in supplication. "This is Antonis Veve…"

"Let him speak," interrupted the Ruler, his dark eyes boring through the young man.

"I am Antonis Vevellis of Chania, and I come to offer my services to your Magnificence."

Halil let out an imperceptible sigh of relief at the young man's measured tone.

The court erupted into a steady laugh of deep bellows, intermingled with the beardless men's giggles.

The Sultan raised his hand and the laughter ceased instantly. "And what services can you offer?"

"I am a competent soldier and I wish to be a ghazi in your service."

The court erupted again.

After an appropriate time, the Sultan casually raised his hand. "What makes you think you are good enough?"

"The last time we met, you wanted to flee the battlefield." Antonis responded calmly.

The court now exploded with anger and two of the palace guards lurched towards him, drawing their scimitars.

Antonis didn't flinch, though his body twitched in anticipation.

"Wait!" commanded Murad.

The guards halted in an instant.

The Sultan let out a long humming chuckle. "If I remember correctly, all of you Infidels died in that charge, including your boy King."

"Some of us survived and I was one of them."

"Liar! Sire, let me teach this Christian a lesson," shouted one of the palace guards who had been halted earlier.

"Well, what do you say to your accuser, Greek?" asked the Sultan.

"A house pet is not worthy of an answer. Are there no real soldiers here?"

The guard itched to attack but held firm.

From behind the Sultan, one of the courtiers stepped forward and whispered into the Vizier's ear. He nodded in understanding and stepped to repeat the message to the Sultan.

Murad's face showed no emotion as he listened. Then, he turned to the guard. "And you? Will you take this?"

"I will kill him for his insolence, your Magnificence."

"He has no weapon with which to defend himself."

"I don't need one for a domesticated pet such as this," interjected Antonis.

"Teach him a lesson," said Murad.

In a flash, the palace guard charged the young Greek and just as quickly lay disarmed on the floor, as Antonis stood over him, holding his sword.

"He insulted you. Kill him," ordered the Sultan.

"He isn't worthy," replied Antonis, lowering the sword.

The guard scrambled clear as quickly as he could.

The Sultan nodded his head in appreciation. "It has been brought to our attention that one of my Janissaries remembers you from the field at Varna. You wore a blue helmet, did you not?"

"Yes, sire, until I lost it in the fighting."

"Most careless. What shall we do with you? Until I decide, you may remain here as our guest."

Antonis bowed and walked backwards away from the Sultan as Halil had instructed. It went better than he had hoped. Now, he just had to wait it out until the Sultan decided where to place him.

As they exited the court, a voice came from Antonis' right. "You are a very brave man."

He turned to see a boy of no more than twelve looking up at him. Finely featured with a pinched brow, strange for someone so young. Yet the feature that stood out the most was his eyes, hazel, almost green, inquisitive, fearless, and piercing.

"Thank you," Antonis responded with a hint of a grin.

"I will need people like you," continued the boy.

"For what?" replied the amused Greek.

"When I become the sole Sultan," said the boy.

Antonis' smile grew broader; he liked this boy's confidence, a rare commodity in one so young. "What is your name, my young Prince?"

"Mehmet."

"Well, we shall see, Mehmet, we shall see."

18

BEGINNINGS OF TRUST

$\mathcal{A}$ntonis sat on the sumptuous daybed in the diplomatic quarters, which, for the present were his lodgings. Generously appointed it was really a house within the palace, replete with bedroom, living and dining areas. However, his favourite was the bath house, which held a large square granite pool.

Incense and flowers were changed daily by his servants. Halil said he must have made an impression to get such luxury, and he couldn't disagree. Yet for all the salubrious surrounding, Antonis knew he was a prisoner; a guard was posted at his door and he was politely asked in broken Greek to stay in the room for his own protection. He was thankful for Halil's daily visits and the time spent on instructions into the Ottoman ways.

He quickly grasped the basics and before long was conversing in an excellent Turkish dialect, vastly different to what he had learned before. Halil was at pains to be as neutral as possible in his tuition, knowing that the palace walls had ears, and he was as much on trial as the young Greek.

"How long am I going to stay here, doing nothing?"

"Patience, the wheels of power turn when they will and there is nothing you can do to change that," replied Halil soothingly. "Besides, you have lodging and I'm sure you're enjoying the daily attention from your bathing girls."

Antonis nodded in agreement and his mind went to Katerina, wondering if she could possibly be so accomplished in that way. He doubted it. Yet, the pain of rejection still seared through him. After indulging in all three girls, he decided to settle on Selima, a lithe Wallachian with a mischievous look, who always wanted to please, and enjoyed bathing him. He found her voice melodious when she spoke Turkish and Greek.

"Yes, but it's been close to four months in this gilded cage," he was by now speaking mostly in Turkish to Halil, who was duly impressed with his capacity for learning. "When will anything happen? I am getting soft and bored here."

"I have spoken with the Vizier and I think they have found something for you."

Antonis stopped pacing and turned with a raised eyebrow to his Turkish counterpart. "Such as?"

"It appears they will be offering you a position in the European army as a junior commander."

"Sounds all right, when do I start?" Antonis replied a little too quickly.

"There is a minor issue, that has to be dealt with first."

"Which is?"

"You have to convert to Islam, if you want to serve the Sultan."

"Why do I have to? Many soldiers fight for the Ottomans who are not Muslim."

"I'm afraid the Sultan has insisted. He says that if you wish to be a ghazi, then you must become one in full."

Antonis could slap that old fool Giorgos for using those words in the letter. *Well, so be it, what is one religion compared to another?* In fact, he remembered that in many ways Islam was more practical, except the five times daily prayer. "Fine, I'll convert then. What do I have to do?"

"You have to learn and accept all five pillars of Islam. The Shahada, the creed of Islam. Salah, daily prayers. Zakat, the giving of alms. Sarwin, fasting, and the Haj."

"I already know most of the creed from my studies, and the others I just have to start doing. I can get around to the Haj later."

"That's good, but there is another thing you must do," Halil paused, "You must undergo Circumcision."

Antonis blanched, the idea of a knife anywhere near his manhood made his abdomen clench into a tight ball. "I didn't know that it was obligatory."

"It is amongst the Sunni, and that is what we Ottomans are."

Antonis said nothing.

"Come, my young Greek, losing a minuscule piece of skin is a small price to pay for the glory and wealth you shall receive."

"I am just worried the knife may slip."

"Let's hope not," laughed Halil. "You will have time to prepare, but as soon as you have done this, and healed, you will be free of this cage."

Suddenly, the cage did not seem that bad after all.

"Well? What will you decide to do?"

He rubbed his forehead as he pondered his options, before finally nodding his head in compliance. "Fine, let's do it. However, give me ten days to prepare, I am going to get as much of those bathing girls as I can, just in case something goes wrong."

Halil laughed, "Ten days it is," then paused, "But wait. First, I shall consult my astrologer to find the most auspicious date for you to start this new chapter in your life."

Antonis nodded, "When will you find out?"

"I shall see him tonight, and then bring him here."

"So be it."

The afternoon dragged on and Antonis began pacing the room frantically, his fevered mind racing. But where could he escape to? The capital was not an option, neither was going home to Crete bearing the brand of a traitor. Subconsciously, he rubbed his fingers on the raised π symbol that had been seared into him. *Would I fare better with the Latins?* He shook his head. He knew this was a momentous step and all that had passed the last four months came flooding back. Nicola's face filled his mind. *Where is this damn astrologer?* he thought, trying to shake the image free. He was not one to believe in all this superstition, but it made Halil more relaxed.

Dusk gradually fell and the servants brought dates, along with a pitcher of lemon water, their scents filling the room. He would have preferred wine. The waiting was making him nervous; he was one for a clear plan of action.

The door opened, breaking his concentration, and Halil ambled in with the wizened mystic, who true to form, was hunched, with a long white beard and wearing ancient black billowing robes covered in strange symbols that obscured everything except for the tips of his spidery white hands.

"This is Magus Ahmed of Baghdad, the finest astrologer in the known world," claimed Halil with out-of-character exuberance.

"Come here, my boy, sit, let me look at you," the man cast an approving eye over Antonis "Do you know your exact birth date?"

"Yes, March twenty-seventh, 1426."

"And the place?"

"Chania, Crete."

"Good, that makes things easier." The Astrologer pulled out three scrolls from beneath his robes, each tied with a ribbon, one red, another blue, and the other purple. He caressed them carefully onto the table.

"What are they?" enquired Antonis, his curiosity getting the better of him.

Unperturbed the astrologer began incantations in a language unknown to the young Greek. Once finished, he meticulously opened the blue scroll, followed by the red. The first was covered in charts and circles and the other a large table of numbers. The old man peered over the scrolls with such intensity as to hypnotise the onlookers. He then opened the purple scroll, which was blank, and started writing down his calculations. After what seemed an interminable length of time, the Magus looked up at his audience. "Given your stars' alignment and the current settings, you should not consider starting a new venture before the end of the third lunar week of March."

One month. Well then, more of the bathing girls, until just after my birthday. What a gift.

"However, you must complete your task within seven days of that date, otherwise the stars will change and you will be doomed to failure."

Antonis rolled his eyes at the doomsayer just hoping he would stop speaking his foul breath over him; it was hard to pay attention.

Halil was having no such issues, hanging on every word. "Is there anything else you see?" he enquired, wringing every drop of information.

The Magus huffed theatrically and drooped his head.

He'll probably ask for more money.

A furrow creased the old brow. "You shall kill your blood, when you think it is of no relation."

"What does that mean?" said Antonis.

"As I said," and with that, he rolled up his scrolls, giving the purple one to Antonis, as a reference, and the other two, he spirited away inside his voluminous robes.

Halil was at pains to thank him and paid twice the usual

amount. The clink of silver rang in Antonis' ears, good pay for a lot of mumbling bullshit.

The next few days passed without incident. Antonis indulged himself as much as possible with his bathing girls, especially Selima, putting all thoughts of the future procedure he would undergo, out of his mind.

He kept the scroll given to him unopened by his bed, but somehow, trepidation of the contents prevented him from revisiting it. He had given it a power, made more so by his reluctance to re-examine the reading. Given the circumstance, he had maintained a high level of fitness, stretching his limbs, hanging from the door to keep his strength, and flexibility as Alexis and Gouzaris had taught him when there was no other option. He particularly liked the breathing exercises for relaxation. Inhaling the floral scents that wafted-in from the garden his quarters overlooked, he focused on what was ahead, circumcision, and then, service to the Sultan.

His mind was still swirling with anger and pain over the events in Constantinople. The hatred for his brother had augmented over time, the vitriol giving him purpose. As for Katerina, he detested her even more for she had chosen Nicola's muscles and handsome face. His logic knew she was not worth this waste of energy, yet his ego refused to let go. Constantly devising new methods of excruciating retribution on his bastard brother and his worthless lover, the all-engrossing hatred pushing him to train harder, offering great satisfaction once completed.

On finishing one of his daily workouts, he wondered irritably why the bathing girls had not instantly appeared. He was cooling down and wanted to be cleansed. In that contemplative moment, it dawned on him how oriental he had become and was still smiling to himself when the door opened, and the customary three girls entered.

Selima was at the fore, with one of the Slav girls, but it was to the third that his eye went as they fanned out to approach him. The opaque cotton dress could not conceal the glorious femininity beneath, large pert breasts lying below square finely formed shoulders. The slender limbs hung by her side with one of her hands gently resting on slim but curvaceous hips and all of this placed upon long muscled legs. Thick jet-black hair surrounded her heart-shaped face, but it was the almond eyes, coal black and infinite that took his breath away.

"A new bathing girl, I see," he said, feigning indifference, though his loins were struggling to keep their peace.

"Yes, Master," said Selima, "Is she not to your liking?"

"What is your name?" he enquired.

"Fatima." Her voice was husky, defiant, and her eyes shone in rebellion. She might be a slave, but her spirit had not been broken.

"Where are you from?"

"I am Armenian," came the short response.

"You will suffice; let's see how well you clean."

She followed the other girls in, getting his bath ready, continuing to stare back at him as he watched them prepare the oils and hot water.

Selima noticed he only had eyes for the new girl and sighed. All things came to an end.

Antonis, with uncharacteristic impatience, disrobed, and stepped into the water where his bathers awaited. "Why have you not entered?" he inquired imperiously to the still clothed Fatima.

She moved to the side of the bath and without losing eye contact, let her dress fall with effortless grace. Standing over him, he could now see her in all her feminine glory, her taut stomach blending seamlessly into her tight fleshy mound, that had been plucked clean in the eastern fashion.

Fatima gave a wry grin as she stepped over the lip of the vessel, her round buttocks quivering like a thoroughbred at the starting gate. Straddling him, she casually picked up the soap and started to wash his shoulders and chest in slow rhythmic movements.

The other girls watched as she took complete control of the room.

Antonis liked her forwardness. "Am I cleaning well enough for you, sir?" asked Fatima as she rubbed his back.

"Yes, it is satisfactory, so far," he replied, his voice carrying only the slightest of quivers. *This is going to be a fun morning.* He sat back and let the strains of bitterness diffuse from him.

"WHAT IS WRONG WITH YOU TODAY?" The old Turk's eyes narrowed. "Have you had a new bathing girl?"

"Why?" Antonis replied a little too loudly.

Halil burst into laughter. "The wolf has become the sheep."

"Why do you worry so?" replied the Greek. His euphoria from Fatima's attention had still not waned. The memory of his savage thrusting into her, and her obvious pleasure still fresh had left him warm inside and out.

The frail old Turk went over the structure of the Ottoman military machine again with his pupil for the third time. "Antonis, pay attention," he chided. "But perhaps it's best we reduce your workload. Why don't you spend some time with her and get it out of your system before the snip? You only have ten more days."

The young man agreed wholeheartedly with his reasoning.

"Now let's get some air, come for a walk with me in the gardens."

The walks amongst the roses were always pleasant as it was the only outside area he was allowed to visit. The rows of flowers interspersed with fountains and sculptures appealed to his sense of order and control. The scents calmed and the chirping birds gave lightness to his being.

Halil gripped Antonis by the arm, breaking his daydream. "Now, listen to me, boy, and listen well. Things have happened that could play very well for us," he spoke in a hushed voice so it would not carry.

"What has happened?"

"What you don't know is that before the great victory at Varna, the Turkish aristocrats rebelled and wanted the return of Murad out of retirement to lead them against the crusaders."

Antonis raised an eyebrow in surprise. "How is this good for us?"

"Mehmet is the only son of Murad. All his brothers died, which means he is the only heir left. That has two possibilities; one, he becomes Sultan on his father's death, or two, the aristocracy lead a revolt to take over."

Antonis vaguely remembered meeting the boy at court and though he showed confidence, the situation didn't bode well for the lad.

"The young prince has been put under the Vizier's tutelage and is due to leave for Nicaea in a few days. I think that you should meet him before he goes."

"Just in case he wins the succession?" said Antonis.

"Exactly. I have been speaking to the boy and there is a lot more to him than the aristocracy realise. It's my business to understand people. He has a sharp mind and knows what he wants. He is also an outsider; his mother was a Greek Christian slave girl."

"So, what are you proposing exactly?"

"Get to know him a little. See if you two get on over the next few days. If you bond, you could consider spending some time in Nicaea with him. Who knows what may come of it?"

It was starting to make sense. "Fine, but first I want to spend a couple of days with Fatima."

Halil laughed, "A wolf, are you?"

Antonis grinned.

"But don't delay, this is a good opportunity for you," the old Turk added as they ambled towards the ever-watchful guards on the balustrade.

A light sheen of cloud distended the waxing moon into a misshaped omelette. The craters appearing as burnt parts of the egg and the fringes melting into the water vapour that screened it from human eyes. The night was chilly, and the dampness made the evening scents cling to his clothing. But he paid no heed to his surroundings, concentrating instead on what had just been said. It excited him; the game was beginning.

In agreement, Halil promised to arrange for the young heir to visit the next day, but first, he must have a visit from Fatima. He could barely contain himself, the warmth in his loins still not fully subsided since the previous day. Lounging on his daybed, all his thoughts were of plunging inside her again and feeling the snug rippling warmth of her womanhood.

The door opened and she stood there in a translucent silken robe, her frame tiny in the oversized entrance.

"Come in," he said as he lay there and watched her enter as if eyeing a prized piece of horseflesh. Her movements were languid and his gaze shifted from her hips towards her breasts, then her full mouth and finally, to her eyes. The darkness of her irises prevented any chance of seeing through them, the wide discs sucking him towards her. He could feel his manhood swelling.

Fatima was nervous as she entered the room, the events of yesterday had taken her by surprise. The way she acted was instinctive and yet she knew she had appeared as an accomplished courtesan. In fact, there had been only the one time before when her slave master couldn't resist himself and taken her, one night; a rough and stubby affair that ended quickly. Mercifully, he had not tried again, as he wanted full price for her. Yet when she saw the Greek, she had felt an uncontrollable urge. His chiselled face, tight black hair, and the haunting deep-set blue eyes, their pensiveness sprinkled with sadness drew her towards him. His slender lithe body, smooth, and muscled was a far cry from the fat-bellied hairy monster who was her first experience. The other girls had told her he was a fine figure of a man, with lots of energy, if sometimes too aggressive. The last appealed to her and when she saw his somewhat cruel mouth it attracted her to him even more. Now though, she was uneasy, as she was alone, the security of the other girls stripped away.

His hooded eyes bore through her as she approached. He stood there in pantaloons and bare chested, his narrow waist covered by a dark blue sash. "How long have you been in the service of the palace?" he enquired.

"I have been here two months, my Lord," she replied.

Her confidence not as strong as before, it aroused him further. "Come closer."

He was taller than she had first thought, as his arm wrapped around her waist and pulled her towards him. She arched her back in surprise at the suddenness and her head fell back. At that moment, Antonis clasped his mouth over hers. At first her lips were tense, but his rhythmic searching relaxed her, and she started to reciprocate with equal ferocity. Her hands clasping at his face as their mouths melded into each other.

Antonis planted a hand on one of her pert buttocks, kneading into her now heated crevice with his fingers. Instinctively, she wrapped her leg around his waist. In one deft move, he picked her up, and she fully enveloped around him; it felt so natural as he placed her upon his aroused member. She felt her body tense around him as his streamlined manhood slid into her with perfection and she rode him at an ever-increasing pace. He couldn't contain himself and exploded inside her, both shuddering together, sweat glistening on their torsos. After the euphoria, his legs felt shaky and he carried her to the bed where they collapsed. Lying together, they stared into each other's eyes, first in wondrous shock then both were laughing uncontrollably.

"So, tell me, how did you come to be here?" he asked, the post-coital ecstasy giving his voice a softer edge.

"I was the daughter of a local village headman and he decided not to pay his yearly tribute to the Turk. He heard of the crusader invasion and thought they would not be able to collect. But he was wrong, and the regional Bey came at dawn with his cavalry force and raided our village, rounding us all up into the square under the plane trees. The Bey did not ask for the tribute, his men just strung him up. As my father hung there quivering in his death throes, he witnessed my brother's castration and my mother's strangulation. I was made to watch."

The matter-of-fact tone made it all the more shocking to Antonis.

"Then they killed all the men and marched the women and children into slavery after they razed the village to the ground, as an example of what happens when tribute is not paid."

Antonis blanched at the description but nodded for her to continue.

"We were taken to the local slave market and sold to the highest bidder. Due to my freshness and beauty I was snapped up by Arkan, the most prosperous of the human traffic merchants. He realised I could fetch a higher price in Bursa, where he hoped to sell me to a rich aristocrat."

Antonis listened with intent, the smell of sex still all-pervading but he was transfixed by this angel's story. "And then?"

"The journey was uneventful, and we were taken to the market where a member of the royal household bought us all. Then I was put into the bathing girls' quarters."

"How do you feel about being a bathing girl?"

"So far, so good, you are my first ward."

He smiled and kissed her on the lips. Aroused again, they made love, this time slow and with more intimacy.

Antonis awoke in fine form. He and Fatima had spent the night talking and making love. When she left in the morning, he felt a yearning for her to stay as if he had known her for years. Only she bathed him that day, and they agreed to see each other again later.

Halil arrived earlier than normal, wanting to make sure all was in order for the meeting with Mehmet. He eyed his young protégé, as he now thought of Antonis. The brooding cloud that usually hung over him had evaporated. The Greek's azure orbs shone as the bright blue of the Ionian Sea. His movements were also more fluid and relaxed. "Have a good time last night, my young Apollo?" enquired Halil.

Antonis smiled.

"Excellent, now that you are finally in a good mood let's get on with it. The prince will be here before noon."

"I know what to do," replied Antonis, the edge in his voice back.

The two men were eating dates and yoghurt when the prince arrived. No large retinue, just a pair of guards and an assistant.

"Welcome, Prince Mehmet," said Halil in his most unctuous tone.

"Hello, Halil," replied Mehmet.

"Your Highness," Antonis said, bowing.

"Hello, Antonis Vevellis," replied the Prince, his precocious gaze resting on the Greek. "How are you finding our living quarters in Edirne?"

"Very sumptuous, sir."

"Well, don't get too used to them, military dwellings are not so respectable."

Antonis smiled. "I am more used to those than this."

The prince sat on the ottoman and one of his guards poured

him some lemon water, which he first tasted before giving it to the boy. "Tell me about the city?"

"Which one, Your Highness?"

"Constantinople of course, I want to know everything."

Antonis described the city, from the magnificent buildings and walls, to the setting on the Golden Horn peninsula. The young prince absorbed everything, asking minute detailed questions, most of which Antonis could answer. How the city worked, what the views were from different parts of it and how it was administered. He was surprised at his perceptive reasoning and warmed to the boy. Halil was right, there was something about him. Mehmet carried on through the afternoon. What was the Emperor like as a man? How his cabinet ran affairs, wanting breakdowns on all the individuals at court. All the while, his scribe noted down everything on vellum scrolls.

"Thank you for your time," said the Prince, as the sun became just a sliver on the horizon. "It would be nice if we could do this again tomorrow, as my time here is limited."

"It would be a pleasure, my Prince," replied Antonis. As the door shut behind Mehmet, he turned to Halil. "That boy is relentless."

"I tell you they are underestimating him," replied the Turk.

Given what he had seen, he could not disagree.

The rest of the week followed the same pattern. Mehmet by day and Fatima by night. The bond really grew between the lovers, both foreigners in a land they only vaguely knew; one making the choice, the other having it thrust upon her.

Fatima lay on the bed, her left leg kicked up in the air, her chin resting on her hands, gazing at her lover; who was pacing again. "You worry too much; the circumcision will be alright. The mullahs know what they are doing."

"Fine for you to say, it's not your cock!"

"Yes, but it gives me so much pleasure, it might as well be," she smiled broadly.

Antonis huffed but couldn't be angry with her, also knowing that once he had healed, he would probably not see her again and therefore wanted to spend every minute he could with her.

"When will it be done?"

He paused. "The Prince leaves for Nicaea in four days, say, three days after." That was still one day within the astrologer's prediction. Why that bothered him he couldn't fathom but best not to tempt fate, he reasoned.

"Fine, then we have no time to waste," she said, deftly rolled off the bed, and leapt into his arms, ready for another bout of ecstatic lovemaking.

MEHMET'S FACE screwed up in thought as he pieced together all the information he had gleaned during the last week. It was the first time he was able to study the prince without the penetrating gaze resting upon him. On the cusp of puberty, he had a feminine quality to him. Slight of build and small-featured, even his hooked nose was finely formed. His skin was sallow but flawless. The delicate fingers with impossibly long nailbeds rubbed his brow and pushed his dark brown hair off his face. Clearly, the influence of his mother.

The prince stopped pontificating and looked up into Antonis' eyes. "What is battle like? Were you scared?"

"It was all so fast; I really didn't have time to be. All I could think of was that I wished I had my bow."

Gone was the penetrating gaze to that of a wide-eyed boy.

"I was petrified the night before. The waiting was very difficult, but once it commenced, my training just took over."

"Did you feel anything when you killed someone?"

"Satisfaction," Antonis paused, then decided the boy deserved to hear the truth. "And ecstasy."

The boy didn't know how to react. "When I become sole Sultan, you will be my General."

"We shall see."

"On what?"

"Whether you become the Sultan."

The boy's confidence cracked.

"If I can help in any way, I will, my Prince."

"Thank you."

THE DAY FINALLY DAWNED, and the Mullah and his entourage arrived for the procedure. Antonis felt the cold sheen on his brow. The assistant laid out the silver bowls filled with hot water, soaps, and towels with care. Next to them, he placed two scalpels and three sets of finely wrought bronze tongs. His preciseness calmed Antonis, who had not slept much the night before. He had instead made love to Fatima contrary to his instructions, but he didn't care.

"Come, rub some of this lotion onto the tip of your penis," said the Mullah, handing him a small earthenware jar.

He took the jar, then carefully disrobing, started to apply the ointment liberally on the soon to be lost piece of skin.

"Good, that should be enough," nodded the Mullah, eyeing his actions. "Now, wash your hands."

Antonis felt the skin and tip of his penis going numb, sensing pressure but not pain. The assistant directed him to sit on the chair and open his legs. The Greek looked down at his appendage and prayed that nothing went wrong.

The Mullah approached with a set of tongs and a scalpel then said in a calm and professional voice. "Just relax, and this will be over in no time." He then clasped the tip of the skin and pulled it towards himself until it was taught and straining against the base of the penis. Placing the scalpel at the top of the foreskin, he sliced it open with a deft stroke and the glans lay exposed, with two wings of skin on either side.

The assistant placed the other tongs on the free piece of skin and splayed them open, whilst the Mullah cut around the base in a smooth stroke, the razor-sharp blade slicing the skin cleanly and, in a moment, the procedure was complete. The assistant had a cloth soaked in another ointment and wrapped it around the freshly cut ring. Antonis had observed the procedure with a sense of detachment and was surprised how little blood there was.

"One of your best, sir," said the assistant.

The Mullah grunted in agreement. Antonis let out a sigh of relief.

"Right, change the bandage three times a day and no intercourse for at least three weeks," ordered the satisfied surgeon, whilst pointing at the assistant to pack up the equipment.

"Inshalah, Antonis Vevellis, as you are now on the path of truth, the beginning of your journey with Allah." The Mullah smiled and touched his hand to his chest, then his mouth, and finally his forehead. Before leaving his freshly cut patient to his own devices.

A constant itching pervaded as the skin healed. This was only the fourth day and he had three more weeks of this. Fatima came every morning and changed his bandage ignoring his protestations, and he quickly understood the futility of arguing with her. Her tenderness and practicality endearing her to him even more. As she was performing one of her daily changings during the second week, she asked, "When are you going to perform the last part; the declaration of faith?"

"A week after this has healed. I am waiting for Halil to visit me, before I find out for sure."

Fatima smiled, though she felt sadness, for once he healed, he would be off, and she wouldn't see him again.

19

NUNNERY

he fear was palpable as she made the short journey towards the place. There were no regrets with her decision, but the ever-present trepidation stemmed from what was impending.

Katerina's mind wandered to Nicola and their tearful parting, as they clung to each other and hungrily kissed, as if bears storing energy for the winter. The sadness sliced through her and yet holding that feeling inside made her stronger and more determined to see this through. A dove hovered above the clattering carriage and finally landed at the open window. She absorbed herself with its pure white feathers, noticing for the first time the fine grey flecks that resided within them, giving the bird a new-found depth and interpreting it as sign of what she was to become. Her spirits lifted at the thought.

The carriage pulled up to the low arched white entrance of Belpia Elpis. Without pause Katerina stepped out. If she was to be this new independent person, she would start as she meant to go on. Vigorously pulling on the bell rope until the door swung open and an expectant nun ushered her in. Her speed checked when she saw Alexis' looming figure in the small atrium.

"Welcome, Katerina, your mother asked that I be here to welcome you. This is an old friend of mine, and your new Mother Superior, Sister Irene," boomed his friendly tones.

The nun smiled at her new visitor and inclined her hand slightly in greeting. "Ours is a humble house, Katerina. Here, we give ourselves to Christ and the spreading of His word." The habit covering her highlighted the zeal in her deep brown eyes. "We shall show you to your cell. There, you will find your habit and all the possessions you will need."

Anxiety again gripped the girl; this was now her reality. The pained look did not go unnoticed by her new patron.

"Don't worry, we come into this world with nothing, and it is with nothing that we leave. Being close to Christ is all that we require."

Seeing her hesitation, Alexis stepped forward and clasped her arm gently. "I will come and check on you from time to time, before Nicola and I leave for the Morea."

The mention of her love's name brought bittersweet feelings. "Thank you," she replied and resigned herself to the fate she had chosen.

Alexis turned to his friend, bidding his leave with unspoken depth. The departing presence of the warrior left a chasm of energy in the room and once again Katerina felt adrift.

Sister Irene smiled. "Come, my dear, let's get you settled in."

Carefully, the petite Mother Superior guided her down a bare corridor, lined with rows of old doors on either side. Through a slightly opened ingress, she glimpsed one of her sisters studiously writing on parchment and wondered if she would be able to write to her beloved during this exile.

Irene seriously doubted the girl's suitability; but Alexis had come to her for assistance, and she could not refuse. This was the pampered privileged child of the Kankileos, whose very realm had crumbled because she could not marry her sweetheart. She had been a seasoned prostitute by her age, dealing with the scum this earth had to offer, and survived. How could this delicate hot-house flower be suited to this life? Alexis insisted there was more to the girl, and his judgement was never wrong, though, there was always a first time.

Putting her misgiving aside, Irene led the young woman to her quarters. "Here is your cell," she said as they reached the penultimate door along the corridor.

"Mother Superior, why do you call it a cell? Is this to be my prison?"

Irene smiled calmly again. "It is what we call our living quarters and always have. Think of this not as a prison but a volunteering of your freedom to serve a higher purpose."

Katerina stared blankly back.

Sister Irene waved her hands towards the door beckoning her to go in.

Her head almost touched the lintel as she entered. A wooden bed, a writing desk, chair, oil lamp, two shelves, and a rudimentary wardrobe greeted her. The white walls and generous windows afforded much light and gave her dwelling a pleasant calming feel. On the bed were two sets of nuns' habits and in the corner, a broom, with which to sweep the red-tiled floor.

"We don't require you to cut your hair, though, it is advisable. Please put on your habit and come join me in my study."

"Do you have any writing equipment I can use?"

"We can sort that out when you come to see me, take your time," said the Mother Superior.

Katerina sat on her bed absorbing her new surroundings. She ran her hand down the fine silk dress she wore as if feeling the cloth for the last time. Tentatively, her other hand went to the neatly folded habit next to her, the wool was coarse and itchy, but at least it had never been worn. It was dark grey, and the coif, pure brilliant white. On top of the pile was a wooden cross on a wooden chain, the only jewellery she was allowed. Though not a girl heavily into adornments it was disconcerting that she would not have the choice. Beneath the habit was a linen undershirt, she wondered if it would stop the itching. Letting out a resigned sigh she carefully undressed and folded her clothes neatly.

Stripped naked, she took the undershirt and slipped it on—surprisingly comfortable—and then the habit. Running her hand through her thick locks, she decided it would not be shorn. She pulled them back and plaited the wild foliage. Once completed, she folded it up and placed the wimple on her head, wondering if Nicola felt the same sense of security when donning his armour. She walked to the Mother Superior's office still unsure of her decision.

She rapped on the wooden door and was bade to enter. The office was much larger than expected, simply apportioned with rows of scrolls neatly placed on shelves either side of the writing table, and two simple chairs to one side.

The diminutive nun gestured for her to be seated.

Katerina looked over the desk's expanse, white and yellow parchments chaotically scattered across it. It seemed strange that there was so much correspondence present; perhaps, the followers of Christ wrote a lot to each other.

The Mother Superior looked at her newest recruit. Her intelligent green eyes assessing her surroundings. The soft set of her mouth showed kindness, yet, she wondered if the right temperament was there for the cloister. "The new habit suits you, Katerina, your true self is now going to shine through."

"Thank you," she responded, but having no idea what she meant.

"As a novice, you will have a guide to show you how things are done; a Sister will instruct you in prayer, mealtimes, and your daily tasks."

As Katerina nodded, a faint smell of lavender wafted through the window behind the Mother Superior.

"We have different areas; the garden, the library, and kitchen, you will work in them all, as do I, there is no hierarchy before God."

A faint knock on the door interrupted Katerina's response. Turning, she saw a squat nun enter.

"Welcome, Sister Maria, this is your novice, Sister Katerina."

She stood to greet her new mentor, towering over the dwarf of a woman.

"Hello, my dear, welcome to our order," said Sister Maria. Her voice shrill and high-pitched, in stark contrast with her looks. Small droopy brown eyes embedded in a puffy white face split by thin bland lips. Her most prominent feature was the large hairy mole on her chin that neatly counterbalanced her dark smattering of upper lip hair.

"Hello, Sister Maria." She hoped all the rest of the nuns were not freaks too.

"Please show our newest recruit our humble abode," gestured the Mother Superior as she stood up and walked towards one of her many shelves. Carefully, she rummaged between the scrolls and pulled out a simple wooden box, along with a ream of parchments, then crossing the room, she handed the package to Katerina. "Here is the writing equipment you requested. I would like you to write three letters, one to your mother, one to Alexis Sartis, and the last to Monk Gannadios. Sister Maria will instruct you on what needs to be written to him. Open it," she urged.

The box was weighty in her hands as she unfastened it, also noticing the crucifix that had been seared into the lid. Inside were three quills, each with a bronze tip, two small glass inkwells, and a linen cloth. Her face broke into a joyous smile, the first time it had done so in a month.

Dutifully following behind the shuffling figure, Katerina

absorbed her new surroundings. Passing through the gardens; she saw a dozen or so nuns busily tending the flowers and vegetables. The two larger ones solidly tilling the earth in preparation for the spring planting. Tucked-in behind were a pair of helpers, each moving the soil to more convenient locations, not noticing her pass by. Ahead to the left, was the Convent's chapel.

"We have prayer there three times a day, morning, noon, and evening. You are not required to attend if you have other tasks to do." Taking Katerina's arm, Sister Maria guided her inside.

Many icons on white walls greeted her. In the alcove hung a large gold inlaid ebony and ivory cross, the only concession to ostentation. Rows of simple wooden benches provided the seating.

"Where does the choir sit?"

"We do our own singing, some well, and others not so good," replied the smiling sister.

Viewing the Chapel, she wondered how many nuns there were, judging by its size, probably not more than fifty.

Exiting the chapel, Sister Maria took her to the far corner of the walled complex, where there was a simple square building with a blue painted dome, the glassless windows boarded with ancient wooden shutters. Generously appointed, she could see through to the tables and trestles within.

"We eat two meals daily, breakfast and the evening meal. Your first duties will be here, washing and preparing the food. Can you cook?"

Katerina shook her head.

"This will be a good time for you to learn then," replied the sister. "Meet me here again when the mid-afternoon bell rings."

Once in her quarters, she pondered over her previous lavish life, filled with luxury and privilege. Opening the calligraphy box, she inhaled the fresh cedar smell and settled down to write two letters, one to her mother, telling her that she was fine, and ending it with the love she felt for her; the second to Alexis, in thanks for his help, and to greet Nicola. Then she lay down in contemplation.

The soft clanging of the afternoon bell roused her from her pensive slumber; at first, she was unsure of her unusually strange surroundings then she remembered her visitation time to the kitchen. Quickly putting on her habit, she hurried to her first duty as a nun.

Sister Maria was waiting for her when she arrived and set about instructing her on the chores, from preparing vegetables for the main cooks—two nuns from Macedonia—to cleaning the kitchen and washing the pans after the meal was prepared.

The delicious emanating smells aroused her hunger and when she finally sat down to eat, thought that never had such a simple vegetable stew tasted so good.

"You are enjoying it, no?" enquired Sister Maria.

"Yes, it's very tasty, do we not eat meat?"

"We do, but only once a week, and on special feasts. Abstinence is part of our life, but I am sure you will find our fare more than satisfactory."

Katerina nodded as she nibbled on the freshly baked bread that accompanied the repast. Mulling that it had been the first time in her life she had ever worked in a kitchen. There was the faintest of murmurings whilst they ate, the focus and discipline astounding her, reminiscent of warriors training; soldiers of Christ. When the meal ended, Sister Maria instructed her to clear up then meet her in the library.

Alone in the kitchen with a pile of dirty dishes, she stared at her shrivelled hands. Her attention turned instantly to a manicure then put it quickly out of her mind, it did not matter anymore. The scent of suds replaced the smell of cooking, turning her thoughts to the library visit. Possibly to write the letter to the monk Gannadios, whoever he was. Carefully placing each washed plate on the wooden drying racks and the cutlery in the earthenware jars, time passed quickly and satisfied with her work, she moved on to the next task.

The library was at the far corner of the complex, diagonally opposite to the kitchen. Reaching the door, she noticed it was different to the others, being oak, and in comparison, much newer. Upon entering, a musty smell of study hit her like a barrelling wave, imbibing her with interest. From floor to ceiling row upon row of books, scrolls, and parchments adorned the room. The maze of shelves was split in two by lecterns at each end with books placed upon them in different stages of reading. Colourfully written Christian scriptures with superb penmanship were surprisingly placed alongside Arabic tomes that Katerina was unable to decipher but marvelled at the geometric designs bordering the script in bright blue, gold, and orange hues. Drawings of long dead men and women displayed scenes of life and her imagination wandered unencumbered by the presence of other people.

"The writings of Omar Kayam, a revered Persian poet, who lived two hundred and fifty years ago," came a voice over her shoulder.

Broken from her daydream, she spun around to find Sister Maria smiling at her. "This is not a Christian text. Why is it here in the Convent?" she asked.

"Belpia Elpis and the order that preceded her, have been the guardians of all literature for nearly a thousand years. During the shameful sack of our city by the Latins, the nuns spirited away all the texts they could to save them from destruction. Luckily for us, they were mainly looking for gold, and not books."

"This is more precious than any metal," said Katerina, running her finger along the leather-bound spine.

Even though it had only been one day, the elder nun was liking her new ward. Perhaps Mother Superior's misgivings were incorrect. "There will be plenty of time to discover the treasures that reside here. First, you must write this letter to the monk Gannadios."

The mysterious monk intrigued her and why did she have to write the letter? "What must I write?"

"Introduce yourself, then ask if any new visitors have arrived at their Father's house and if so to describe them as you were hoping it's your long-departed cousin who had joined his order."

"That's it?" Katerina asked with unmasked surprise.

"For now. Seal it and take the letter to the Mother Superior, then you are free for the rest of the day."

The following days passed in a mixture of prayer, chores, and contemplation. She gradually met the other nuns, all of whom were pleasant and welcoming. During moments of solace, her mind drifted to Nicola, wondering how he was faring. It would not be long until he left, and she hoped that seeing him was a possibility before then. Alexis and her mother visited on different occasions, as promised. Proudly, she showed her mother the skills she had learnt in the kitchen. To Alexis, she enquired about Nicola, and the letter that came from her beloved, she read again and again. Time gave her the space for the pain to subside.

Sitting in her cell one afternoon, there was a knock at her door.

Sister Aliki entered carrying a sealed letter. "This arrived for you."

Perplexed at the lion's head seal she did not recognise, she carefully opened it.

Greetings, Sister Katerina,

Yes, your Cousin has arrived at our Father's house and is well. He was received with open hospitality and we have provided room and board for him.

We are sure he is now here to stay and will join our order.

May Christ be with you.

Monk Gannadios

Only Sister Maria or Mother Superior would understand, so she went in search of them. Spying her mentor hard at work pruning the flowerbeds, she glided over to her clutching the letter. "Sister, I have a response from Monk Gannadios."

"Very well, my dear, what does it say?" replied Maria without pausing in her work.

As Katerina read out the message, her audience's rhythm did not falter.

Only after admiring her horticultural labour did she speak. "I think we should go tell the news to Mother Superior."

Poring over the letter, Irene looked over the desk at the two seated nuns. "I shall request the benefactor to visit us. Katerina, please return tomorrow after breakfast, to visit with me and one of our Patrons."

Throughout evening prayer, she wondered what this meant. Undoubtedly, there was a hidden message but as to its meaning, it was fathomless.

Arriving promptly after a hurried breakfast, she knocked on Irene's door in anticipation. To her surprise, Alexis was in the room. *Is he the Patron?* They had clearly been talking for some time. She proffered her greeting, which Alexis acknowledged.

"You are I'm sure curious to understand the meaning of this letter," said the Mother Superior.

Katerina nodded sheepishly.

"The Father's home is the court of the Ottoman Sultan and the cousin you enquired about is Antonis Vevellis."

Her eyes widened in surprise. "And who is Monk Gannadios?"

"Oh, he is real, one of our fellow brothers in Edirne," replied Irene. "The letter says that Antonis Vevellis has gone to offer his services to the Sultan and is preparing to convert to Islam to further his ambitions."

Katerina's mind went back to their last meeting and remembered his offer. *So, he has done it.*

"No one outside this room except Nicola and Thanos will know of this information, is that understood?" Requested Alexis.

"Yes," acknowledged Katerina.

"You are probably wondering a great many things at this moment."

She nodded silently.

"Irene and I have been acquainted for a very long time, since we were children in fact," Alexis knew it was a slight exaggeration but, in this context, true.

"I was not always a nun, but since joining this Order, I have used my previous life skills to develop a network of informants," chimed in Mother Superior.

"Like Monk Gannadios?"

"Exactly. As members of the cloth we are given freedom of movement throughout foreign lands that is not afforded to others. The Greek Church has taken it upon itself to help preserve our liberty."

"Which is being eroded little by little every day," added Alexis.

"We supply the best information we can of what our enemies are doing to the meagre military we have so they may be as effective as possible."

"You spy on the Ottomans?"

"They are not our only enemy. The Latins have their political interests, which do not necessarily align with ours. They desire our city as much as the Turk and all they really want is their precious commercial rights."

"What about your trip to Florence, General, was that not about trade routes?"

Irene was impressed. How could she have doubted Alexis' judgment?

"Aye, but not on the surface, the powers that influence the Pope are Genoa and Venice."

"So, you gather information on this disposition and present it to the Emperor?" Katerina asked Irene.

"Not exactly, Alexis here is the conduit."

"There are countless subversives at court who would expose us. Hence, secrecy is our best protection," added Sartis.

The realisation was mind-boggling, but exciting; her life here was not just going to be passing time. "I assume my father knows nothing of this?"

"Absolutely nothing, upon Alexis's recommendations," said Irene, waving her left hand in his direction. "I have recruited you. Do not disappoint us."

"I won't," came the firm response.

Alexis stood to his full height, satisfied that she would be a valued addition to their cabal. Perhaps this was her calling. He stole a look at Irene and wondered if young Katerina would end up paying such a heavy price. "Nicola and I will be leaving the city in the next few days. We shall arrange for you to say your goodbyes. You must tell him nothing of this conversation. He has his own path to travel."

The novice nodded.

"Additionally, you say nothing of this to your mother," added the Mother Superior.

Again, on cue, the faint waft of lavender filled the room. Katerina wondered if Irene created it. Given what she had just discovered, she wouldn't be surprised.

"You may speak freely with Sister Maria, though, only whilst you are alone. Careless talk costs lives."

Katerina murmured agreement and promptly left as ordered.

"I told you she has the right abilities for this."

"Yes, you did, and I did not believe you."

Alexis smiled, "Still you doubt me?"

Irene looked at him. "I have never doubted you, my darling, just on occasion, I question you."

His booming laugh filled the room. "Have we had any news from our brothers in Attica about the state of the Duchy of Athens?"

"Not yet, but I am sure it will be through soon," replied Irene then continued, "What are you going to do about Antonis Vevellis?"

Alexis' face crumpled in pain. "What can I do? He has been shamed and exiled. Is it a surprise he has gone to the Turk? I kept my vows to keep him alive, and I succeeded as best I could, given the circumstances. My worry is that he is a capable young man and now filled with desire for vengeance. God knows where that will lead. Let's hope that he doesn't advance too far, or better yet, a skirmish puts an early end to his new career. I will inform Nicola of his brother's new life."

"But not his parents?"

"I know Andreas Vevellis well and the thought that his only son has done this would break him. That I cannot do. Better he thinks Antonis has gone to hide and lick his wounds rather than betray the very fabric of his being."

"Very well," concluded the Mother Superior.

HER WORLD HAD CHANGED in a month but life had possibilities again; the path laid out for her was unknown, yet energising. It seemed strange to be greeting her beloved in a nun's habit, but she was excited at Nicola's imminent arrival. Sister Irene gave permission to meet in the guest quarters, where they would have privacy to say their goodbyes, and it was there she headed with a spring in her step. She entered without knocking.

Nicola turned upon hearing the door, and it took him a second before he recognised the person in the habit. He strode forward and clasped her shoulders with both hands, his eyes delving deeply into hers. They moved to kiss but an invisible barrier had sprung up between then. They embraced awkwardly, cheek touching cheek, yet feeling each other's energy. Pulling back, he finally spoke, "It's good to see you again. Though, I admit, it's strange to see you like this," he smiled.

"At least I don't have to think about what to wear every day," she replied. "Like your leather breastplate."

Nicola shrugged. These were their uniforms now, he a soldier and she a nun, but he was finding it hard to say anything, his emotions clouding his thoughts. "How is it in the Convent?"

"The nuns are nice, and I have a daily routine that involves a lot of reading and prayer."

Looking into her eyes, he could see she was happy and that lifted his spirits. "Do they have a good library?" he asked.

She wanted to tell him what she was really doing, and he would be so proud of her, but she kept her secret. Gently, she touched his face and smiled. "Don't worry, my love, it's going to be fine. I am happy here and will wait for your return."

"It could be a long time before I do."

"I know."

Nicola stared into her emerald eyes, his dilated pupils absorbing as much as he could of her. Life was unfair. He leant forward and kissed her, his arm clasped around her waist, the habit masking her slender form from his touch. Katerina's fingertips rested gently on his jaw as she turned her head up to greet him. "I will write," he said.

"I will read," she replied, "I love you."

"I love you," he clasped her hand. "It's time for me to go." Turning swiftly, he walked away, closing the door gently behind him.

The poised nun remained surrounded by a faint masculine essence.

2 0

CONDOTTIORE

*T*hanos was busy ordering his servants to pack his 'essentials'. Heavy oak chests, pitted, and scarred with use weighed down the mules in the courtyard. Others had yet to be packed. Goblets, weapons, and doublet, all scattered in chaos.

"No! I want the Florentine fabric and the Toledo steel swords!" said the fussy Greek in a raised voice.

"Yes, Mastre," responded his servants and hurriedly changed the contents of the trunk.

"You've grown soft with all your possessions. Don't forget your face powder," said Alexis.

"Oh, shut up," he replied.

After the debacle of the last few weeks, Thanos realised how stagnant his life had become and decided to accompany Alexis and Nicola on one more adventure. However, he had become accustomed to his luxuries, which gave his packing for campaign, a whole new meaning.

"You can never be too prepared, Alexis," came the delayed response.

"We are going on campaign, not a feast," Alexis' mocking tone grated.

After an interminable amount of time, all the mounts were finally loaded. Four with Thanos' equipment and one with Alexis' and Nicola's.

Watching the theatrics lightened the sadness that had enveloped him since leaving the convent. Katerina appeared happy, although seeing her in a habit felt strange. And losing Antonis had been hard to take, he still could not truly grasp it.

The task ahead seemed daunting. Where was he going to acquire a fortune so they could be together? Alexis assured him it wouldn't be a problem, just that it would take time. Nicola looked longingly around the courtyard of Thanos' house, taking one last look at the pristine walls and flower trellis clinging to them. Imbibing the scents that he had become so familiar with and listening to the calming tinkle of the water fountain. In such a short space of time this house had come to feel like home and his mind instantly wandered to his parents. How sad they must be at losing their only son.

The letter he wrote was stilted and difficult to compose, extolling Antonis' bravery, and how much he missed them. There had been no reply. That was two months ago. The clattering of the horses' hooves jolted him out of his daydream and after a cursory backward glance, left the house and headed towards the Eleutherion Harbour for the return to the Morea.

Fluttering pennants clapped the masts of the two carracks docked at the harbour. Nicola subconsciously rubbed his shoulders as the icy Bosphoros wind slated his back, grateful to be heading south and shorter winters. The now fully recovered Sergeant Themis, coordinated the loading of the Laconians and their mounts. Forty-eight men returning, out of the two hundred who had left four months earlier. Catching the eye of the odd soldier, he occasionally received nods of recognition. His miraculous escape at Varna had earned him a grudging respect from the men, but he knew it took more than one act of skilful courage to be truly accepted.

With the troops and their baggage on board and evenly divided between the ships; Nicola joined Thanos whilst Alexis was in command of the other.

"Whose boats are these?"

"They are mine," replied Thanos. "I have three ships in total; the other is delivering a cargo to Sicily. If we are going on campaign it is good that we are as self-sufficient as possible and three carracks can provide invaluable support."

As the ships pulled out of the Harbour, Nicola was surprised with the speed that the city shrank away, and wondered when he would see Katerina again, her loving words echoing in his ears. Instinctively, he straightened his shoulders and let the brisk sea breeze course through his hair.

They took the fastest route possible to the Morea as the men were impatient to return home.

Intrigued at Thanos' industriousness, Nicola pointed at a collection of small knives. "What are these for?"

"These are throwing knives. Never know when they'll be needed. Rarely a killing tool, unless you are very accurate, but useful nonetheless when you need a diversion to gain time."

Nicola had come to learn that for all his quirks, the effete mercenary knew his weapons and how to use them. "How do you and Alexis know each other?"

Thanos arched his brow in surprise. "Well," he paused dramatically, as storytelling was his forte. "I was once in the Laconians. In fact, your father, was my Commanding Officer. Alexis and I were both young soldiers in the tagmata. We became friends during the first Ottoman siege of the city, and that's when the big man earned his laurels. I stayed on with the Laconians for another four years but decided to go my own way as a Condottiore. You see, Alexis is a patriot, whereas I am far more pragmatic and decided to create some wealth with my skills. We have always stayed in touch and since my retirement into a life of plenty I have been bored senseless, until Alexis returned into my life."

"So, you knew my real father too?"

"Aye, that I did, but not well, he was a senior officer, very private and withdrawn. A good soldier, respected, but not loved by his men. He was killed in a skirmish in Thessaly around the time you were born."

"I know, my father Andreas told me what happened." Nicola's eyes bore no sadness, he never knew his blood father. All his guidance and knowledge came from Andreas.

He felt for the young man, cast adrift without a rudder.

"How come you never had a family?" asked Nicola.

"Never had the time, too busy enjoying myself," smiled Thanos, whilst he polished the stubby pointed blades. "Now, let me show you how to use these."

ALEXIS WAS with his own thoughts on the other ship. He was grateful Thanos had decided to accompany him, his resources and experience would be invaluable in the coming months. He opened the small chest filled with his personal possessions. An icon of St. Demetrius, patron saint of soldiers, his writing box, a leather pouch of Venetian ducats, a pair of fine pigskin gloves, and two packets of letters from which he pulled one that had the embossed imperial double-headed eagle cipher and re-read it.

The plan he had hatched with the Emperor and his brothers had taken a severe blow. Yet reading this letter, Constantine did not think so. His confidence never ceased to amaze Alexis, but doubt gripped him. The defeat at Varna showed how resilient and strong the Turk was. He quickly put those doubts aside and focussed on the plans they had devised, staring out at the wine-dark waters of the Aegean, that felt as infinite as the tasks ahead.

. . .

"Finally, Alexis is returning to Mistras," exclaimed Constantine. His lithe physique pacing around his desk.

Plethon looked on bemused. *If he has energy enough to waste, good on him.* His mind wandered to the boys, how they must have grown, for surely, they would still be with Alexis. "Yes, it will be good to have him back in our fair city."

"And not a moment too soon, we have many tasks ahead of us."

Plethon had become privy to their 'Big Idea', as Constantine called it. It was audacious, the type of scheme that only a younger man would concoct. But all men were younger than him as he was now well past his ninetieth year. When Constantine asked for his opinion, he paused. Knowing what he knew about all the parties involved, he did not think it would stand the test of time and to his everlasting shame, he did not say so, merely nodded and encouraged Constantine to proceed, whose reasoning was, 'better to do something than to sit and do nothing.' He admired his zeal and dedication. Perhaps in another time, he would have been a great ruler, but alas, fate, he felt, would not be kind to him. "Are you going to proceed immediately with the implementation?" asked Plethon.

"Within two moons," came the curt response.

The old man shifted in his chair uncomfortably, his dowdy woollen clothes starting to itch. He noted how he had no ability to shut out discomfort anymore; the inevitability of growing old. The last trip to Rome had made that clear to him.

Glancing out of the window to his left, he could see down the mountain of Mistras. The white-daubed houses interspersed with olive and pine trees that stitched the buildings to the slope. Down the main thoroughfare, he noted a column of horses making its way to the citadel. At its head, the unmistakeable figure of Alexis stood out and just behind, a man nearly as large with long brown hair streaked with blond. It took a moment but then he knew it was Nicola. He looked for his brother but could not make him out at that distance. "My Lord, I think Alexis and the Laconians have returned."

"Ah, at last," Constantine exclaimed, and the frustration started to dissipate from his body.

Nicola had mixed feelings on his return. The smells and the vibrancy felt the same, the fresh thyme and rosemary wafted in abundance, and the happy faces of its citizens lifted him, bringing back memories of happier, more innocent times. Gently, he patted his mare's neck as if to imprint those better memories on his burdened soul.

The head of the group had passed the lower city and entered the citadel. The remainder of the Laconians stayed under Themis' command and went to the barracks to unload their kit and reunite with their families.

Constantine watched as the three men continued, his excitable energy returning. Plethon judged that he should be more reserved in his behaviour, for he might one day become Emperor. They rode to the foot of the palace and dismounting, entered through the main entrance; Alexis in the centre with Thanos and Nicola on either side of the wide steps.

"It's a pretty little town. Seems a bit low on interesting company though," said Thanos irreverently.

"I am sure you will find some fun here, you always do, you should try nearer the barracks," offered Alexis.

"Back to basics then?" countered Thanos.

They climbed the wide staircase to Constantine's office, each guard nodding to Alexis as they stood to attention as he passed. At the final stage, the household guards opened the door.

"Welcome back, Strategos," said one of the guards.

"Good to be back, Yiannis," replied Alexis, who knew the name of every man under his command.

The guard gave the faintest of smiles in return; it was for gestures such as these that the men loved him.

As the three strode into the ruler's quarters, Constantine stood to greet them. "Alexis, my old friend. It has been a long time."

"Yes, it has, my Lord," replied Alexis, bowing.

He clasped his old confidant in unabashed pleasure then turned to the others in the group. "Nicola, you have grown. You are as big as our general here, and growing a beard I see."

The young man was glad the scar wasn't mentioned. The smattering of hair had covered it well enough from all but the most focused of scrutiny.

"This is Thanos Mavroides, an old comrade in arms, who has decided to join us on our venture," said Alexis introducing his friend.

"Welcome to my humble city," said Constantine.

"Thank you, sir," replied a slightly awestruck Thanos.

Plethon, who had been seated, shuffled towards the standing party.

Nicola noticed a slight loss of sprightliness in his former teacher, although his eyes had lost none of their zeal.

"Where is your brother, is he still in Constantinople?" asked Plethon.

"I am afraid he is no longer with us," replied Nicola.

Alexis noticed that his words were controlled now. Time had that effect.

"I am sorry to hear that," Plethon said, intending to enquire more later. "It is good to see you again," he added with a laconic smile.

Constantine wasted no time and dragged his general to the table at the far side of the room, where many rolls of paper were ordered neatly in a box by its side. The tall ruler bent down until he found the correct one and pulled it out, unfurling the yellow leaf, which was a map of southern and central Greece.

Nicola marvelled at the attention to detail; passes, mountains, and lakes, were all clear to see. There was none of the usual flowery patterns around the edge, only a north-pointing arrow.

"Gentlemen, this is our task for the coming season," Constantine announced and with a theatrical gesture, raised his finger then brought it down on the eastern shore.

"Athens!" exclaimed Thanos, his tongue clearly overcoming the presence of royalty.

"Yes, the Duchy of Athens. Hasn't been in Greek possession for over two hundred years and it's time we brought it back into the fold." He then set about explaining how he planned to use a combination of guile and tactics to take the prized treasure.

Alexis was impressed, his leader had been busy planning. Soon, the table was covered in a jigsaw of interlocking parchments showing the whole Balkans from the Adriatic to the Aegean.

"My Lord. You are missing the inescapable fact that the northern armies of Hunyadi have been destroyed, so the enemy can divert all its energies towards us," interrupted Nicola.

Constantine noticed the scar under the beard. *So, he is marked.* "Skanderberg."

"What is Skanderberg?" queried Nicola.

"The Prince of Albania, who has been a thorn in the Turks' side for years. Defeated every one of their generals sent against him."

"Then why wasn't he at Varna?" countered Nicola.

Constantine shrugged. "Doesn't matter now. More importantly, he has a full army at his disposal protected by mountains, and through our network, we have been in regular communication with him."

"So, the plan hasn't changed, just some of the players?"

"Exactly, Strategos, and given his track record, he couldn't be a better bet."

The discussions went on late into the night. Food was brought and when they finally broke, the birds had begun their chirping.

"He really thinks this is going to work," said Thanos as they wandered to their quarters.

"Yes, and I think it has a real possibility."

Thanos slowly rubbed his chin. "What the hell! It will be an adventure, whatever the outcome."

The following morning, Nicola awoke feeling positive and upbeat about the forthcoming mission. Constantine's intelligence on his enemies and allies' disposition impressed but he speculated where he got all his information. His scar itched, for though it had healed well, a phantom pain manifested when he thought of Antonis.

Now, back with the Laconians, he was given a command of twenty-four men and horses, with the formidable Themis as his sergeant. The now famed escape at Varna gave him an easier ride, for he was not some entitled milksop.

The next month was a mixture of drills, planning, and military strategy. Alexis and Constantine were busily rounding up all the men they could muster, conscripts from the Peloponnese, displaced Greeks from the conquered territories, and even a few bandits from the hills of Messina flocked to the cause in the hope of some booty.

Letters to Katerina were his only relief. Sworn to secrecy, he talked about being back with the men and the bond that he and Themis had developed from their common experiences and always ending with how much he loved and missed her. The end of the ritual was to reach into his pocket and touch the handkerchief that she had given him all that time ago in the mock tournament.

"There is real energy in the air, Strategos," said Constantine.

"Yes, my Lord."

"Have we had word from Skanderberg?"

"My contacts have sent us positive news of his intentions, as well as the Turk's disposition."

Alexis' information was unnervingly accurate. Though extremely curious as to who these contacts were, Constantine never asked, knowing that he would never get an answer. "So, are we sure that he will tie down Ali Pasha's forces in the north?"

"He is relishing another successful campaign against the Turk."

"He has certainly had more success than anyone else," grunted Constantine.

Alexis agreed and thought ruefully how useful he would have been at Varna.

"At least we have the Hexamilion to protect the heartland of the Morea from any flanking Turkish surprise."

"That pile of stones has never held anyone back."

"This time we have put in extra trenches and some other special surprises for any would-be attacker," replied Constantine with supreme confidence.

Alexis had no such faith but held fire on any further negativity.

Following another exhausting day of planning, Alexis retired to his quarters for some necessary solitude. Beside his baths, the other place of peace for him was at his desk. Reaching into his cedar writing box, he pulled out the two packets of letters and read the most recent. Absorbing the information and cross-checking the map that the plan made sense, his instincts leaned towards the likelihood of success.

Looking at the second batch, he pulled out a faded letter and went over it slowly. The discoloured sheet was dated March 1423, the emblem of the crucifix clearly visible in the heading. As he read it, a smile crept across his face. It was one of the first letters Irene had written to him, relaying her new life at the convent. Gradually, he closed his eyes, placing himself in her world, feeling her joy of liberation at finding a purpose in life. He had memorised the contents years earlier and let his mind wander to the events of a generation before. His emotions were mixed; happiness for her but tinged with regret that he had not committed to her. Life took over and never again did he find anyone who could match her in spirit, courage, or beauty. His chest crumpled in sadness as he daydreamed.

A strong knock at his door snapped him out of the reverie and placing the letter on the desk, he bade the visitor to enter.

"Strategos."

"What can I help you with?"

Nicola strode purposefully into the room.

His protégé had grown both in stature and maturity during the last months, a fact made startlingly clear in the confines of the small room. "What's on your mind?"

"How sure are you of the intelligence reports that we have full support of Skanderberg and his Albanians? I mean, if they don't do their part, we will be terribly exposed."

"Aye, that we will, but my sources are extremely reliable."

Alexis could see the conflict. *There will be a time to know but not yet.* "Get some rest, we march the day after. Make sure your men are prepared and we will discuss this another time."

The younger man showed disappointment but obeyed. Turning to leave, his eye caught the letters on the desk and briefly, felt a sense of familiarity. As he returned to his quarters, the last image in Alexis' study niggled at him, but he soon put it to the back of his mind, as he took to his bed with thoughts of his duties for the morning.

"They look impressive, General, don't they?"

"Yes, sire," replied Alexis as they inspected the troops marching out of the city and northward to Athens.

Nicola rode ahead of his Lokos, his chest bursting with pride, seeing all the Laconians marching in symmetrical formation. Followed by the infantry, not as splendid but formidable nonetheless and mercenaries in their variegated uniforms, and finally, the siege engineers with their machines. The clanking of metal filling the onlookers' ears and the swirling dust clogging their airways as the tagmata pounded by. Themis rode to his left, and with Alexis leading the army, he knew that success was a strong possibility. Katerina would be so proud of him, going on this mission to liberate Greeks and bring them back into the fold of the Empire. He looked at the throng gathered to watch them leave, wives, mothers, sisters, children, each of their faces glowing with expectant hope.

THE ARRIVAL of nearly four-thousand men at their gates put the fear of God into the Florentine rulers. A brief skirmish ensued, during which Nicola and his troops acquitted themselves well but it was an uprising in the city that forced the Duke to send a representative under a flag of truce to parley with the besiegers. Nicola waited in the purple tent with his commander and ruler for the delegation, thinking they had achieved a lot in the two weeks since they arrived.

The envoy was ushered into the Byzantine lines and pulling up to the headquarters, dismounted with effortless grace and strode with utmost confidence to meet with his conqueror. "Lord Paleologus, my master, the Duke of Athens, sends his greetings and wishes to discuss the terms of his surrender."

Watching him closely, Nicola knew the confidence was a veneer. He, and most probably his comrades were spent.

Constantine, resplendent in full armour, looking every inch the conquering hero, waved his hand magnanimously. "We are Christian brethren, and as such, have no wish to inflict more loss of life," his voice brimming with success. "The Duke shall surrender the city to me, acknowledge my over-lordship for all his domains, including Thebes, and place his troops under my command."

The herald's eyes widened but knew his master had no choice. "I shall relay the message to the Duke."

"We shall await your response. If, however, we receive no news before sundown, we shall take that to mean refusal of our terms and resume the siege," replied Constantine. "Our terms will not be so favourable should there be a next time," he added, the blandness in his voice giving the last statement added menace.

"Do you think they will accept the terms?" asked Alexis.

"They would be foolish not to, but who knows what's in his mind. Men do stupid things under pressure."

Alexis nodded in agreement.

"Additionally, it's our people in the city and he knows I have no wish for them to suffer. Though, I will not flinch to take this city by force if I have to." A pained look came across his face as he turned to face the walls of Athens.

Nicola sensed that Constantine cared for his people. This was not solely about power but belief, and why he commanded such loyalty, and why the Morea flourished under his rule.

The sun was starting its slow descent and still no answer came from the city. A look of resignation showed on Constantine's face, accepting that more loss of life was to come until his objective was fulfilled.

"Sire, look, they are lowering their standard."

The group of soldiers all looked in unison at the city and saw the red and white flag making its slow descent to the ground. As the pennant fell below the height of the wall, the front gates of the city opened. Nicola stared in anticipation of what would happen next. Three horses and riders appeared and trotted out to meet the Greeks for the second time that day.

The Duke was at the head of the party with his standard folded up in front of him. Slowly dismounting, he took the folded cloth and walked to his conqueror. With great care, he handed the symbol of his power to Constantine. "The city is yours and I acknowledge your over-lordship," he said.

As Nicola looked on, Constantine towered over the diminutive Florentine. The Count's pallor made him appear older and the dye in his beard did him no favour.

"A wise decision, your grace," replied Constantine as he took the standard.

A cheer went up from the soldiers.

Alexis ordered one of his men to take the double-headed eagle standard and raise it upon the walls. Only then did the army make its way through the open gates of Athens.

As Constantine and Alexis rode at the head of the column, he turned to his general. "So far, so good, and we suffered fewer than thirty losses."

Alexis couldn't dispute the statement and for the first time since Varna, thought that this outrageous plan might work.

The ecstatic populace mobbed their liberators; flowers were thrown at them as they paraded past. Women hugged the soldiers, partly out of happiness at being re-joined with the Empire, and relief that there had not been a bloody siege.

Perhaps Constantine is what he seems. Everything he said has come to pass, and with the minimum loss of life, thought Nicola. He looked up towards the Acropolis and saw the Parthenon in all its glory. It had been the palace of the Dukes of Athens and it was there he was headed.

The handover was a quick and simple affair. Alexis tasked Nicola to secure the treasury. The captains had differing roles, some to account for all the Latin knights, and others to secure various government buildings. When Constantine was informed of the vast quantity of gold in the city's coffers, he was delighted, and ordered some of it to be meted out to his soldiers.

Nicola received a large bonus for being the victorious commander of the only skirmish during the campaign. The three pouches felt pleasantly heavy in his hands and were more than enough to buy a small farm in Crete. He was now well on the way to earning his right to marry Katerina. Thanos was right, it was now just a matter of time. A smile broke across his face and his thoughts turned dreamily to his beloved and the future they would have together.

GROWTH OF POWER

Antonis had chosen Goran, a tall Croatian to be his sergeant. His imposing presence galvanised the men into a coherent team and they performed their tasks efficiently. He had desperately wanted to get involved but held himself in check as he remembered Alexis's leadership lessons.

By the end of the third day the stalls were free of debris, their gates repaired, and ready to have the horses housed. Pleased, Antonis decided to collect the animals personally, accompanied by Ahmad, regarded as the best judge of horse-flesh in the army. Carrying letters of authority given to him by Mehmet, he went to the royal ranches on the edge of the city.

At first, he thought he had made a mistake. Palatial buildings, with ornate marble façades gleamed in the spring sun, until the familiar smell of horses filled his nostrils. The two men were greeted at the gate and shown to the Sultan's equerry, to whom Antonis handed the letter.

The short hairy man read its contents. "One hundred mounts? Well, you certainly have friends in high places."

"Where are your horses?"

The old Turk eyed the upstart up and down as Antonis'

reputation preceded him. Rumours abounded with his arrival at court, his swift elevation, and of creating a new military for the young Sultan. If one of their finest was betraying them, what hope did the Greeks have.

Gesturing to the visitors to follow, he took them through the narrow white-walled passageway towards an old oak door. Cranking it open revealed a vast expanse that was bordered by hills to the north and east and the city by the south and west. The plain was teeming with equine magnificence from the fast-Asiatic ponies to the lumbering draft horses beloved of European knights.

Antonis gawked in amazement; there had to be close to two thousand on display. The resources at the Ottomans' disposal only confirmed he had made the right decision. Ahmed and he wasted no time picking out what they wanted.

The equerry then ordered his stable boys to round them all up. "I think we are done here, let's retire to finish the paperwork."

Antonis had finished signing the receipts for the hundred horses when one of the grooms entered, telling the equerry that they were having issues.

"What's the problem?" enquired Antonis.

"One of the stallions is playing up, would you excuse me."

Curious, Antonis followed him out to the paddock, where a groom was struggling to control a huge chestnut of at least eighteen hands with wild, defiant, and imperious eyes. His coat gleamed, heightened by the rays of the morning sun, changing hues as his muscles strained against the bridle.

"Ah, Zoza, a most unruly stallion. No one can break him in," said the equerry in exasperation.

"May I?" asked Antonis and without waiting for a reply, walked up to the rearing horse, showing neither fear nor hesitation, his palms facing upwards. He breathed out slowly and held the stallion's wild glare.

Astonished, the groom released his grip on the tether and to everyone's amazement the horse didn't bolt but held the stare of this new visitor, who in turn was humming an unintelligible sound.

Antonis knew the animal simply needed to be shown a firm unthreatening manner. Inching closer, he gently patted the horse's flank, calming him down, then in a flash leapt upon and in an instant, was trotting the stallion around the paddock.

"How did you do that? No one could break him," asked the incredulous equerry.

"That's a secret," replied Antonis. "I shall name you Xenophon, and may you lead me and my ten thousand to glory," he shouted triumphantly.

The equerry nodded. Perhaps this Greek truly was something special.

CASUALLY, Fatima stroked the top of his arm as he lay gazing at the ceiling after one of their exhaustive bouts of lovemaking. "What are you thinking, my love?"

He sighed deeply. "I'm still not sure how to create this unit. The fusion of horse-archer and knight is not as easy as it sounds."

The concubine's forehead creased in thought. "Perhaps you should consider what they will most likely confront and tailor their style to that."

"Yes, well, we would most probably encounter mounted Latin knights and their yeoman infantry, heavily armoured and slow."

"So, speed and distance would be preferable, with some protection," she countered. "Isn't that how your Laconians are structured?"

Grudgingly, he admitted she was right, that the solution was staring him in the face. Just Ottomanize what he had already learned; decorate the unit with Islamic symbols but essentially keep the Byzantine military teaching. A smile broke across his face followed by a frown. "What do I call it?"

"The Thracian Cavalry?" she responded.

He leant over and kissed her softly on the lips, then rose from the bed and strode towards his sword belt that rested in the corner of the room. Reaching down, he pulled out his sfakion and casually played with it in his hands as he continued to pace around the bedchamber.

Fatima observed his movements with interest. Whenever he was in contemplation he always held onto his dagger. However, it was the first time he had risen and grabbed it. "What is so special about that knife?" she asked, curiosity getting the better of her.

It broke her lover's concentration and he turned to face her. "Nothing really," he replied absent-mindedly.

"Then why do you always caress it when you are deep in thought?"

"I don't know, habit I suppose."

Fatima glided over to him and took the knife, which weighted heavily in her hands. Casually, she ran her thumb along its razor sharpness and gasped as it broke the skin, drawing blood. She sucked to stem the bleeding, now also noticing the letter embossed at the bottom of the handle. "Is that for Antonis?"

He nodded silently.

"When did you get this?"

He let out a sigh as he collected his thoughts. "One was given to me and another to Nicola on the day we passed through the school at Mistras. It was a symbol of our rite of passage from boys to men."

Fatima noticed the pained look cross his face, his hooded eyes developing a dark scowl. "Do you miss your brother?"

"He is not my brother," came the fast response, his usual self-honesty disappearing in his bitter speech.

"Well, you did grow up together and shared a lot."

Antonis ignored her last comment as his jaw set from his clenched teeth.

She saw this as her opportunity to pry for information. "What happened with your brother? Why did you leave the Empire and come over to the Turks?"

Antonis smiled at her question, it was nearly a year since he left Constantinople and he still had not spoken about that time to anyone.

The conflict was evident in his face and Fatima knew this was not the right moment. Giving him back the knife, she clasped her arms around his taught waist and rested her head on his branded chest, feeling his struggle within as they stood in silent reflection.

It was a fitful night's sleep, he kept waking and remembering the painful experience surrounding his sudden departure from his homeland. He had no regret, yet the anger of rejection still seethed, and he was more determined than ever to show Nicola that he had chosen the correct path. As he mulled this over, an idea germinated that would prove it, and give him the glory he desperately craved. But first, he had to attend to more pressing issues, such as his men and the naming of his cohort.

The young Greek strode confidently into his men's barracks for the weekly inspection. The entire troop stood to attention by their beds as he walked past them, followed by Goran. A glimmer of satisfaction stole across his face as he saw their armour and weapons were oiled, polished, and hanging above their bunks. They were beginning to have the look of soldiers. Balkan Slavs mingled with Anatolian Turk in a truly cosmopolitan unit. "You have done well so far, men, and now we have more good news. Each man shall receive new armour befitting an outfit such as ours."

Smiles broke across the men's faces.

"You will all start to use the bow as standard from now on. So those of you who haven't much experience had better start practising." Turning to Goran, "Concentrate on the European troops to improve their marksmanship."

"Yes, sir," he replied.

"That will be all," he added, before leaving his men in the care of his trusty sergeant.

Arriving at the stables, he found Xenophon saddled and ready. Wasting no time, he rode to the palace to begin the germination of his idea.

THE YOUNG SULTAN sat on his sumptuous chair; his fine features screwed up in confused thought. Opposite him, sat a middle-aged man dressed in the voluminous black robes of a Muslim cleric, his stern features framed with short grey hair and sallow skin. The huge head was tilted downward to emphasise the point he was trying to get across to the boy, whose face relaxed as he finally understood the lesson and Mullah Guwani's eyes glowed as he saw the spark of comprehension.

"So, Christians and Jews are still people of the book, and yet are infidels as they do not follow the one true God?"

"Exactly, my Sultan," said the Mullah in his rasping tones.

"I mean, they don't seem that different to me. The Jews eschew the eating of pork and drain the blood of their livestock before consumption as we do. We all believe in one God."

The elder nodded in encouragement.

"I think religion is just a means to control people, by binding them together under just one banner."

The Mullah couldn't help the sharp intake of breath at such heretical talk, at the same time having admiration for the fourteen-year-old boy. He would make a formidable Sultan.

"Is that not what we believe, sir?" asked Mehmet, as he

looked up to the teacher with his penetrating hazel-eyed gaze. He had grown to like his tutor a great deal.

The cleric never patronised the boy, simply giving him the facts with reasoned argument. In turn, Mehmet would constantly try to goad him with outrageous statements and every time the response was calm and measured. So that now, after a year of theological and philosophical instruction, they had regular discourse on a great many things.

"What do you think of the Greeks, Mullah?" asked Mehmet innocently.

"They were once a great race. In the Qur'an, we praise them highly for their intelligence and resourcefulness, but in the end, they will succumb to the will of Allah."

Mehmet smiled enigmatically.

The doors to his apartment opened and the young Greek strode in to greet his benefactor.

"Antonis!" exclaimed Mehmet, leaping off his chair to rush and greet the captain of his newest guard.

The Mullah sighed, still a boy, with his love of Antonis, an entity he couldn't reconcile himself to. It was possible he was a true believer, a zealous convert, or maybe there was a dark side to him, but only time would tell.

"And is this one of the intelligent resourceful Greeks our Holy Book was talking about?" Mehmet queried.

Antonis and Mullah Guwani nodded brief greetings to each other.

"Tell me, how is my new unit coming along?"

"Very well, your Magnificence. The men are forming into a cohesive unit and I have some able lieutenants to aid me."

"That's good, I will come and inspect you very soon. If they ever let me out of these lessons," grinned Mehmet.

Antonis returned the grin. "Lessons are important, my young Sultan," he paused. "I have a request, sir?"

"Yes, what?"

"Our tactics require a certain type of uniform to work effectively and I would be most grateful if the palace armourer could make some for the troops. I have the design so I would merely need to instruct them on what it entails."

"Of course, it will be done. What is the design?" asked a curious Mehmet.

"It will incorporate overlapping fish scale armour for lightness and maximum movement."

"What about helmets and weapons?" countered the boy.

"We will use the traditional spiked helmet with chain-link protection for the neck. As for weapons, the compound bow will be standard. Though, I will allow the men to choose their own blades. Soldiers can be very precocious about things like that."

Mehmet laughed, "I look forward to seeing the new unit."

Antonis nodded.

"Also, we must have some more of our talks again, as we did a few months ago."

Antonis smiled imperceptibly.

With his robes trailing on the ground, the surprisingly diminutive Mullah waddled over to his pupil to bid leave of him. The avuncular look turned to undisguised animosity as his gaze caught an approaching slim elegant man.

The young ruler turned to see what had made his teacher's face turn so. Candarli Halil Pasha was undoubtedly a brilliant politician and ruthless, but his inconsistency always put everyone around him on tenterhooks. The mullah hated him passionately.

"Your Majesty."

"Candarli Pasha, good morning," replied Mehmet. He had no such misgivings, the man was his father's most trusted person, the now retired Murad II.

"There are some documents that require your signature, sire."

"Of course, what are they regarding?"

"Nothing to interest you too much, general administration for the building of Alms houses for the poor," replied the Vizier offhandedly.

The Mullah bristled at his condescension.

Mehmet didn't notice and put out his hand to receive them. The young ruler did not sign immediately; instead choosing to read what he was putting his name to.

The Mullah smiled, now that was a good trait in a Sultan.

As Mehmet read the documents arranged before him, he looked up at Antonis. "We shall come visit you the day after tomorrow, and then we can have one of our chats afterwards."

"That would be a pleasure, sir," replied a relieved Antonis.

It was the Vizier's turn to bristle internally. This young Greek was an unknown quantity and he couldn't discern a way to control him. This made Antonis dangerous. It would take some time, he thought, but he would find his vulnerability. He would see reason, or be crushed, a necessity for the coming events.

Mehmet resumed his reading then began signing the documents before him. "I want to be informed when they are completed, as I want to visit them," he said as he finished the last signature.

"Of course, your Magnificence."

Mehmet looked up and bore through his First Minister, holding the stare for more than a minute in complete silence. "When are they due to be opened?"

The Vizier had a look of surprise at the boy's attention to details, "I'm not sure."

"Well, find out, and report it to me on our next briefing," came the assured response from the fourteen-year-old.

Candarli Pasha acknowledged the order, making him more positive of his decision. The news his spies had sent him of the resurgent Greeks in the Morea along with a down but not broken Hunyadi, filled him with worry. Additionally, Skander-berg had resumed his campaign in the northern mountains, and he was nigh on impossible to beat. The possibility of the three antagonists joining forces was all too real, and this boy king did not have the strength or experience to handle it.

ANTONIS FELT FLUSHED after a most productive day, Mehmet's inspection was a resounding success and the chat with him afterwards was good, though, it did not seem like the right time to suggest his idea yet.

The sight of Halil waiting for him upon his return, filled him with slight concern. Fatima, resplendent in a shimmering pale blue silk robe, her luscious black hair pulled back by a long plait, had the old smuggler totally enthralled in their discourse.

"Ah, my young Achilles, I have been wonderfully entertained by Fatima. Such a keen mind and so knowledgeable," said Halil, rising to greet his former ward.

"A pleasure to see you again, my friend, what is it that brings you here? A social visit by chance?" replied Antonis, dismissing the slight pangs of jealousy he felt from seeing another man chatting and laughing with his woman.

"I have some news from your benefactor."

Antonis' mood changed sharply. Knowing the old man talked in riddles, he clearly had something of importance to say and privacy was unquestioned. He sighed, for all he desired was to make love to the fiery woman by Halil's side.

"Well, gentlemen, I think it's time I took my leave as the day has been long," interjected Fatima.

As soon as she left the room, Halil's face turned conspir-atorial.

"How is Giorgos? Still as mad as ever?" asked Antonis.

"He is doing well and sends his best."

The Greek knew this was small talk before the real message. "Send him my best, and that I hope to see him."

"He asked if you remember your walks amongst the gardens with him?" continued Halil.

Antonis looked quizzical for a moment, as it was with his present guest he had that talk, not Giorgos. "Yes, why?"

Halil lowered his tone even more so Antonis had to strain to hear. "Because what you discussed is about to happen and you, my boy, have a choice to make."

The news was momentous. How Halil got his information he did not know but he knew it was accurate. He rubbed his hand across his chin as his brows furrowed in thought.

"Don't think upon it too long because this is imminent," added Halil, reading his mind.

"I will have a decision within two days," replied Antonis.

Halil murmured his approval, knowing the Greek would make the right one.

2 2

GREEK CONFIDENCE

Nicola listened intently as the argument raged. Each of the men raised their voices a fraction in turn to talk, though, they did not cut the other off as they laid out their reasoning to the gathered nobles.

They had been in Athens close to four months now, planning the next part of their campaign. Alexis rose to his full height as he impassioned with Constantine for caution. The General's shoulders were set back straight, his bulk blocking Constantine from Nicola's view.

"This is going to be interesting," said Thanos, who was nonchalantly eating grapes while observing the proceedings.

Nicola casually looked at his colleague, his dry observations never ceasing to intrigue. For his part, he was uncertain where to place his opinions, knowing Alexis would not recommend caution unless he had good reason, but his heart went out to the idea of recapturing central Greece. As the voices battled to win their minds, he turned to stare through the columns of the Parthenon and gazed out to the city below.

The cross streets of Athens cut the slopes and valley with the brown and white scabs of houses and workshops filling the spaces between. The wind had picked up and the smell of the city's cooking wafted into the high vaulted temple of Athena. His thoughts turned to his brother, wondering how he was faring amongst the Turk, with no doubt in his mind that he was doing well. Antonis' keen intellect and utter ruthlessness would see to that. Would fate decide if they were to meet again? Even after all that had ensued, he couldn't help but miss him.

He mulled over the events of the past two years and wondered what he could have done differently. Plethon and Gregorios had always taught them that a man was responsible for his actions, yet he could not help but feel that he had been ignorant of his brother's feelings since the incident with the bandits. He had been fêted as the warrior, his brother over-looked, and the pursuit of Katerina had produced troublesome results. Sadness welled up inside. Shouting men snapped him out of his daydream.

"Attacking a Latin Dukedom is one thing but to take on the might of the Turk without support from Skanderbeg is suicide," repeated Alexis for the third time. "I have very reliable information that the Ottomans will be ready to move if we enter their territory."

"Their territory? It is Greek land! We are reuniting with our brothers," exclaimed Constantine.

"I understand, sire, but let us get confirmation of Skander-beg's support before we push on through. That is all I am suggesting," countered Alexis.

Thanos tapped Nicola lightly on the shoulder, "great enter-tainment, don't you think?" Then picking up a goblet of wine, "this is thirsty work," he smacked his lips, and turned back to the performers.

Alexis was trying his best to keep his cool in the face of such stubborn resistance to the information he was sharing. All correspondence he had received from Katerina pointed to there being no co-ordination between the different Christian forces.

The events at Varna had showed the courage and strength of the Turk and this meagre force was no match for what they would confront. He lamented the ease with which they had recaptured Athens as it had given Constantine a false sense of their abilities. There was no use in trying to change his mind, all he could hope for was minimising the danger to the troops. "Sir, we need to corroborate that Skanderbeg will attack from his mountain stronghold and we as yet, have not had verification on that," he implored.

"Very well, we shall wait for another two weeks for a response, but in the meantime, we shall prepare the army to move on Larissa," replied Constantine, rubbing his creased forehead, "Time for lunch."

Thanos sighed, "I think the Despot just edged that, so we have two weeks until we move again. Time to delight in some of these Athenian ladies, as we don't know what Larissa will bring. Fancy joining me?"

Nicola shook his head and made excuses about seeing to his men, when in fact he did not want to sully the emotions he had for Katerina by carousing with a whore or two.

"Very well, your loss," said Thanos, and left the palace for the taverns below.

THE SEALED LETTERS lay on the pitted wooden table, the owl signs embossed in the red shiny wax staring out at him. He had a sense of foreboding with the simultaneous arrival of the missives. Belpia Elpis was not given to hyperbole when corresponding information. At least there was a two-week reprieve until any decision was made but he knew he could not hold Constantine indefinitely. His thoughts were interrupted by a loud knock on the door.

Thanos ambled in and flopped into the free chair. Tugging at his beard, he looked at the stress showing on his friend's face.

"Come on, Lexon, it's not that bad. We have Athens, they can field over one thousand cavalrymen alone, and coffers full of gold. What's more, there is a lot better entertainment here than Mistras."

Alexis smiled humourlessly; his friend could always be counted upon to make light of a situation whilst stating facts.

"What is worrying you?" continued Thanos.

"These," replied Alexis pointing to the three letters.

His old friend's gaze rested on the neatly ordered embossed owls staring at him. "You haven't even opened them; how can you possibly know what they contain?"

With a sigh, Sartis reached out and picked up the first letter. Ripping open the seal, he perused the short message and put down the paper. He repeated this action twice more, then sat back to digest what he had just read.

Thanos leaned over, picked up the missives, and eagerly scanned them. Finishing the last, he turned to his friend. "This is excellent news! Skanderbeg is in, the Turks are in disarray, and the city of Larissa is awaiting our arrival to revolt. What is there to be worried about now?"

"It just feels too easy, that's all," stated Alexis.

Thanos understood that old soldier's gut instinct and had learned to his detriment not to ignore it. "So, what are you going to do?"

Alexis pushed his lips into a thin line and clicked his tongue to the roof of his mouth. "Are your boats ready to sail?"

"Yes."

"Good, let me think on this information for a few days, and tell no-one of our conversation."

Thanos shot him an exasperated look, as if he needed reminding.

"By the way, how is Nicola doing? I haven't had a chance to speak with him recently."

"Pines for his girl too much and refuses my offers of diversion. Otherwise he's doing fine."

"Yes, well, we are not all cut from the same cloth, Thanos."

"Life would be boring if we were," he countered as he took his leave.

Once alone, Alexis sat at his desk deep in trance-like thoughts as he pondered how to overcome the gnawing feeling inside. Then furiously wrote his response to the letters and sealed them with his Lambda. Calling his servant, he gave instructions to deliver the letter to the Laconians' messenger rider, who would know what to do with it. Satisfied that was all that could be done for the moment, he poured himself a goblet of wine, and walked outside to survey the evening bustle of the freed city below.

KATERINA POURED over the information in front of her, the candle barely giving out enough light to be able to read it. Her eyes stung and she could feel the welling of pain inside her head. She glanced at the tips of her index finger and thumb black with ink. How that would have bothered her in her previous life.

Quickly, she returned to the task at hand; letters from their controls in Edirne; detailing the fury of the Turks over the Greek's recapture of Athens. The hawks were screaming for a lesson to be taught to them, few were counselling caution. Missives from Skanderbeg's domain showing his vacillation over joining forces, after he had agreed to do so. The information arrived just after sending the positive details to Alexis. She hoped the new information reached him in time. Her mind went to Nicola, she had promised that she would write, and include it in the next dispatch, which would leave before dawn.

. . .

ALEXIS CLIMBED the deep steps of the Parthenon. Casually, he wondered if ancient Athenians had been giants to build it in this manner, or simply the conceit of rulers who wanted it stamped this way for time immemorial? The nagging feeling had still not gone but he decided to bury it, hoping it was not a decision he would regret. Everyone was present as he entered unusually late, even some of the junior captains, Nicola among them.

"General, I am glad you could make it."

The patronising tone piqued Alexis' already fragile mood. Constantine went back to detailing the next part of the campaign. All were listening intently.

Nicola looked over to the new entrant with the harried look on the usually sardonic face. He was no longer a boy but a man with responsibilities to attend to and it left little time for conversations with Alexis. The huge vaulted space inside the Parthenon felt claustrophobic and he wished for his previous life.

A cheer went up as they finished the briefing, zeal re-ignited amongst the commanders. Even the Duke of Athens seemed pleased with it, though why he should, God only knew, mused Nicola. As the captains were leaving, Alexis asked him to remain behind.

"So, General, have we had any news on the disposition of our northern brothers?" asked an ebullient Constantine.

"Yes, we have, sir," came the curt response.

"Well, what do they say?"

"It seems they will aid us in our venture."

"And what of the Turks?"

"The information I have says they are not going to retaliate anytime soon."

"Excellent, we shall prepare to move the day after tomorrow, there is no time to waste."

Alexis knew he could not argue the point here; it was on his information they were acting.

Constantine's energy doubled and he buzzed around giving directives.

With a flick of his hand, Alexis summoned Nicola, who was silently waiting for him to do so. Their eyes met on the same level and Alexis was shocked that he had missed the final part of Nicola's rite of passage into manhood. "How are your men doing?" he asked.

"Well, sir," came the response, though Nicola knew this was not the reason for him being summoned.

"Themis is a good man to have as your sergeant?"

"Yes, sir, he is."

"I want you to prepare your men as I may call upon you to undertake a little mission for me. Keep it quiet and be ready to move with half a day's notice. Is that clear?"

"Yes, sir, what is this all about?"

"I will tell you nearer the time, just make sure they are ready."

Nicola nodded and walked away, confused at his commander's request. Dutifully, the young captain returned to his troops and instructed Themis to have the men prepared and equipped for one week's travel. Who, in turn, quickly set about instructing them. Nicola noticed how his sergeant never raised his voice, yet always had the utter obedience of those he ordered. Satisfied, he retired to write the letter to his beloved that he had been meaning to do for some time.

There was a curiously muted mood as the army prepared to leave. The gaudy pennants of the Italian knights that now swelled their ranks fluttered in the strong early morning breeze. Constantine had left a small detachment to safeguard the city, though, it was purely symbolic.

Nicola, placed at the rear of the column, watched as the neat rows of men, horse, and machine snaked its way through the valleys of northern Attica. The strong sun and arid summer had left the hills parched and the brown hues made the brightly coloured pennants stand out even more. He knew he had a long wait until his troops moved and sat in idle daydream wondering what Katerina was up to, probably at morning prayers. It was still strange that she was a nun, yet, he was grateful that she had chosen that and not followed her father's orders to marry the suitor of his choosing and vowed once more that he would make good on that promise. A yearning welled up inside him to feel her in his arms again and the sweet floral scent of her skin came flooding into his pleasant daydream.

CONSTANTINE SET A VERY fast pace and the army reached the plains of central Greece within a day. As they prepared to camp for the night, he sent out a messenger to inform the people of Larissa that their salvation was due in two days and to be prepared to rise up against their occupiers.

By the time Nicola brought up the rear, the plain was dotted with campfires and the smell of roasting meat wafted toward him. The mood was jovial, as the Greeks were experiencing success for the first time in years. Decades of defeat had imbued them with a subconscious acceptance that things would not go their way. In the space of a few months Constantine had changed all that. After attending to his men, he joined the rest of the junior captains in the commander's tent.

The tall elegant figure dressed in black, held court, "We will arrive at the city by tomorrow evening and we shall array ourselves along the Southern and Eastern sides of the citadel."

One of the infantry captains raised his hand. "Why don't we surround it, sire?"

"Good question. First, we do not have enough troops, and second, the city lies on a hill. We could not hope to attack that side. We shall, however, leave a small force there to prevent any of the Turks from escaping."

The rest of the briefing went through with ease and even

Alexis was starting to feel confident about this campaign. Realizing it was useless to worry about something he could not control, he decided to enjoy the evening and prepare for their arrival at the city the next morning.

THE THREE RIDERS felt fatigued and their commander decided that after the last hill, they would return to rest their horses and fill their bellies. So it was with vacant minds set on returning home that they rode over the lip of the small range of hills that bordered the plain. Their jaws dropped open aghast. Hurriedly, they took an approximate count of the fires they could see and assumed five men per fire. The three conferred their estimated numbers and all being close to each other, plumped for the middle figure. Azad knew the city could never withstand the onslaught of more than twelve thousand men, so where had the Greeks found that many? Wasting no time, they rode back to the city to deliver the bad news.

Kerim Bey stood ashen-faced as he received his scouts' information, his stubby fingers wringing themselves as he knew he was in a no-win situation. To lose the city meant his head and there was no chance his meagre force could withstand what was arrayed against them for long. His mind spun in thought, beads of sweat appearing on his pasty brow. He would need to hold out for at least two weeks, but there were not enough provisions to feed the populace. In any event, he certainly could not trust the Greeks who resided within the walls.

He looked around the great hall, cursing the Byzantines who built the city some four centuries earlier. Then he cursed the old Sultan, for giving it to him, and finally cursed himself for having taken it. Resigning himself to his fate, he set about making the best of the situation. Messages were sent to Edirne and the city Garrison was put on full alert. All provisions were hurriedly pulled into the city, soldiers, and populace worked equally through the night, taking what they could.

It was with a strange feeling that Alexis crossed the ravine that marked the border of Thessaly from the south. He had not returned home in over thirty years. His mother had long since passed and without siblings there was nothing left for him here; it was just another territory to reincorporate into the Empire Yet, along the road to the citadel, he found himself looking out for familiar landmarks or buildings. He smiled as he lost himself in childhood memories. Thanos, riding next to him, saw the change of mood in his old friend. "Strange to come back to the place of your birth, Lexon?"

"Well, I was actually born north of the city. But, yes, it is a little," he replied.

"Should have figured you for a country boy, It's that bumpkin grin of yours."

Alexis laughed, "Aye, that it is."

The two men fell back into their silent thoughts as the invading host inched closer to its destination.

The sun was well past its apex as the city-watch saw the beginnings of the army come into view, but the dust trampled up by horse and men had heralded their arrival long before. However, the realities of gleaming spears and fluttering pennants made the young Turk gulp before he sounded the alarm. Soon, bells were clanging all around the city.

Kerim Bey was having his afternoon tea and pastries as the cacophony emanated throughout. He finished his repast in utter calmness with the fatalism of a condemned man before climbing onto the walls to gaze upon his impending doom. He had sent messengers to Edirne as soon as he learned of the invading force, and looking along the walls, saw that every able-bodied man was at the ready. The food provisions had been stored as best as possible. Satisfied he had done everything, given the circumstances, he retired to his residence to prepare for the next phase.

Constantine was in his tent reading letters and issuing missives. The large oil lamps on the stands blurring out a bright smoky light, the strong smell of burning olive oil filling the canvas structure. The guards at the open entrance parted as Alexis entered.

"Strategos," he said without stopping at his administration.

"Sir, I have some worrisome news."

Constantine put down his quill and looked up. His General had been unusually agitated during this campaign, fretting about the whole venture. He nodded for him to carry on.

"I have news that Skanderbeg has decided to remain in his mountain stronghold in the event of Turkish reprisals."

"Well, whatever the Turks do, we have at least two weeks to capture the city. We need to finish this rapidly and prepare for their response. We knew this would come."

"What about Skanderbeg?"

"As soon as we have the city, take your Laconians north, and persuade him to join the fight."

"In anticipation, I prepared some of my men for this under the command of Nicola Vevellis."

The Despot shook his head. "No, I want you to command, it requires an experienced leader. Talented as Vevellis is, he is too young. Also, the full brigade will be more persuasive."

"But what about defending here?"

"There are enough men, and more are flocking to our cause daily. You will be of more use in the North."

"Understood, sir," he did a quick mental calculation of the transfer of six hundred men and horses. One of Thanos' ships was still at sea and the other two could only carry two hundred and twenty each, at most. The land route it would be.

"And remember, we always have the Hexamilion to fall back to," added Constantine with a confident smile.

His faith in that six-mile stretch of stone will be his undoing. At least he wouldn't be there to witness it and twinges of guilt entered his conscience.

The Bey was in deep sleep when the first clash of steel occurred. Initially, he thought the Greeks had started their assault, however, he soon realised that the commotion was from inside the city. The sun was breaking over the horizon as in horror, he watched the armed citizens of Larissa making a concerted effort to break open the gate to their liberators outside. The outnumbered and unprepared sentries disintegrated under the onslaught. With a sense of detached observation, Kerim Bey saw the gaudily dressed Ottomans being rhythmically devoured by an amorphous mass of shabby town dwellers. Two huge Greeks with long straggly beards, wielding clubs, made it to the gate, and with a heave lifted the crossbar. He cursed his luck yet again and gripping his scimitar with sweaty palms prepared to greet what came through the now open portal. As he saw the double-headed eagle banners enter, his last thought was for his family and hoped that they would be spared in the aftermath.

23

PRINCE MEHMET

Candarli Pasha's lips trembled as he stood a full two minutes in silence as he tried to make order of his emotions. The news that Larissa had fallen in just two days was too much to bear but a man who prided himself on self-control, was not about to break it now. Assembled in his palace chamber were the leading heads of the old Aristocratic families, who between them commanded over two-thirds of the army. He had called them there for a very specific purpose; treason. Though, he did not see it that way.

Carefully, he spoke about the need for an experienced ruler in this time of unrest, reminding them how a generation ago the empire almost collapsed. At pains to state that this was temporary, he laid out his reasoned argument for deposing the young Sultan and bringing back Murad from retirement. One by one the fifteen men gave their assent to his plan as each remembered the chaos that ensued all those years ago. With their pact sealed, the Grand Vizier put his plan into action, and prepared to confront the young Mehmet with the news.

Antonis started to believe Halil was misinformed. Nothing had occurred in weeks and soon he had relaxed into his daily routine of training with his men and the weekly chats with Mehmet. It wouldn't be long now until his 'Thracians', as he decided to call them, would be ready for the field. Still he had not broached the subject of his idea to Mehmet, but there was plenty of time for that.

His uncontrolled anger had subsided into a cold hatred, he just hoped his brother was still alive to appreciate what he was about to do. A flicker of pleasant childhood memories from Crete entered his mind, giving him a pang of sadness, which he quickly dismissed. *We've made our choices.* Reminiscing was for the foolish and weak.

A palace messenger approached with a request for his immediate presence at Mehmet's throne room. Thinking nothing of it, he accompanied the man to the palace. As he walked towards the building, he noticed a different set of guards at the gate; the hair on the back of his neck tingled. With trepidation, he approached the throne room, wondering from which corner the assassin's dagger would come but the guards pulled their spears aside and he walked into the nerve-centre of the Empire.

Candarli Pasha smiled as he saw Antonis enter, the only person who could have been a fly in the ointment but was now safely within his control. A forlorn-looking Mehmet sat upon his throne, surrounded by the greater part of the Turkish Aristocracy. The Vizier stood in the heart of them with a proclamation sheet. Behind the throne and to the right stood the glowering Mullahs, Guwani and Aks Semseddin, their impotence making their scowls fiercer.

There were still more captains of the palace troops due to arrive and thus Antonis waited. He glanced over to Mehmet, trying to catch his eye but the boy king merely looked straight ahead.

Holding his paper and his horsetail whip, the Vizier addressed the gathered audience. "You who are gathered here do not yet know, but the Greeks have recaptured Larissa, and are now in complete control of the Thessaly region." He raised his hand to quieten the gathering. "Given that we still have the Hungarians to the north, we must crush this insurrection before it gains pace and becomes permanent."

Murmurs of agreement emanated from the gathering.

"In our time of need, we require a strong and experienced leader to command the army. So it is with great reluctance that we, as the clan chiefs, request the reinstatement of Murad as Sultan. This time, until his death, or the insurrection has been crushed in its entirety. We have spoken with the young Sultan and he agrees to stand down in the face of this threat."

Mehmet was furious but presently powerless, he vowed to teach the Vizier a lesson when he was able to do so in the future.

The speaker continued, oblivious in his triumph of the enemy he had created. "During this time, Prince Mehmet will continue his studies under the guidance of the Mullahs, and myself in Nicaea. Sultan Murad has agreed to lead the army and will be returning within the week."

Antonis noticed the slightest of flinches in Mehmet as he was called by his new demoted title of prince. His own head spun at this turn of events, and he wondered where it would leave him. Undoubtedly, the Vizier would be quick to inform him of his choices.

A court herald informed all the captains present they would be seeing the Vizier to receive their new orders and whilst waiting for his turn, the Greek played out his options. He desperately wanted to prove his men in battle, and he was sure Nicola was among the Byzantines. He relished the chance for them to meet again but Halil's words kept ringing in his ears about strategy. Finally, his turn came, and he was shown in to see the Vizier.

The elegant figure was waiting to greet him with glazed reptilian eyes, betraying nothing. "Captain Vevellis, we have given some thought to your situation and have decided to keep you stationed in Edirne under the command of the war council."

Antonis paused before responding. "Candarli Pasha, I respectfully request another assignment."

A look of surprise registered in the Vizier's rising eyebrow. "What is that?"

"My sponsor was the Sultan Mehmet and I would like to repay that generosity by serving him and being stationed where he is. Furthermore, my troops still need more training until they are ready to fight in the field." Antonis knew this to be false but hoped it would swing the Regent's decision.

Candarli wondered what was behind this, as the Greek opposite him was too calculating to make decisions based on loyalty. However, it did not matter, as he would be out of the way. "Very well, you shall join Prince Mehmet in Nicaea. You do understand that this had to be done for the good of the Empire?"

Antonis looked at the Vizier, beneath all his finery and jewels he truly believed he was doing the right thing, but he had signed his death warrant, for Mehmet would never forgive this slight. As he left the chamber, he did not notice a servant blending seamlessly into the background. The innocuous man made a mental note to enter what had transpired in his next report. The monk always paid well for extra titbits of information.

THE ARMOUR FELT heavy on Murad's shoulders as he rode into the capital with his personal guard. It was with great reluctance he came out of retirement but the impassioned plea of the Vizier, with the support of the clan chiefs, was too strong to ignore, and he had not strived his whole life to see his empire collapse into civil war. His mind went to Mehmet, certain he was livid with the circumstances. His first task would be to calm the boy and reassure him this was only for a year, or two at most. Indeed, he had no wish to remain Sultan for the rest of his life, much preferring his library and gardens in his Nicaean palace to the court intrigues and power politics of Edirne.

What was the point of ultimate power unless you could enjoy its fruits? But presently, he had to set about crushing this invasion and put Constantine in his place. The portly ruler dismounted and ruefully thought that he had not expected to return to this place so soon.

"Welcome back, your Magnificence." Candarli Pasha greeted his old master.

"Where is my son?"

"He is in his quarters."

"Good, inform him of my arrival and that I want to see him this evening."

"Yes, your Magnificence."

The Sultan nodded his head and headed towards his rooms without another word, leaving a perplexed and slightly concerned Vizier standing there.

The fresh scent of jasmine filled the Sultan's senses, making him feel cleansed and refreshed. He had donned his favoured silk gown with pantaloons beneath, and the slippers felt soft on his feet as he walked towards his son, who was eating some of the dates that had been put out.

Mehmet watched intently as his father approached, they had never had a close relationship, and what little common ground they had was being put to the test.

Murad felt was unsure how to proceed with the boy, deciding to appeal to his logic rather than appease his bruised ego. "Do you understand why the nobles did this?"

"Because they don't trust me, or think I am unable to rule," Mehmet replied.

"In part, but mostly out of fear," replied his father in soothing tones.

Mehmet eyes widened in surprise, "What do you mean?"

"People are weak and driven by fear and greed. The nobles are panicked this invasion will turn into a rout and they will lose their lands and power. What they fail to appreciate is that we are strong and cohesive, and this is but a blip, but in their panic, they have turned to someone they know to lead them."

Mehmet said nothing.

"We Sultans have always held onto our power because of the support of the clan chiefs. It has been this way since our nomadic days. To ignore that is to invite dissention and civil war, for they control their own troops."

In that moment Mehmet decided that he would alter the way the army was structured as soon as he had the chance, but resigned to his fate, changed tack. "What are you planning to do with the Greeks?" he asked.

His father shot him an exasperated look. "They are a constant thorn in my side; however, I have committed to peace as long as I live. So, I will recapture our land and then invade the Morea."

"You will conquer it?"

"No, I will just raze a few villages and sack one of their cities, to teach them a lesson. Have Constantine sue for peace and then pay what meagre tribute he can."

"Then?"

"After that, I will go home to my garden and library in Nicaea."

Mehmet considered how different he was to his father. Murad had no tangible ambitions except his learning and horticulture, whereas he felt he was destined for greatness.

The old sultan could see the young mind at work and thought it best to offer his advice. "Continue with your studies and you will soon be Sultan again, and when that time comes, you will be better prepared."

Looking at the boy—whom he had never wanted to become Sultan but had no choice with the death of his brother during a riding accident—he shuddered involuntarily. His mother was a beautiful Greek slave girl, who produced this effeminate child; too much of her had gone into him. Yet, he saw fire behind those eyes and knew for the first time that Mehmet would be a powerful ruler. He only hoped he would be a just one, as he patted his son's shoulder in the most paternal way he could.

Antonis considered, this truly was the most bloodless of coups and had a grudging respect for the Vizier's handling of the situation. It had taken no more than a few days to prepare his men, a fact that pleased him for they were now becoming a cohesive force. When Mehmet discovered that Antonis had chosen to be by his side as opposed to staying in Edirne, he was truly grateful.

As the Greek stood in the throne room, he felt life was being repeated. Murad again sat upon the throne, Mehmet by his side, and the nobles and eunuchs vying for prominent positions. Yet, it was much different. He now commanded his own troop and his relationship with Mehmet was growing daily. He was truly in a position of power if he used it wisely.

Seeing the boy and his father on the Dais reminded him of his own family; it was a long time since he had thought of his father. His decision to come to the Turk had effectively cut all ties, for Andreas Vevellis would never forgive this betrayal. He wondered if he could have forgiven the branding. His mother would be more forgiving, but then, they always were.

Murad had spent a great deal of time pondering on how he would speak to the clan chiefs, who now stood before him. There was always his cousin Orhan, waiting in the wings to claim the throne, but the wily old ruler was not about to let that happen. "I am deeply honoured that you have asked me to lead the armies against the Greek threat," he scanned the room as he spoke his lie. What he truly wished was that they had never asked him, but now he had to make the best of the situation. "We shall deal with this swiftly and efficiently."

Shouts of 'Crush the Greeks' emanated from the back of the room.

"We shall not conquer their territory, as I promised peace during my lifetime," Murad added, quashing any mob mentality. "However, we will teach this leader of the Morea a lesson, so he never does it again." Cheers erupted from the gathered crowd. "I have one further thing to add, once this is dealt with, I shall retire again, and my son Mehmet will rule in my place and be OBEYED!" He then put out his hand and gestured for the young prince to join him, sending a clear message to all present, of his full intent.

The nobles raised a deep bellowing chant to their old Sultan. Mehmet looked on and wished they loved him as they did his father.

ALEXIS STOOD at the head of his men relieved, as they prepared to move northward. News had arrived of Murad's return to lead the army and he feared the worst at this news and knew the Laconians would be in a safer place with Skanderberg in the mountains. His guilt was not assuaged by the supreme confidence of Constantine, his faith in his men, and that ludicrous wall.

"Speedy journey, Strategos, and bring Skanderberg into the fray," said the Despot at their departure.

"I shall, sir," he replied.

Thanos watched as the Laconians left. Not given to superstition, he nonetheless had the strange feeling that he would not see his friend again. Dismissing it as foolish and sentimental worry, he lingered on a little longer as they rode into the distance before returning to his ships. As he walked towards the port, he chuckled, realising he would miss Nicola. Such wasted talent pining after a girl. Besides, he would see him soon as Alexis asked him to wait for his last carrack and then sail them up the Ionian coast to Epirus, from where it would be easy for them to join up. Thinking no more of his fears, he busily went about his tasks.

Relishing their recent successes, Nicola felt a twinge of sadness at departing. Riding north on some errand for Constantine, felt as if they were missing out on glory, no matter how important the mission. The saddlebags felt heavy next to his legs, laden with his prize money, from Athens and now Larissa. He almost had enough to ask for Katerina's hand in marriage. Dreamily, he thought of the large farm in Crete, with olive and citrus groves, knowing she would love it there. Doubting there would be much chance for any prize money in the Albanian mountains, a twinge of envy crept in regarding the remaining Byzantine forces, for their next objective was Thessaloniki, and that was a rich prize indeed.

KATERINA's initial reaction reading the letter was pleasure at hearing him doing well, quickly followed by concern at how much information he leaked. Nicola was open in his dislike of having to leave the main force on a nefarious diplomatic errand. Katerina smiled, that sort of mission would never sit well with his warrior spirit. She felt the urge to be enveloped by his masculine arms, the feeling of safety and completeness taking hold of her.

Glancing at the array of letters on her desk, she accepted that people depended on her and she couldn't simply leave the order. She put the conundrum aside, relishing the moment of warmth the letter brought, yet ever more determined to resolve it when the time came, and resumed her correspondence from one of the monks in Edirne. As she read its contents, her eyes widened, it was the first news of Antonis' activities in months and judging by this, he was now at the centre of power. Strangely, she felt detached from the discovery and glanced at the pile of other missives to plough through. Wasting no time, she drafted a letter to Alexis. He had requested to be kept informed of anything to do with Antonis, if it materialised. Three letters more, and then she hurried to attend evening prayer reflecting on how different life now was.

FATIMA HAD NEVER BEEN HAPPIER EVEN as the carriage rattled down the narrow road, dust welled-up, and crept through the thick blue curtain, covering the passenger and everything inside with a fine sheen of powder. Antonis' self-imposed exile along with his prince was a stroke of genius. Mehmet would not forget this act of loyalty. When he revealed his decision, she had made love to him with extra passion.

Peering out of the curtain, she saw her lover riding ahead of the column, his posture rigid and demeanour dark. She knew he desperately wanted to join with Murad in attacking the Greeks, as the fires burned strong within to prove himself. Riding next to him was Mehmet, another frustrated traveller on this journey. The two were in conversation as they approached the harbour opposite Gallipoli. Fatima strained her ears, but the noise of the horses prevented her catching anything clearly. Resigning herself, she sat back in the carriage, in contemplation of life in Nicaea.

The retinue looked splendid in their shiny new uniforms, their polished armour glistening in the afternoon sun. The pennants of a white crescent and star on a bright red background fluttered merrily in the wind as the procession wound its way down the hill to the port below. Mehmet elected only for Antonis and his chosen men as escort for him and the

Mullahs Guwani and Akshamsaddin. The young prince was grateful for the loyalty the Greek had shown and vowed to place him highly in the new order he would create.

Looking down, Antonis saw two carracks waiting in the port and noticed they flew the personal ensign of Murad; they were going in the Sultan's ships. There was much commotion in the port, ropes carelessly strewn about, barrels of dried fish, and spices being stacked on the side.

"This is my father's personal port, no other ships may dock here except the Sultan's," he said and pointed to the royal ensign. "That is why it doesn't have the usual dregs floating about."

Antonis acknowledged and set about getting his men on board, ordering Goran and Ahmed to split them evenly. He could see the land in the distance, so it would be a ferry ride at best, and with luck, they could be at Nicaea at sundown. Glancing over, he saw Mehmet's look of repugnance as he scanned the horizon towards his exile. "It won't be that bad, sire," he said, trying to soothe the boy. But he also knew how it felt to be rejected and the anger and venom that could fester from it.

"It is a jail sentence," replied the forlorn prince.

"Then we should use this time to plan," countered the Greek.

"Plan what?" Mehmet asked.

"Your destiny."

The boy snorted his disbelief but was curious as to Antonis' meaning. But before he could utter anything further, the two Mullahs had disembarked and were approaching their pupil.

Antonis turned his attention back to his men, satisfied he had planted the seed of his plan.

THE PALACE in Nicaea shone like a beacon of Byzantine light, the previous Sultans had left its fusion of Roman and early

Christian grandeur untouched. It was here amongst the beauty of the low-slung domes upon perfect marbled walls, where the first council had met some eleven hundred years before, endeavouring to define what Christianity was to be. Antonis laughed to himself at the contrived nature of it all.

Fatima loved the palace the moment she laid eyes on it; the sheer opulence taking her breath away. It felt as though she were in the bathing quarters back in Edirne but without the vagaries of duties. Antonis took one of the diplomatic guest apartments as close to his men as possible but very much within the sphere of Mehmet's realm. It suited her perfectly. As the trunks arrived, she busied herself settling into her new home, humming melodically, and for the first time since she had been taken from her village, she truly felt happy.

24

CONSTANTINE'S FOLLY

*E*xhaustion was clear on the men as they marched in the midday sun. The demons of defeat had returned. Constantine paid it no attention, only focusing on getting his army to safety at the Hexamilion before the Turks caught them. Humourlessly, he contemplated the fickleness of the fortunes of war. They had reached the walls of Thessaloniki and were preparing to lay siege when the Ottomans under Murad appeared in full force. The anticipated support of Skanderberg didn't materialise, and in the face of overwhelming odds, the Greeks were forced to retreat.

Now, all that was left was the wall, and safety behind its thick stones. These last two years, Constantine had rebuilt and improved its defences, sure it could withstand anything that was thrown against it and he had enough men to defend its entire length. Looking back, he could see the dust clouds of the enemy billowing on the horizon and encouraged his men to greater speed with the hope of the wall and protection.

Murad gave orders to execute on sight anyone suspected of being involved with the invading force, and his guards obeyed with their customary zeal. Concerned that he could be trapped in a pincer movement from the north, the Sultan drove his men relentlessly. He wanted this concluded swiftly, his back ached, and his hips were sore from too long in the saddle. The dusty smells were too much to bear and he longed for the sweet scents of his gardens and their calming fountains. It was with relief when he realised the Albanians had deferred their attack and the Greeks would retreat behind Constantine's wall, relishing the surprise he had in store for him.

ANTONIS STORMED INTO THE ROOM, his face a heavy cloud, and the blue orbs blazing with anger. Fatima sat bolt upright in a reflex action as he entered and found herself wondering what had happened.

"I knew it was a mistake not to stay in Edirne," he muttered to himself.

"What has happened now?" she enquired as she stood to calm him with her touch.

"Murad caught Constantine unprepared approaching Salonika and has been chasing him south ever since. I will now miss the chance for glory, and most likely meeting Nicola in battle." He landed on a sofa with a thump, overacting, in the hope his lover would shower him with concerned attention, which she duly obliged.

Fatima stroked the curly black locks that had grown since his conversion to Islam. She nuzzled his neck and he was awash with pleasure, marvelling at the instant effect she had on him, her sweet musky scent encircling him in this most feminine of incarcerations that he willingly accepted. Running her hand down his perfect abdomen her fingers felt the hilt of his beloved sfakion. "You seem very keen to see your brother again. Yet you chose to leave," she asked innocently.

"He is not my brother," he snapped.

"But why do you want to meet with Nicola?" she corrected herself.

He wavered for a moment, biting his cheeks in thought. Putting his arm around her, he was aware how he had grown accustomed to her presence, yet, was under no illusions as to their mutual need of each other.

Sensing his indecision, she pressed, "What happened in Constantinople?"

"All right!" he said angrily, rising suddenly, and brushing her aside. Pacing around the room, he gradually collected his thoughts before commencing the tale. Sparing no detail, he recounted from the bandits, to meeting Katerina, and the feelings of jealousy that welled-up, culminating in their divergence of where their future lay, and finally the battle and its aftermath.

His lover listened transfixed; pitying his insecurity, reviling his pettiness, fearing his anger, and admiring his courage of conviction, however distorted it might be.

The catharsis was imperceptible at first, but the relief at voicing it all took hold. It did not change his opinion, merely made it less emotional.

Fatima was at a loss for words. Whilst understanding his pain, she couldn't fathom why it had engendered such an extreme reaction within him to turn his back on everything he knew and cared for, over a girl. It was stupidity, especially in one so intelligent. The silence became uncomfortable and she needed to break it. "Do you hate Nicola?" It sounded inane as it came out of her mouth and she dreaded the reaction.

Antonis responded matter-of-factly. "No, I don't hate him. I just want to show that I was right, and his betrayal will be punished." As he spoke, he realised that was no longer what drove him. He had made his decision out of a desire to succeed and joining the strongest power was logical. Katerina was the catalyst, Nicola the enabler, and his benefactor made the choice clearer.

Giorgos' words on the boat came flooding back, "Power or the poutana."

He smiled, for now he could see clearly. He was in a position beyond his wildest hopes, as the potential power behind the throne. Never more certain was he of his decision and if he could in the process exact his revenge for the betrayal on Nicola and his whore, then that would be an even sweeter bonus.

The calm that washed over him as he stood there contemplating the future, filled Fatima with an indescribable dread, that his overpowering desire for vengeance would be his undoing. "But you have everything you want now, there is no point in seeking retribution," the fear evident in her voice.

His smile was cold as he placed his hand on his hips and said resolutely. "It is only the beginning; revenge is but a small part of it all."

A WHITE PENNANT fluttered from the tip of the lance as the rider lowered it to strike into the straw-filled sack hanging from the thick-pitted wooden beam. Behind, another rider followed in his wake, but left it too late, thereby missing the target.

"Fucking Anatolians, great with a bow but useless with a lance," muttered the exasperated Croatian under his breath. Since being promoted to Lead Sergeant, he had taken on his role with gusto, driving the men to perfection in training. Firm but fair; he had earned their respect. "Right, you four, do it again, and make sure you all hit the target, or it's latrine duty," he shouted at them as they pulled their horses out for a second attempt. Some of the onlookers laughed.

A sense of purpose enveloped Antonis as he rode into the training ground. The flat dirt field was bordered by stables and barracks and was closed in by low-slung white-washed walls. The previous evening, he had suggested to Mehmet that he come train with his Thracians. The young prince happily jumped at the chance. It would be the first time they would engage in martial pursuits.

"Morning, sir," said Goran.

"How are the men doing today, Sergeant?"

"All right, but some of these Turks cannot seem to get a handle on using anything but a bow."

"Very well, keep them practising until they get it. We will be joined by Sultan Mehmet this morning, who wants to train with us," said Antonis to a surprised Goran, as he coached the hapless four to repeat their lance drills.

Mehmet was unsure which weapon to take to the training ground and decided on his bow—as it displayed his best ability —as well as a light scimitar blade that was tucked neatly into the red sash around his waist. He had cancelled his daily lessons with the Mullahs; which pleased Akshamsaddin , as he thought the young man did not practice the ways of war enough, though he consented with his usual solemn tone.

His nervousness was palpable as he approached the parade ground. The ruler-in-waiting he might be, but he was a boy entering a man's domain, in which he would need to prove himself, if he were to command them. As he neared the troops, he consciously straightened his back and squared his shoulders. At first, none noticed the elegantly dressed boy riding towards them but as one did, the others quickly followed suit and before long eighty pairs of eyes bored down on him before prostrating themselves to their Prince. He put on his mask of entitlement as his horse walked towards the waiting crowd. The taste of animal and leather seasoned with dust sat at the back of his throat, and the desire to flee rose inside, swiftly followed by the stronger urge not to show weakness. The chestnut mare ambled through the gate, carrying the slight figure. The two hundred yards between them may as well have been two hundred leagues, with the nervousness he felt.

Every inch the Sultan. "You honour us with your presence this fine morning, your Magnificence," Antonis said, walking his horse to meet him.

"I thought I would join you, to see how my newest unit is faring," replied Mehmet in his most regal tone. He liked how Antonis still used his title of Sultan.

"We are just finishing lance training and will be doing the bow next. May I see?" Antonis indicated towards Mehmet's weapon.

The young warrior obliged and handed it over.

The recurved bow was made of layered strips of alternating woods of different hardness, bound over time with resin then polished and smoothed until it appeared to be one piece. The balance was perfect, he then drew the string to his shoulder. It was truly a masterful weapon.

Taking his own quiver off his saddle, Antonis slipped it over his shoulder and with a quick turn and dig in the horse's flank, galloped towards the hanging dummy at full speed. He knocked the first arrow and drew the string back. At thirty yards, he released it, instantly reached for another, and quickly released it at twenty yards. He drew for a third time and released it at ten yards. Pulling the reins, the horse slowed its gallop and he turned and trotted back to where Mehmet stood.

There was a hushed silence across all those present.

Mehmet looked at the dummy, the Greek had placed three arrows in succession in an area the size of a man's heart; he couldn't hide the look of astonishment on his face. "How did you do that?"

"Would you like me to show you?"

The young prince nodded with eagerness. Antonis smiled.

Mehmet was flushed with exertion by the time they stopped for the afternoon, displaying the same voracious determination as when he was learning about Constantinople, though, improvement to his strength and stamina were needed, if he were to be able to perform well. "With an army of these I could conquer anything I wanted," he said, holding his bow.

"To what end?" replied Antonis.

"To expand the Empire and my power."

"To create a lasting legacy, is to achieve true greatness," countered the Greek in a calm voice.

"How do I do that?"

"To take the ultimate prize, the thorn in every Muslim heart for the last seven hundred years. Conquer the Red Apple."

"But no-one has ever succeeded in over a thousand years."

"That is why if you triumph, your legacy will last a thousand years too."

Mehmet fell silent and his adolescent imagination went into overdrive. Dreaming of the reverence and accolades he could receive, the true love and respect of the people, and clan chiefs.

So, it begins. The smell of the evening air had that extra piquant taste as he rode with the daydreaming prince back to his palace.

Looking out of the granite mouth of his winter lair and onto the snow-capped peaks sent Nicola into a deeper depression. The damp cold sliced through the leather soles of his boots; he clenched his toes to invigorate them but to no avail. For eight months they had been holed up here, eking a meagre existence, pinned in by the Ottoman forces of Ali Pasha.

Then news came of the near annihilation of Constantine's army at the Hexamilion. The wall in which he had placed so much faith, lasted less than three days against Murad's new cannon.

The stew pot bubbled away, and Nicola ladled some mutton onto his plate; it was unpleasant, but hunger drove him to consume two bowls. The sweet eager face of Katerina flashed in his mind. There had been no correspondence in five months.

How could there be? They were skipping between mountains with occasional forays down into the valleys.

"It's not that bad, sir, it will be spring soon and we can leave this place," said the sergeant in-between mouthfuls.

Nicola smiled weakly. It astonished him that all Themis wore was a simple tunic, with his only concession to the harsh winter a scarf wrapped around his neck. The long black hair, beard, and his generous layer of fat kept him warm like a bear in hibernation. "And not a moment too soon."

The rider glanced towards the summit and could not see any signs of life. He had never known such a harsh winter; almost April, and still no sign of the throes of spring. He was doubting that anyone was up there and began berating himself on wasting good coin in following these directions. This was the fourth valley they were travelling through and his patience was wearing thin, but orders were orders and he would carry on until he found them.

His helmet clattered against his chain mail armour, and he opted instead for a woollen cap to keep his head warm. Spying the small plateau above, he decided they would rest once reaching it. Approaching their destination, he felt a change in the wind's direction and with that, the faintest of odours reached him. At first, he thought it was wishful thinking but after a few moments, he was sure it was the scent of horses. Finally, they had found them. No doubt they were already under observation, for no-one that well-concealed would be lax in detecting intruders. Turning through the final twist of thorn bushes, onto a small plateau a dozen spears appeared through the scrubs surrounding them.

"Who are you?" demanded the tall handsome soldier with a long scar on the right side of his face.

"I am Janus Fekete, we bring news from John Hunyadi." Replied the rider to the strangely familiar soldier.

It took a moment before the scarred soldier ordered his men to lower their weapons. The Hungarian let out a sigh of relief.

After stabling the horses, the new arrivals were led up towards the summit. Curious eyes watched them as they passed. The Hungarians were impressed at the number of concealed men.

"What is your strength here?" asked Janus.

"We have approximately twelve hundred men and horses on the two slopes."

The Hungarian let out a slow whistle of respect as he was shown into the headquarters of the concealed army. Alexis stood with his back facing the new entrants, engrossed in oiling his sword. He tuned at the sound of footsteps.

"Strategos, may I present Janus Fekete, a messenger from Hunyadi."

"I thought I recognised the standard outside though I never suspected you would be here," said the new arrival as he took off his woollen hat and scarf.

"It's been a while."

A glistening bald dome shone where the hat once sat. Intelligent alert eyes were surrounded by deep wrinkled sachets and a purple gash of a mouth divided his off-white face. "Yes, nearly four years. Don't you have a drink for an old friend anymore?"

Alexis smiled and reached behind him, pulling out an old gourd of Raki.

"The hard stuff. Good!" said Janus as he took the flask, uncapped it with his teeth, and took three big gulps. Satisfied with the warming effects of the liquor, he sat down loudly on the nearest chair. "I thought Skanderberg was up here?"

"He is on the other slopes," replied Alexis.

Nicola stood there puzzled with this dynamic, not recognising the man who sat before him.

"You're one of the boys from Varna," he said interrupting Nicola's thoughts. "You have grown some and I see you have now been marked by battle. Have to admit, you did make me a touch nervous when we met," he added with a deep laugh.

"Why are you here?" Alexis interrupted.

"Hunyadi is planning another attack, this summer, and recruiting support wherever he can."

Nicola's ears picked up at the thought of getting out of the hellhole.

"You would have thought he would have learned from the last fiasco," said Alexis blandly.

The Hungarian raised his eyebrows. "This time, we won't have a foolish boy king to screw things up."

"There is always someone who fucks it up," replied Sartis as he gestured for the flask and took an uncharacteristic swig. Then turning to the still-standing Nicola, he ordered him to go fetch Skanderberg, whilst the coarse Hungarian and he caught up on their differing pieces of news. The young Greek obeyed and went in search of the Albanian leader.

A sense of disquiet was about Alexis, the usual energy and vigour seeming muted. Nothing outwardly noticeable, nonetheless, it was evident to Nicola.

Upon hearing the news of the messenger, Skanderberg made haste to meet him. Nicola left the three men in deep discussion, which went on into the night. He could not help but feel excited at the thought of leaving these dark gloomy mountains.

SPRING FINALLY BROKE through during the middle of May, bringing a lighter mood amongst the Greeks. Relations between the two groups improved, as now they had common purpose again and the Albanian had sent out his messengers to incite the uprising in the occupied Balkan lands.

Nicola found himself humming tunes as he prepared to break camp, tasks were completed more quickly and the friendly banter between the men returned. Themis made sure the men were ready for travel down to the flatlands, each soldier responsible for his horse, weapon, and armour, plus provisions for the first part of the journey.

Prior to departure, the eight tagmata commanders crowded into their general's tent for the last time to await orders. Their beloved Strategos stood looking at his men before speaking, streaks of white scattered in his dark hair.

"As you are all aware, we are going to strike at the Turk again. Due to unforeseen circumstances, we have been stuck in the north for over a year without the chance of re-joining our comrades in the south. However, this will be to our advantage for we have all the Laconians in the right place to make a difference, unlike the last time."

Some murmured agreement, especially those present at Varna. Chills ran up Nicola's spine as he recalled that day.

"I have gone through our strategy and where we shall be of best use. Keep tight discipline and we will see through this campaign season with success." Even as he said it, Alexis was full of doubts as to its chances of victory, but he would not show that to his officers. When the briefing ended, he asked Nicola to stay behind and pulled out the flask of Raki. "What is your opinion of this campaign of Hunyadi's?"

Nicola was taken off guard, not by the question itself but with the clear indecisiveness in the general's voice. "Well, it's preferable to being stuck up in these mountains, sir."

Alexis smiled, and looked upon Nicola as the son he never had. "Aye, true. But whilst there is willingness on the side of the Christians, what do you think can go wrong?"

"If we and our allies do not work together, it will be our undoing, just like last time."

"I agree. Therefore, this time, we will use our full force to bear and the Laconians will be in the centre of the action."

"Understood, sir."

Nicola noticed the drawn look and deep furrows on his

mentor. He had taken the news of the destruction of Constantine's force very hard, whilst grateful that he still had his finest troops intact, the feeling of helplessness gnawed at his spirit.

"One further thing, I am promoting you to second-in-command. You have shown your worth and are the right choice."

"Thank you, sir."

"You have earned it, Nicola."

25

———————

KOSOVO

It had been nearly two years and still he had not managed to relinquish his duties as military leader. Just as one insurrection was quelled another sprang up to replace it. *When will these Christians realise, they are beaten?* This time though, news arrived that Hunyadi had raised an army and was thirsty to avenge the defeat at Varna. Whilst the Court was in a fluster, Murad could not have been happier, finally he could settle this once and for all.

Candarli Pasha entered with his daily briefing.

"Send word to my son in Nicaea, I want him present for this campaign, it is time for him, now," said the sultan.

The Vizier knew better than to question his ruler when in this belligerent mood.

"Let's get the army together and crush this Hungarian insect!" bellowed the old man.

SMOOTHLY, the young man released his final arrow as his horse thundered past the row of hanging dummies, each one displaying the result of his accuracy. Antonis looked on, pleased with Mehmet's progress. Just as in his studies, the lad was a diligent and fast learner. The relationship between the two had grown closer the months since he had planted the seed of his plan in Mehmet's thoughts. This was to be their final practice, as word had arrived that the young prince was called to lead part of his father's army, a task which filled him with great excitement.

Antonis was pleased too, as this would be the blooding of his Thracian unit. They were to act as the young prince's personal guard during the campaign. As Mehmet rode towards him, he still looked frail, though the slender limbs belied his stamina and strength, reminding him of himself at that age.

"Getting better," said a flushed Mehmet.

"Yes, you are, sir," replied Antonis truthfully.

"Well, I am going to need it where we are going," added the Prince as he beckoned to his commander to ride with him. He had been mulling over the idea of taking the Red Apple. Gone was idle dreaming, in its place logical reasoning, and the Greek was the foil to his discussions.

Antonis was careful during these sessions, to let the notions appear as if they had come from Mehmet, though, to be fair, his strategic insight was superb.

He had also brought it up with his teachers, which they in turn wholeheartedly supported. For them, it was the one glaring failure in an otherwise illustrious march of Islam across the known world. Guwani had no doubt this young prince had the desire and ability to make that happen and was filled with pride at his development.

Nicola felt joy wash over him as the Laconians reached the flat lands, not least because he could now communicate with the outside world again. In pleasant confirmation, he was greeted at the first village they arrived at by a messenger bearing a small bundle of letters from Thanos.

Still, there was no correspondence from Katerina and he

fervently hoped that everything was all right. He thought of Antonis, and sadness gripped him at the image of him as an enemy across the battlefield.

Alexis, true to his word, parted with Skanderberg, and joined with Hunyadi and the main army, but to his consternation, the Hungarian had become reckless. His desire for vengeance clouded his judgment and he marched the small force directly to meet the Turk, with all the nobles blindly following his lead.

Nicola saw the frustration rise within Alexis as his lone voice of caution to wait for the Albanians was ignored. So, it was under this premise that the two armies finally met on the field of Kosovo, the Laconians positioned in charge of the left flank.

Antonis and Mehmet watched as the crusaders came into view. Stationed on the right, Mehmet commanded the light cavalry. The Greek surveyed the forces arranged before him, his eye taking-in the impressive cavalry to their left, a familiarity about them; then he saw the flag flutter open in the light breeze, the red lambda of the Laconians. He could not fathom why they were here, but he was sure who would be among them. His lips curled in anticipation.

Thick clouds blanketed the sky, giving a grey sheen to the field and its inhabitants. Antonis used this to look closely at the men from the Laconians; Nicola was easy to spot, his size making him stand out, and the large man to his left looked like Themis. *The only three survivors from Varna meet again.* Gently, he rubbed his fingers on the raised brand he carried.

Nicola rode up to Alexis, full of concern the Christians were outnumbered at least two to one, and he was under no illusions as to the outcome on this field. "What type of unit is that? I don't recognise it," he asked.

"Neither do I, but it carries the Sultan's standard so a

member of the royal household commands it," replied Alexis, he too sharing Nicola's assessment.

"I wish he had waited for the rest of the crusaders," added Nicola.

Alexis gave a carefree laugh for the first time in months. "Well, we will all die sometime." He had awoken that morning with a feeling of dread, but his mood had brightened rapidly and now staring across the field at the horde before him, he felt carefree. Trapped in the mountains for a year, due to the incompetence of his allies, they were now were outgunned due to the same folly. Hearing the birds flying overhead, he envisioned the carrion feeders feasting on the bodies of those about to be slain.

Nicola took up his place at the head of his tagmata and waited for the orders.

THE ENERGY of the soldiers both eager and fearful to fight, imbued Antonis with calm, taking his mind back to his first battle. The clarity he felt was an emotion he wished he could always have. He chuckled to himself.

"What is so funny?" asked a nervous Mehmet.

"The troops facing us is my old unit, the Laconians," replied Antonis.

"I thought you said they were the best."

"They are," replied the Greek, calmly.

Mehmet shifted uncomfortably in the saddle, totally unsure of what was to come, and it was taking all his strength to appear outwardly calm in front of his men. He had an audience with his father the previous evening, who gave him some paternal words of advice. It didn't help but when he joined Antonis around his fire, who, after some persistent questioning, told him of his first time, Mehmet slept more easily. That peace had all but disappeared now.

The trumpets sounded on the crusader side.

"Well, it seems we are going to be the first into the fray," Nicola told his servant as they started to walk, preparing for the charge.

Antonis saw his old unit come lumbering in and knew the Rumelians would stand no chance. Along with the light Wallachian cavalry, the two allies crashed into the awaiting Turks, who reeled under the onslaught. His orders had been to stand by the Prince and protect him at all costs, but he could see Nicola's figure as he charged and desperately wanted to engage him.

As the whole of the left flank began to crumble, he saw the chance for a counterattack and urged Mehmet to lead it. The young prince had already decided. He smiled at the boy's courage and took off his helmet. Mehmet turned to him in shock.

"I want the Laconians to see who I am," Antonis said with a cruel smile. He only cared that Nicola saw him, so he would know his executioner.

Cheers went up as the Muslims broke and fled, but alarm bells rang with Alexis. He shouted at the top of his voice for his Laconians to keep their ranks as the Wallachians, filled with bloodlust, gave chase.

A small group of Anatolians had stood their ground and Nicola's force was tackling them. Thick black smoke from the cannon drifted across the field muffling any sounds of approaching horses. The first of the red-tipped lances came through the dark cloud, smashing through the side of the Greeks, and drove on through. At their head rode a long-haired Turk, with something familiar about his riding style. As the warrior turned, he recognised his former pupil. He saw Antonis' gaze rest on his brother and without thought rushed towards Nicola, shouting at him to gain his attention.

Antonis spurred his horse on after his second run-through and espied his brother's impressive figure intently trying to break the will of the resistant Anatolians. He paused, took his bow, drawing a bead on his target.

Nicola couldn't hear the warning shouts until Alexis was upon him. He turned his head at the sound coming through the chaos of battle, to see his brother in the distance with an arrow poised for release, and watched in slow motion as it flew in his direction.

Antonis' pleasure was short-lived by a cavalryman who had ridden into the arrow's path and now swayed in the saddle as his horse slowed, before dropping to the ground. Both brothers looked in horror as they recognised the fallen man.

Instantaneously, a pang of sorrow filled Antonis, as that was the last place he intended the missile to strike.

Nicola rushed to reach his mentor, leaping off his horse in the chaos to attend to the stricken general, who seemed small as he lay on the churned ground. "Mastre," he cried in anguish as he looked to see where the arrow struck. The barb had penetrated the shield and entered between his neck and collarbone, pierced his lung.

Alexis looked at his captain as his face grew paler. "It's nothing, take command of the men," he rasped with effort.

Nicola stayed there, holding him, screaming for the surgeon's helpers.

"Now," Alexis gurgled out louder as the bright red froth bubbled out of the wound.

Antonis had seen enough and started to draw a second bead on his brother, just as a Laconian bore down upon him. Spinning, he released his arrow and felled him at ten yards then saw more following and realised with bitterness that he had missed his opportunity and turned to face the ensuing melee.

Still holding his dying commander in his arms, Nicola took stock of the chaos surrounding him; Christian and Muslim engaged in vicious hand-to-hand combat. He saw his brother fell a Laconian and engage another. Some of the men had rallied around to protect him, forming a defensive circle, but he knew they were outnumbered and ordered a retreat.

The prince's cavalry had taken this round and Antonis looked to see where Mehmet was.

Seeing that the Turkish counterattack had been successful, Hunyadi decided to order a final charge at the forces in the centre.

The Sultan watched as the remaining might of the crusaders galloped headlong towards him and smiled. For now, he knew he would soon be returning to the peace of his gardens.

26

ZAGANOS PASHA

Mehmet planted himself on the leather stool in his tent, his face a blank mask as he absorbed what had just occurred. He let out a slow chuckle as the realisation of survival began to sink in. Curiously, he allowed himself a certain amount of self-praise before he dissected the battle piece by piece. The outnumbered crusaders had fought well, but in the end, it was futile in the face of their larger and more disciplined force. He intently scratched at his budding beard, recollecting the fray and his first kill. Euphoria got the better of him and he slipped back into the thrill of battle, but his daydream was punctured by the sound of men approaching and he snapped his composure together as two Janissary entered his tent.

"Your Highness. The Sultan requests your presence in his quarters as soon as possible."

"I will be there directly."

As the Janissary left, one of the servants silently appeared, and began to prepare for the appointment. A tiny smirk of pride was etched on his face, for everyone in the army knew it was his young master's cavalry that turned the tide.

Relieved laughter mingled with music around the blazing Ottoman campfires. Some soldiers loudly relaying their deeds of bravery whilst others silently gave thanks for being spared. Antonis had seen to all his men first, making sure he touched their consciousness. He was proud of their first engagement and they had acquitted themselves well, an undoubted match for the Laconians, of that he was now sure.

The men crowded around him, full of praise for his leadership, and naturally, for his fatal wounding of the great General Sartis. A few other commanders also came by to voice their praise. Goran, the giant Croat, declared how their leader felled the opposing general as he charged across the field at full gallop. Someone piped up saying he was already fleeing and Antonis put him out of his shame. But through the raucous laughing, all agreed the difficulty of the shot was indisputable. Antonis mused over the irony; the tale was being glorified, when it was an accident. Of course, no one knew of his sibling, nor of the feud between them.

But the belittling of Alexis saddened him, and once or twice he bit his tongue to stop himself from making stinging remarks to the exhilarated men as they heaped praise upon him. His mind drifted back to the day he met him, a terrified boy in a walled garden in that village in Crete. His presence was all-pervading, a naked man taking on three armed thugs in what he saw was an injustice. Remorse began to grip him; this was a man who had trained him, nurtured him, had even twice saved his life, and this was how he repaid the honor.

He felt the need for a drink for the first time in months and quietly made his way to his tent, where he kept a flask of Raki amongst his belongings. Pulling out the skin sack, he opened it, and gulped the strong liquid that burned as he swallowed. The fluid calmed his guilt and rationalisation took its place. It was combat and he got in the way, an unfortunate accident but such were the casualties of war, he reasoned to himself. As the warming effects took hold, he knew he had been in his tent too long and needed to re-join the victorious army. It would not be good for him to be seen drinking alone, especially with a sad face. There could be no opportunity of bringing his loyalty into question.

Exiting the tent, he walked through the orderly rows of canvas structures towards the centre of the camp. Anatolian lute music played throughout, accompanied by the aroma of roasting lamb. The Christian units drank un-watered wine to release the day's exertions. Soldiers who saw him walk by shouted out praise. It has already become legend.

He espied two giant white-capped janissaries guarding the entrance to their master's quarters. Their synchronous nods of respect as they pulled their halberds apart, said a thousand words. The tent was decorated like a palace, silks hung from the ceiling, covering the sides with bright shades of red and yellow. Two long trestle tables were laden with food, roasted lamb and chicken lay on one with sweet delicacies on the other. Pitchers of lemon, pomegranate, and lychee juice were placed around at intervals.

Antonis saw Mehmet as he entered, his demeanour more self-assured. Survival had that effect. Two fellow captains from the Anatolian regiments came up to congratulate him. Effusive displays of back slapping and loud praise for saving their men from annihilation. Undoubtedly, meant from the heart, but a touch irritating to be on the receiving end. He noticed that he was the last of the captains to join the victory feast.

Still in his battle fatigues and looking grubbier than the rest, Murad caught the Greek's eye, and beckoned him over. "The great hero graces us with his presence," he said, his joy undisguised, though for him, that was due to his impending return to his palace gardens, a feat made possible in large part to the actions of the man before him.

The Sultan eyed Antonis as he stood in mud-splattered leggings with sprays of blood on his sky-blue tunic; at least he had washed his hands. The long curly black hair had a wild appearance to it and his hooded blue eyes burned with fearless energy; still, the wily ruler detected a haunted sadness behind them. *Why has Allah put this man in my path?* He was still an enigma and he could not fathom why he had chosen to join his own people's mortal enemy. His actions though, spoke of zealous loyalty, that only converts had and his son would need men like him when he was to rule again.

In that moment amongst the sweaty odour of his tent, the old Sultan decided. He rose and the lute playing instantly stopped. "Captains, we have won a great victory, Allah be praised."

Cheers went up from the gathered officers.

"And this was made possible by the actions of my son's brigade."

More cheers followed, though with less gusto.

"His trusted lieutenant was the man who cut the head of the deadliest snake the crusaders had." Murad raised his hands to prevent further cheering. "It is our decision to reward this achievement, and as such, I raise Antonis Vevellis to Pasha and Commander of the European Army."

This time the cheers were so loud it rattled the plates on the table.

Mehmet smiled at Antonis' good fortune and the Greek stood there dumbfounded. This was the last thing he had expected, and the surprise was humbling.

Murad knew he had made the correct decision as he noticed the change in the Greek's bearing. "Henceforth, you shall be known as Antonis Zaganos Pasha," he stated as he stepped down from his dais and clasped the newest member of his nobility in an act of solidarity.

As Murad released him, the perfumed captains crowded around their newest hero with dazzling smiles of praise. The Muslims saying, "Inshallah," and the various Christians congratulating in their own ethnic style, some with a handshake, others with hugs and kisses.

27

<hr>

ALEXIS

The smell of death filled the tent as Nicola sat next to the listless Alexis and mopped his fevered brow. The colour had drained from his face and been replaced by a ghastly greyness. To see the powerful figure of his mentor reduced to an ailing sack of skin and bones was devastating, but to know his condition was due to the act of warning him from danger was too much to bear.

Alexis' eyes opened in a moment of lucidity and saw the forlorn face of his bedside companion. "Death comes to us all, Nicola," rasped the general.

Nicola noticed the looseness of skin around the neck and ears and how the body had wasted away. It was testament to Alexis' strength he had lived so long.

For four days, the Laconians had marched westward, toward the safety of the mountains and finally made camp as close to the Adriatic as they could. Nicola decided to rest there for a week, to allow his general as peaceful a death as possible. Riders were sent to the port at Tirana, where Thanos had left the ship for their use should it be needed.

Now, they were back in one of the bleak Albanian caves.

Candles were placed throughout the granite to give as much light as possible, incense was found to take away the stench of decay, and orders were given to find an herbalist who could concoct a potion from the seeds of the poppy flower to make his onward journey more comfortable.

Alexis fell back into unconsciousness and Nicola went outside, inhaling the cool mountain air and taking stock of the situation. They had lost many men, but the bulk of the force was intact and provisioned. Discipline had held and no one questioned his command. Fortunate, considering many knew their beloved general's killer was his brother.

Recalling the cold look in Antonis' eyes brought chills, as he knew the deadly arrow was meant for him. The fact remained, he had killed Alexis, but worse, it was to be a lingering death. Strangely, he felt no anger toward his brother, just sadness and loss by this total betrayal. His thoughts went to his parents; now, he had to tell them what their son had become. The heavy emotions clawed within, as he fought to keep them in check.

"Sir, the herbalist has arrived," said the approaching the trooper.

"Show him to the Strategos, I will be there shortly," replied Nicola.

The old crone examined her patient. *He was once a fine warrior,* she thought, but the infection had spread into the blood and now there was no hope. She had seen this numerous times in her one hundred and three summers of life, and set about preparing the potion to ease his journey to the underworld. Reaching into her small leather knapsack, she pulled out two earthenware jars bound with rope—to prevent them from cracking and spilling their precious contents. The string was blackened with years of handling, so it had the hardened appearance of a beetle's carapace. She lay them on the side with a small wooden bowl and two spatulas. Pulling off the wooden lid, she scooped out some of the thick black buttery liquid into the bowl, its cloying sweetness filling the room. She added two spoons of white powder and began stirring them together until it became a dark brown paste.

Nicola, who had joined halfway through the process, watched fascinated and started to feel lightheaded.

When ready, she placed the paste on the wooden board as if laying out small biscuits to bake. The rest, she put in a cup of wine and dissolved it. "Once I start to burn this, it will fell you quicker than a janissary's spear, young man," cackled the old witch. "Perhaps you should wait outside until it is complete."

"I shall remain," insisted Nicola.

With a grunt, she continued her preparation and burned the small piles of paste, wafting their smoke under the nose of the sleeping Alexis. The fumes filled the area and feelings of euphoria gripped Nicola.

"Soon, he will feel no pain. When he wakes make sure to give him this," said the herbalist, handing him the wine goblet. "I shall stay till his time has passed, as you may have need of an embalmer."

He nodded in understanding.

The potent fumes did their work and Alexis stirred in his sleep. And after a time, he came-to with a little more vitality, beckoning to his protégé to approach.

Grasping him by the hand, Nicola felt his general's cold and clammy wasted flesh.

"It is my time," Alexis whispered.

"You will be fine and strong again," said Nicola.

Alexis smiled weakly at the lie. "Take the men home and use them to protect the city for as long as you can."

Nicola tried to say something, but the dying man waved for silence.

"Follow your heart, Nicola, be with the woman you love. Nothing is worth that sacrifice," he continued as he gripped him with the strength that comes from impending death. "Don't make the mistakes I made. But take care, for your brother means to destroy you, and our way of life." His eyes burned fanatically as he spoke, his last breath rattled, then he fell back abruptly onto the bed, staring blankly into infinity.

Nicola carefully closed the dead man's eyes and prayed for his speedy onward journey, tears welling in his own as he did. Fighting back his emotions did not prevent two rivulets from running down his cheeks and soaking into his beard. He kissed Alexis' hands in loving respect, and placed them across his chest, before leaving to inform the men of their leader's demise.

RETURN TO THE CITY

The usual turquoise colour of the Ionian Sea had been turned to white froth by the power of Mother Nature, buffeting the carrack in the raging water. Men were vomiting from excessive motion, whilst some prayed for safe deliverance.

Nicola was too engrossed in his own discovery to have any concern for the gale outside. As the new commander, he had gone through Alexis' papers. Expecting the mundane, he was astounded to discover the source of his excellent intelligence had come from Belpia Elpis, this, his first opportunity to read the box of letters in their entirety. Eagerly, he poured over them, some from Katerina and the others from Irene, whom he remembered was the Mother Superior. As he reached the final missives, he smiled and patted Alexis' embalmed body lying on the table next to him. *So, this is what you meant with your dying breath;* he realised how precious life was while reading the love letters sent by his mentor some twenty years earlier.

His heart burst with pride for his beloved and it made him more determined that they should be together upon his return. Along with the gold he had gained from the campaigns, Alexis had left him all his possessions, except for a small wooden chest, his sword, and the silver amulet he had carried upon his person which were bequeathed to Irene.

Once the ship docked in Patras, Nicola learnt of the death of Emperor John VIII, no doubt due to the final crusader annihilation. Constantine was the new ruler and had made his way to the capital to claim the crown. After leaving most of the men and horses at Mistras, he too sailed onwards to Constantinople.

Thanos was there to greet them as they entered the Golden Harbour; having given explicit orders to be told when the ship was in sight of the city. News had reached the capital of the great General's death, and rumours abounded of a Greek traitor who led the fatal charge. The old soldier knew it was Antonis they spoke of and waited with trepidation for confirmation.

They embraced as he stepped onto the dock, Thanos noticing the pain of loss on Nicola's face, and his heart reached out to the lad, as he still thought of him as such, then said, "Good to see you again, even if the circumstances could have been better."

They watched as four Laconians carried the linen-bound embalmed body off the ship on a wooden pallet.

"You too," replied Nicola, his face brightening for the first time in weeks. "Many things have changed."

"Yes, they have," came the laconic reply as they made their way back to the house.

It took two full days before Nicola picked up the courage to even contemplate visiting the convent. He simultaneously dreaded and desired to go to Belpia Elpis. It was Thanos who finally told him he must go. He had decided to walk as penance. Carrying the box, his boots felt like anvils as he trudged up the hill to the small door under the white archway.

Welcomed by the attendant nuns, he requested an audience with the Mother Superior and was ushered in to see her. He stifled a shocked gasp. Gone was the radiant glow; Irene looked tiny and frail as the chair and desk overwhelmed her. Only the constant scent of lavender had familiarity but even that felt lacklustre.

"I wondered who it was to be paying me a visit," she said. The rock to which she had anchored her spirit all these years was broken, and she was drifting in agonising hollowness.

The visitor did not know how to start, made more difficult by the knowing gaze that pierced through him. Instead, he placed the box on the desk in front of her, putting the amulet on top.

A wistful smile broke across the nun's face as she saw the silver locket. Reaching out to clasp it in the palm of her hands, she cradled it for a few seconds then opened the frame and gazed into its contents. "You know, we were little more than children when we made this pact." She looked up at Nicola. "That beautiful man saved my soul."

"He died saving my life," he replied.

"You mean your brother's arrow was meant for you?" A slight hint of surprise in her voice. "Undoubtedly, you now know what we are, and do here. You think I would not have found out what happened by now?"

"Alexis also requested that you have his sword."

She shook her head, "I think you should keep it, it would be best."

Nicola reached into his tunic and pulled out the old frayed yellowing papers. "He left no instructions for these," and handed them to her.

The Mother Superior's hand covered her gasp as she saw what they were. "Thank you. And now, I think you need to see someone; she is waiting in our guest quarters. There, you can have the privacy you need."

Nicola bade his leave and strode through to the other side of the convent.

. . .

Katerina waited with trepidation for her love's arrival, knowing he was seeing the Mother Superior first and without a doubt the secret was out. She was not sure how he would react to the news; would he think her duplicitous in not telling him all this time whilst she declared undying love to him in countless letters? It was not the action of an honest lover. She said a small prayer of forgiveness under her breath.

The wimple felt constricting on her head and she wanted to take it off, the harsh fabric not sitting well with her. There were just some things she would never become used to, she reasoned, taking off the coif and letting her long thick auburn hair fall free. As she ran her hands through the tresses, she realised how much it had grown; in vain she looked for a mirror. Her hair smelled bland as she held it and an urge for almond oil presented itself for the first time in ages. Unconsciously, she was preening herself in anticipation of Nicola's arrival.

It had been three years since she had last seen him, she wondered how he had changed. Pulling out her simple wooden brush, she passed it through the locks, hoping to at least give it a little sheen. Holding the long ends with one hand, she brushed it out with the other and noticed how her hands were stained with black ink. Making the best of what she had, she scrubbed at her nails, attempting to make them as presentable as possible, then sat down and waited.

Walking through the corridors and towards the guests' quarters, his chest was tight with nervousness, palpable excitement blended with apprehension of what she had become, for she had not been sitting idly by merely saying prayers these past years. Approaching the old oak door, he recalled in his trepidation that it was in this very room he had last seen her, and gingerly knocked.

"Come in," said the feminine voice on the other side.

As he walked in, his heart jumped into his throat as their eyes met. Her luscious hair had grown even longer. Without pause for conversation, he strode towards her and embraced her.

Katerina buried her face in her lover's neck as she hugged him with years of unrequited emotion, the familiar scent flooding back into her psyche. They stood in an embrace losing track of time.

"It's good to see you again, I have missed you," said Nicola.

Katerina gazed into his eyes expectantly, "and I missed you."

There was so much to say they did not know where to begin.

"Thank you for all the letters, the ones for Alexis, and the ones for me," he said with a smile.

Katerina gave a sheepish grin. "I'm sorry I never told you, but I was sworn to secrecy, and I keep my vows."

He held no anger but pride for what she had done and become, taking adversity, and creating something positive. His love for her only becoming stronger because of it. "I understand, and your information was invaluable, though, our leaders did not always use it wisely." Looking at her, he knew that keeping the flame lit for all this time had been the right decision. She was truly a worthy partner. "So, tell me, how did this come about? I mean, did Alexis have a part in this? It cannot have been an accident."

She hesitated a moment then consoled herself in the fact that he was now the new recipient of their information since their benefactor's death and reasoned it would be fine to tell him the story, sparing no details about all that had happened and how her position came to pass.

Nicola listened transfixed at the convoluted tale, noticing how her confidence had grown, and that she was now truly a woman. He felt a stirring in his loins as she spoke of her contacts in other monasteries around the Balkans. An electrical charge built up in his body and taking the back of her neck in one of his massive hands, he pulled her towards him.

The sudden movement made Katerina tense for a second,

then relenting, she allowed herself to be drawn towards his searching mouth, her soft white hands clasping around his sinewy neck as they pulled each other closer. Years of pent-up emotions exploded as their lips touched, consuming them as they forgot their surroundings and station.

Soon, Nicola lifted Sister Katerina's habit, his fingers running up her legs until reaching her linen undergarment. For a moment, she hesitated as she realised her surroundings then gave in to her full carnal passions.

With care and attention, Nicola slipped a hand around her ample buttocks, feeling the saturated heat coming from between her legs. As his fingers found the thick thatch of hair, she shuddered in anticipation. With his free hand, he undid the belt and let his trousers slip to the floor, revealing his prodigious manhood in all its glory. Instinctively reaching for his erect penis, she gasped in her inexperience, it was thick, and the weighty feel felt intimidating. She stared expectantly into his eyes.

He had seen that look of surprise and anticipation on the women he had been with before but this was different, for she had been the very centre of his thoughts even when he tasted the occasional female during the last years. Finally, he had the object of his desire in his hands and wanted to see her in all her splendour. Slowly, he lifted the habit, pulled it over her head, and her soft pale skin came up in goose bumps. Her petite breasts stuck out under her square shoulders, her slim torso melding into her rounded hips, which were punctuated by a bush of light brown hair, all set atop her slender long legs.

Picking her up, he carried her to the pallet in the corner of the room and carefully laid her down. Unsure what to do, Katerina gently stroked her lover's face. Nicola felt the nervous tension in her body and for a moment, wished he had taken Thanos up on his offer of those nights of carousing. Tenderly, he kissed her lips then slowly moved down her neck. She shivered in unknown anticipation each time he planted his tender greetings all over her belly. Unable to restrain himself any longer, he finally parted her pliable body and entered her. Katerina's face exclaimed in pain, bit her lip to hide the agony, and her fingernails dug into his powerful shoulders as he began frantic thrusting movements. The sensation was all-consuming for Nicola.

Gazing into her eyes, he saw the pained look on her face and softened his power. Slowing his strokes gave Katerina pause from the agony and allowed her to feel the pleasure of his manhood. Now she wanted him even more and shyly urged him on again as if she was straining to reach a mountain summit. The encouragement spurred him on, he lost himself totally within her, forgetting consideration, joined with her to reach the peak together. Gasps of pleasure emanated and Nicola containing himself no longer, let out an uncontrolled moan, and released his seed inside her.

Katerina's body tensed in surprise as she felt his warmth spread throughout her. Then they flopped together, still conjoined and holding each other close, as their scents entwined with indescribable feelings of satisfied ecstasy.

Lying there together, time lost its meaning. All that mattered was the heat and energy they shared. Katerina marvelled at the intensity she had felt from the man in her arms. The novel sensation had her basking in a temporal haze but as she fell into the abyss, she abruptly became aware of her surroundings and with a spasmodic jerk shook her blissful lover back into the reality of Belpia Elpis. "You have to go," she said gently.

"What? Again?" Nicola replied, remembering their last encounter.

"Yes, do you realise where we are?"

"But we are to be together, I have everything we need, just come with me now," came the impassioned response.

"I cannot just yet," she paused, "Let's arrange to meet in a few days."

"Why? Come now to my place."

Katerina hesitated as her mind calculated the issues that lay before her; the heart yearned to leave, the head counselled patience. "No, we have to wait, I will arrange to see you in three days."

Nicola was crestfallen but knew he could not argue the issue and grudgingly agreed. Hurriedly, they dressed, and carefully checked that the other looked respectable before going their separate ways, both thinking of the next time they would meet, three days hence.

As he floated back towards his house in the Elafonion district, the city's stillness only encouraged the tumultuous thoughts of the future that lay ahead, resolving they would now be together. Never had he been so sure of anything before. Approaching the weathered oak door, he let himself in and passing through the dimly lit atrium, wandered towards his chambers, playing over in his mind the sensations he had felt earlier in the evening. Entering his room, he crashed on his bed, and fell into a warm dreamless sleep.

PLANEDES LOOKED CONTEMPTUOUSLY at the stuffed scented-peacocks vying for their master's attention. Lukas Notaras trying to dominate the proceedings with his imposing stature, Lascaris yapping at his heels. Only George Sphranzis, Constantine's old friend, showed no effort, as he knew his position was secure. What were they fighting for? Not even scraps from the master's table but scraps from the master's dog. Regal and majestic Constantine might look, as he sat upon his throne, but he needed the approval of Murad to take it. The great title of Emperor reduced to nothing more than a city governor.

The last four years had been hard, Katerina's departure to

the convent affecting him deeper than he cared to admit. At first, he thought her petulance would last only a few weeks, but as the months rolled on and she stayed, he realised he might have lost her for good. His wife began showing open hostility towards him as she lay the blame squarely at his feet. The last remaining strands of hair fell out and the jowls began to droop on his face. Added to his malaise, Constantine did not appoint him Kankileos upon his elevation to Emperor. Only the news of Alexis' death, brought any pleasure into his otherwise miserable life.

Due to his visit to the convent and events that transpired, Nicola waited a few days before requesting an audience with the Emperor. Thanos fussed over him like a mother hen, which irritated the young man slightly, as he prepared for his visit to the Blachernae.

"Constantine and I go back a long way," said Nicola. He knew though, that saying so was his way of getting himself ready, for neither of them knew if the Emperor would accede to their wishes. He stole a glance at the embalmed body lying on a trestle table in the corner of the atrium.

The Palace's familiarity instantly put Nicola at ease as he walked towards the imperial chambers. Thanos, however, was full of nerves; a private audience with an Emperor was intimidating. Passing through long corridors adorned with deep red Italian tapestries, the younger man noticed how few guards were posted along its length. Idly, he wandered if that was due to Constantine's destitution or his overtly confident style of rule. Wearing his beloved simple faded brown leather jerkin and matching leather britches, Nicola comfortably entered past the last two guards and into the private quarters.

"Nicola," bellowed Constantine in greeting as he clasped the shoulders of the larger man in the most avuncular fashion.

"Your Majesty."

Constantine smiled at the new title, still unfamiliar with it.

"Getting used to it. The treasury is depleted, and all the council members are at each other's throats vying for pointless titles."

Nicola listened intently as his new ruler bemoaned the state of his domain. "I've come to request a favour," he said.

"What is it?" asked a curious Constantine.

"It is regarding General Sartis. I humbly request that he be interred in the city among the great figures from our past, as befits his achievements."

Constantine stiffened and stroked his beard as he pondered the request.

The silence grew uncomfortable and filling in the void, Nicola stated that Alexis had saved the city almost single-handedly in the siege of 1422.

The Emperor nodded in agreement. "Quite right, my boy, quite right. And as such, we shall honour him with a tomb in Aghoi Apostoloi."

Thanos gasped in amazement, for Alexis was to be buried amongst Emperors; an honour that had been accorded to only four other men throughout the Empire's eleven hundred years of existence.

"Thank you, sire," Nicola beamed contentedly.

"It is the least we can do for one of this ancient Empire's greatest sons," replied the Emperor. "And now, we have a funeral to plan."

Sitting at her writing desk, Katerina's mind floated nebulously as she struggled to focus on her correspondences. The warm feeling inside her still had not waned after nearly a week since last seeing Nicola. She had contrived to see her lover again and that time, in the full privacy of his house. The awakening of her emotions had taken full control and a major dilemma presented itself, for how could she simply leave her responsibilities at Belpia Elpis. Her heart was torn when she told Nicola it was not the right time to get married.

He couldn't hide the hurt he felt but recognised that both had responsibilities to others and life was not that simple anymore. His masculinity filled her memory as she recollected the gentle way he made love to her. The safety and security she felt in his arms sent her again into a warm haze.

A loud knock on the door dissipated her comforting miasma, jolting her back to reality. Before she could answer, the solid oak planks swung open, and the infirm figure of Mother Superior stood in the doorway. She knew this was not a social visit. "Good morning, Mother Superior."

"Good morning, Sister Katerina. Are you busy this morning?"

"No," she lied.

Irene entered the room, moved closer to her protégé, and asked, "Why are you still here?"

A look of surprise came across Katerina's face. "I don't understand."

"Nicola has returned, he is wealthy, and you are free to marry him. I know you have spent a few nights with him of late."

Katerina sat back in her chair and her eyes squinted in thought. Finally, she spoke. "I do love him, but I also have a duty to the work we are doing here. It is important and we both know we are crucial if our city is to survive."

With pride, Sister Irene listened and remembered Alexis' words, that this girl had something special. Though, she vowed she would not let Katerina sacrifice her heart for duty. "Very well, but there will come a time soon when you must choose your path. Now, tell me, what news from our friend Gannadios?"

Katerina turned to the piles of correspondence on her desk; rummaging through the organised chaos, she pulled out the pertinent letter, and relayed the relevant details of what was occurring in the Sultan's domain. After the full debrief, she enquired as to whom the information now went in lieu of Alexis' death.

Mother Superior replied, "The new Laconian Commander will be the natural recipient."

The young nun smiled, as it meant that she would be seeing a lot more of her beloved now.

29

FUNERAL

An eerie silence filled the Church of The Holy Wisdom. The patriarch had finished his blessing of the departed soul, who lay encased in the lead-lined oak box in the centre by the altar. Arrayed before him, were all the great and the good of the city. Standing in the front row, the Emperor, resplendent in full imperial dress, looked downcast and sad. All those who knew Alexis checked their emotions, as one of their greatest sons was being laid to rest. To Constantine's left stood the imposing figure of Nicola, his countenance set like stone. Contrary to custom, he had shaved his beard off, and the scar down his face glistened in the reflective light. It was his form of penance in exposing his disfiguration.

A few rows behind sat the only person who reaped any joy from the proceedings. Planedes held back his smiles at Alexis' misfortune, his only wish that he had died slower and more painfully. As he surveyed the congregation of genuine mourners, the light feeling quickly evaporated as he spied his daughter at the opposite side of the church. Her elongated physique standing out between the other nuns. A lump of yearning filled his throat, soon replaced with venomous bile at her betrayal.

Sister Irene shuddered as the patriarch finished his sermon, the finality of Alexis' parting hitting home; one could only hold back tears for so long and soon, torrents ran down her cheeks.

Katerina gripped her hand in solidarity and to assuage her helplessness in the situation. She also had seen her father as they all filed into the church, chose not to acknowledge him, and strangely, realised her mother was not present. Glancing up, she saw her beloved's imposing physique, and her heart went out to him. She could only imagine how alone he felt in his profound loss.

Nicola stared at the gold double-headed eagle embossed on the coffin. Childishly, he imagined the lid popping open, and Alexis springing out and announce it was all a prank as he so often did amongst his men on campaign. He daydreamed over their shared experiences, from the time of Mistras with Antonis, throughout their adventures in Central Greece. The many successful campaigns, his kind and generous instincts, great leadership, and infinite courage. His mind rested on his brother's fateful shot and that it was not intended for his mentor; the jerking body in the saddle, the smell of decay in the Albanian cave, and finally on the sweet pungent odour of the potion to ease his passing. He thanked God that he was there in his final moments, yet still mourned the loss of such a friend and leader of men.

The tinkling bells of the incense holders brought him around and the opiate scent of his reverie was replaced with the reality of the church's frankincense. So lost was he in his thoughts that he missed the entire eulogy delivered by Constantine and now the procession was making its way to the final resting place of his General amongst the Emperors, who had been entombed there for a thousand years.

30

MISTRAS

Katerina awoke with the first crow of the cockerel. As she gained full consciousness a feeling of nausea enveloped her and she lurched to the chamber pot vomiting profusely. It was the fourth time in a week it occurred, she felt panic welling up inside her. After rinsing her mouth out, she dressed, taking care with her robes as her breasts felt swollen and sore.

Fortunately, she had no tasks before breakfast and so was able to take her time as the sun began its daily ascent and ambled over to the refectory. Sitting at the opposite table, Irene espied the strange behaviour and instantly knew what had come to pass. She had seen this, many times before, in her previous life and letting out a knowing sigh finished eating her breakfast.

As soon as she was able, Katerina absconded herself to the privacy of her study. The tranquillity of the musty scrolls soothed her nausea and promptly she set about her daily routine of letter writing and the reading of correspondence. Deep into her third missive, she did not hear the door softly open.

"When was the last time you had your woman's curse?"

enquired the voice behind her.

An inkblot appeared on her letter as she froze in her writing. "Nearly three months."

"You are with child," replied the mother superior.

Powerful emotions overwhelmed Katerina. Elation at the thought of carrying Nicola's progeny was quickly followed by worry. "Are you sure?"

"Yes."

"What am I to do?"

The Mother Superior went over to her protégé and gave her a reassuring hug.

The faint smell of lavender gave clarity and strength to Katerina. Nonetheless, how she wished Nicola were here, having departed just over a week ago to Mistras with his Laconians, of whom he was now the General. The farewell had been tender and tearful, but both had to follow the paths set before them. With this news, her heart wanted to shout out with joy, yet her head counselled temperance.

Irene could see turmoil in the young woman's face and ironically thought that such a lady was bred for a pleasant, uncomplicated life, not this.

With her arms around Mother Superior's waist, Katerina buried her face in her bosom and began the slow uncontrolled sobbing of despair.

Gently, Irene stroked the thick golden-brown hair in a futile attempt to calm her, then giving up, she gently whispered. "Cry, my dear, cry. But we shall find a way through this." And looked out of the cell's window to the beautifully pruned rose bushes outside.

NICOLA FELT LONELY BACK in the mountain-citadel of Mistras. He shuddered as he recalled the thick granite slab being placed on Alexis' sarcophagus. The void left in his life was still a huge chasm. The cool February air rippled through the open window as he gazed down the mountainside to the Laconian plain below, dressed only in the thin white linen shirt, as the southern lands had far milder winters than the last two he had experienced in the high Balkan Mountains.

The cacophony of cicadas switched his thoughts to Katerina and their emotional last visit; a warm glow engulfed him as he reminisced on the sweet lovemaking they had enjoyed. Still, it rankled him that she insisted she stay for the time being at Belpia Elpis. But how could he argue? The service she provided was invaluable. And now, as Alexis' successor, he understood just how much. The pride he had for her sense of duty was balanced with the sadness he felt with the insistence upon delay. His mind clouded, trying to find a solution.

"Good morning, General," said Thanos' jolly voice as he barged into his quarters.

"Don't you know how to knock?"

"My apologies, General," he replied in mock subservience.

"You know, I could have you flogged for your insubordinate tone."

"Yes, but you're so poor, you would need me to buy the whips for you to mete out the punishment."

Nicola laughed as he was brought back to reality. He was still getting used to his new position. "Why have you graced us today?"

"Just coming to see how my lovesick little Nicola is doing."

The General smiled. "He's doing fine."

Thanos ignored the lie and enquired as to the last time he had seen Plethon, suggesting that perhaps they should go visit the ancient man. "He must be nearly a hundred years old, so we'd better get the time in now."

So preoccupied with administration and emotions since his return to the Morea, Nicola had not yet been to see his old teacher. "Good, let's arrange to see him."

"Should we not invite him here?" replied Thanos.

"The mountain goes to Mohammed."

STANDING NAKED, Katerina looked at the swelling of her belly; it had grown significantly during the last few days, the skin developing a translucent sheen where it had stretched to accommodate the life growing inside. Her breasts felt weighty and uncomfortable as she put on her linen undergarment. Pulling the fabric taught over her body, she noticed how the bulge protruded rather than spread; even she thought this to be the old-wives-tales, that she carried a boy. Whatever it was, it felt heavy.

After the initial shock, she set about the task at hand with her customary resolve. Talking it through with Irene, she decided to have the baby in secret and enlist Agatha's aid, her old handmaiden, to look after it. Originally, she considered her mother but since leaving home, Sophia's health had deteriorated, and she wasn't sure how she would take the news either. Once that was settled, she would broach the subject with Nicola. Soon, she would undertake a journey out of the city to give birth to her child. Thankfully, the nun's habit covered any expanding midriff, but the sounds of a wailing new-born could not be muffled in the convent.

Irene suggested she visit the nunnery in Thrace in an official capacity about a month before the baby was due, where, afterwards, she would go to the house of one of Agatha's distant cousins. It was arranged the house-maiden would receive a letter urgently requesting her presence, due to a family bereavement. There, they would wait until Katerina gave birth, whereupon Agatha would return with the baby, as if it were her distant cousin who had died in childbirth, and therefore entrusted her with its care.

Katerina smiled feebly to herself. Hopefully, Mother Superior had left nothing to chance. Feeling somewhat calmer, she busied herself with the daily chores as her mind wandered to Nicola and how he was faring.

"I FORGOT how steep this slope is," exclaimed Thanos, all the while huffing and puffing theatrically. "The house didn't look that far away."

Nicola agreed but would never admit it. It was unsurprising that Plethon rarely ventured from his mountain perch. "You are just out of shape, Thanos, all those town whores have made you soft."

"I think it's the exact opposite, my young lad," came the quick counter.

Conversation died again as they conserved energy inching upward towards the white-painted stone house perched precariously amongst the wild thyme bushes. Cicadas went noisily about their business and the strong scent of wildflowers gave a pleasant aura to their tiring work. As the sun entered its apex, they finally reached the antique pitted wooden door.

The loud knock was met with silence. Nicola knocked once more, again no response. Concerned, they opened the door to find Plethon catatonic in his chair. Rushing to his side, Thanos shook the ancient body gently.

Plethon gradually opened his pale-hooded lids fringed with white eyelashes.

"What do you think you were doing, old man? You had us worried," admonished Thanos.

"I was sleeping," came the curt reply.

"We came up in the noon day sun to see you and you didn't even hear us."

"Well, you should have waited till the late afternoon, all civilised men have a siesta," Plethon retorted with a smile.

"It's good to see you again, Mastre," said Nicola.

"Why didn't you come visit me earlier?" Plethon's pale yet vibrant eyes blazed at Nicola.

The rest of him had visibly aged. His skin was translucent and his cadaverous appearance was topped with brilliant white hair that fell about his shoulders, but strangely, he didn't exude the peculiar smell that was so prevalent in persons of his years.

"Apologies, but I've been busy with my new administrative responsibilities."

Plethon grunted disapprovingly as he eyed Nicola, noticing the pressures of obligation etched in his face, though inwardly, was very pleased to see him.

Thanos felt the dynamic change in the room and sensing the need for tutor and pupil to be alone, barked. "Have you any wine, old man?"

"No, only Raki."

"What sort of host are you? Don't you know civilised men drink wine in the afternoon?"

"You'd better go find some then."

"I will, and there are some ladies in the lower city who know how to treat a man. I bid you both farewell," Thanos added in a flourish and promptly left.

The old philosopher turned to Nicola as the door slammed theatrically and pointed to the blue and white striped cloth in the corner of his modest house. "The wine is under that."

The young man took the clay cups that rested next to the bottle. Pouring two healthy portions, he handed one to Plethon, and sat down on the stool opposite him. "Yammas," he said and took a large swig of the deep red nectar.

Un-watered wine, the lad really needs to relax.

Looking into the empty cup and then at his host, Nicola hesitated as how to begin. Seeing his old teacher reminded him of simpler times, when the future seemed bright and clear. Now, he felt clouded and confused, a luxury he could not afford. "Exactly how old are you, Mastre?" He asked.

The old man chuckled, "I am in my ninety-sixth year."

"That's a long life and during that time you have seen and done much."

"Tell me, boy, what is on your mind and how can I help you?"

Nicola let out a sigh of relief, then slowly ordering his mind of hopes and fears for the future, began to offload on the last remaining person alive whom he could truly trust.

SPRING CAME EARLY THAT YEAR; the mild winter gave way to a glorious bloom and the usual April rains were light so that towards the end of May there was a parched look to the surrounding countryside. Katerina checked her small trunk again, making sure everything was accounted for, ticking off her mental list as she did. Finally satisfied that nothing was left out, two of the more robust nuns picked it up and carried it to the waiting mule to be loaded. It had been at Katerina's insistence that both she and Agatha travel light.

The journey was quick and without incident and within two sunsets the heavily laden Katerina arrived at the quiet house overlooking the Sea of Marmara—a coastal retreat for her uncle. It was rarely used nowadays and best of all, there was no permanent staff in the house, which suited the ladies perfectly. The dark stone construction was cool and passing through the atrium, she came to the platform that overlooked the wine-dark sea. Gazing out onto the white flecks that spotted the water, she knew this to be the ideal place to have her child.

The mule carrier brought in the trunk and as Agatha instructed, took the luggage to the main guest quarters. "I will prepare everything for you, my lady," she said, as she paid the transporter and dismissed him.

The clear blue sky gave way to a reddish hue as the sun sank into its nightly slumber and the thickness of the stones protected the walled house from the hot breezes, making the evening repast pleasant. Staring across the long rectangular oak table, the soon-to-be mother toyed at her plate of figs and cheese, which was making her nauseous. Her awkward size made sitting in one position uncomfortable. The only relief was the discarding of her nun's robes and wearing in its stead a light linen dress that felt soft and smooth against her skin.

Agatha looked across at her mistress and thought how strange these circumstances were. To be sitting with her superior as an equal was most unfamiliar. It was getting late and after clearing the table, bade her leave, as she wanted to walk along the clifftop to clear her head.

With a lurch of the heart, Katerina realised it must be almost the first time in her entire life that she was experiencing solitude. A privileged child and even protected when she went to the convent, she had always been surrounded by people. Now, she was alone on an island, in a sea of quiet; the only person nearby, her faithful Agatha, taking an evening stroll. She felt the baby kick and uncertainty welled up again. Her instinct was to cry out for her companion, but her pride kept her counsel. Again, she mulled over the plan and wondered how this would work. What would become of her child, questioning her decision to stay in the convent, and to continue with her duties.

Sighing at her predicament, she walked to the open archway at the end of the room, inhaling the strong scent of thyme wafting through the open door. Having taken two steps, she felt the rush of liquid flow between her legs and waves of panic engulfed her, making her stumble, and cry out; her yelp coming out muted. Drawing upon her inner strength, she staggered towards the bedroom, where her legs finally gave way. She lay there trying to find comfort, wanting to scream but quietly waited for Agatha's assistance.

The Meltemi blew hard and the warm evening air pushed the hair off Agatha's face as she walked along the clifftop. She pondered over the responsibility she had been entrusted with. Flattering for sure, but daunting nonetheless, and she vowed to do her utmost to honour the trust placed in her.

She leaned against the heavy oak door to compose herself before entering, then realised Katerina was not present. Hearing the groan, she raced up the winding stone stairs to her mistress's room. "I'm here," she shouted and rushed to help the stricken girl.

Katerina did not answer but stared at her wild-eyed, moaning in agony.

"Not to worry, my lady," continued Agatha, who had seen many births in the crowded dwellings of Constantinople and knew what to do.

"Come, another push," she said later in an uncharacteristic voice of authority.

The pain was close to unbearable for Katerina as she lay screaming and groaning, and with every fibre in her existence lit up with the effort of expelling this life from within her.

Agatha saw the head push through then the shoulders eased out, one after the other, and the little body came sliding into her hands. It was done.

Katerina fell back exhausted as her servant tied a piece of string around the cord then cut it with a knife. "What is it?" she rasped.

"You have a son, My Lady."

"Healthy?"

"Perfectly, and he's a strong one."

And as if on cue, the lungs burst forth and Agatha passed the screaming naked infant to his mother, who instinctively put the child to her exposed breast, the sweet sensation all-consuming.

"What will you call him?"

"Alexis," she replied. In her maternal ecstasy, her thoughts went to Nicola, and how happy he would be to see this.

31

SULTAN

The palace was awash with muted concern once the news broke of Murad's illness. The ashen look on the royal physician's face each time he left the chamber ample confirmation that change at the helm was coming. Mehmet, as the only son was the heir presumptive, however, there was also the Sultan's brother, Orhan, exiled in Constantinople, who could cause another war of succession. All these issues flew around the Grand Vizier's head as he walked to see the ailing ruler. His large blue and white turban feeling particularly heavy on this crisp, scentless morning. Leaving an hour later, his mind was made up, and his direction clear.

Antonis stared blankly at the chessboard in front of him, the move by his opponent catching him unawares. "Looks like you have me again." and he tipped over the black king.

"That's three this week," Mehmet pointed out, a smirk on his thin lips.

Since the victory at Kosovo, the young prince had grown in confidence and stature, become a highly proficient horseman and archer; however, his greatest skill was strategy, something they both loved. This precocious eighteen-year-old was already planning his legacy, a matter he was only too happy to assist with.

"Another game tomorrow, my Lord?" asked Mehmet.

"With pleasure, and I will be paying more attention this time. Now, if you will excuse me, I need to attend to my affairs."

They bade farewell in an oddly formal manner, a quirk in an otherwise very close relationship. Riding out of the palace gate, Antonis spotted a horseman galloping towards him, his steed streaked in white froth. Raising his right hand, the rider skidded to a halt. "What's the hurry?"

"Apologies, Zaganos Pasha. I have an urgent message from the Vizier for Prince Mehmet," said the messenger.

"Show it to me," he ordered.

Reluctantly, the man handed over the scroll.

Antonis began to open it.

"My Pasha, upon pain of death, I must deliver the scroll directly to the Prince."

The rider's fear was palpable, and he wondered if it was his wrath or the Vizier's that he dreaded more.

"Very well, I shall accompany you," he conceded.

Mehmet was pacing on his veranda, his long silk robes flowing in the January breeze when he recognised his erstwhile opponent's footsteps. "Wanting another match so soon, my lord?" he said nonchalantly.

"There is a message from the Grand Vizier for you." replied Antonis.

Mehmet extended his hand to the oncoming messenger, hastily opened the wax seal, and read the contents of the scroll.

"It appears that my father is dying, and the Vizier suggests that I return to Edirne in haste, to secure the succession." His voice was calm, but his eyes burned with anticipation.

Antonis let out a low whistle, after nearly three years in provincial exile, they would now be in the centre of power.

. . .

FATIMA COLLAPSED on top of her lover as she came to a shuddering climax. Still entwined, they shared the post-coital glow, relishing their respective heated scents after a particularly vigorous bout of lovemaking. Her thick raven hair spread across his arms and shoulders and he inhaled her sweet almond scent. With her ear pressed to his chest she could still hear the elevated heartbeat and his continued arousal pleased her.

Their connection had grown strong the last months of self-imposed exile. Absorbing fully the news from earlier in the day allowed her to finally let her imagination take flight. She was returning to the capital, only this time, not as a captive slave girl but the favoured concubine of a great warlord. Whom, would very soon, be the second most powerful man in the Empire.

Openly, he spoke of his desire to make 'his city' the capital of the new Islamic Rome. His slighted pride had been replaced with a clear strategic plan for power. Now, she had to make sure her lord felt she was indispensable to him; physically, emotionally, and mentally. "Will you accompany the Prince to Edirne?" She asked innocently.

"Of course."

"Will the Thracians go with you?"

"Only a small group. It is civil war they are most afraid of and the Vizier will be keen to have a smooth transition. Bringing a horde of troops will only add to any possible tension."

Kissing his neck tenderly and stroking his clean-shaven face, she pressed her ample breasts into his chest. "Will you need a companion to help you relax at night?" she whispered sweetly then lifted her head with exceptional grace and fixed her large almond eyes upon him, her lips in full pout. "I am only thinking of your wellbeing, my Lord."

Antonis let out a hearty laugh, "of course you are, my dear."

Fatima flashed her warmest smile, knowing she would now

accompany him. Feeling his arousal again, she willingly, focused all her energy upon her lover.

"Sire, I think we should only take fifty men, anymore would create unease," said Antonis.

Mehmet digested the morning's conversation; his dreams were nearing fruition. The countless months he spent with his friend and trusted lieutenant planning what he was to do when he acquired the reins of power, now seemed dauntingly real. "Very well, but we shall be taking all our personal household," he said then added mischievously. "I am sure you would want your concubine to join you."

Antonis nodded, recollecting the conversation with Fatima the previous night. Gently repeating this was the opportunity he had craved, to be the power behind the throne. Yet he could clearly see he meant more to Mehmet than being a mere stepping-stone to ultimate power. They truly were cut from the same cloth.

The heir apparent saw Zaganos Pasha deep in thought and thanked Allah for this man crossing his path. Looking at the tight black curls of hair, he knew this was the only person he could trust for he had repeatedly demonstrated personal loyalty, yet he still did not know what drove him. Deciding there would be time enough to discover the Greek's secret later, he turned his attention to the impending visit to the dying Sultan. "I still do not trust Halil Pasha, for it was his actions that forced me into this exile," said Mehmet coldly.

"The tables have now turned. Soon you will have the upper hand. I suggest we leave at dawn."

"Agreed," said Mehmet as he carefully finished his breakfast.

.   .   .

PAIN SHOT through his body as he struggled through rattled breath. The throat infection he had contracted six weeks earlier had spread to his lungs. The fawning surgeons on their daily visits only made him more irascible. He threatened them with execution unless they healed him. The black humour of his empty threats one of the only things that gave him respite from his impending demise, the other was the succession.

Whilst it pleased him that his Grand Vizier cared so much about the sultanate, he had no worries about his son. The boy had steel running through him, something the Turkish aristocracy did not understand. Furthermore, his heir had loyal people around him, especially Zaganos Pasha, still an enigma, yet his achievements for the kingdom could not be disputed. The cool January breeze wafted through the open window. *At least I'll die in pleasant temperatures.*

The elegance of Candarli Pasha had been replaced with worry over the past few weeks as he agonised over the succession. A member of his clan had been Vizier for the last sixty-one years. They had made sure they survived the existential collapse fifty years ago and now it rested on his narrow shoulders to make sure it did not happen again. He would not be remembered as the Vizier who let the Empire crumble, he reiterated to himself as he entered the royal chamber. "Good morning, your Majesty."

"What news have you for me today?"

"Your son, the Prince, is en-route to the capital, sire. He should be here in three days."

"Good, so you can finally stop your fretting."

Candarli Pasha smiled humourlessly.

"Anything more you wish to say to your dying ruler?"

"Nothing of importance, sire."

"Good. Now leave me until my son arrives."

. . .

RESPLENDENT in a bright gold frockcoat with matching suede boots and sky-blue britches, Mehmet confidently approached his father's inner sanctum. On either side of him, walked Zaganos Pasha and the Grand Vizier. The young prince relished the enmity between them as they were soon, after him, be the most powerful men in the Empire. As they reached the bedchamber, he told them to remain outside, as he wished to see his father alone.

"Come here, my boy," rattled the Sultan, "let me take a closer look at you."

Mehmet inched closer, feeling like a child again. The grey pallor of the Sultan's skin and water-filled bloodshot eyes instantly struck him, but it was the cold clamminess of his hands as he kissed them that confirmed the mark of death was upon this padisha.

"Take off your hat," ordered Murad. The son duly obliged and after removing his headgear, the rheumy eyes inspected the visitor. "You have grown into a man, and soon, you will be Sultan. Do you think you are good enough for the role?"

Mehmet shot him a look of defiance but remained silent, noting that his father was only in his mid-forties. Not a very long life and he wondered if he would live as long or perhaps longer and with such achievements.

The Sultan let out a low cackle, "Thinking about your legacy already? Will you do better than me?"

"No, sir, I was thinking about your health," he replied a half-truth.

"Good to see you lie so well, a very important quality to have in a leader. Remember, you are always alone at the top and can never rely on anyone. There is no such thing as unconditional loyalty."

Mehmet nodded and listened; for it was the first time he was receiving any real paternal advice; he never counted the eve of Kosovo.

"I can see you have big plans, my young Prince, but first, you must win over the aristocrats, and secure your base before doing anything ambitious."

Locked in the palatial bedchamber, the Sultan dispensed all his acquired wisdom to his successor, this going on for a full two days from dawn until dusk, with only the interruption of servants delivering refreshment. Mehmet hung on his father's every word, absorbing as much as he could; the Sultan dispensing insights with alacrity before his time ran out. On the third day, satisfied he had imparted all that he could, he ordered that his top three Viziers be present when Mehmet arrived that morning.

"I have gathered you three as the top-ranking officials in the kingdom."

Candarli Halil Pasha and the other Viziers listened intently. None of them had any doubt what was to come next.

"Wait, father, I would like Zaganos Pasha to join us too as he is my trusted aide," blurted Mehmet.

Murad raised an eyebrow in feigned annoyance. *He's already thinking like a ruler.*

The servant propped the Sultan on luxurious brightly coloured pillows, so he sat almost upright. His once chubby face had a gaunt look. Taking the goblet of lemon water proffered to him, the ailing man drank greedily in preparation. Finally satiated, he turned to his waiting audience. "My lords, I have gathered you here at my bedside today to declare my dying wishes."

The Viziers looked on expectantly, their excessively perfumed hair and skin clouding the Sultan's thoughts momentarily as he took his next laboured breath.

"Prince Mehmet is my designated heir. He will, upon my death, become the ruler of the House of Osman. As such, I want you to now, in my presence, swear your allegiance to him." With a subtle wave of his hand, he guided the Viziers' gazes to his son.

Mehmet turned to face his ministers and held out his hand as they each in turn knelt, kissed it, and swore loyalty.

Antonis looked on bemused at the ceremony unfolding before him; the inscrutable look on the young prince's face, and the fawning courtiers all presiding over by the dying ruler.

"Zaganos Pasha," said the Sultan. "It is your turn now, but before you do so, I promote you to Fourth Vizier."

Candarli Pasha used all his years of diplomatic training to contain his surprised horror. *An upstart convert is now a Vizier!*

Antonis hid nothing, the news was incredible. *How many more accolades will this Sultan give me?* With due ceremony, the newly promoted Greek took his friend's hand, knelt, and swore undying fealty to him.

Probably the only one of the four who actually means it, thought the Sultan.

UPON MURAD'S ORDERS, the news was made official later that day. The Sultan's household scribes sent sealed letters to all governors, beys, and ancient tribal headmen of the officially sanctioned succession. The next few days were uneventful. Mehmet did not change his daily routine, except for spending more time writing at his desk, not even telling Antonis what he was so hard at work with.

The newly promoted Vizier whiled away his time with an elated Fatima, who showed her happiness in a myriad of ways. There would be no administration overhauls until the Sultan died, so he relaxed for the first time in years, finally feeling comfortable in his skin. Looking at the beautiful woman in this opulent setting, his life in Constantinople, Mistras, and Crete seemed so far away; pedestrian and dull compared to where he was now.

He wondered what his bastard brother was doing, and smiled; it would not be long until they saw each other again. An idea sparked and he quickly penned a letter to Halil, his old smuggler friend. As he dripped the wax on the letter, he knew he had to change his seal, to reflect his increased status. Satisfied, he turned his attentions back to his mistress, deciding to indulge himself once more.

THE COLD DEW had not left the ground on this particularly chilly February morning and the wail of the call to prayer sounded as usual through the city as the faithful began their daily rituals. Yousuf, Murad's loyal eunuch, entered his master's chamber with a pitcher of water, figs, and some olives on a heavy gold tray. The still slender forearms of a man castrated before puberty, carried the weight with ease. Placing the dish carefully by Murad's bedside, he went to draw the curtain. He gasped as he caught the wide-eyed stare of his now departed master. Touching nothing, he hurriedly left to inform the palace dignitaries.

The wail of mourning soon trumpeted across the city rooftops. Town criers, merchants, and imams all broadcast their lamentations of their beloved Sultan.

Groggily, Mehmet opened his eyes to see one of his servants looking at him wide-eyed. Instantly, he knew why. What surprised him was how unaffected he was. "What is it?" he asked.

"Sire... your Majesty. The Sultan passed away last night."

The realisation spurred him into action. He rubbed his face to order his thoughts. "Fetch Zaganos Pasha," he barked.

Hurriedly, the messenger left on his ordered errand.

Inhaling the faint perfumed scent of his lover, the usual dawn cacophony sounded different this morning. At first, he thought it was a new prayer then it hit him that they were lamentations. He strode over to the shuttered windows, pushing them open, the nascent light flooded in, accompanied by the clear wailing. Instantly, he understood what it meant, and his thoughts went to Mehmet. Hurriedly, he dressed, leaving a dozing Fatima undisturbed. Not forgetting his sfakion, he briskly headed for the Prince's quarters. Passing the standing Thracian guards with a curt acknowledgment, he spied the fretting figure of Mehmet's servant hurrying down the dawn-lit corridor.

As the man slowed to address him, he put up his hand. "I know, where is the Prince?"

"In his quarters, my Lord."

Without breaking stride, he headed towards the new ruler of the Ottoman Empire. A sense of destiny absorbed him; all his years of loyalty would now come to fruition. The brightness of the rising sun had an extra intensity as he approached Mehmet's chambers and with the imbuing sense of success guiding him, he entered the rooms.

The young Sultan was at his desk writing a beautiful calligraphic missive. With a flourish, he signed his name at the bottom of the parchment, and carefully dusted it with powder. After a quick glance of satisfaction, he handed the letter to the waiting Greek.

Not sure what to expect, he read slowly and as he reached the end, let out a deep belly laugh. "You waste no time, my Sultan," said Antonis.

"We have talked about it often enough, now is the time to act, Zaganos Pasha."

32

THE LETTER

Constantine's shook as he read the contents of the message. The rage inside him wanted to tear the beautifully calligraphed letter to shreds but he knew that would not make the demand it contained go away.

George Sphrantzes and Lukas Notaras looked on concerned. No one in the council knew what he had just read, only that it came from the new Sultan, Mehmet II. There had been great rejoicing in the new Sultan, but he was a mere boy, and had been toppled once already, so what threat could he be?

"What does it say, your Majesty?" asked Notaras.

"The little brat," he snarled, "has asked me to leave my city as he desires it to be the new capital of his Empire."

A hushed tone descended on the listeners. Hands were wrung and shoulders slumped. All knew what this implied and in unison their thoughts turned to their families and survival.

"Sire, our walls have never been breached in a thousand years," said Sphrantzes.

"Except through treachery," shouted one of the wags in the gathered crowd. Another shouted that Mehmet was just a dim-witted boy and further that he would not risk war with Venice and Genoa. Soon, the whole chamber was in belligerent uproar, challenging the young Sultan to do his worst. Constantine was unsure, he only knew he had to respond and refute the demand.

Stroking his full dark beard, Lukas Notoras, the Megas Doux was in no doubt as to the seriousness of the letter. One of the richest men in the empire, his family had spent generations acquiring wealth in the different domains of the Byzantine world and was not about to lose it. Amongst this pack of braying dogs, there would be little chance of getting his voice heard for any meaningful discussion but hearing all this insane shouting was driving him to distraction. "Sire!" bellowed his deep voice as he stood. The power and pitch cut through the crowd's noise and for an instant they quietened.

"Yes, your Grace," replied Constantine, welcoming a point to focus on.

Seizing his initial advantage, Notaras pressed on. "What do we know of this new Sultan? Does he have the support of his Aristocrats? How real is this threat?"

The pertinence of the questions subdued the crowd.

His only information came through correspondence with Halil Pasha and he was not sure how much power he would yield in the new order. Why wasn't Alexis still alive so he could access his network of informants, idly wondering if Nicola had picked up those reins. "Sire?" repeated Notaras.

"Before we respond, we shall look into it, Mega Doux," said the Emperor.

George Sphrantzes, the Great Logothetes, had been listening with intent at the shouts and arguments. As the First Minister, it was down to him to guide his old friend and ruler in the best possible way. His portly frame trundled towards the Emperor, who was standing on the dais and gently requested they speak privately.

Constantine said they would speak later and opened the floor to debate on what should be the next step. A lord from Trebizond threw in his florin's worth of opinion as the hall once again erupted into pandemonium. Planedes decided he had heard enough and knowing he would not be included in any private discussions, left to make his own preparations for the future.

Feeling the heat from all the anger spewed, made the Emperor weary. It had now descended into a pointless ranting and he decided greater sense would be wrought from his inner council. Once back in his private chambers, Constantine felt more at ease, yet the nagging fact that he had not been crowned in the great Cathedral of Aghia Sophia lingered. Consoling himself that it was purely symbolic, it was these very symbols that made men believe in him when he sat on his dais in the throne room.

Gone were the ornate adornments and clutter of furniture, to be replaced with a simple but beautifully crafted wooden table around which were placed seven chairs; four along one length, one at each end and his solely on the other side. Each of these placements were allotted. The facing seats were for his two most senior lords, the Megas Doux and Grand Logothetis, the other two for the patriarch and the leading general.

Wistfully, he glanced at the last, which remained empty since Alexis' death. There was no real army in the city that warranted a general, he thought bitterly, his only real troops were the remnants of the Laconians in Mistras. From the large arched windows, he gazed over the outer walls and the flat plain beyond towards his opponent's capital, out of sight but very much in mind. He needed allies, but at what cost to the dominion? Who could he send that would be heard without being sullied by politics? There was only one man he trusted and had that ability. It looked like that seat would be filled once more.

· · ·

THE FLAMES BEGAN to flicker on the collection of oil lamps around the room, warning its occupants they needed to be refilled. The debate, sometimes heated, raged on through the night. Options and counterplans flowed between the five middle-aged men seated around the table.

Planedes felt flattered to be allowed into such exalted company, though in truth, it was simply the measure of their desperation, he thought cynically. The facts were depressing; near-empty coffers, a few hundred professional soldiers, no navy, and their defensive walls in serious need of repair. Even he had not thought the situation was so dire, which at least confirmed that his planned course of action was the best to follow.

"So, it is agreed, we will send an envoy to raise help from our Christian brothers in the west. Repair our walls promptly and call in all our troops from the outlying protectorate," said Constantine.

Planedes stopped himself from laughing at the absurdity of it all. It was like trying to stop a charging bull with a peashooter, but gravely, he agreed along with the others. With the actions settled, the next phase was to apportion the tasks, which happened with relative ease. Notaras had the walls, Sphrantzes the Genoese at Galata. The patriarch to soothe the populace, and Constantine would try the diplomatic route with Halil Pasha, whom he regarded as being a wise counsel of caution in the Ottoman court and could be trusted. Planedes was to help Notaras with the strength of the city's defences. The only issue had been who was to be the envoy in the west.

The first choice was clearly Constantine, but he knew that leaving the city now would inspire panic and unrest. Furthermore, there was one other person in the kingdom who had fought alongside them and was respected in his own right. The mention of Nicola Vevellis' name brought an unforeseen tirade of objections. He could not fathom why, as he had made up his mind, and determinedly convinced each of those present until they concurred. Finally, all in agreement, they prepared themselves for the task ahead.

33

THE THROAT-CUTTER

A deluge of correspondence filled Katerina's small desk, as since the new Sultan's accession there was conflicting evidence of what was happening in Edirne. Through all the mire, she was sure of one thing, the young ruler was not content with the status quo and along with General Zaganos Pasha, his heart of stone desired more power. Her city was the logical choice. She focused her mind on Nicola and happier thoughts. Her feelings quickly turned to guilt as she still had not told him of their son, preferring to wait until she could tell him in person.

Agatha had played her role to perfection and her family allowed the child into the household. At least it restored a glimmer of life in her mother, Katerina thought, and hoped the connection would not be made. But it might soon happen, as the Emperor had sent for Nicola, and with the thought of only a few more days to that revelation, she returned to her duties with a renewed feeling of hope.

· · ·

NICOLA IMBIBED the clear salty sea air, the gentle motion of the carrack relaxing him. The dispatch he had received from Constantine was perturbing, but at least it meant he would see Katerina again and hopefully this time, she would leave with him. Subconsciously, he touched the letters in his breast-pocket. She had, as promised, written to him regularly, though, her last three letters had seemed different, in a way he couldn't quite fathom.

"Always thinking, my lad. Not good for the health, you know," said the ever-jolly Thanos.

The constant presence of his friend had a way of lightening his burden. "You should have been an actor, Thanos, you give people humour."

"Nicola, we are all actors in the play of life."

The younger man let out one of his booming laughs. "Well, you certainly are no philosopher."

"No, my brains are well below my belt," came the quick retort.

The two men stared across the wine-dark Aegean, content in their silence with only the fluttering of sails as accompaniment.

"ZAGANOS PASHA, have you gathered the men as we discussed?" asked Mehmet.

"Yes, your Majesty, including the stone masons and labourers among them. If we require further manpower when we're there, we can hire locally," replied Antonis.

The young Sultan smiled thinly, once this action became knowledge, the other Christian states would have to react. In truth, he sensed they would prevaricate and be appeased with trade rights. "Good. Then go with the blessing of Allah, and I shall meet you there in three moons, by which time I expect there to be significant progress."

Antonis had no doubts he would achieve their ambitious aims in the timeframe they had set themselves. He intended to surpass them. It was time to enact what he had conceived and created.

Nicola awaited the Emperor's news with trepidation. "Sire, my Laconians are at your disposal."

"I am making you the Imperial Envoy and task you with raising the assistance we need from the Latin kingdoms. Letters have been sent to the Italian states, France, and the Spanish kingdoms, heralding your arrival."

Nicola was speechless.

"However, first we must make your status proportionate to the role, and as such, I promote you to Grand Chamberlain of the Treasury, Kyrie Vevellis."

Ennobled and promoted in one swift move. Surely, Katerina could now have no impediment to their marriage. He stole a glance at Planedes standing amongst the throng and caught the faintest glimmer of a smile. Was that acknowledgement? A politician such as he would always approve of power just as a moth was drawn to the flame.

Constantine had left nothing unprepared, having his new seal ready and an imperial ring for Nicola to wear with immediate effect. Even the best ship was placed at his disposal, which Nicola politely declined, as it would be needed in the defence of the city. Glancing at his ruler's greying temples, he wondered if he had the stomach or the skill for the fight ahead.

Thanos felt pride for the lad. Admittedly, it was a hollow title; but it carried a thousand years of tradition and he could now forever banish the stain in his mind of being only the adopted son.

"Lord Vevellis, when will you be ready to depart?" asked the Emperor.

"Three days hence, sire."

Constantine smiled and hoped his ploy would work.

"How long will you be away?" asked Fatima forlornly.

"The whole project will take a few months, at most," replied Antonis, surprised as his voice softened with emotion.

"Will you return at all during that time?" she knew better than to ask to accompany him.

His brooding face creased into a smile and his blue eyes sparkled. "It's not that far away."

She just stared at him with her deep almond eyes, her full mouth pouting in sadness.

"You will be able to visit after we have set the foundations."

Fatima's face broke into unabashed delight as she flung her athletic limbs around his neck, showering him with kisses.

He was finding it increasingly difficult to resist her, and it went beyond her sexual beauty, it was something deeper that felt just right. However, decorum took hold; he firmly gripped her arms and told her to control herself.

In mock admonishment, she obeyed to let him go and complete what he had set out to do, comfortable in the knowledge he had eyes only for her. Each day she fell in love with him a little more, and for the first time, she permitted herself to think of marriage.

Pacing around the courtyard of Thanos' house like a caged animal, Nicola contemplated the task ahead. He was a soldier, not a diplomat. Feelings of sadness overwhelmed him as he picked up each of the five imperial letters he was to take to the Latin states in the west. The Emperor's instructions kept invading his thoughts, it would take at least a year to visit all those cities. He had riches and power now, yet it came with heavy responsibilities and high price.

He had only been in the city one day and the Emperor asked him to leave post-haste. But before he did, he had to see Katerina, even if for only one hour. What were three days in the twelve centuries of the Empire's history?

Satisfied with the instruction to his household regarding his packing, Thanos made his way to see Nicola. Feeling relaxed in his green silk robes, he decided a night of drinking together in his house would do the trick. He also thought about inviting some female company, but Nicola was too honourable for that and he dismissed the idea. The huge frame swiftly pacing around brought home his friend's predicament. "Why are you so worried?"

"Me? I'm fine."

"Then why the pacing?"

"It's just… there is a lot to do and so little time," replied Nicola.

Thanos nodded and took a swig of wine from the fine silver goblet he was carrying. "You mean too little time to see your nun lady friend?"

Nicola shot him an angry look.

"We don't have to leave immediately. We can delay a few days."

"I already decided that."

"Good, now let's have a drink or two tonight and enjoy the smells and sounds of the city."

A servant appeared laden with prepared fruits, sweetmeats, a pitcher of wine and two goblets. Thanos filled his goblet and settled into a relaxing evening of drink and conversation.

Katerina sat idle at her desk for hours, her thoughts elsewhere, for she knew Nicola had entered the city and was waiting for word from him. Finally, at sunset, a note arrived, asking her to go see him at Thanos' house the following evening. Her heart leapt in anticipation and she resumed her correspondence with renewed energy.

THE ARRIVAL of hundreds of peasants from the Balkan hinterland placed a strain on the available resources, the ever-present smell of human refuse mingling with the smoke of the burning vegetation. Antonis set a unit to create living space and order in the camp, running it as he did his Thracians, with military efficiency. It was testament to his strength of personality that it held together as he opted only for a personal guard of sixteen to accompany him whilst governing and managing nearly one thousand disparate people. Even in his most arrogant thoughts, they could never control a full-scale rebellion, therefore, the use of intelligence and show of power would have to suffice.

After one week, they were ready to lay the foundations and soon, the quarried stone would be arriving, as would masons, carpenters, and draftsmen, who would undoubtedly be trailed by the usual hawkers, thieves, and whores.

Looking at the large parchment on the trestle table, Antonis listened as the main architect described how he could begin to lay the foundations in the shape of the Mohammed calligraphic, taking everything into account. The topography allowed for the construction of the shape and decided that three large towers would be all that was needed to anchor the curtain wall of the castle. They were to be simple round towers, built quickly and economically as the most important thing was to have this 'throat-cutter' as it had become known, constructed and in use as soon as was humanly possible.

Strangle their supply routes, the oft-repeated words of Mehmet came into his head.

Finally, with the camp swelled by another few hundred, a

squadron of cavalry arrived with green and golden banners fluttering high above. The horsemen imperiously rode into the bustling camp. Threading their way through the ordered lines of tents and workstations, the Sultan's guard with Mehmet at their fore, headed towards Antonis, who was busy delegating the daily tasks. Deliberately delaying until the last moment to acknowledge his ruler's arrival, Antonis did not notice the two Viziers who accompanied the cavalcade.

"Zaganos Pasha, we are pleased to see such progress," said a buoyant Mehmet.

The fierce blue eyes accepted the praise then settled on the elegant figure of Candarli Pasha.

"Congratulations on your supreme efforts in getting this 'Throat cutter' commenced," said Halil Pasha in his condescendingly grating tone. As he spoke, two men brought forward a large wooden chest with shiny metal bands around it and carefully placed it at Antonis' feet.

"What is this, my Lord?"

Before Halil Pasha could answer, his Sultan interjected. "Our Grand Vizier has offered to build one of the towers of the Rumeli Hasara."

Antonis bent down and opened the chest, filled to the brim with gold, hiding his obvious pleasure that the old fox had resorted to this grand gesture. Sensing a moment in which he could be magnanimous, he offered the Vizier his choice of tower to build and have it named after him.

Mehmet watched as the play acted out between his two most powerful Lords.

Out of the corner of his eye, Antonis saw the Sultan's cold smile as he accepted the choice of tower from Halil. There was no forgiveness in Mehmet's heart and at that moment he knew the Grand Vizier's fate was sealed. A brief pang of pity for the old politician, who had aided him to reach this exalted position, struck him, before he resigned it to the order of life.

By the end of the first month, all the foundations had been laid and the stone edifices started to rise from the ground, block by block. Not wanting to miss out, the second Vizier, Sadic Pasha donated a small fortune to construct the third and last tower, so that by the coming of the second full moon, three pillars of Ottoman power graced the skyline and began the ominous domination of the strait.

"Sire, we have a slight problem," said a concerned Master Builder.

Enjoying his breakfast of yoghurt and figs after a particularly energetic training session, Antonis was not in the mood for difficulties. Fixing his gaze on the engineer only worried the poor man more. "What issues do we have, Stepanek?"

"The work has progressed so fast we have used up our supply of stone and are still waiting for the next deliveries from the quarries."

"Well, you had better hope some arrives very soon," replied Antonis and went back to his breakfast.

A low cackle sounded behind him, making him freeze in his repast.

"My, haven't we come a long way?" said the familiar voice to his rear.

A waft of stale fish flew over him as the man drew closer. "Yes, I have," came the cool response as he turned to see the approaching figure of Giorgos.

"Is that how you greet me after all this time, my boy?" The eyes were as wild as ever and wearing a crooked smile, but at least he had covered up his leathered skin with a grey woollen blanket.

Swiftly, two Thracians grabbed the scruffily dressed man who shrieked his abuse at them.

"Leave him!"

"Sorry, sir, we didn't see him creep in," replied one of the guards.

"It's fine, I will speak with him alone." The unexpected appearance of the old smuggler had caught him off guard. What did he want anyway? "Are you hungry?"

The guest declined, only asking for water. "I have been following your progress with interest," said Giorgos, gazing warmly on the younger man.

Antonis felt surprisingly relaxed at this abrupt reminder of his moment of weakness.

His men looked on puzzled as to how this vagrant could command their Pasha's attention, then dismissed it, as they were sure he had his reasons.

"Why have you come, old man?"

Ignoring the hostile tone, Giorgos picked up the goblet with his misshapen hand and drank sparingly. "To see how you are doing. I did say I would check up on you from time to time."

"This is the first time in ten years, I thought you would be dead by now."

The old man chortled, "I will probably outlive you, boy. Halil mentioned that you have begun spying on your enemies."

"What of it?" He replied and unconsciously, his hand went to the branded scar on his chest.

"Be careful of revenge. It has a way of showing you things you don't want to see."

The clarity in the round brown eyes unnerved the younger man. "How is life as fisherman treating you?"

Giorgos ignored the fake pleasantries. "I think it's time I leave, but it's good to see you." The wizened man stood up shakily then as he turned to depart, looked at Antonis again. "Remember what I said," his tone was ominous.

Zaganos Pasha waved his guest away with a pleasant smile, but the leaden words rattled heavily inside his head. The visit from Giorgos distracted him, not with a sense of dread, but instead galvanised him into action.

Satisfied at the pace of construction, he made his way back

to see Halil, to find out if there had been any interesting discoveries. Leaving his trusted Goran in charge, he returned to Edirne, which also had the added benefit of Fatima.

THE DUST-COVERED RIDER quietly approached the side door down the alley of the maids. Under strict instructions to be totally inconspicuous, he kept his black-hooded cloak firmly secured so it did not flap in the summer breeze. Beads of sweat ran down his temples, soaking the fine woollen cloth, and sticking it to his face. Further down the alley, he spied the chink of light that was his destination and slowly crept in through the unbolted entrance.

The lank thinning grey-haired man who greeted him was his paymaster. "Well," he said expectantly.

The messenger held out his hand, "Payment first."

Holding two bags of coins, he gave one. "You get the second when I hear the news."

Bringing himself closer to the paymaster's ear, he recounted the events going on just a few miles north of the city; the mysterious appearance of the fort, the presence of the Sultan, and the operation being driven by the Vizier, Zaganos Pasha.

The unflinching porcine eyes masked the calculated turmoil in his head; knowing this, his course of action was the only one that could transpire now. Pulling out a sealed letter, he weighed it carefully in his hand and investigated the man's face; his breath smelled of stale wine and garlic, and his clothes of being too long in the saddle. He tipped the scroll into his hands. "Deliver this to Zaganos Pasha personally and await a reply. Return and you shall receive six bags of gold. Discretion is a must."

The messenger nodded; six bags was a hefty sum for what would be no more than three day's work. "Agreed," he said and left as quickly and quietly as he came.

Satisfied he had done all he could for the moment, the odious man returned to his bed.

Katerina lay in her love's arms, the naked heat making her feel secure. The joy at seeing him again after all these months was overwhelming, but her mind turned to reality. Nicola as Envoy meant another year apart, and she still had not told him of their baby. But to do so now, might jeopardise his expedition. She fidgeted as she wrestled with the dilemma.

Nicola stroked her thick hair as for him too, this reunion was bittersweet, and he felt her sadness. "When I return, you will leave the Order and we shall be married. I have wealth, influence, and power. We can go anywhere," his voice was calm but determined.

Circumstances were beyond her control, all she could do right now was feel her love for him and their child, and silently agreed, she too did not want to miss any more time from either of them. "Yes, hurry back, and we shall be married, and together always," she replied with tear-filled eyes, desperate to divulge her secret.

Nicola sat up suddenly and smiled broadly. It made him look childlike and innocent again. Then leaping off the bed, he went on bended knee and pulled off the gold ring from his smallest finger. "Will you marry me, Katerina Planedes?" he said, holding out the yellow band encrusted with polished rubies.

"Yes, my love, I will."

With careful ceremony, he slid the ring onto her middle finger. Surprisingly, a perfect fit. "I am so happy; we shall marry as soon as I return."

Katerina put a finger to his mouth to silence him. This was not the time for talk, but expression, and she brought her lips forward to kiss him.

34

DISCOVERY

The icy grip of fear was slowly taking hold in the city. Word had spread of the mission to raise help from the west and a throng of onlookers gathered at the Golden Harbour as Thanos' squadron of ships departed, some in curiosity, others for support, all in hope. The port fishwives could be heard wailing until the last of the carracks passed the outer boom.

The blazing summer sun felt muted under the blanket of the north wind. Nicola was under no illusion as to its silent power and kept his cap firmly on. Entering the Sea of Marmara, the mini fleet sailed past the Ottoman fort at Gallipoli, the flags fluttering proudly in the breeze. For a moment, the crews worried about cannon fire but nothing materialised and they passed through without incident. Nicola had no doubt that upon their return, the enemy would not be so accommodating.

The ships clung to the coastline sailing between Anatolia and the Genoese-held Aegean Islands until they reached Chios on the second day, ostensibly for resupply of water, but Nicola also had a hidden agenda. Approaching the main harbour, he briefed Thanos of his plan.

His comrade let out a low whistle as he heard the scheme. "Well, I suppose it is worth a try."

"He is the best they have, and the visit is en-route," replied Nicola.

"I hear he's quite big and his temper notorious, so even you might have a problem handling him if he doesn't take kindly to your proposition," said a wary Thanos.

"Let me worry about that." But approaching the governor's mansion, doubt abounded within Nicola.

The man who came striding forward to clasp their hands and greeted them was extraordinary. Although the same height, the Genoese's shoulders were nearly a third as wide as Nicola's, the face open, and honest, with large brown eyes set upon a strong square jaw, finished atop with short curly black hair.

"General Vevellis. Your reputation precedes you," said the host.

"As does yours, Giustiniani," replied Nicola.

"To what do we owe the pleasure of your visit?"

In silence Nicola handed the letter that was destined for Genoa.

Intrigued, the giant Italian took the scroll, broke open the seal and read it. His face turned from curiosity to concern. "When did all this start?" he asked.

"The Sultan sent the ultimatum over a month ago. Already they have started construction on a fort to block the Bosphorus."

"To strangle the shipping routes from the north," completed Giustiniani, stroking his beard.

His demeanour reminded Nicola of Alexis. How he wished he were here now.

The Genoese ordered his servant to assemble his lieutenants. "Come, let us have some breakfast, whilst we wait for the others to join us. You can tell me about your famed Laconians. If they are anything like you, then they are most formidable," bellowed Giustiniani as he eyed Nicola.

They could not argue with his hospitality and followed him to the terrace where a simple meal of bread, olives, and fruit awaited. Before long, the two lieutenants of the Condottiere Company joined them, Giovani Testoni and Paolo Braga, both seasoned veterans peppered with scars and hardened eyes. After brief pleasantries, they charged headlong into strategic discussions; the number of men the Greeks could raise, the state of the city's defences, the mood of the people. Sanguinely they took the bad news.

"So, your Emperor's plan is to ask for help from the Latin states to defend the city?" piped up Testoni.

"Yes."

"You are going to need a further ten thousand men to have a middling chance of survival. I don't think you are going to do it," responded Testoni.

"Well, you have seven hundred already, and I am committing my men to the fight," said Giustiniani.

His gathered lieutenants smiled wolfishly at the prospect.

Nicola nodded appreciatively, only nine thousand three hundred to go.

"You will have a great deal of difficulty in persuading the councils in Venice and Genoa to commit troops. They will vacillate in fear of losing trade rights with the Turk. Gold, it seems, is more important than beliefs nowadays."

"It always has been," replied Nicola.

All the warriors laughed.

Braga, a short dark man from Puglia, offered, "Before you go to the cities, visit the Bocciardi Brothers in Ponte Negro. They are crazy, but good soldiers, and love any chance to fight the Turk. Also, they do as they please and pay no mind to their superiors in Venice."

Nicola noted that and decided to stop there on the way west.

Curiosity got the better of their hosts, and they enquired about Alexis Sartis. His reputation was renowned, and these fellow soldiers held his achievements in high regard. Who was he to argue? The rest of the morning was spent in conversation about his deeds and praise of the man's character. With free-flowing wine, the time passed most quickly.

Nicola was itching to leave, but upon the Italians insistence, stayed a further three days. During which they showed him their military might and discussed ways in which he would be best placed to persuade their fellow Genoese to join the fight. Which notaries would be in favour, which would not; he was bitterly aware it all revolved around who had the most to lose financially.

Re-stocked and supplied, the three ships once again set sail to their next destination. After a brief visit to the mad Bocciardi brothers, who were most willing to join them, Nicola and Thanos made the two-day journey to the port of Mistras to prepare their men.

"We have a thousand committed so far," said Thanos.

Nicola baulked at his friend's enthusiasm and held out little hope for the mission's success.

Neither did Thanos, but he was not about to let Nicola know that.

"Thanos, I will take one of the ships and sail to Crete, it's time I go see my father. It has been too long, and I need to personally tell him the news of what has happened." Nicola's voice was tinged with sadness as he spoke.

"I wondered when you were going to do that. Now is as good a time as any, and we are not far." As he finished speaking an idea sparked in the old rogue, "Whilst you are there, see if you can get some troops too. Your fellow islanders in the Lefka Mountains would be most useful."

Nicola turned and smiled, having already decided on that course of action.

Clasping his shoulder, Thanos wished him luck, telling him he would have the men ready to sail to the city within two weeks, and could return within the month. "Take your time, nothing will happen till next spring."

STEPPING on home soil for the first time in years brought mixed emotions. He bought a fine-looking bay mare from the old horse trader by the Venetian boatyards and wasting no time, took the coastal road west, towards his home village.

Snaking along the road, nothing had changed; still the same fishermen's huts that clung to the rocky outcrop. The tiny caiques rolling in the sea, waited at their tethers to go out at dawn again. Passing the white sands of Maleme, the countryside opened into the gentle rolling hills covered in olive trees and citrus groves towards the Tavronitis River. In the far distance the stark peaks of the Lefka Mountains thrust into the air.

Nicola's thoughts went to the events of twelve years past. It seemed so long ago, the sadness was muted. Those bandits had been frightening but what he had experienced since made the incident seem insignificant. Letting the mare walk at her own pace, he imbibed the familiar smells, for he was in no rush to confront his father with the news he was carrying, acting like a procrastinating adolescent trying to avoid a chore rather than the veteran warrior he was. But time passed quickly and before long, he crossed the River and was at the foot of the valley leading up to his family's home.

The pale stone house shone out like a beacon surrounded by tall cypress trees with the kitchen garden to its left. The well-trodden red dirt path gave way to pebble paving as he approached and entered the pillars that buttressed the walls. He noticed very little signs of life. Tethering his horse at the steps, Nicola walked in, shouting greetings to anyone present. Finally, a maid appeared, whom he did not recognise and asked for the owners of the house.

She replied that Kyrie Vevellis was on the terrace that overlooked the sea and hurriedly, he strode to find his father.

At first glance, he thought he was mistaken. The shrivelled old man asleep in the chair was nothing as he remembered. Carefully, he approached without waking him to look more closely. Andreas' hair was brilliant white, and he had lost all his bulk so that his skin hung loose under his chin. The joints in his hands were swollen with a thick covering of age spots and long yellowed nails. Nicola did not expect anything this severe. Gently, he placed his hand on the now bony shoulder and shook his father awake.

The old man grunted and came to, slowly opening his eyes. "Nicola, is that you?" he rasped.

"Yes, Papa, it is."

"Come here, my boy, help me up," he said in disbelief.

Nicola bent down and pulled his father out of the chair, surprised at how light he was.

As he came to full height, Andreas hugged his boy with all the strength he had, the spindly arms digging into Nicola's sides, sobbing at the joy of seeing him again. "I cannot believe it's you after all this time." The wrinkled face regained some of his prior vigour as he gazed upon his son and saw how he had grown into a man. "Where did you get this?" he asked, pointing to the scar running along his neck and in front of his ear. "Not over a girl, I hope?"

"After Varna, a rogue Turk caught me by surprise with a knife." Not a full lie but kinder than the truth.

"Lucky he didn't finish you," replied his father.

"Enough about me, where is mama?"

Andreas' shoulders slumped and his jaw set at the question. "She passed away a few years back."

Pangs of guilt hit Nicola at his lack of communication these past seasons. "How? What happened?"

The maid reappeared with a tray of lemon water and some fruit. Andreas asked her to bring wine as he sat down and recounted what occurred after they received his letter.

"Maria was heartbroken at Antonis' banishment and her joy for life left her. Her health began to fail, she died two years later."

Nicola wondered if she would have had the same reaction if it had been him, but he already knew the answer. Now, he started to doubt what he had to say, for this would surely break his frail father.

The wine arrived and Andreas gulped the greater part of a goblet. "Now, tell me about you. What has happened in your life?" He no longer wanted to go over old sad news, instead wanting to hear good tidings. "Do you have a wife, children?"

"No, I don't," replied Nicola, "But I am the General of the Laconians now."

A look of pride came over his father's face and he demanded more news.

Nicola obliged and told of his adventures with Alexis after Varna and their success in capturing Athens, the tragedy at Kosovo, right up to him being made Envoy for the Emperor. Carefully, he omitted anything relating to Antonis and as he chattered on the fear of breaking the difficult information grew. Once he finished his tale, he saw the energy of life flowing in his father again.

"You have done well, my boy," said Andreas but his intuition told him Nicola was hiding something. "Why have you come to see me?"

"It has been a long time and I wanted to visit home."

His father's eyes bored through him as of old.

"Also, we need to raise troops and I thought our countrymen would want to join the fight," he added lamely.

"What is the real reason?"

Nicola bit his lip apprehensively. "Antonis has gone to the Turk. It was he who secured victory for them at Kosovo and caused Alexis' death," he paused to see his father's reaction. There was none. "He is now general of the Sultan's armies and is known as Zaganos Pasha."

That name flickered recognition, for everyone in Byzantium knew of him. Andreas rested his chin on his closed fist and went into deep thought. Stroking his white hair with a gnarled hand, he absorbed what he had just heard. "Well, if it was to be either of my sons, Antonis was the more likely one, his frustrated ambition always lay bubbling under the surface, and the Turk offered him more chance for advancement."

The matter-of-fact tone seemed strange to Nicola, "Papa, I cannot know how you feel about Antonis' betrayal. I understand that I am only an adopted son, but I will strive to do this family honour and defend our city to the best of my abilities."

The old man started laughing, much to the younger's confusion, who took a nervous swig of wine. "There is something that you should know." Andreas paused. "I am your real father."

Nicola choked on his drink.

"Upon my return to Crete, I fell in love with a local farm girl, called Helen, and she swiftly became pregnant. However, during that time, I was ensnared in a betrothal of marriage agreed between my father and Maria's."

Bewilderment abounded within Nicola, as he tried to comprehend what he had just learned. "Then where is my mother now?"

"Your mother died in childbirth and I was too weak to embrace you as an illegitimate son, knowing Maria would never accept you in our family. So I arranged for Zenon to adopt you. Only the two of us knew the truth, as Helen had no immediate family. I watched you grow into the image of your mother, a constant reminder of my true love, and my weakness."

"Then Zenon died in the riding accident," said Nicola.

His father nodded. "Yes, and God gave me a chance at redemption, so I adopted you to raise as my own. Maria, knowing no different, accepted you because of what she imagined my act of kindness."

"When would you have told me?" asked Nicola, surprised at his lack of anger.

"There never seemed to be a right time, until… now, that Maria is gone. I vowed to tell you the next time we saw each other."

It was too much to absorb. He was truly of the Vevellis bloodline, something he always wanted to be. And although his father had shown weakness, fate allowed him to make amends. Then, Antonis… Would they ever unite again? Would this knowledge influence his decision? Of that, he was not sure.

His father seemed so small and frail that his heart went out to him. And now, they only had each other, as he had lost everything else, true love, a son, and a wife. Nicola went to him, hugging him in forgiveness.

The old man, overcome with emotion, sobbed in his son's arms.

35

ORBAN

The sun beat down on his head as he rode into the city. To his surprise, the buildings by the wall were deserted and overgrown. Urbanity had been replaced with fallow fields. Half a mile on the road and then the familiar smells of sweet curried stews mingled with the filth of humanity. It had been a long journey to come here and now all he could think of was rest as he made his way to his brother's house in the southern part of the city. Though not a salubrious district, as the middle-aged man arrived at his destination, he noticed that they had fallen on hard times. Laughing to himself as his timing could not have been better, he rapped on the door.

The small wooden peephole opened abruptly and a fresh-faced young woman with piercing green eyes appeared.

"Natasha, is that you?"

"Who wants to know?"

"I am your uncle Orban."

Her eyes widened in long-lost recognition and instantly the sound of sliding bolts preceded the opening of the thick wooden door.

Has it been that long? For the child he recalled now stood before him a handsome woman. "Where is your father?"

"He passed away last year." Natasha told him then sensing her lapse in manners, asked, "Do you have any luggage, uncle? I can prepare a bed, so you can rest."

"This knapsack and satchel are all I have but I would be grateful for a place to rest. Thank you, my dear."

Natasha showed him to her father's old room. The house was kept clean but it was clear how close to poverty she lived.

Helping him settle in, she was curious as to what the leather bag contained.

"That, my dear niece, is our salvation."

Natasha smiled for the first time in months.

THE EMPEROR PORED over the inventory of the city; barrels of grain, olive oil, and flour. At least they had sufficient provisions for a siege, but only just, he reflected; certainly, better than the Empire's coffers, which were nearly empty. After council with Notaras, Sphrantzes, and Planedes, he decided to strip the minor churches of whatever valuables they contained, which would at least pay for any mercenaries who showed up. And there was the additional cost of repairing parts of the walls that had fallen into disrepair. Deep in thought on finding solutions, his concentration was broken by one of the courtiers.

"Sire, there is a gentleman requesting an audience."

"Why are you disturbing me with this? Tell him to go through the proper channels."

"Sire, he says he can bring a Tagma's worth of troops to the city's defence."

The Emperor stopped looking at his books. "Who is he?"

"He calls himself Orban, from Hungary."

Probably a tribal chieftain who wanted some famed Byzantine gold. "Bring him forth."

A short middle-aged man entered, clutching a leather satchel. Droopy hound-dog eyes sat in gnarled grey skin; his jowls covered in a salt-and-pepper matt of hair. Certainly, not the wild warlord he was expecting.

Theatrically, the man bowed, spilling the contents of his bag. "Your Majesty, I am Orban of Tzizot."

Constantine raised an eyebrow in surprised amusement. "My people tell me you can bring a tagma of men to the defence of the city. I have never heard of a clan chieftain from a city."

"Your Majesty, I can do better than that, for I am a maker of cannon. The best there is," said Orban with supreme confidence.

The Emperor's interest was piqued, having experienced first-hand their devastating effect at the Hexamilion. He motioned the man to proceed.

Orban bumbled forward, set his satchel on the table with a thump, rummaged inside, and pulled out one of his parchments, carefully unfurling it, to show the diagram of the most immense cannon anyone had ever seen, explaining how it would be constructed.

It dawned on his attentive listener that this creation could shatter his walls, even if he doubted its safety.

"For only ten thousand florins I can build this for you."

The Emperor laughed, "A princely sum, my cannon builder, but I don't think we will need something so massive. We have our walls, Greek fire, and our own cannon, if not so large. I thank you for your time and please take some refreshment from one of our courtiers outside."

Seeing the sloped shoulders leave the room, Constantine wondered if he would regret the decision. But he did not have the resources to commission it.

Walking along the tapestry-lined corridor, Orban's mind went to his niece. He had built up her hopes and now would let them down so cruelly. His appetite left him.

"Have you just been to see the Emperor?"

"Yes," he replied.

"With what?"

Orban looked at the man dejectedly.

"Perhaps as one of the council members, I can help," said the dignitary.

What was the harm in telling him? And Orban explained his gun briefly to the porcine man in his path.

The man listened with intent, his scheming mind thinking of possibilities. As Orban finished, he instructed him to go to his house and wait whilst he made the Emperor see reason. Emboldened, Orban left to return to his niece with some news of hope. The shrewd man felt buoyant as he entered the Emperor's chambers.

ANTONIS LAUGHED COLDLY as he read the missive. *How rats leave a sinking ship.* He gazed across the Bosphorus from Zaganos Tower; the Throat-cutter had sprung up in a few weeks and now dominated the narrowest point of the vital water channel. No one had dared run the blockade yet, but he was sure it would only be a matter of time.

Scanning the letter again, he pondered. He certainly had use for an inside man of influence, but the irony of his identity was not lost on him. This was the third such communication but unusually, the traitor informed him he was sending a person of great interest, following on from his assurance to assist with the forthcoming siege. Who was he to argue?

Halil's spies had also returned with news, his mouth twisting cruelly at the thought of Nicola pleading with the Latins for troops. Dispassionately, he thought of Katerina performing the pointless cycle of Christian prayer in that convent. Then it occurred to him to expand the parameters of his operations to include Planedes, for one could never have too much information. The sound of clattering hooves entering the courtyard below broke his train of thought and he saw it was another unexpected visit from the Sultan.

Mehmet was ecstatic, never in his wildest dreams had he expected the fort to be completed so quickly; this meant they could take the city a full year earlier than planned. "Zaganos Pasha, Praise Be to Allah for your stunning feat," he said as he went to clasp his friend's hand.

"For the glory of the Empire," replied Antonis.

"Your work here is done, and we have plenty to do in Edirne."

Antonis nodded and replied with his choice of garrison commander on his departure.

Mehmet agreed with the appointment and with a boyish twinkle in his eye, an act that was reserved only for those closest to him, he requested to see the cannon fire across the Bosphorus.

Antonis was more than happy to oblige.

Within a short time, the stone balls splashed into the middle of the channel in an orderly procession from left to right as the thick black smoke wafted across the parapet.

THE DARK STONE fort ramparts were foreboding to the approaching Orban, who was still processing all that had occurred these past few days. The meeting with the mysterious council member had not gone as he intended. Yet, the man was adamant that his new benefactor would not only be reliable but would pay far more, assuring him the Pasha would receive him and his knowledge gladly, and gave the Hungarian a gold coin as proof.

Orban declared to the sentry at the main gate that he was there to see Zaganos Pasha. From inside his shirt, he pulled out the sealed letter and asked that it be delivered, as he was expected. Before long, another official arrived and ushered him in to see the Pasha.

Large pots in the corner wafted the scent of tea across the courtyard, which was abuzz with soldiers busily going about their duties. Red and green banners fluttered overhead as he was led towards the largest tower. He felt as if he were being shown to a cell, letting out an audible sigh of relief, as they turned left to climb small spiral steps. Running his hands across the hewn stone calmed the nervous engineer, and with each step gained confidence. By the time he was shown in to see the Pasha, a buoyant, if out of breath Orban performed his customary bow with far more grace than the last time. The dark-haired man with piercing eyes and cruel mouth bade him to be seated, as his companion looked on amused.

"Our mutual associate in Constantinople says you have something fantastic to show us."

"I do, my Lord, I most certainly do. This is an impressive castle; how long did it take you to build it?"

"Four months."

"I admit that is incredible, but I can build a machine that could destroy it in three weeks."

The companion spoke. "Tell us how you propose to do this?"

For the second time in as many days, he pulled out his drawings and explained his theories. On this occasion however, his audience was enraptured, and began asking questions as to how he could prove it.

"Explain to me how you can keep the integrity of the bronze at that size?" demanded the companion.

"We mix it with a copper powder in the forge to give it better rigidity. With ten thousand florins I can build this," said the cannon-smith, hoping this time for success.

"You shall build me two and as many of the smaller ones as you can in the next six months."

"But, my Lord, that will require far more than ten thousand florins."

"You shall have unlimited funds and manpower at your disposal."

The Hungarian looked on confused. "Surely, only the Sultan can authorise that?"

"I am the Sultan," said Mehmet.

The canon maker beamed, for now all his years of hard work were about to pay off. How proud Natasha would be of him.

SIEGE

The sounds of cavalry arrived before the lookout at the top of the Circus Gate Tower could see them. Carefully, he scanned the horizon to wait for the first of the invaders to come into view. Outriders appeared with their red and white pennants and horsetail plumes, riding straight towards the walls, seemingly without a care in the world. The sentry let out a sigh, as he saw no further men; probably a scouting party.

Then, it came. A low murmur imperceptible at first, growing slowly into a constant rumble, followed by the shuffling of thousands of feet as they marched steadily forward. Turbans appeared at the brow of the final hill before the city plain, morphing into a fluid bobbing mass, the line gaining depth again and again. Soon, red tops of bouncing nectarines gave way to green tops of bouncing apples, followed by the straining oxen, as they pulled the large wooden siege towers behind them.

Bells started to sound throughout the city and those brave enough clambered up the sparsely guarded parts of the land defences to get a better glimpse of their foe. Slowly, the horde before them unfurled like a coiled snake and the horrified onlookers watched as the reptile continued its long spread.

Turbans gave way to the white peaks of the Janissary, marching purposefully with pike and harquebus towards the Gate. Behind this elite, followed the rest of the army; Bashi Bazouks from Anatolia, in their red tabards, and Levymen from Bulgaria with their long beards. Conscripted Greeks from the occupied territories flanked the clanking wagons carrying covered supplies.

The rhythmic marching lulled the shocked observers into a trance, which snapped as the Janissaries halted in unison three-hundred metres from the walls. The body behind fanned left and right, like a wave breaking on a rock.

Dressed in full armour, Constantine stood at the Romanus Gate to inspect the arrival himself, his display of leadership a calming beacon to his people who had flocked to the walls to see the approaching beast that had come into view just after daybreak, and was still pouring over the hill at noon.

"So, the teetotalling bastards and their Christian whores show themselves to us," bellowed Giustiniani.

Constantine found his constant guttural language offensive but conceded that the Genoese had been invaluable in the preparation of defences. His seven hundred mercenaries had arrived just after the New Year, closely followed by groups of Venetians. Even a company of Catalans had made an appearance along with the Laconians, and the city militia, made up nearly eight thousand. Short of what they needed but made the best use of them that they could. He was thankful to Nicola—wherever he was presently—for his efforts, hoping he was successful in Venice and Genoa.

"Let's hope General Vevellis had success with my countrymen," said Giustiniani, as if reading Constantine's thoughts.

The Emperor looked on forlornly and prayed to his ancestors that he would not let them down and keep their city alive. Turning to his left and right, he saw the ashen faces of the thinly-spread defenders along the wall.

But he could not help but admire the precision in which the

organism moved. There was no shouting, bells, or whistles, only the hypnotic thud of drums splintered by the clash of cymbals as a regiment changed direction to fit its allotted space. "This show will take some time to complete and I think my time is better spent walking around the city," he announced.

"Yes, your Majesty, I will stay at the walls," Giustiniani said as he watched the Ottoman soldiers in the centre busily erecting a large tent bordered by pennants and other eastern trappings.

AT THE HEAD of his Thracians, Antonis manoeuvred into his place, opposite the Genoese colony of Galata, exactly where he wanted to be; the hill overlooked the Golden Horn and the safe sea wall of the city. Under the Red Cross of St. George, the occupants looked on, fearful that the Sultan might breech his truce. Antonis smiled as he saw their city walls, their time would come and set about positioning his army for the siege.

Riding straight to the lip of the hill, the Greek could see all the might of the Ottoman State arranging itself before the walls of the besieged city. Scanning to his left, his eye wandered along the Golden Horn, first to the small cross atop the square red brick tower of the Belpia Elpis convent, then into the Phanar district, where Planedes' house lay, and finally to the imposing dome of Aghia Sophia, the end-point of Mehmet's ambition. He wondered where Nicola was stationed and looked in vain for the Laconian banners. With a sigh of resignation, he returned to overseeing the deployment of his men.

The stars shone brightly on the clear night at the end of the first day of the siege. Two Ottomans got too close to the walls and were shot by one of the defenders, which raised cheers on the Byzantine camp. The mood was buoyant in the Sultan's tent as the various commanders gathered for their ruler. Antonis, resplendent in his signature blue coat with fur trim, glanced around at the assembled generals. Kasapoglu, Admiral of the Fleet, a caricature of a seaman, short and bow-legged was talking with Herziq Pasha, a General of the Anatolian levies as one of the old clan chiefs, who was dressed in traditional eastern dress, his yellow turban blending well in the gaudy opulence of the tent's interior. Halil Pasha, looking frailer than ever, caught his eye in discussion with the Serbian commander and the returned bland stare affirmed his dislike of the old aristocrat.

In the centre of the tent was a map of the city with the location of their forces arranged at the defences. Blocks of red-coloured wood signified infantry, and yellow, cavalry. Black for the cannon regiments, and small wooden ships for the fleet peppered the blue of the Bosphorus and the sea of Marmara. Finally Ahmed Buzogla, the clan chief of the Eastern Turks arrived with his messy beard and stench of garlic to complete the roster.

Mehmet, conspicuous by his absence had the generals soon wondering where he was. As the concern grew, the young Sultan strode into his command tent. In silence, he looked each of his generals in the eye. "My Lords, our date with destiny has arrived. Praise be to Allah," he said.

"Allah Akbar," they replied in unison.

Antonis marvelled at how he used piety to control his people.

"Which one of you luminaries can tell me how I will take this city?" said Mehmet, catching their attention fully, and pointing to the map on the floor in front of them.

All present looked around perplexed, unsure what he asked. Antonis stood in silence, as he knew what came next. Mehmet did like his theatre, he reflected.

"Well? Anyone?" demanded the Sultan. Still, they said nothing, and he ordered them to stand back. Leaning forward, he gripped the edge of the carpet and rolled it up, along with the map and models that were set upon it until it was a neat tube. He then ordered two of his Janissaries to pick it up and carry it out of the tent. The onlookers gawped in amazement.

"That is how we will succeed here," said Mehmet triumphantly, and with that left the confused room to discuss what had happened.

Antonis stayed behind to observe and immediately saw the room split into two, wonderment and belief came from the Janissary generals and Christian conscripts, whilst scepticism abounded from the Turkish aristocrats with Halil Pasha being the most cautious of the old guard.

Looking from behind a secret curtain, the Sultan's face screwed up in dislike, his Vizier had undermined him once too often, and had now decided his fate. After this siege, things would never be the same, he determined.

Large brass stanchions blazed out the soft yellow candlelight onto the darkened walls of the great hall in the Blachernae, casting shadows across Giustiniani's face, giving him a sinister countenance. Each of the gathered men looked on expectantly.

The Emperor was thankful for the giant Genoese. Organising their meagre forces as best they could, camps had clearly formed, yet he kept the disparate groups together. The Greeks under Notoras, Sphrantzes and Lukas opposed by the Venetians and Genoese contingent. Clearly, the scars of 1204 had not healed.

"The chain has done its job and kept the Ottoman fleet out of the Golden Horn, which means we can keep it lightly defended. The bulk of our forces needs to be concentrated here and here, the Romanus and Circus Gates on the land walls." Constantine jabbed his finger at those points on the leather map on the table.

"The Emperor and I shall be stationed at the Romanus Gate, as that is where the Sultan has placed his command tent. The Circus Gate shall be covered by the Laconians, with help from the Bocciardi Brothers' company of men."

"They might be of use if their General was in the city," piped up one of the Venetians.

Murmurs of agreement concurred.

"It's because of General Vevellis that half of you are here, and he will be returning soon," growled the Genoese.

The crowd silenced but Constantine wondered where Nicola was. It had been nine months and still there was no definitive support from the Latins. He wished he shared his lead General's confidence.

Giustiniani ploughed on. "Prince Orhan, your company shall guard the Golden Harbour."

The Turk nodded his agreement.

The Genoese understood that no quarter would be given to the pretender of the Ottoman throne, so his loyalty was assured. Then one by one he confirmed each of the commanders' allotted places. His no-nonsense approach calmed the worried crowd. Once he finished, they were dismissed, including the senior Greeks, who showed their displeasure. No one noticed the strange-looking man still sitting silently in the corner, who remained so once the room cleared.

"Johannes, how are your supplies looking?" asked Giustiniani.

"They are looking as best they can, General," he replied.

Constantine turned to look at him, no one really knew where he came from; some said Germany, others Holland, though, he did not speak with a Germanic accent. The rumour was that he was a Scotsman. But wherever he was from, his genius with explosives, tunnels, and Greek fire was divine.

"Good, keep me informed if there is anything you need."

"I will, General, but for the moment I am fine."

. . .

PLANEDES HURRIED as he left the Blachernae taking the short walk towards his house. He had more important matters to attend to; the impending visit of his contact from the outside. The final climb up the steep hill left him out of breath as he entered the courtyard.

"You need to do more exercise, dear," said his wife, holding the toddler in her arms.

He smiled humourlessly at her. Since Agatha returned with her cousin's baby, Sophia had been invigorated, her maternal instincts re-ignited, and existence had meaning again. Frankly, he did not care, but at least it kept her from moping around the house, which he found infuriating.

"Alexis, go say hello to Uncle Spiros."

The child duly obeyed and walked over. With his large brown eyes and mop of golden hair, he looked up at him expectantly with outstretched arms.

Planedes patted the child's head like a puppy. Irritated that the child's name reminded him of his now dead nemesis.

"Spiros pick him up and say hello properly," scolded his wife.

Reluctantly, he scooped him up, and the boy ecstatically gave him a hug. Duty done; he handed the child back to his cooing wife who promptly took him away for his evening bath.

"I am expecting a visitor soon. Please show him into the dayroom when he arrives and bring me some wine," said Planedes to his servant as he went to collect his thoughts.

The man in the hooded cloak preferred nights like these. Cloud cover afforded him the luxury of the shadows as he passed noiselessly by the Greek and Italian vessels in the Golden Horn. Pulling his caique up to the Phanari Gate, he efficiently tethered it, and slipped silently into the city through one of the unlocked sally ports. Even with his experience, it still astounded him the laziness that came with a sense of security.

He made the short walk up the steep hill, his feet light and swift, his breathing hardly noticeable. At the peak, he arrived at his destination, and forcibly knocked on the door.

Opening the peephole, Agatha was presented with a grey-hooded man, only his stubbly pointed chin showing.

"I am here to visit Lord Planedes," announced the emotionless tone.

About to ask his name, she thought better of it and opened the door. The man gave off a frightening aura that sent chills down her spine and like an automaton, she showed him directly to her master. The guest waited until the door shut behind him to uncloak himself, revealing a surprisingly pleasant face, large intelligent brown eyes deep-set into a wide full face. The only sign of his profession was a livid scar just at the hairline above his left ear. "My master has weighed your proposal and finds it acceptable," he said, discarding pleasantries.

Planedes nodded gravely, betraying none of the elation he felt inside.

"However, he would like a detailed breakdown of how you plan to do this."

"There is a small entrance on the outer wall after the fosse at the Circus Gate, only large enough for a grown man to squeeze through. If your master can have a squad of men ready, I will make sure that at a pre-arranged signal, the door shall remain unlocked."

"I shall relay this and will return with his reply." With his business concluded, he opened the door just as a naked child with a big beaming smile ran into the room, and straight into the seated host's legs.

"Alexis! What are you doing?" said Planedes in a raised voice.

"Your son?" asked the guest.

"No, it's our housemaid's, but my wife indulges him, so he runs around, to my displeasure."

As the boy leapt onto Planedes' lap, the stranger noticed the unusual birthmark on his lower right kidney area. Agatha appeared, sheepishly scooped up the child, and whisked him away. Thinking nothing more of it, he let himself out, and stealthily returned to his moored boat.

3 7

CRETE

"**S**ire, there is a ship sailing south through the Bosphorus."

"One of ours?"

"No, sir, Venetian."

The commander rose tiredly from his snooze and walked along the battlements to see what the ship was all about. A lone carrack was at full sail southward through the strait. Probably en-route from the Crimea, and did not know of the blockade, but rules were rules. Absent-mindedly rubbing his eyes, he turned to the gunnery sergeant. "Sink her and bring the survivors to me." Then turning around, he went back to his afternoon siesta. Lying back on his cot, he heard the report of cannon, a loud cheer followed the third, and satisfied, fell back into his dream-filled sleep and the memory of the wonderful whore from the other night.

Mehmet was deep into administration regarding Orban's cannon, having ordered them constructed under wooden canopies so the defenders were not aware of their true size and power. The first salvo had to not only smash stone but break spirits too. A messenger entered, disrupting his concentration.

"Your Majesty, a Venetian carrack has been sunk by the guns at Rumeli Hasari."

"Any survivors?" asked the Sultan.

"Yes, sire, and the commander asks what you wish to do with them."

Mehmet stared blankly for a moment then fixed his piercing gaze on the messenger. "Bring all the survivors to our side of the Golden Horn and have them flogged, then executed. The Christians have to understand that rules are there for a reason."

The messenger nodded and left Mehmet, who had already returned to his logistical conundrum.

Large flaming beacons burned brightly on the Turkish side of the Horn. The eight-surviving crew of the Venetian carrack were strung across wooden frames. The hapless captain cursed his arrogance as another searing bolt of pain coursed through his back, the thick stench of pitch burners filling his nostrils, making it hard to breathe, and his throat became too dry to scream his agony. Now, all he wished for was for this to end.

Mehmet set the location perfectly, for not only did the defender sailors see, so could the bulk of the land forces in the north and the 'neutral Genoese' in Galata, lest they had any ideas of helping their fellow Christians. In the end, the executions were a swift beheading, but the effect was achieved. The city's soldiers and citizens were left in no doubt as to where they stood.

That night, Constantinople slept badly.

"It's beautiful country," said Thanos, looking towards landfall.

"Aye, that it is," replied Nicola.

Their journey around the cities of the west had taken eight months and achieved nothing. The Council of Genoa vacillated, the Doge dithered, and the French were of no use as they were fully engaged attempting to expel the English from their lands. The Pope made noises, but his demands came at a heavy price. Only the brave Spaniards showed any inclination to help, as a company of Catalans had left almost immediately upon his request for assistance. Now, finally, the two remaining ships entered the Cretan town of Sfakia to collect their final contingent.

Charmingly apportioned white houses surrounded by lush dark green trees adorned the steep slopes of the crescent bay, in perfect contrast to the clear deep blue water. The carracks docked at the port where Nicola and Thanos were met by clan chief Yiannis Skordilis and his brilliant white whiskers.

The tanned weathered face greeted his visitors warmly. "Welcome, Vevellis."

"Thank you, Kyrie Skordilis."

Thanos was surprised at the formality, had to be a provincial thing.

"We have been awaiting your return; everything is ready." Gripping his guest by the arm with considerable strength, Skordilis guided him to the seated group of expectant men under the vine trellises on the seafront.

They stood in turn, as Skordilis introduced his sons, brother, and nephews; each of them with outlandish moustaches and fierce eyes to complement their majestic physiques.

"Are they all like this here?" said Thanos.

"Yes," replied Nicola.

"I'm starting to feel sorry for the Turk."

Skordilis laughed as he poured out shots of tsikoudia, to seal the agreement.

With the warming feeling filling his stomach, Nicola asked how many men they had mustered.

"We have four hundred of our finest, that is all we can spare," said the clan chief.

"It is more than we could have hoped for. When will they be ready to leave?"

"We will be able to depart tomorrow."

The sun rose behind the mountain to the east across the deep crescent bay and Thanos awoke as the rays of light shone through the porthole. His head pounded and his mouth was dry. Staggering, he lurched to the bowl of water, and splashed his face to infuse some life into himself. "What is that firewater these mountain men brew?" he asked aloud.

"Talking to yourself again?" came the reply.

"Would have been talking to a lady if I had the choice, but I think your countrymen would have gelded me for it."

Nicola laughed. "Right, we must load two hundred men plus equipment on each ship, but luckily no horses. We should split them evenly and when we reach Chania, the third ship can take some too. It will be a tight squeeze for a day but no more than that."

Thanos could smell the alcohol oozing from his pores. "I'm afraid you will have to take a few more on yours as I have some cargo in my hold that we did not get a chance to unload in Mistras."

"What?"

"I loaded a few personal items when we left Constantinople."

Nicola headed to the nearest hatch and opening it, clambered down to see what the items could be. To his surprise, he found statues, furniture, and works of art. Four old wooden chests, which when opened, revealed gold and jewels.

Gingerly, Thanos finally made it down.

"This is from your house. What have you done?" said Nicola.

Rolling his eyes in mock innocence, Thanos took a moment to answer. "I sold some things before we left."

"Four chests of gold worth? That must be everything you own."

"Well, I thought we might need the funds," Thanos paused,

"so I decided to sell my house to Isaac the Jew, he offered a good price."

It dawned on Nicola what his friend was really saying. "You don't think the city is going to survive this time, do you?"

The old mercenary shrugged nonchalantly. "No harm in hedging your bets."

An awkward silence descended, which neither was willing to break. And for the first time, Thanos also saw visible doubt on his friend's face.

"Very well, we will load most of the men on my ship and we can sort it out when we reach Chania," said Nicola.

Admonished, the sobering Thanos nodded his agreement.

Going back on deck, the two men saw the Cretans filtering down from the mountains. Each of the hardened hill men was dressed completely in black. The monochrome broken by a maroon or purple sash across the waist into which were tucked their fearsome daggers, their unstrung bows looped over their shoulders, and each carried big bundles of arrows rolled up in white linen cloths. The crew of the ship welcomed them aboard and instructed them where to stow their gear.

"Formidable, aren't they? Why haven't you enrolled them in the Laconians?"

"They don't like rules very much," replied Nicola.

Thanos thought better of offering them grooming tips and instead greeted his passengers in an effusive manner.

As the Cretans boarded, Nicola could not help but feel it was too little too late. Absent-mindedly, he thought of Planedes, whose opinion would not change or be impressed. A tinge of anger welled up, quickly replaced with happier thoughts of Katerina. His mind wandered to the time he spent with his father; still absorbing what the new knowledge meant, and felt the urge to take care of him. Over the past few weeks, he had processed the revelation, finally understood, and forgave his weakness. There had already been too much loss to let pride get in the way. He made a note to see him before they left for Constantinople.

"Vevellis, we are nearly all aboard. Just these last few pieces to be loaded," said Skordilis.

Nicola turned to see the chief's sons and nephews carrying barrels. "What are they?"

The headman laughed, "We don't know how good the liquor is over there. A dozen barrels of tsikoudia should cover us."

Nicola shook his head, baffled.

THE CITY HAD BEEN under siege for two weeks, but no attacks had ensued. An eerie sense of quiet had descended across the populace. *Perhaps a negotiated peace will occur,* Katerina thought even as she missed Nicola and the safety of his strong masculinity. Her thoughts quickly turned to guilt over her son. It had been almost a year and Alexis did not even know she was his mother, although, she visited as often as she could, under the pretext of seeing her mother. Now, with the city surrounded, she was just another anxious daughter wanting to be with her family.

A cock crowed outside and she made her mind up that this malaise had to stop, deciding to bathe then visit her son. Standing naked, she felt the added weight of her breasts that had not rescinded since childbirth and her hips had never regained the svelteness of before. With a sigh of resignation, she entered the filling bath, a sharp intake of breath her only reaction to the cold water. Sliding into the invigorating liquid, her mind calmed, and feelings of peace began to wash over her. She wondered whether he would come in time to save them.

THE SAILS BILLOWED in the wind as the carracks cut through the choppy water. Since leaving Crete, a sense of urgency had descended, as there were no more stops until their final and vital destination.

"Land, ahoy," shouted the lookout high in his perch.

With amusement, the experienced Yiannis saw his sons rush to the gunwales to get a better look at the Gallipoli fort, and the foe they were about to face. *There is time enough for that,* and he watched with paternal patience as his young warriors grew more excited in anticipation of meeting their adversary.

"Eager lot, aren't they?" said Thanos.

Nicola nodded in agreement as he scanned the horizon for any potential threats. Surreptitiously crossing himself, he hoped there wasn't a squadron of Ottoman galleys in the fort's harbour.

In the event, the ships, along with an imperial transport they had picked up on the way, sailed calmly past the narrow straits into the sea of Marmara, without a shot being fired. Thanos was buoyant at the ease with which they passed. Nicola felt only trepidation, as they entered the calmer water. He always found it fascinating how the smell changed as they passed from the Aegean. The pond, as he called it, had a bland scent, devoid of any character. Even after all these years, he had never become used to it.

"I think the city is under siege," he announced.

The finality of his tone sent a shiver down Thanos' spine. "What makes you think that?"

"There were no ships at the fort, which can only mean they are blockading Constantinople."

"If you're right it's going to be an interesting last leg. So, I'd better go sharpen my sword."

"Kyrie Skordilis, you should get your men ready for an imminent battle."

"My men are always ready."

Looking him straight in the eye, Nicola had no doubt that

was a true statement and went to join Thanos in sharpening his weapons down in the hold.

For thirty days the sentry sat on his perch, looking south for the possible arrival of any relief force. Boredom was taking hold as he registered nothing but flat blue water. A fleck appeared in his vista. Indiscernible at first, it grew and soon three fluttering dots came into view. Realisation dawned; those were not his compatriot's galleys but carracks from the west.

Fumbling, he stood up for a clearer view. The large deep red flags flew high, most likely Venice. The sentry's mind ached as it raced for the first time in weeks; perhaps this was the vanguard of the Latin relief fleet that so many Turks feared. Emboldened with a sense of urgency, he began to ring the big brass bell beside him, and soon, the alarm was raised across the whole of the army. The complacent sailors, Greeks in the pay of the Sultan, jumped to life and hastily made their galleys ready.

Nicola and Thanos stood at the prow scanning the distance for the sight of sails as the city came into view. The soft undulating hills of Constantinople rose over the sea wall and to the left of their capital, the clear line-up of the besiegers was evident.

"You were right, it has begun," said Thanos.

A flash of light accompanied by billowing black smoke appeared from the Ottoman lines and was followed by flying stone of the city walls as the projectile hit. Then the awful sound, like the cracking of bone hit them. Their faces grew pale at the sight of such swift destruction.

"The walls won't last long with that pounding," observed Thanos.

Nicola's thoughts went to Katerina and her safety. The desire to see her spurred him on and he turned to the captain to give more sail into the wind; they had to round the Horn before any galleys appeared.

Obediently, the sailors wrought what they could from the wind and the four ships sailed headlong to safety.

Nicola relaxed as the headland came closer and there was no visible enemy fleet, but the feeling soon evaporated as he saw square sails appear close to the waterline. He urged his captain on.

"Don't fret, we have the wind at our backs and these treacherous currents are in our favour," replied the captain.

The sailor's calmness amazed him, as a fleet of forty galleys and fustae approached, armed with cannon and soldiers, and this Venetian laughed it off. The Greek looked to the full-billowed sail and marvelled at how the breath of the gods blew them along to safety. Something deep inside him instantly regretted thinking that and in dreaded confirmation, he saw the tautness of the sails relax.

A sense of urgency descended upon the crew as the wind dropped away; the carracks were losing momentum and began to drift into the treacherous currents towards the middle of the Bosphorus and the fast approaching Turks.

Sensing prey in their sight, the sounds of the Ottoman drums and horns grew louder and more menacing. The crews prepared for the ensuing melee as their admiral, standing on the prow of the lead galley, urged them on to surround the Christian ships. In response, the crossbowmen ran to the sides and began firing bolts at the approaching armada.

"We need a miracle to outrun them and make it to port," said Thanos.

Grim faced, Nicola nodded.

Skordilis sported a demonic grin in anticipation of the forthcoming confrontation. Nonchalantly, he drew a bead on the lead galley some two hundred paces away and released his arrow. Nicola and Thanos followed the missile as it felled a Turk as he stood on the deck.

"That's a good start," said Thanos.

Without pause, Skordilis had already cut down another Turk, before turning to encourage his men to find their targets.

Watching from the shore on the hill of Galata, Antonis felt mixed emotions as the four hapless ships were surrounded. He knew from the pennants that his brother was on one of them and it deflated him that he would not be able to confront him personally. With a sigh of resignation, he took a swig of wine from his goblet and watched the events unfold on the water. The lifeless sailing boats were soon surrounded by the low-slung galleys, their oars raising foam in their eagerness to be the first to board. Even at this distance, he could see the frantic activity of his fellow besiegers clambering up the high sides of the carracks like ants swarming around their prey.

Goran went to join him in viewing the spectacle. "Looks like this round is going to us."

"Don't be too sure, the sea is a fickle mistress." He then ordered for some light refreshments to be brought as the battle raged on through the afternoon; his desire to be facing his brother constantly in his thoughts.

Mehmet dashed down to the beach at the foot of Galata and uncharacteristically not caring about appearances, shouted instructions at his Admiral, whilst the sea soaked his robes. The ships were now so close to the shore that the sound of clashing steel and dying men was clearly audible.

Munching on the light repast of olives and bread, Antonis watched in amusement Mehmet's unusual display of emotion. Glancing back, he noticed that the carracks had somehow managed to lash their boats around the imperial transport and were now a floating platform of four ships. It would give them a bit longer, but their end was inevitable, unless the wind picked up.

Nicola was tiring from exertion and glancing over saw the looming Galata shore with the Ottomans present and waiting. His fellow Cretans were ferociously repelling the attackers, and he was impressed at the few casualties they had sustained. One of Yiannis' sons drew a bead on the shouting Admiral and struck him in the face. A cheer went up from the Christians as he fell. The acrid smell of gunpowder hung like a heavy cloud on the windless deck. Jolted back to reality, he struck a clambering Turk in the throat and pushed him back into the water. A sharp glance from Thanos signalled his concern and Nicola fervently wished the wind would pick up.

A rousing roar came from the Admiral's galley as he stood again to shout orders. His left socket was a bloody mess, but his courage was indefatigable. Again, Nicola prayed and in response, felt the thick smelly cloud of battle lift. Instinctively, he looked to the sail, and saw life being blown into the limp fabric. In unison, the combatants felt it too, at once giving hope to the Christians, and urgency to the Turk. Within moments the sails billowed and with a sudden lurch, the heavier carracks broke the fragile stranglehold of the smaller Turkish fustae.

"Hard port," shouted the captain to his helmsman as one of the four lashed ships turned towards the safety of the chain and the Golden Horn. Oars snapped like brittle twigs, each crack making the Admiral shout ever more frantically. Within minutes, Genoese ships came out to escort the powering juggernaut to safety, leaving the broken galleys behind. Exhaustion had taken its toll and the Turks gave up the pursuit.

Glancing over to the shore, a dishevelled Thanos saw the gesticulating Sultan screaming orders for his sailors and marines to follow. "That is the young Sultan? Looks like he's having a bad day."

A humourless grin crossed Nicola's face, he was just grateful they had reached safety, though the thought that he had jumped out of the frying pan and into the fire could not escape him.

Sitting atop the Galata hill, Antonis watched in hope as the carracks made it to safety. Looking down, he saw his ruler stunned into silence then climb upon his horse and ride away. The safety of the Horn presented too much security for the Greeks, he mused. Just then an idea came to him. It was insane but achievable and its effects would be shattering to the morale of the defenders. Retiring for the evening, he decided to speak with Mehmet in the morning.

3 8

THE ATTACKS

Katerina stood at the sea walls overlooking the Golden Horn, the knots in her stomach still present even after watching the carracks enter the harbour's safety. The lambda flags flying on the masts confirmed the return of her beloved but worry gripped her as to whether Nicola was alive. She yearned to row out in a caique and see for herself but her natural self-control took hold and she resisted the urge. Reasoning that he was busy with his men and no doubt relieved that they had survived, a nun in a small boat was the last thing he needed.

She walked down the steep steps of the sea wall towards the convent along the low part of the defences and spying one of her couriers, instructed him to deliver a verbal message to the arriving ships, specifically to Nicola Vevellis.

Nodding understanding and repeating the contents for confirmation, the leathered sailor hopped into his boat and rowed across the Horn to deliver his missive; the small vessel weaving its way through the clusters, a mixture of Venetian galleys, Genoese carracks, and imperial transports. Pulling alongside one of the three lambda-flagged ships, he shouted up to enquire if General Vevellis was on board.

A sailor looked down over the steep side to see who was asking and pointed. "He is over there."

In thanks, he rowed over to the last of the carracks and hailed to go aboard. Clambering up the lowered rope ladder, the messenger went on deck; splintered wood soaked in blood greeted him, the odour of battle masking his fisherman smell. "I have a message for General Vevellis."

A tall man came to greet him, clearly showing the fatigue of the day's events. "I am General Vevellis."

Momentarily, the messenger felt overawed and paused before speaking. "Belpia Elpis send their greetings and hope that your journey was fruitful."

Nicola's heart leapt for joy, she managed to get a message to him as soon as possible. Maintaining his composure, he replied, "The Laconians thank Belpia Elpis, and yes, our journey was as fruitful as could be hoped for. We shall pay our respects as soon as we have returned to a semblance of order here."

His task complete, the fisherman returned to his boat to deliver his reply, leaving the exhausted new arrivals to their tasks. His last view, as he climbed down was the General furiously ordering his men to clear the decks.

FLICKERING oil lamps in the tent played tricks with his vision. Creeping shadows became Christian spears and shimmering reflections became drowning Turks. Mehmet gripped the sides of his head to steady himself, the burden of history weighing heavily upon his narrow frame. Islam had attempted to take the City on three occasions and failed. His navy was made to look ridiculous against four transport ships; seeds of doubt started to sprout.

He had learned from the mistakes of his predecessors and

yet luck still favoured his opponents. A letter from Aksham-saddin, his trusted teacher, lay upon his desk in confirmation of the fragility of his people's beliefs in their ultimate victory and that warned of the discontent in the camp. The young Sultan knew defeat was not an option; he was not loved by the army as his father was, nor could Zaganos Pasha's troops protect him if they decided to revolt.

Next to it, lay another missive, with a gold embossed double-headed eagle; an offer of peace from Constantine. It was almost laughable if it didn't have to be taken seriously. The possibility of the siege lengthening and help from the west was becoming more apparent daily. Today's events brought it into sharp focus. He felt foolish for his open display at the shore.

One of the servants entered his tent.

"I told you I was not to be disturbed," snapped Mehmet.

"Your Magnificence, Zaganos Pasha requests an audience."

He was the only person Mehmet would even be willing to entertain this night. Nevertheless, he deliberately paused before telling the equally relieved and terrified messenger to show him in.

Upon entering, Antonis saw the heightened state of anxiety in the Sultan's demeanour. "Your Majesty," he began.

"Zaganos has come to console me on my failure?" his voice dripped with bitter disappointment that only Antonis could understand.

"No, I have come to offer a solution," came the confident response.

"Really, you're going to fix my navy?"

Antonis ignored the petulant reply and appealed to his higher intellect. "Which is the one area where our forces apply no pressure?"

"The Northern shore, but that chain prevents us taking the Horn."

"Then our ships can bypass the chain, the fustae are small and light, and my forces control the shore around Galata."

A flicker of comprehension dawned in Mehmet's eyes. His prodigious intelligence already grasping what was being proposed and now was working out the implementation.

"Even a small force appearing as if by magic, would rain fear and confusion upon them," continued Antonis.

"It would have to be planned in utter secrecy to have maximum effect."

"Agreed. The route from the double columns to the Valley of the Springs is not long. Twelve hundred paces at most."

As he sifted the variables through his mind, a smile broke across the young Sultan's face. Confidence reappeared and looking at his friend, he thanked Allah for placing him in his path. "First, though, I must deal with my Admiral," said Mehmet.

"That is your decision, your Majesty."

"Then, we proceed."

A crisp dawn started the day and a determined Mehmet, with his personal guard and ministers in attendance, rode to the double columns to deal with his Admiral's failure. From the shore, he summoned Bataoglu from his ship to answer for the previous day's debacle. During his sleepless night, he knew he had to make an example of the man, if he was to keep any respect, and fear needed to be instilled in the troops.

A bedraggled Admiral came ashore, his left eye socket a gaping bloody hole, as he had deliberately removed the bandage for he feared the worst from the Sultan. The cowed man prostrated himself before his ruler, who was surrounded by the four chief Viziers and tribal headmen.

"Why could you not take those few carracks on a calm sea? How do you expect to take the Christian fleet in the Horn?" Mehmet demanded.

"I tried my best, your magnificence, but I cannot control the wind!" pleaded the admiral.

In his heart, he agreed, but an example had to be made. Turning to his Janissaries, "impale him," he ordered.

The courtiers gasped in horror.

"Sire, he has lost an eye, is that not proof enough of his bravery?" pleaded Halil Pasha.

Mehmet seethed; his authority was again being challenged; something he would not tolerate.

Although Antonis thought the forlorn Admiral to be a puffed-up fool, execution was too harsh. Bataoglu's courage was undoubted and the army's fragile confidence did not need such a display, and the incident could escalate out of proportion if he didn't act quickly to diffuse it. "Your Majesty. As the man has lost half his sight, a commuted sentence would perhaps be more clement." The clear reasoning in his voice and confident tone cut through the cacophony.

His friend's piercing blue eyes betrayed no emotion, yet Mehmet knew he had an impossible situation, but he could not lose face. He pursed his lips in strained emotion, feeling vindicated in his judgment, but still his entire entourage did not see it that way. The imploring faces before him could easily revolt. "Very well," he said finally, and turned to look at the bedraggled Bataoglu at his feet. "You shall be stripped of your rank, your possessions shall be distributed amongst my Janissary, and you shall receive one hundred lashes."

Purposefully, a Janissary strode forward, grabbed the prostrate admiral roughly, and tied him to a makeshift diagonal cross of two ship planks, which had been propped against a wagon.

It was still harsh in Antonis' mind but at least he had taken heed of his council. He did not have the appetite to watch and deftly extracted himself as the crowd surrounded the hapless Bataoglu. His mind was on more pressing matters, such as the upcoming war council to discuss the peace offer from the Emperor. The courtiers were wavering in their resolve and there was no way he would let years of careful planning slip away now. Walking away, he noted grimly the lack of sound from the victim as the leather cut viciously into his skin.

NICOLA STOOD on deck and surveyed the damage of the previous day's events. His sailors and the Cretans had performed a minor miracle in making the ships look presentable. They had worked tirelessly throughout the day, uncomplaining, and efficiently. Now, he had to see his Emperor to bring him the news, and then, finally go visit his beloved Katerina. It had been months since he had seen her, but these last few hours of waiting felt never-ending; being so near and yet not together.

"Thanos, get Skordilis, his men, and their equipment ashore, leave them in the Venetian quarter until I find a place to station them," said Nicola.

Passing through the steep hill of the Phanar district, Nicola walked close to Katerina's convent. It took all his willpower to resist a quick visit; but it was better to have time to see her, he reasoned, than have the spectre of duty disturb his long-awaited reunion.

Walking through the middle way and entering the flat part of the city toward the land walls, the signs of war became more apparent. Overshot cannon balls had smashed the few houses in the quarter and rubble was strewn over the fallow areas. Ahead, he saw the Emperor's camp at the highest point behind the wall with his purple double-headed eagle standard flying proudly high above. Just below it was the Red Cross of St. George, denoting the presence of Giustiniani.

Entering the communal area, there was distinct confidence. The armour-clad imperial troops had a purposeful step to them.

He looked for his Laconians but could not see any, might be at the Blachernae, the other weak spot on the wall, and in confirmation saw the deep red lambda flag flying above the Circus Gate some thousand paces away.

"Vevellis," came the booming voice.

Nicola turned to see the smiling face of the giant Genoese coming towards him.

"Decided to join us finally, have you?" resonated Giustiniani.

"I had some errands to run," came the response.

"Well, don't worry, there is still plenty of fighting left to do. Come, the Emperor is in council and will be eager to hear your news."

Nicola smiled blandly, they would not want to hear it.

The flurry of activity grew as he approached the tent with Giustiniani; nods of respect accompanying the sentries' salutes as they entered. The Emperor stood over a table with a map of the city and its hinterland. A long purple cape covered his shiny eagle-embossed breastplate and his chain-mailed legs. Arranged around the table were the other notables, Notaras, Cardinal Isodore, Theodore Paliologus, Minolto, the Venetian Bailey, and of course Sphrantzes, the Emperor's trusted friend. In unison, all turned to greet the new entrants.

"Lord Vevellis," exclaimed the Emperor. Instantly ignoring his briefing and turning his full attention on his returned envoy; his expectant face betraying his desire to hear promising news.

Nicola subtly took a deep breath to prepare himself.

"It seems your escapade yesterday has silenced their cannon," said the Emperor but the strain was clearly showing through his upbeat display. His skin was a shade greyer, and furrowed.

Nicola knew this reprieve would not last long. Silently, he reached inside his doublet and pulled out four sealed letters. "These were the responses from the Italian cities, and the Pope," he said, and handed the missives over.

Unceremoniously, Constantine opened each, read them in turn, and did well to hide his disappointment as he pored over the messages. Folding and holding them firmly in his hand, he finally turned to his Envoy. "How many men did you bring with you?"

"I have brought two hundred and fifty of my fellow Cretans."

"Archers?"

"Yes."

"Good, we will need them. Anything else?"

Nicola paused, then added. "They brought a dozen barrels of their native liquor, fearing there would be nothing good to drink in the city." The room erupted in laughter with one commenting on the idiosyncrasies of provincial islanders. A piercing look from Nicola quickly silenced them and showed the others where his loyalties lay.

It was late afternoon when a fatigued Nicola finally left the Emperor's command post, wanting to see Katerina, yet first he had to visit his men. He had been teamed with the Bocciardi Brothers; that would be interesting, he reflected. The millstone of his responsibilities was weighing heavily, but he duly went about it before their meeting. Walking down the undulating hills behind the inner wall, he ambled northward to the Circus Gate, contemplating what he must do. A messenger was sent to them to inform him that the Cretans were to be stationed at the Horia Gate near the Horn. He was pleased with the decision because if the city fell, it would be a good escape route from there. He mumbled a reproach to himself for his lack of conviction in final victory, followed by a quick rationalisation that he was merely planning for all eventualities. Though, looking at the destruction the Ottoman cannon had wrought on the walls in such a short span of time, his heart knew the likely outcome, however bullish the Emperor and his council were.

. . .

EACH OF THE Sultan's Generals waited in trepidation for their ruler to speak. His display of ruthlessness earlier in the day had seen to that. Mehmet inhaled the smell of fear and it calmed him. "My Lords, we have received a peace offer from Constantine. Clearly, the events of yesterday have emboldened him."

"Sire, I think we should look at his proposal with seriousness. No army has breached this city's walls in a thousand years, except through treachery. Countless armies have tried and failed a dozen times," said Halil Pasha, breaking the silence. "The Red Apple is not yet ripe for our picking though the time is close, and a punitive peace settlement would hasten that day."

The heads of the Anatolian army and navy murmured agreement, whilst the non-native converts remained silent. Halil feared defeat and the rebellion that would undoubtedly follow and knew this to be the correct path.

Antonis was enraged; that old fool might ruin everything given half a chance and judging by the split of opinion, he could pull it off. He was not about to let that happen. "My fellow Lords, this is not about religion, that is for the masses. This is a battle of wits and resources and on those factors, we are clearly the winners. The arrival of these new ships means we must hasten ourselves for the decisive blow."

His comment on religion drew sharp intakes of breath.

Before indignation could be voiced, he continued. "All we need to do is hold our nerve. Orban's cannons are pulverising their ancient walls, our navy has them blockaded, and our ghazis are eager for the fight." His calm voice, steady pace, and piercing gaze held his fellow generals.

Once again, the young Sultan was grateful that his loyal friend was there in support. He let the debate rage on before putting it to a vote, confident the pendulum had swung in favour of a continuance; as the loud crash of cannons could be heard wreaking their havoc in the distance.

. . .

THE LACONIANS SHOWED their pleasure at the return of their commander, and for his part, the order and efficiency with which they occupied their position filled him with pride. But it was a flying visit to his troops, as there was time enough for that in a day, he reasoned; there was still the pressing matter of Katerina.

Nicola's ears were still ringing from those damned cannon. Relentlessly the brass tubes brought noise and fear when they resumed their fire. He put it out of his mind as he hurried back into the city and his long-awaited rendezvous with Katerina. Without the luxury of Thanos' house they had decided to meet in a quiet tavern deep in the Phanar district. One of Nicola's regular haunts; it was quiet, clean, and discrete.

Katerina shed her nun's robes and opted for an understated linen dress and shawl, the dark red giving a healthy glow to her skin as she walked to her tryst. The knot of excitement was tight in her belly as she kept her head down and descended the steep hill purposefully. She had already planned what she had to say; tonight, she would tell Nicola about his offspring, prayed he would forgive her omission, then rationalised this was her first opportunity to do so.

Turning into the cobbled street at the foot of the slope, she almost walked into a couple coming towards her. Something about their countenance broke her concentration and she could see a young married couple taking an evening stroll in apparent oblivion to the state of affairs. About the same age as her, the husband was in his military garb and the wife dressed in a somewhat matronly outfit. Sadness overcame her as she saw them exchange intimate glances of familiarity between them. It had been nearly eight years of unrequited time between her and Nicola and never once during that time had they developed this most sacred of matrimonial bonds. Tears of frustration and self-pity welled up as she passed them by.

The couple imagined Katerina must have recently lost her

husband and offered comforting smiles as their paths crossed. Wiping the tears off her cheeks, she carefully dabbed at her eyes with her silk handkerchief to prevent her eyes puffing up, quietly denigrating the vanity act she was performing. Spying the sign of the ram above her, she entered the cave-like tavern and sat herself in the corner of the deserted eatery to wait for her love's arrival.

The fat innkeeper waddled over to take her order.

Garlic odour filled her nostrils. "Water, please," she asked.

"This is not an alms house, lady," grunted the man.

Green eyes flashed him a fiery look, preventing further questioning, and he went to fulfil the request, muttering to himself how this siege had been the ruin of his business. Anxiously, she hoped Nicola came soon.

Ancient wooden tables lay silently waiting to host entertainment once more. Idly, she wondered what had passed here before, then quickly shut it out of her mind. A large hand rested gently on her shoulder. Startled, she turned, and her heart fluttered as she looked into the large leonine eyes of her beloved.

"Hello, apologies, but it's been a busy day." His face creased into a warm smile as he spoke.

"Well, I will forgive you this time," Katerina replied.

"May I sit?" asked Nicola.

A look of incredulity was the response and he duly took a seat. In just those exchanges, it was as if they had last seen each other only yesterday. All memory of lost time vanished and once again they were reunited, rapt in their intimacy. Katerina rested her hand on one of Nicola's huge thighs, a tingle of anticipation shooting through her as she girlishly fidgeted next to him.

Putting one arm around her waist, they turned to face each other, Nicola leaned forward, and passionately kissed her slightly parted lips. Whilst full of emotion, there was a pause in fully expressed passion, like a hunter circling his prey. His musky smell mingled with that of the leather jerkin he wore, invigorating her deep in the pit of her stomach and forgetting her surroundings and worries, as the world became just the two of them in a warm and longing embrace.

The tavern keeper thumped the earthenware jug on the table, bringing them back to reality.

Nicola looked upon Katerina's adoring eyes as they pulled away.

A discreet cough from his server, reminded him that he was in a tavern.

"A pitcher of your best wine." Nicola placed two coins on the table.

With a grunt of satisfaction, the fleshy hand picked them up and went to fetch the order.

"I cannot remember the last time I have not seen you in your nun's habit."

Katerina smiled, "Well, I thought it best to change into something more innocuous. It wouldn't be seemly for a nun to frequent a place such as this."

Nicola boomed out a laugh that filled the grotto-like room.

She clasped her hands over his and locked her gaze again into his eyes. The memory of the panic when she saw his three ships surrounded by the Ottoman galleys flooded back, making the happiness at seeing him again that much sweeter. The crashing of one of the big cannons filled the room, making her flinch and she dug her nails into his hand. "I don't know how much more I can take. Seeing our people wander aimlessly in a haze under the weeks of continual bombardment. The convent has been giving food to the poor. We only have a month's more supply."

Nicola smiled knowingly.

In the forefront of her thoughts was how to break the news of their son's existence. Would it change his behaviour during the siege? Almost definitely, and probably not in a good way; he needed to focus on defence and lead his men.

"This will be decided within forty days, one way or another. The Turk will have sanitation issues and the likelihood of some relief coming or at least on its way would be most real," he lied calmly about the possibility of rescue. "So, they must take the city or leave by then."

"What happens if the city falls?" asked Katerina.

"The end of our Empire, and the yoke of the Mohammedan Turk," replied Nicola guilelessly.

"No, I mean to us."

Nicola shook his head in contrition. "I've made plans for that. My Cretan brothers are stationed at the Horia Gate, where our ships are moored. If the time comes, it will be the place to which you must go and the headman, Yiannis Skordilis, will take care of you if I cannot. Don't worry, I will introduce you to him in the next couple of days, so he knows you." Meticulously, he laid out the full escape plan should the day ever come, complete with back-up options.

Fear gripped her as he spoke so matter-of-factly about the advent of Armageddon, but it did resolve the question of their son, and she decided to wait to break the news. Her indecision assuaged, she felt the welling of desire within her and put a finger to his lips to interrupt him. "Does this tavern have rooms?"

"I was beginning to worry you would never ask, it's why I chose this place," he replied.

Smoothly, Katerina gripped his arm and pulled herself towards him. "It's about time you showed me then."

Silently and with a beaming smile, he took her hand and led her toward the step at the back of the cellar-like room. Time for words was over, now was the moment for expression.

39

OMENS AND PORTENTS

Agony was clear on the face of the stumbling figure as it lunged towards her, blood gushing from a wound to the side. His piercing blue-eyes glazing over as his legs gave way and the life drained out of him.

Fatima shot bolt upright in her opulent bed and let out a yelp. Her body was drenched in perspiration and her hands shook as she put them to her face. It was the third such vivid dream in the last week. Not one given to superstition, it still unnerved her; that pit of feminine intuition was telling her something. Wearily, she called for one of her servants and ordered a revitalising tonic. Dawn was still hours away and the cloudy sky had made the night claustrophobically black.

The young servant swiftly brought a jewel-encrusted goblet of water with a small amber box containing the powder she needed. Scooping two big spoonsful and quickly stirring it, she handed the beverage to her mistress.

Thirstily, Fatima drained the cup and quickly felt the calming effects of the drug and began to drift. Groggily, she vowed she would consult the soothsayer as soon as possible then fell into a dreamless sleep.

.   .   .

ANTONIS WALKED down the hill from his camp towards the shore by Galata. A team of fifty sailors and carpenters were busily laying out all the pieces of wood in the orderly fashion as they had been instructed. Planks laid to the left, masts and sails to the right. The Greek looked at the small group working tirelessly. Both he and Mehmet had agreed to keep this clandestine, their only concern the lookouts at Galata. He had suggested firing their bombards over the city walls and the ships on the Horn and to the other side, saying that would keep them occupied and not too curious at the movements of the small group of men. The trails of black smoke drifting from his cannon's redoubts and the acrid smell of sulphur left him satisfied on this early morning.

Looking at the progress, he calculated it would take another three days of preparation before they could exact the coup de grace. *Another nail in the coffin of this defunct Empire, and I'm the hammer.* Content, he walked toward the man in charge of the operation and asked. "Will this be completed by the day after tomorrow?"

The head shipwright was a Greek from the Ionian coast; his compact robust stature suggesting he was bred from countless generations of seafarers. "Yes, my Lord," came the terse response.

He felt confident they would finish by dawn but knew better than to over-promise. Zaganos Pasha was not a man whose displeasure he wished to incur. Something about his eyes filled him with apprehension even though his reputation in the army was of exacting but fair command.

Antonis saw the anxiety on the man's face and it pleased him. Walking away, he allowed himself a little chuckle, imagining the look of horror on the Greeks' faces when they realised what was happening.

. . .

THERE WAS a marked decline in sister Irene's sprit since Alexis' death, which meant Katerina was the defacto head of the convent, organising the distribution of their resources. Considering what Nicola had said, she opened the cellars of Belpia Elpis; reasoning that if the siege ended within seven weeks, it was best they were fed. Each person was given a loaf, a lump of cheese, and a handful of olives. Every third day they would receive some cured meats.

The doors opened just after dawn and were closed at noon; the queue formed in the dead of night in anticipation of the charity they were to receive. One of the sisters came up with the idea of daubing the left hand with a different coloured paint for each day of the week, making it easy to see who had tried to scrub their hands clean to gain more. The system was efficient; people were ushered into the courtyard and funnelled into a single file where three nuns stood. One gave bread, the other cheese, and the last olives. One of the enormous Macedonians stood at the start of the line to impose order, and at the end was Katerina with the coloured paint to mark each hand as the person left.

If it was just that, she could have coped, but the constant crack of cannon and shattering stone frayed her nerves. In the dead of night, there was no respite, the continued loud reminder of the deadly threat that lurked on the other side of those crumbling ancient walls. Seeing another rough hand doused with the yellow paint, she wished this would end soon. She chided herself on her momentary weakness, smiling hollowly at the grateful recipient of her convent's charity, even as she made a mental note to go see her son that afternoon.

. . .

HEAVY CLOUD COVER and lack of wind gave a claustrophobic feel to the evening. Sounds were muted and smells lingered longer than usual. Antonis knew they could complete the task on the following night and had his select band ready to mobilise. The aroma of fresh grilled lamb filled the air, which reminded him of his need for sustenance. His servant had left a tray under the oil lamp stand filled with meats and bread, and he took his well-earned repast.

Taking a piece, he sunk his teeth into the still warm, juicy meat. After the first bite, he looked for lemon and liberally doused the remainder with the acerbic liquid. He found himself devouring the food at a rapid rate, somewhat out of character; it reminded him of his brother and his fast eating habits. Strange how such a mundane action could bring thoughts of people into one's consciousness. Not that he yearned for it; this was his conduit for reminiscence.

He had always marvelled at Nicola's vast appetite and with half a smile, picked up the goblet of wine to wash the food down. Consciously mimicking his brother, he wolfed down a second chunk of meat, slapping his lips as he did so, enjoying the momentary loss of control he so prided himself on. Four pieces of meat and three goblets of wine later, he sat back licking his fingers, his stomach full and distended. His servants came and poured a cup of sweet tea. He had no room for it but knew it would aid in digesting his gluttony. As the food coma hit, he lazily dreamed of the day he would triumphantly enter the city.

The gentle hand shook his shoulder and a voice called repeatedly. "My Lord."

Antonis' eyes opened.

"The Sultan is here to see you."

"What time is it?" he demanded.

"About two hours before dawn."

Antonis smiled, knowing the Sultan was without his retinue,

and wondered why he had even waited outside. "Well, you'd better show him in."

Mehmet's slight frame entered the tent, his usual composure replaced with excited anticipation. "My Lord, are we set for tomorrow night?"

"Yes, your Majesty," replied Antonis.

"How many do you think we can do in one night?"

"If we could get thirty of the smaller vessels, that would have the desired effect."

The Sultan rubbed his hands together gleefully as he thought through how it would play out.

"Remember the prophecy, 'ships which travel across the land will portend the doom of the city'," said Antonis. "But prophecies are for fools, we cannot afford to leave anything to chance."

Mehmet was aware of his precarious position, and how fragile the bonds that held his army together were. "Very well, tomorrow it is," he sighed and promptly left.

The Greek calculated the logistics in his head, but in the deepest reserves of his consciousness, was the anticipation of seeing his brother again. Sleep evaded him and before long the cock crowed, signalling the start of another day.

IT HAD BEEN ONLY ten days, but Thanos regretted selling his house. Whilst this tavern was passable, it lacked the creature comforts he was used to and the knowledge that his old abode was less than a mile from where he lay, made it that much harder to endure. Scratching his thigh, he suspected there were bed bugs under the linen sheets. Fully awake, he arose to see who was in the same predicament.

The Laconians resided in the three lodging houses next to the Circus Gate, the officers had their own billet whilst the enlisted men rotated their beds.

Putting on his leather britches and simple linen shirt, he

walked down to the empty eating room. The remnants of smoky embers assaulted his senses and the eerie silence was broken by the blast from the dreadful cannon. Stepping outside into the pre-dawn, he made his way to the main hexagonal tower on their section of the wall, deciding to go see what was happening on the other side. He marvelled at the awesomeness the huge structure projected, because even under onslaught from this new-fangled technology, the stone curtain still kept the enemy at bay. Reaching the top of the tower, he walked out onto the parapet of the inner wall.

"You're up early," said a deep voice in the morning darkness.

"Did the noise also disrupt your beauty sleep?" came the quick response.

Nicola did not answer.

Thanos leaned on the crenulations and gazed out to see the besieging army below. They had been spared direct bombardment, but to their left and right, two huge cylinders had been spewing their load the last few days. The wall in front of the Emperor's position was reduced to rubble and only the quick thinking of Giustiniani and his earthen barrels, had prevented a successful storming some three days earlier.

Hunched on a drum of tar, Nicola watched his old friend assessing the view. "Doesn't look good, does it?"

"They haven't got in yet, so I guess, so far so good."

"They are up to something, I can feel it, just don't know what. One thing I am sure of, my brother is directly involved with whatever it is."

Since returning to the city, his brother had been weighing heavily in his thoughts. He supposed it was the knowledge that he lurked so close by. Undoubtedly, Antonis knew he had arrived with the four ships so spectacularly a few days before; he also wondered what he made of that. The revelation they were brothers by blood brought him turmoil, for he knew it would affect his actions should they meet again. He doubted

Antonis would feel the same and shuddered at the image of piercing blue eyes cold with purpose drawing a bead upon him.

Thanos saw the pained look and knew better than to ask, instead, he reasoned that getting him to think about the current issues rather than letting his mind dwell over worries was better. "How long do you think before they break the walls?"

Nicola stroked his chin. "At this rate, not more than four weeks, by the next waxing moon." The matter-of-fact reply enhancing the accuracy of his prediction. "Soon, they will turn their cannon to our position, it's the logical choice." Heavy-footed, he joined his friend on the parapet. Gently resting his hand on Thanos' shoulder, he too gazed at the besieging horde below.

In the far distance, orderly rows of white tents came into view with the breaking dawn. Closer to the walls, were the entrenched cannon protected by earthen booms and guarded by archers. They were silent. For a few hours either side of dawn, the city was given a brief respite from their destructive resonance. Wide boulevards of ground had been formed between artillery emplacements, where the infantry fodder had marched through to hurl themselves at the walls. Directly in front, were a few of the smaller bombards that scarcely dented the stone.

Secretly, he was pleased his men had been stationed here, though, for how long? Feeling the sun on his back, he turned to greet the dawn as his gaze rested a fraction longer on the pennants of his brother's tent, high on the Galata hill across the Horn. *The Great Zaganos Pasha,* he thought bitterly.

FATIMA FIDGETED in the chair as she sat facing the wizened old man, the nightmare had been plaguing her for days and this seemed the only way to placate her intuition.

The seer started his chanting once the incense was lit.

Theatrics for the gullible, yet here she was hoping to get

clarity from him. Her nose crinkled as the floral-scented smoke mingled with his own zesty aroma, creating a pungent odour.

Finally, with his vocal preparations completed, the seer looked up at his anticipating audience of one and cracked a black-tooth smile. "Tell me child, why have you come to see me?"

"I had a disturbing dream and want you to interpret it."

The old man let out a knowing sigh. "Tell me what you remember, omitting nothing, however trivial it may seem."

Fatima screwed up her brow as she tried to recall all the details of her vision. His request clouding her usually ordered memory. "There are two eagles flying high in the sky, it's daytime but I can see the clear crescent moon and it's a translucent white."

The magus nodded in encouragement.

"They spy prey on the ground, I am not sure what it is, just that it's surrounded on three sides by water, they both dive to catch it. The hunters start to jostle, their talons scratching each other as they near the target. At the final approach, the smaller of the two swoops in and catches a mole, or some type of rodent. As that happens the sky darkens, and the moon turns a deep red. The larger eagle turns and flies across the water empty-handed and disappears," Fatima paused to catch her thoughts.

"Go on, my child," encouraged the seer.

"As the victorious bird catches its prey, I am suddenly standing on the ground and the eagle has turned into a man, stumbling towards me, clutching his belly with blood gushing forth." She starts to bite her lower lip in emotion. "I gaze directly into his eyes as life starts to fade from him. Then I wake up."

The listener sat back as he absorbed what he heard.

"No, wait, one more thing. As the other eagle swoops past,

the bright red moon starts to drip blood as I look into the wounded man's eyes."

The seer pursed his lips and squinted his lined watery eyes at her.

"Well? Does it mean anything?" asked the impatient Fatima.

The man started humming, irritating her, and again she regretted her superstitious weakness.

"The eagles denote rivals fighting over their claim, which is the prey. Their claim has the moon as its symbol and the smaller eagle wins his prize, but in doing so death occurs for his victory. The other escapes free."

She understood what he was describing but was unsure as to whom each participant was.

"The turning of the moon means, the place that had the Lunar crescent as its protector, will be no more."

Fatima's face drained of colour as she understood with horror what it all meant. Hurriedly, she thanked the seer and gave him an extra silver coin, before abruptly leaving to digest what had been revealed.

40

THE NOOSE TIGHTENS

A sense of foreboding engulfed Nicola as he listened to Giustiniani briefing his commanders. The Turk was surely up to something and needed the silence for it, but looking around the command tent, he sensed that only he had any concerns. Greek sat with Italian, it was testament to the Genoese that they were working together; how he reminded him of Alexis.

To the left was a table piled high with food and wine that had barely been touched. With the people starving, such wastefulness annoyed Nicola. It was only the efforts of Katerina and her ilk that had prevented riots. He made a note to distribute all the food as soon as the briefing ended.

"General, how is your station at the Circus Gate?" enquired Giustiniani.

"We are in good shape. Having been spared the full force of their cannon both the walls and my men are pretty much intact," replied Nicola.

The General nodded and turned his attention to another commander.

Sitting towards the back of the room, Planedes smirked at

Nicola's confident response, seething at his success and his daughter's continued love for him. Death was too good, only destruction of his reputation and legacy would suffice, and if the city fell at Nicola's station it would vilify him for eternity. Deep in his vindictive daydream, he almost laughed aloud but quickly muffled it by coughing, whilst furtively glancing around to see that no-one had paid it any heed. Satisfied, he sat back and listened to the others droning on.

As all the reports were covered, the Emperor rose to give one of his motivating speeches. Since the success of the ships, he felt confident for the first time in this whole episode, even with the rejection of the peace offer. The multinational force was keeping its cohesion. The plan of integrating the different troops seemed to be working.

The meetings always occurred at night and continued until dawn. Each of the Gate commanders exchanged his experiences, and suggestions on how to counter the attackers were eagerly shared. These moments were the true barometer of how the Christians were faring.

The various captains and generals consumed more wine and their masks dropped, revealing their true nature. Nicola was often silent at these exchanges, preferring observation to locution. Boredom gripped him as the tone of discussion turned to horses and women; he decided to venture out of the tent and into the breaking dawn.

Facing east, he knew it would be a hot day, the steely creeping of bright blue gradually illuminating the crisp morning. The faint clash of cymbals and drums drifted over, accompanying the approaching light. It seemed odd for the noise to be coming from that direction and initially he thought the wind was playing tricks. The noise grew steadily louder from Galata's direction and he peered to see what was causing it.

Astounded, he saw a galley's mast, complete with oarsmen moving overland behind the walls of Galata. He shook his head in disbelief, thinking he was hallucinating from tiredness. A second mast appeared behind the first and incredulously, there were four in a row, steadily moving towards the Horn. His surprise was replaced with curiosity as he tried to ascertain how they were doing it. They must be dragging the boats on logs, he reasoned, as there was no chance there was a wheel strong enough to support the weight. The oarsmen and trumpets were purely for theatrics. Grudgingly, he gave respect to their plan.

Raised voices around him confirming others had also seen the events unfolding and soon shouts of alarm sprang up across the city, made more penetrating by the absence of the cannon's roar. He managed a grim smile, knowing the last little touch had come from his brother's furtive mind.

He made his way to his station at the Circus Gate, which afforded him a grandstand view of the operation. As the morning passed, he saw the procession of boats popping into the Horn; like leaves on a pond they spectacularly covered the dark blue water. The Venetians in their boats stared transfixed at the events unfolding as the first of the bombards landed in the water, directly hitting a Genoese merchant vessel that sank with alarming speed. The populace had now flocked to the sea walls to gawk in horror at the emerging carnage.

ANTONIS LET out a slow laugh each time a ship sank into the water, knowing his brother was watching and wished he could see the look on his face.

"Things are going according to plan," said a buoyant Mehmet.

"The first part of our holy trinity of victories," replied Antonis.

The deliberate Christian reference did not go unnoticed. "We do not have many more days left to achieve it." The Sultan's febrile mind was already thinking of the next part of the plan.

Antonis nodded, "Time for celebration will be at the final victory, my Sultan. We have tightened our grip on the sea, now, to topple those great walls."

The force in the voice and curling of lips that bared teeth surprised the absorbed Mehmet. He wondered what drove his Vizier to such emotion and thirst for conquest of this city. Even now, as the Sultan, he hesitated to ask, for when around him, the great ruler still felt like the outcast boy he had been when they first met.

"The Saxons are ready, my lord?"

"They have already begun their work," replied Antonis.

Mehmet looked over to the Horn. Now, his red and white crescent pennants ringed the city in its entirety. For the first time, he felt a deeper confidence as to the final outcome.

"Do you still think it was a mistake selling my house?" Thanos asked.

Nicola looked up. "This is my brother's work and he will not rest." Remembering their rigorous training as children he knew Antonis would follow his idea with another killer blow; he was too strategic not to. He scratched the top of his head, recalling that even with his advantage in size and speed, his brother always had a way of evening the odds. His thoughts clouded as he tried to work out where the next move would be. "Thanos, go down to Skordilis and his Cretans, go see how they are faring."

The sharp tone troubled Thanos, Nicola's nerves were finally fraying. "Yes, General."

"While you are down there, find out what the Italians are planning to do about the Ottoman ships that are now in their lake."

Thanos screwed up his face in annoyance as he left, his feet dragging for dramatic effect.

Nicola held his head in his hands, staring at the ground. Still confused as to his brother's next move, he sighed and wished there was someone who knew him that he could speak to. Realisation dawned and he jumped up, resolute to follow his train of thought.

KATERINA WAS RELIEVED at the Turk's actions, as it meant there were only half the usual number of alms-seekers that morning. Her legs and back ached and she was enjoying the quiet time. The convent was near-deserted; the nuns had followed the other citizens in flocking to the Horn to the magical appearance of the Ottoman fleet in their 'safe harbour'.

Back in the calm of her study, she removed her headdress, and ran her fingers through her limp hair, trying to imbue life into it. Ignoring her vanity, she relaxed, thinking this present life must end and whatever came next would be better. Finally, she would get what she craved for but was afraid to allow herself to dream. Staring at her now dormant piles of correspondence was another confirmation.

"I think this is the happiest I have ever seen you."

Startled, Katerina looked up to see a frail Mother Superior standing in the doorway.

"You forgot to close the door." Irene said then shuffled into her deputy's study.

Resigned sadness filled the younger woman at the visible decline of her visitor, who seated herself with deliberate precision in the chair opposite.

The dullness of her once bright eyes rested upon Katerina. "What makes you so happy amidst all this chaos?"

"I was thinking of Nicola."

The Mother Superior smiled at the half-truth. "You have done well running the convent and I approve of you giving provisions to the people. Your selflessness and charity are admirable but when the time comes, and it will soon, you must think of your child and his father."

Katerina opened her mouth to speak but was cut short by Irene's raised hand.

"You were never meant to live this life and you must return to where you belong. Soon, I shall tell you to go to your boy. My decision is final." Irene looked at her protégé and her eyes blazed again for the first time in years. With her piece said, she rose, and promptly left.

Katerina was perplexed, feeling elation at being given permission, which was swiftly tempered with the innate fear of oncoming change, and the uncertainty it brought.

THE STREETS WERE DESERTED; the populace was either still watching the fleet at the walls or staying indoors in a vain attempt at safety. Either way, it suited Nicola as he made his way towards his destination. He wondered how long Thanos would be with his errands. But before he had even finished his first train of thought, he stood before the low white arched doorway. He assumed the keepers fared the same as the rest of the populace and rapped loudly on the door. To his astonishment, it was promptly opened, and he faced the tiny figure of the Mother Superior and her genuine smile as she saw who it was.

"She is in her study; the convent is empty, apart from the three of us."

Nicola nodded and returned her smile then strode in to see his beloved. "You're not at the walls with everyone watching the Turkish spectacle?"

"And miss all this peace and quiet?"

His heart burst with emotion as she twisted her mouth down in mock seriousness. Walking around the desk, he leant down and picked her out of the chair, giving her an ursine hug then hungrily searched for her mouth.

Katerina melted, giving herself unreservedly to the safety of his arms. It became harder each time they had their brief meetings.

Pulling away, he stared at her with his leonine eyes then casually stroked his fingers through her hair. "I need you to come with me."

"Now? I thought we discussed this."

"It isn't what you think. I want you to meet the people I mentioned, for when you need it." Nicola smiled. "And judging by your dress you have a bit of free time."

She reached down to pick up her headdress but he shook his head. She protested then realised the futility of disagreeing with him. Her shoulders relaxed as she acquiesced to his demand, went to change, and reappeared in a sober grey dress; her thick luscious hair tied back at the nape of her neck.

Nicola's imagination wandered as he envisioned her bedecked in finery and jewels.

She noticed the strange look and asked again what was so important that they had to hurry.

He ignored her inquiry and gently taking her hand, led her out into the empty city streets. As he pulled the door to, Irene's diminutive figure stepped out of the shadows, her hands clasped in prayer with barely an audible whisper emanating from her moving lips.

The clandestine action piqued Katerina's curiosity as she obediently followed her lover to their unknown destination. Disappointment was evident as she realised, they were heading towards the Horn. *Is all this simply to show me the enemy fleet that appeared this morning?*

Nicola ignored her reaction and hurried her along to the tower in the Horia Harbour. The imposing circular building loomed high over the sea wall but more perturbingly, there was hardly anyone around it.

Entering the open doorway, Katerina finally relented. "I really don't need to see the ships. It doesn't serve any purpose."

"We are not here for that," replied Nicola as he gripped her hand and led her inside.

To her surprise a group of fifteen or so men casually sat around drinking, in idle chatter. In the far corner a goat was roasting on a spit, attended to by two men. All wore a uniform like nothing she had ever seen. Bereft of armour, each had a sleeveless sheepskin over voluminous white shirts and black pants. Except for the younger men, they sported large flowing whiskers, and all had fearsome-looking daggers tucked into their belts. "Who are these people?"

One of the younger men walked over to the new entrants. "Vevellis, have you come to see my father or to observe the excitement on the pond?"

"I am here to see your father." Nicola smiled and clasped the younger man's outstretched hand.

Though not long out of boyhood, this animal-skinned man presented an imposing figure, already practically as tall as Nicola. A further two young men joined them, each as tall as the first and greeted the General. Nicola introduced them to Katerina and with a sincere serious tone they greeted her. Never had she felt as petite as now.

The nonchalance in the face of all the chaos confused her but not as much as to why Nicola had taken her there. Yet for all their apparent fierceness, their hospitality was impeccable and within moments, a plate of roasted meat was offered, along with some strong-smelling liquor. Graciously accepting the first, she declined the second, and asked for water.

Nicola drained two cups in quick succession. Hurriedly, a space was made for them on one of the long trestle tables that adorned the courtyard of the walled harbour.

"Vevellis, you grace us with your presence. You have just missed Thanos," said the greying moustachioed man approaching them then his tone turned conspiratorial. "He said he needed to see the Venetians; I think he's a little scared of us."

Nicola laughed. "Skordilis, may I present Katerina Planedes."

His normally squint eyes opened in full roundness. "I see why you have gone to such lengths now," exclaimed the older man as he gallantly took her outstretched hand and kissed it lightly in the 'presence of such dignified beauty'.

Katerina stifled a giggle as he did so.

"I have brought her here so you know each other if the time should come."

Skordilis nodded seriously as his guest continued speaking.

Katerina was confused.

"As we discussed, should the city walls be breached, you make your way here, where Skordilis and his men will protect you and evacuate with you to their ships."

"But I thought…"

"Don't fret, my dear. We are clansmen from Crete and we always take care of our own, even if they spend most of their lives away from home," interjected the older man.

It was not what they had discussed but she thought better of arguing the point in front of these people and quietly nodded her understanding.

With everything agreed, Skordilis called out to the men present in the courtyard, and instructed them to memorise the woman's face, and ordered she be treated as if she were their sister. The conversation soon turned to the day's events and Nicola along with the Cretans walked along the low wall to observe the newly arrived fleet. Curiosity got the better of her and she followed in their wake.

"You have to admire the bastards. No one saw it coming," said Skordilis.

All murmured in agreement.

"General, what does our navy have planned?" asked Sakis.

"Not sure, but you can be certain they will do something by dawn tomorrow."

Another bombard landed in the water as Nicola finished his answer, quickly followed by a cheer. They saw a small group of men swimming by the shore in front of them, without a care in the world.

Sakis laughed but was cut short by his father. "Costas is uncontrollable, get him and the rest of them out of the water. This is not the time for play."

Katerina was confused, as the rest of the Cretans appeared to be lounging around just as much. Sakis obeyed his father and swiftly went down to urge his brothers and friends to come ashore. Moodily, the young men swam back towards their gesticulating countryman.

"They are good swimmers," said Nicola.

"The best," replied the proud father.

"Then why don't you get them to swim over to the Turkish boats and break holes in their hulls with those terrifying daggers of yours?" suggested Katerina jokingly.

The old man looked at his guests and let out a deep belly laugh. "Perhaps I may just do that, my dear."

The hair raised on the back of Nicola's neck as realisation dawned. "Kyrie Skordilis, thank you again for your hospitality, however, I have to return to my duties." His desire to follow his hunch became overwhelming.

"With pleasure, Vevellis, and worry not, your woman will be safe with us if the time comes," replied the Cretan solemnly.

Swiftly, he escorted Katerina back to the convent under the guise that her fellow nuns would soon be returning, and it would not be prudent for her to be seen in non-ecclesiastical garb.

The journey across the city felt like an eternity and his mental state seemed incongruous to her. She put it down to all the stratagems swirling around in his head, and insisted he leave her to walk the last few hundred feet to the convent alone, to which he was more than happy to consent.

Finally, free of obligation, Nicola made his way to the Emperor's position. After Katerina's comment, he was sure of his brother's next move. Inwardly, he cursed his stupidity, hoping he had time to rectify it.

IT WAS TAKING all of Fatima's self-control not to panic at every obstacle that prevented her departure. The servants busily packing her trunks seemed to be taking twice as long to complete their tasks and the sun slipped towards the horizon before she even had her carriage loaded. Her shoulders tweaked painfully at every enquiry she fielded, fear looming constantly in her mind that she would be too late. Looking up to the sky, the full moon shone in the afternoon. Tomorrow, it would begin its fourteen-day journey into nothing.

The feeling that her destiny was linked to the lunar cycle was inescapable and she redoubled her efforts to get the entourage ready. A few shouts followed by threats and her confused household had the caravan ready for departure. Her maids had never seen their mistress like this and knew that something was gnawing inside. Fatima did not sleep the night through, checking and rechecking that everything was completed according to her meticulous instructions. It was an exhausted household that boarded the carriages at dawn for the journey south.

AS NICOLA EXPECTED, the Emperors tent was deserted. Giustiniani was most likely with his fellow Italians, deciding what to do with this fleet that had so abruptly appeared, and Constantine no doubt, was reassuring everyone with his active presence.

The command post, bereft of its occupants, appeared tired and dilapidated and Nicola quickly decided that someone at the walls could help him. Once outside, he stumbled into the avuncular figure of Lukas Notaras.

"Lukas. Do you know where I can find Johannes Grant?"

The old politician stared at him incredulously. *Why at a time like this does he seek that crazy man?* "I wouldn't know but you can try his lair near the fourth gate. Why are you looking for him?"

Ignoring the question and with quick thanks, Nicola left the bewildered Notaras to pursue the mercurial Scotsman.

A flurry of activity greeted him and at its centre the diminutive red-headed man he sought boomed out orders to his Saxon helpers. Metal-looped wooden barrels were being filled with the thick black liquid and meticulously placed in rows, ready for delivery. Nicola was impressed by the industrious efficiency that radiated from this group of misfits.

With the faintest of nods, Grant acknowledged his new arrival and continued barking out orders for a while longer. Once satisfied that the production line was running smoothly, he handed over the duty to a stout blond-haired Saxon and came over to greet his visitor. "General, what a surprise to have you here."

"I found this and thought you might be able to put it to use."

Johannes let out a low laugh and took the proffered flask. "Aye, not as smooth as mah whisky but I've ne'er drunk anything stronger than ye sigooodia. How is that Yiannis doing over by the Horn?"

"He's fine and you are welcome to drink with him anytime." Nicola smiled at his terrible accent but except for the Cretans, he was the only man in the city with a strong enough constitution to handle this fire water.

The wily old engineer immediately took a swig, smacking his lips, followed by a sharp intake of breath.

Nicola liked his no-nonsense approach, even if the strong

smell of alchemy surrounded Johannes' body, making him light-headed as he shook the calloused pallid hand; he wondered how they could think clearly in these conditions. Not surprising many thought him mad.

"How can I be of assistance, General?"

"Has there been any unusual activity at the walls?"

"No, nothing, their cannons destroy our walls by day, and by night we rebuild them. We distribute our meagre resources to the front line."

Something still did not feel right. "How long has this been going on?"

Grant rolled his eyes. "Nothing has changed this last month."

Nicola pursed his lips and tried to place himself in his brother's shoes. "Where are the weakest points in the wall?"

"The military gate because of the river, and the Blachernae, because of its single wall. But you already know that."

"We have had cannon, land assault, and strangulation by their navy. What is the one thing they haven't tried?"

The Scotsman rubbed his ginger beard, producing a rasping sound, that slowed the more he thought about his response. Comprehension dawned in his pale blue eyes. "How old-fashioned. Besides, to attempt it with the size of ditch we have would be virtually impossible. Do you realise how much lumber they need to support the lengths and depths of those tunnels?"

Nicola's silent implacable stare began to convince the engineer that it was a possibility as he made the mental calculations. "Just look into it, will you?"

Grant clenched his jaw and unceremoniously went back to his work.

Watching the ordered chaos, he knew that if anyone could find them it would be the Scotsman. Satisfied he had achieved all he could, Nicola returned to his men further along the wall. To his astonishment, he found them most relaxed being entertained by Giovanni Bocciardi with one of his tall tales of female conquest. His usual disciplined reaction would have been for them to stand-to, but a combination of the Venetian raconteur's ability and the bonding it engendered, persuaded him to let it pass. Finally, after a tumultuous two days, he was able to relax a little as the storyteller mimicked the horrified but hapless father in the story and tears of relief mingled with genuine laughter ran down his face.

Unnoticed, Thanos saw his friend unwind and was happy.

41

REVENGE IS NIGH

She stared into the child's expectant eyes, the innocent light brown irises filling her with guilt at her actions. Consoling herself that it would not be for much longer, she cast aside her insecurities and picked up the smiling toddler, who unwittingly taunted her with his father's resemblance.

"I think he knows who you are," said Agatha as she approached the seated mother and son.

"Let us hope he never remembers this time," replied Katerina.

The melancholia that engulfed her mistress had much to do with how she had disavowed herself of her child, filling her with shame, yet Agatha felt it showed great strength and intelligence to wait. "He has been back for weeks, why don't you tell him?"

"You know as well as I do this siege will end before the month is out, then I shall tell him."

Alexis started to gurgle in his mother's arms and straightening his legs, restlessly bouncing up and down on her lap, demanded more of her waning attention, his noises becoming louder until she did so. Willingly, she let the time pass in the moment.

Planedes stared at the sealed letter before him. The boldness in delivering this missive in the Emperor's tent astounded him and the spy's subtle smile only confirmed to the politician that he was taking the correct course of action. He had tucked it away fearing discovery, but now, finally alone, he opened what he knew would be the final message from Antonis.

Written briefly on the thick vellum were the instructions he had to carry out, the signal moment clearly set down for him. He knew a good part of the Ottoman plan and if he chose, could betray it to his fellow defenders. Furtively, he speculated if this was a test of his loyalty? He could assume nothing. Either way, it did not matter, his decision was made. After memorising the contents, he casually passed it over one of the candles and watched intently as all evidence of his treachery was purged. Walking out to the courtyard, he nodded confirmation of his acquiescence to the awaiting spy, who promptly melted away into the evening throng of the city.

Perhaps it was his nomadic heritage that found the lack of air and sky so foreboding but he noticed as he stood hesitantly at the entrance to the main tunnel that these troglodyte Saxons had no fear. Just large enough to take two medium-sized men shoulder to shoulder, meant they needed to be packed densely to have any effect at their final destination. Mehmet shivered at the thought. The smell of damp ancient soil wafted in his face as he saw his returning general.

Clods of mud clung to his clothing and through the ghoulish covering of reddish white dust Antonis' blue eyes shone in the half light of the tunnel. "The Saxon miners are doing a splendid job, we should reach the main wall in less than a week."

Mehmet smiled, "Then we burn the supports and the walls fall?"

"Exactly, sire," Antonis' thoughts darted to his own plans he had to accomplish. Time was running out and there were still many pieces that needed to fall into place. The bustle of miners behind him snapped his attention to the present.

Willem, the Saxons leader, approached. He had grown to respect this Pasha, who was unafraid of getting dirty with the men he led. In contrast, the Sultan feared entering the claustrophobic labyrinth. The thick-set man straightened up to his full height as he reported to Antonis.

Mehmet felt aggrieved that the man ignored him but thought better of it. As long as this succeeded, that was all that he cared about, and sat back to listen to the report.

"We like what we see here, Zaganos Pasha, and look forward to our eventual success," said Mehmet as the miner finished his update. A strange race, he thought, and lucky for them, he did not desire their northern lands, for he would have shown them no mercy. Exiting the canvas-covered entrance into the afternoon sun, he inhaled the fresh warm air that greeted him, and journeyed back to his tent satisfied with the progress.

The Saxon let out a sigh of relief as his paymaster left. Preferring to deal with the Greek General.

THANOS WAS RELAXING with some of the men in front of the fire when Nicola entered. Everyone stiffened slightly as their commander appeared. In the past few days, his friend had become more agitated as he tried to fathom his brother's next move. He had thought it would be under the walls, but Johannes Grant and his men had found nothing. Perhaps they were looking in the wrong place, so they had searched for anything that appeared like a possible entrance to a tunnel. The only conclusion he could draw was that they had hidden it from view by one of the gun emplacements.

"Thanos, could you join me for a moment."

"Yes, General."

Nicola gestured for him to follow to one of the lookout posts.

Thanos was loath to leave the fire's comfort but knew this was no fool's errand he was being asked on. The strain was clear on his friend's face; dark circles ringed his leonine eyes, though, his energy was undiminished as he looked purposefully across to the Turk.

"Tell me what you see."

The effete mercenary was puzzled for a moment as he turned his lethargic gaze to their besiegers. "Death and destruction?"

Nicola huffed in exasperation, "No. I mean, analyse it. Does anything seem out of place?"

Thanos stared again at the rows of barricades with soldiers behind them and the cannon emplacements that broke the lines. Nothing stood out. He shrugged his shoulders.

Nicola nodded and pointed to a position directly opposite. "What about that canvas covering by one of the large cannons?"

"There are few extra barrels and a bit more canvas."

"Look again."

Thanos strained his eyes to observe more closely at the men moving around and something seemed incongruous. Imperceptible at first, he then realised it was their dress, all green, colours that did not fit the Sultan's army. Comprehension crept across his face as he recalled where he had seen them before.

Nicola broke into a grim smile of vindication. "My brother has been subtle, but not quite enough. I think we should pay a visit to the mad redhead with this discovery."

Before he could respond, Thanos found himself being marched southwards along the wall to Nicola's desired destination. Giving up any hope of relaxation, he decided to enjoy the walk in the afternoon sun, admiring the dark stone in the distant tower of Galata.

The Scotsman cursed under his breath as the beads of sweat

fell from his forehead and down his eyelids. Looking up as he cleared his eyes, he saw the unmistakable figure of Nicola walking along the top of the inner wall. He cursed to himself again, no doubt coming to enquire as to whether he had discovered the tunnels he was sure the enemy were digging. As if he did not have enough problems with supplying the defences, now he had this giant Greek to deal with. Though, he gave him latitude, if only because he had introduced him to his hard-drinking Cretan brothers, the only respite he had found in this madness.

Choosing to ignore his impending visitor, he turned back to the porters carrying their barrels of pitch to their allotted destinations. The citizens who volunteered to help with logistics, although enthusiastic, needed careful overseeing, something the Scotsman was at pains to attend to. They could be careless and drop a barrel, spilling its precious cargo into the earth, or deliver the wrong combinations to the defences at the walls.

A murmur started to grow with a few of the porters outside the staging area. One by one they put down their loads and stopped moving.

Grant hurried over to see what the commotion was. "Why have you stopped working?" he exclaimed as he approached them.

One of the Greeks turned to face his irate overseer and pointed to the derelict house. "We heard a banging noise down there by the wall."

The Scotsman shouted for everyone to stop. Within seconds, the whole area was in silence and the rhythmic thuds could clearly be heard. Hunching his shoulders and crooking his head in the direction of the sound, there was no mistaking to his trained ears what he was listening to and concern was quickly replaced by rapid action. Screaming in his heavily accented dialect, he ordered barrels of Greek fire and diggers to be brought immediately.

Nicola arrived and ordered two dozen fully-armed soldiers to be brought from the walls, while the area was cordoned-off and the fearful defenders stared at the red soil in preparation for a breakthrough.

The Scotsman ordered the barrels cracked open and ready as the soil began to give and the glint of metal poked through. Quickly, he raised his hand to stop the expectant rush. "Wait until the first man fully breaks through," he said in hushed tones.

The pick worked its way through and soon the crown of a dirt-covered head appeared.

"Now," yelled Grant.

In unison, the defenders grabbed the entering man and pulled him out of his burrow. The Saxon's surprised scream was quickly snuffed out with a fatal club to the head. The barrels were tipped into the hole and the thick black liquid poured down to the sound of shouting below. The miners scrambled to get out into the air, only to be met with kicks and blows.

Solemnly, Grant carried a torch to the entrance and threw the flame into the abyss. Wide fear-filled eyes were the last thing he saw as the flame ignited the fluid into an intense inferno. Screams accompanied the smell of roasting flesh. Whilst many of the Greeks made the sign of the cross, a few laughed cruelly.

Nicola's countenance set grimly as he felt the heat on his face, knowing his brother would be angered at their failure, but there would be more attempts.

"It seems you were right, General," Grant said begrudgingly.

"This hasn't finished. We need to send men down there to block it up and undoubtedly there will be others."

The Scotsman sighed, "that will be dirty work."

"It always is in the bowels of the earth."

· · ·

THE TWO MEN stood over the map that lay on the table, Mehmet listening as his General detailed his plan of attack on the walls.

"Their defences are severely compromised, here and here," said Antonis, pointing on the map. "Along with our miners, they will soon be ready to collapse, and we can finally enter the city."

Both knew time was running out and it was unlikely the army could maintain this siege much past two weeks. Supplies were running low and even with the cremation of the dead the chance of disease was increasing daily.

Antonis felt the beginning of panic as he contemplated failure, which quickly turned to cold anger as he imagined the look of triumph on his brother's face if the city held.

"They will pull reserves from other parts of the city."

Antonis shook his head, he had good estimates of their numbers from his spies. "They have no reserves left."

Mehmet had heard that finality in his friend's voice before and knew better than to question it. In private moments like this, all rank was discarded, and honest equal discussion happened. However, he had his desires too and he pointed to a place on the map. "This is where we break them, and with it, the myth of Byzantium."

Antonis looked at the spot and smiled. Symbolism was always important but never more so than at a juncture such as this. The two men revelled in their daydream and for a moment were unfazed by the world outside. The Greek knew where his brother was stationed, and that knowledge gave him mixed feelings because he wanted to see the defeat in his eyes as he claimed victory. However, in a rare moment of faith, he vowed to stick with the plan, hoping the gods granted him revenge.

A commotion sounded outside the tent, bringing them back to reality. A Saxon was shown in to report his message. The Sultan and his General kept their composure but knew instantly the news was not good.

"Sire, the Greeks discovered one of our tunnels and destroyed it."

Antonis clenched his jaw and took a deep breath.

Mehmet swiped his hand in anger on the table, knocking over a candlestick, spilling thick wax over his map.

"How many men have we lost?" asked Antonis.

"Nearly all, I think."

The Greek placed his hand on the petrified messenger's shoulder. "Come, let us see what has happened," he said calmly.

Exiting the Sultan's tent, Antonis' mind filled with a mixture of anger and trepidation. Plumes of thick black smoke billowed from the entrance to the tunnel. He gripped Mehmet's arm to make sure he kept his composure. "This is just one part of the plan, sire."

The Sultan's downcast look signalled his acquiescence.

Soot-covered Saxons wandered aimlessly amongst their dead countrymen. Willem, their leader, was forlornly shouting instructions to bring order to the bedlam. Spying the arrival of the Sultan and his General, he instantly feared for his own survival.

Cold fury welled up inside the Sultan and approaching, he muttered curses under his breath.

Antonis knew instantly this avenue to success had been firmly closed and set about mitigating the fallout. "Has the fire been stopped in the tunnels?"

"Yes, sire. After the initial ignition, they entered our diggings and attacked. Fierce fighting ensued but we were overwhelmed and eventually they collapsed the tunnel."

He wondered how they discovered their operation, when shouts erupted from the entrance and a wounded defender was dragged out. On closer inspection, he recognised the dark red tunic of the Laconians and silently cursed his brother. Out of curiosity, he went to see if he knew the captive, he didn't, but the shock of recognition on the prostrate prisoner's face betrayed his knowledge. Coldly, Antonis drew his dagger and slit his throat. "You will see your General soon," he added as the life drained from the Greek's body.

RELIEVED EUPHORIA ENGULFED the city that evening as news of the failed tunnel spread amongst the populace. The conversations were louder, and in some corners, music played. Constantine was under no illusion as to their situation but seized the opportunity to motivate his flagging troops.

At the commanders' meeting, Sfrantzes suggested a religious ceremony would unite everyone in the City in their faith, and the Emperor was quick to congratulate him on a 'splendid idea'.

Nicola thought it a waste of time and resources, while counting the loss of forty-two men in their subterranean victory. He had brought a thousand Laconians and now, two months into the siege, there were less than eight hundred left. Bitterness engulfed him as he knew those losses could be ill sustained. The Emperor asked his opinion on this show of faith and he agreed, just to keep with the motivation. It was scant consolation his brother might know it was the Laconians who defeated them. At least his Cretans were largely unscathed, and their archery skills would probably be needed very soon.

ANTONIS COLLAPSED ON HIS PALLET, physically and mentally exhausted. He gripped a piece of the executed Laconian's tunic as if somehow that would bring him luck, and his brother, disaster. They had found another Greek and he took pleasure in drawing out his execution. His sobbing pleas to die a catharsis for his failures in the tunnel.

The path was now clear, one final assault on the weakened city's defences. He rested as he readied himself for the council of generals; for both he and Mehmet, failure was not an option.

This setback was sure to give voice to the Turkish aristocrats' strong desire for retreat, led by that snivelling old fool Halil Pasha. An image of the triumphant look on his face clouded his thoughts as he mulled over the issue. Meticulously, he analysed every possible objection of a final push, and formulated a worthy counter.

THE STRONG SMELLS of the camp hit her long before it came into view. The short journey from Edirne had seemed an eternity. Her carriage carried Zaganos Pasha's seal and was swiftly guided through the ever-increasing groups of soldiers and equipment. The cacophony of commanders shouting instructions, braying mules, and the clash of hammer on steel assaulted her ears. Curiosity got the better of her and she carefully pulled the thick red fabric covering the window, to be greeted with the profile of a gnarled soldier's face. Quickly shutting the curtain, she sat back and waited for the squeaking wheels to halt.

Silence conveyed trepidation; the coachman opening the door brought open fear. Tentatively, she stepped out of the carriage and composing herself walked purposefully towards the large tent ahead. She noticed how unimposing the guards were, how like her beloved to be so understated with those worthless baubles of power.

The Thracian instantly recognised her and ushered her inside. The waft of her divine scent as she passed, invigorated him.

Antonis was poring over the maps strewn across his desk. "Fatima! What are you doing here? I told you to wait for me in Edirne."

Undeterred, she glided towards him, breaking into her warmest smile before seating herself on his lap. She wrapped her arms around his neck and looked deeply into his eyes. "My

Lord, I missed you, and couldn't wait any longer," she replied in her most sensual tone.

Antonis felt heady in her presence and her aroma excited his dormant loins. But he was not fooled by the theatrical show and speculated what her true reasons were for being there. "That's most flattering, but I am accustomed to my orders being obeyed."

Fatima placed a finger on his lips to silence him and followed it with a passionate kiss. In that moment he forgot his worries and indulged himself with the delight that had unexpectedly resurfaced.

The spartan sleeping pallet overflowed with the two entwined bodies resting upon it. Lying on his back, Antonis felt the serene calm wash over him as Fatima rested her head on his arm and felt the strong deliberate beating of his heart telling her of his calm state.

"How is the siege coming along?" she asked.

"We've had our successes and our failures."

"This will end soon, won't it?"

"Yes."

"Before the next waning moon?"

Antonis frowned at the question, "Most probably."

"Where will you be on that final day?" she asked.

"What does it matter? I will be where I am needed," he replied tersely.

"I know you have a strategy, my Lord, and I humbly request you humor my inquisitive mind," her voice became controlled and deliberate.

Antonis sighed in frustration but how could he refuse her? "My forces are arrayed in Galata and will attack the palace and the Phanar wall."

"Do you know which troops you are up against?"

He smiled, "Of course. The Bocciardi brothers and elements of the Laconians."

Fatima's body tensed at the mention of his old unit, her dream becoming ever more real. "Nicola will be there, won't he?" Her mind swirled at the path she was taking. How he would react to her request was uncertain but following her heart was the only course of action, no matter what the response was.

Antonis turned his head to look at his lover directly, the worry clearly on her face. "More than likely. After all, he is their Commander." He kept his voice as calm as possible, suppressing the reprisal in his heart.

"You will be careful?"

He responded gruffly, before turning to kiss her pouting lips. At least it kept her quiet and he could not think of a more pleasant diversion from all this disorder.

As she melted under his onslaught, she vowed that she would tell him her fears before the full moon.

Nicola's body ached from the exertions of the last few days as Johannes assured him, they had destroyed the last of the tunnels. He looked at his hands covered in a fine red dust; was it from all the blood spilt in those subterranean melees or was it mud? He put the fingers to his nose, the earthy scent gave him the answer. But as tiredness overcame him, he hoped they had staved off the last of the miners' tunnels.

He awoke with a start, to hear wailing coming from the street. Fearing the worst, he scrambled off his bunk and grabbing his sword hurried outside towards the top of the walls. Coming out into the cleared area at the foot of the palace, he saw a small gathering of citizens staring skywards with looks of absolute horror on their faces. Certain dread filled his chest as he slowly followed their gaze.

"You clearly don't know your prophesies, General."

Nicola spun around to see Thanos standing there with an exhausted smirk on his face.

"Enlighten me."

"It is said the city will never fall on a waxing moon, and today is the full moon."

Nicola's brow creased in confusion, "Yes, but it's not even full."

Thanos nodded. "Just informing you about the superstitions, General. I don't control the moon."

Nicola found all this reliance on omens tiresome. Soldiers, tactics, and not to mention luck, won battles, not prayer and hocus-pocus superstition. However, his thoughts quickly went to someone who did, and he promptly hurried away to find out the state of affairs in another part of the city.

FATIMA LOOKED SKYWARD and knew that was the sign for her to say her piece, justifying to herself that it wasn't quite yet full moon until the disc completely showed itself. She called for her maids and instructed them to prepare a bath and her finest dress. Then she wrote a note to her beloved, asking him to join her that evening.

The Sultan's mood lifted as news of the 'magical moon' reached him. Antonis in turn observed how superstition was beginning to take hold. Whatever worked.

"Zaganos, do you really think I believe all these stupid signs?"

He raised his eyebrows in silent agreement.

"Well, I don't, my General. However, my soldiers do and anything that will motivate them I believe in."

Antonis pursed his lips at Mehmet's indisputable logic.

"Is everything in order in the valley of the springs?"

"Yes, sire, the Genoese are being quiet, and our ships are keeping the Christian fleet at bay in the Horn."

Mehmet nodded approval whilst Antonis' mind went to the next few days. He knew the final assault had to be before the new moon, two weeks hence. Casually, he wondered what his brother was up to; probably keeping the morale up of the beleaguered defenders. He saw how loyal, even under torture, that Laconian had been. No doubt Nicola would use his considerable magnetism to spur the populace and its leaders on.

CONSTANTINE SAT in his chair and gripped the handles with a shivering dread. He gazed out of the open entrance eastwards, towards the heart of his city. Hope was quickly replaced with resignation when news arrived on a Venetian brigantine that no Christian fleet was coming. He let out a quiet sigh as he pondered. Yet, it was the moon that drove him to this despondency. For a full six hours, he watched in horror as the crescent shape stubbornly stayed high in the sky. It was the early hours before the full disc revealed itself. Ever-increasingly superstitious, he took it as a catastrophic sign and remained firmly seated in his tent until the dawn had fully broken.

Nicola felt surprisingly short of breath before he entered the Emperor's tent enclosure and on seeing his ruler slumped in his chair, knew his instincts had been right. "Sire, why do you sit alone?" Already knowing the answer and abandoning all forms of protocol, he picked up a stool, sat beside the Emperor, and silently followed his gaze out onto the city.

The undulation of the hills clearly visible with their peaks was dotted with church domes. His eyes rested on the crisp blue water that surrounded the tip of the peninsula. The warm feeling quickly cooling as he saw the collection of white sails that glided on the surface like sharks surrounding their prey. "She is worth fighting for, your Majesty, and the people will shed every drop of blood to protect her. But we need our symbols and our leader to show us."

The Emperor turned his head to face his General.

Nicola continued. "Is there not something we can use to unite the populace in hope and faith that our strength of arms will see us through?"

A flicker registered on Constantine's face as he mulled over the suggestion. "Yes, there is one thing. We shall parade the Hodegetria to give the people a symbol to unite under with renewed faith."

Nicola let out a low hum, "What is that?"

"The Icon that shows the way." Energised, Constantine leaped out of his seat and set about his new mission with his customary zeal.

Nicola was at a loss but whatever the icon was, it had reinvigorated his ruler and that was what he had set out to achieve.

4 2

DENOUEMENT

The slender figure knelt silently in prayer, raising his hands each time he made a proclamation to God. In the corner stood Antonis, holding the embroidered silk shirt that had been given to him by Mullah Guwani. He read the verses from the Qur'an that had been embroidered upon it. 'The Greeks have been defeated in the near part of the land.'

The irony was not lost on him, as the Arabs had failed twice to fulfil this prophecy, as well as the two Turkish fiascos. *Fifth time lucky?* Rising after his final decree, he faced his General, who stepped forward, and placed the silk shirt over his upstretched arms.

Mehmet flexed his shoulders as the fabric rested upon his body, briefly emphasising his muscled torso. In the darkened tent, he looked at his loyal General; the only person apart from the Mullahs who had stood by him in the dark days of exile. Now, it was these three who were present during this most intimate and precious of moments. He peered past Antonis' shoulder and beckoned the hidden men to show themselves. From the darkened recesses of the tent the two holy men stepped forward and he broke into a childlike smile. Mullah

Guwani noted with satisfaction what a rarity that was nowadays.

"I know you don't always agree with each other, but you have always been loyal to me. Today is our date with destiny. Something only you men truly understand. Whether it be for the glory of Islam or revenge upon a brother."

The Mullahs murmured agreement and Antonis could not hide the shock on his face.

The Sultan rested his hand upon his arm. "My friend and most loyal General, I know what happened to you, the betrayal of your people and especially your brother. Allah be Praised for He has delivered you to me so that we can fulfil our destiny together. This I promise, you will have your justice," he said and hugged the Greek.

A tear of emotion betrayed Antonis. Since when had he known?

Mehmet turned to the Mullahs. "My teachers, I thank you for your guidance and wisdom. Today, I shall erase the eight hundred years of pain, and capture the Red Apple for our people." Solemnly, he clasped his hands together and bowed his head in reverence before stepping forward and kissing each on the cheek. Moving back, he straightened up.

Antonis ceremoniously dressed the armour on his Sultan, checking that each buckle was fixed, then murmured his approval that his Ruler was ready.

"Come, let us claim our destiny."

Resplendent in his uniform, Mehmet rode to the head of his army and observed as the felt-clad boots of the European conscripts marched silently in unison towards the looming silhouette in front of them.

Outwardly, he appeared calm but underneath he furiously calculated all the different aspects of the attack. Hamsa Bey, with his navy, was to pin down the Greeks at the sea wall. Zaganos would attack the Circus Gate and he, with the bulk of his forces, would strike directly at the Emperor's position. Orban's creation had done its job as the bite marks of his cannon showed on the walls' outline. Shame about his death, but money well spent, he thought.

In an ordered row behind the advancing troops stood heavily armed Janissary, who had orders to kill anyone who retreated through the line of Chavushes stationed in front of them. Mehmet knew the power of the sword to be far more persuasive than any speech. Silently, he turned back to his advancing throng and waited.

The distant clash of steel and shouts of men brought Nicola swiftly out of his light sleep. The source was soon confirmed as he saw an explosion of Greek fire on the attackers down at the Military gate. Thankful he had decided to sleep on the walls, he sprang to his feet to alert his troops. A smirk of pride broke across his face to find the Laconians already standing to.

"This is it, my big Greek friend. Judgment day!" shouted Gio Bocciardi, before dashing along the wall towards his men.

Nicola was bewildered, how did this made the diminutive Venetian so happy? But he certainly made up for his lack of stature with his love of violence.

"Glad to see you're awake, General," said Thanos grimly.

Nicola growled as he scanned along his thinly stretched forces. Another flash of light caught his attention, and he was grateful that at least his part of the defences was built on a solid outcrop of rock. "They will be coming, keep your eyes and ears open," he boomed, before he secretly made the sign of the cross.

Antonis silently prayed as he watched his army advance towards the land walls. Not for them, but in the hope Nicola survived the onslaught. He had issued strict orders that anyone fitting Nicola's unique description was to be captured alive; his warning of a fate worse than death to those who did not follow them working well-enough, though, he was under no illusion that the prize of his weight in gold to anyone who succeeded in the feat, was the more persuasive.

Standing safely on the northern side of the pontoon bridge, he heard the clash of steel as his men climbed their ladders on the single wall of the Blachernae Palace. "Goran, fetch me six archers and have them ready with their flaming arrows."

The tall Croat nodded and went off to carry out his master's orders. Antonis let out a sigh as the pieces he had so carefully engineered, were now finally moving into place.

KATERINA CLUTCHED Alexis tightly as the sounds of activity in the city began to reverberate throughout the house. Her thoughts went to Nicola and how he was faring at the wall, grateful she was not in her nun's habit. If she were to die, at least it would be in comfort.

Agatha entered the room wide-eyed. "It has begun?"

Katerina nodded whilst she stroked her son's curly brown hair, the action calming her; thankful that at least he was too young to understand what was truly happening. She glanced around the room and drank in the sights and smells of her family home. It felt alien to her now, from a different lifetime. Her father was cold to her when she turned up the previous evening. She sighed, knowing at least this life would soon be over. Her ears strained at the faint sounds of battle that filtered through the darkness.

Her worried mother entered the candlelit room and sat down next to her and the child, silently giving her a hug.

"Where is papa?"

"Downstairs. He will be going out soon to help with the defence."

Further conversation did not seem appropriate and the three of them sat in silence.

Planedes rubbed a hand across his forehead, wiping away the greasy sheen that had collected. The other hand went to the key that rested upon his neck as he went over the things he had to do. The spy had given him a banner to unfurl from the house to prevent any ransacking. He panted heavily as he padded through the deserted streets towards the staging post of the city's reserve. The sounds from the walls though clear seemed distant and incongruous in the quiet space of the interior of the city. He barely had the energy to shake his head as he saw the pitiful force that was gathered; three hundred yeomen were assembled in the sloping space between the Mese and the Lycus River. And that fool Constantine thought they could win.

Spying Nikephorus Paleologus in his full-peacocked regalia, made him feel a little saner. At least he knew he looked ridiculous, that old fool imagined himself Achilles. Planedes nodded whilst clumsily adjusting his sword-belt, his breastplate feeling heavy and rubbing on the shoulders and under the armpit. Scanning through the men, he saw the reserve was made up solely of Greek volunteers, not a professional soldier amongst them, their uniforms and weapons nearly as unkempt as their long beards.

"My Lord, it has begun," said Nikephorus.

"Yes, my Lord."

"I suppose we wait here until called upon?"

An explosion of light broke his concentration and he looked up to see what it was. Nothing much yet, he realised, and then searched the open sky to get his bearings and to note the location where the signal would come from. "Our glorious Emperor will hold them at the walls, and all we shall be needed for is to shovel away the dead bodies."

. . .

A SENSE of disquiet filled Nicola as he directed his men at the defences. They had repulsed repeated attacks, yet it just felt too easy, too straightforward. Looking over the battlements into the darkness contorted bodies of attackers lay strewn at the base, evidence of the Turks' courage, and their failure.

He was confident they would not be breached here yet there was the nagging doubt he had missed something. His brother's army was attacking at the weakest part of the defences but judging from the dead it was the pressganged European cannon fodder he was using to soften them up. Another lull occurred and a thought crossed his mind.

Without hesitation, he ran along the walls to see what the fleet was doing in the Horn. As he suspected, it was engaged with the Turks, but nothing seemed right. There was no way his brother would be this one-dimensional and he searched his mind for what other surprises he might have. Scratching his head in vain, his moment of reflection was quickly broken as the top of a ladder thudded against the crenellations. He shouted at two of the Venetians nearby to stand to with poles. Another thud occurred a few yards to the left of the first.

"Wait for it," said Nicola calmly. The first Turkish head appeared on the crest and he swiftly dispatched him, the headless body falling to the ground. Then he shouted, "Now!" With a heave, the two Venetians pushed the ladder away from the wall. Yells from the falling men accompanied their fast descent as they attempted to counter the drop, but the timing was perfect, and it teetered for a second before crashing down with screams on the rocks below. Nicola did not wait for the result and was already dealing with the second group with his customary efficiency before calling upon the Italians to echo their actions. The grim play of slash and shove repeating itself until all the ladders were toppled.

The Venetians laughed in relief as their commander, Gio Bocciardi, came to join them. The diminutive captain bounced onto the lip of the wall and looked down at the groaning and dying men below, letting out a slow whistle at the carnage. A scream penetrated through the others and Bocciardi screwed up his face in annoyance. "Shut up and die, you prick," he shouted as he spat at them. The noise did not abate and the little man unslung his crossbow, put in a bolt, took aim, and fired, then grunted satisfaction at the silence. "The three of you took out thirty of them? Remind me to never piss you off! And, Vevellis keep up the good work," he added with a friendly slap on the shoulder and trotted into the darkness along the wall to tend to his other men.

Nicola chuckled, did the man have no fear? A tinge of envy came across him, realising he probably did not.

The distinctive Venetian's curdling scream cut through the night, as he joyously killed another attacker.

During a lull, he looked around in the pitch-blackness of the pre-dawn, precluding him from seeing anything past a few paces, the only respite being flares of flame at flashpoints along the defences. Nicola wondered how his Cretan brothers were coping by the Horia Gate; judging by the direction of the noises they were not that challenged presently. The sound of that cannon's awful blast reached his ears and he spun around, towards his men at the Blachernae Palace.

ANTONIS WATCHED the sand-timer he had started when the attacks began. It had reached past the halfway point and still there was no sign of an actual advance. Anxiously, he rubbed his chest scar and in a rare moment of doubt vacillated about what to do next. His assaults had been repulsed, but they were merely a diversion. The question was whether Mehmet would break through. As for himself, he did not want to be trapped inside the city. He paused for a full minute before punching the air force-fully then calling to one of his Thracians, he ordered him to instruct the archers to fire; it cured his indecisiveness and he prepared for the next part of his plan.

Mehmet shouted encouragement at the heavy infantry as they poured wave after wave of the mail-clad men into the stockade. Their courage was undoubted, he didn't need to place Chavushes behind these troops to motivate them, but he could not see how they were going to make the breakthrough. The Greek resistance was super-human in the face of such overwhelming odds. The dead piled up so high there was now a gentle sloping ramp that almost reached the lip of the makeshift outer wall.

An idea sprang to mind. Rapidly turning his horse back towards the rear of his lines, he knocked his own troops out of the way, and sped towards the protected earthen mounds. As the horse slid to a halt, the young Sultan leapt off and ventured to the emplacement. "Are the big cannon loaded yet?"

"Yes, your Majesty."

"Good, I want all of them to fire at the centre of the wall."

"But, your Majesty, it could hit our own men," said the bewildered Sipahi.

"Now," he screamed.

Without hesitation and in fear for his life, the captain ordered the two remaining tubes to fire. In an instant, the great stone balls smashed into the outer stockade, littering Greek and Turk alike, stopping any momentum the attack had in its tracks. After a few moments as the smoke and dust settled, a clear opening was visible. Before Mehmet could say anything, the howling of his men signalled what they were about to do as they charged headlong into the opening, pushing Greeks and Italians back into the Mesitocheon.

"Well done," Mehmet shouted to the relieved captain. Then excitedly, he mounted his horse, and sped back towards the front line.

The sight of their Ruler galloping towards the enemy further spurred the soldiers on and they rushed headlong into the yawning space that had been created; each man knowing the honour that would be bestowed upon him if he distinguished himself before his Sultan.

Animated, Mehmet stood on his stirrups and urged them on. To his excitement, a few hundred broke through the space between the walls and pushed the defenders back. The flames of the exploding Greek fire illuminated the proceedings and he could see them clearly being thrust against their final line of defence. But just as he believed that his Anatolians would secure the advantage they had created, the red and yellow Greek banners appeared from the sides of the gap and inching closer, trapping them inside. A triumphant roar emanated from the defenders as the surrounded Turks were butchered to the last.

His shoulders slumped, knowing they had failed yet again, and saw the infantry general pull his soldiers back from the walls. Darkness began to wane and looking along the ramparts, he spotted the lion of St Mark, and the infernal Lambda of the Laconians fluttering clearly in the advancing dawn. Turning back to his position, the Emperor's eagle taunted him still. Doubt mixed with fear gripped him for the first time since he had begun this venture. Twisting in his saddle, he saw the decimated and beaten troops of his Levy men and Anatolians and behind them, waiting in orderly rows, stood his last hope, the white-capped Janissary.

This was the moment, and rashly, he urged his horse in the direction of his personal guard. "Men, glory beckons. I promise you this. The first of you who plants the flag of Osman on that wall, will be made Governor of any province in my Empire, that he chooses."

Thunder reverberated from the five thousand, who, as one, ran towards the beleaguered defenders at the stockade. Mehmet's shouts of encouragement now lost in the melee.

· · ·

PLANEDES' saw the dozen flaming arrows high in the sky.

"What the hell was that?" asked Nikephorus.

He shifted uncomfortably. "Perhaps I should go check it out."

Nikephorus was too agitated to realise how incongruous that sounded coming from the slimy politician's mouth. "We are under instruction not to move until called upon."

"I will take one man as a runner, to notify you if we need reinforcements."

Nikephorus hesitated momentarily before nodding in agreement.

"You, come with me," ordered Planedes to one of the soldiers and confidently marched towards the location of the flaming arrows, leaving his co-commander feeling sheepish for having doubted the politician.

In total silence the two men made their way through the deserted streets. Passing one of the torches, which illuminated the soldier's side, Planedes smiled at his good fortune; a youth barely out of boyhood. "What's your name, boy?" he barked.

"Jason, my Lord."

"You're doing well. Don't worry, it's going to be fine. Let's take this street."

The youth looked down the narrow alley Planedes pointed to, thinking it was a strange choice. "Weren't the arrows fired from over there, my Lord?" he said, while pointing to the other, wider, more inviting alley.

Planedes put on an avuncular face to mask his contempt at the boy's yokel brogue. "They were, but this is a safer route, as we will come to it from the side as opposed to the front."

The soldier gulped his apology and nodded wide-eyed in fear as he stepped into the narrow lane.

"Boy, you'd better draw your weapon before you start down the alley," said Planedes, who felt the sweatiness of his palm as he rested his hand on the hilt of his own sword.

Obediently, the conscript did as ordered but felt a sharp pain in his exposed rib, the scream muffled by the gurgling liquid in his mouth. Through the shock, he could hear the grunting exertion of his commander twisting the blade ever more violently into his collapsing chest.

Planedes felt his hand slipping in the boy's blood as he continued the spiteful murder but eventually, the lad slumped to the ground. He leaned against the narrow alley's stone wall wheezing at the unusual amount of energy he had expended; the pain of his beating heart sweetened by euphoria. He soaked up the new sensation momentarily, before stepping over the crumpled body, and continued his journey towards his destination.

Walking elatedly through the alley, he came into a square where the sounds of battle were audibly nearer. Clutching his bloodied sword, he slowed his pace as he approached the small door nestling at the foot of the palace, lest he was taken for a random Turk by a battle-crazed Venetian. The sound of boots thudding on stairs quickened his pulse again as some of them were returning from a sortie out of the postern gate. He clutched the key around his neck, smiling at his cleverness in insisting to Constantine that the Bocciardis get the key, so they could defend the city; after he made a copy. His furtive glance confirmed he was alone as he silently moved his portly frame into the small alcove that shielded the hidden wooden door. With a calmness that surprised even him, he firmly placed the solid iron key into the lock, turning it to leave the wooden slab ajar, then quickly hurried away back to the safety of his house.

ANTONIS LOOKED at the sand-timer yet again and with another order put the last part of his plan into action. He took out his sfakion and held it in his hand, studying the hilt with the letter alpha ornately engraved upon it. Running his finger lightly along the edge, he sniffed in satisfaction at the blade's sharpness, and ended his reverie by deliberately piercing his finger on the tip. A speck of red grew, and he sucked it to stem the flow, the first of much that he intended to spill that morning. Sheathing the knife, he walked towards the Golden Horn, leaving the sand-timer on his table to run out of its grains.

"THIRSTY WORK, THIS," said Thanos, as he scooped another ladle of water from the oak cask.

"We seem to be holding them," replied Nicola as he took the ladle from his friend. "They will need more than this effort to get past us. Not to mention those lunatic Venetians." He scratched idly at his scar.

"Any news on the casualties?" added Thanos.

"Could be worse, we have lost around a dozen. Gouzaris bought it from a Turkish bowman."

"Poor bastard," said Thanos, making the sign of the cross.

They heard the thud of boots coming up the stairs. Nicola's head spun around.

"Must be the Italians coming back from one of their raids," said Thanos, opening the door to let them up. But the glazed look turned to shock as his eyes focused in the pre-dawn light at the sight that beheld him, drawing his sword just in time to block the slashing blow of a Turk's scimitar.

The second Turk shoved Thanos off balance, knocking him backwards and down the inner stairs, his sword clattering to the ground.

Nicola turned as he saw his friend fall from view and bellowed in defiance, dispatching three attackers before he had finished his scream.

Within moments, there were two dozen Turks upon the ramparts as the Laconians struggled to stem the tide. Shoulder to shoulder, Nicola's troops stood with him, preventing the invaders pushing into the palace walls, but on the other side of the attackers, the fewer numbers of Greeks proved costly as they began to give ground.

Nicola saw two blue-clad Turks rush toward the fluttering Laconian pennant, tearing it down, and replacing it with the red and white crescent of their Sultan. Dread gripped him for if that flag could be seen elsewhere it would cause panic amongst the defenders.

"Get that flag down now," he yelled, charging forward with his remaining Laconians, cutting off the Turks from their stairway escape route.

The surge was too great and with regrouped Laconians led by Themis, they were engulfed and were soon slaughtered. Thrusting in to confirm that the last of the attackers was dead, Nicola tore down the red flag, replacing it with the fallen Lambda. He ordered someone to check the sally port was secure but also wondered who had seen it placed upon the ramparts. He stole a glance towards the Emperor's position. Battle was fully joined, the Emperor and Giustiniani's men were holding the line against the rolling avalanche of the white-capped janissary.

"I don't think it was noticed, my friend, so we may have gotten away with it," spoke a familiar yet unexpected voice.

"You live! I saw you fall."

"I was shoved off balance and slipped down the stairs, lucky not to break my fucking neck," replied Thanos with a sheepish grin.

"That wouldn't have been very glorious, would it?" said Nicola.

"Wasn't my time, my friend."

Nicola hugged him in unabashed relief.

One of the Laconians returned, "Sir, they came in through the Circus Gate. We've repulsed them and sealed it."

"Good work." Nicola knew this was his brother's doing, just not sure how. "Thanos, go to the Emperor's position and tell them we have the wall, then return if they need reinforcements. I will have my Laconians ready to assist."

"Yes, General," replied Thanos and hurried off the eight hundred paces towards Constantine's position.

The relief he felt at his friend's survival was matched only by this deep sense of disquiet about Katerina's welfare. He hoped she had listened to him, desperately wanting to go to her now. His only consolation was that she was in Yiannis Skordilis' capable hands.

ANTONIS LINGERED at the water's edge, his fustae resting calmly in the water amidst all the chaos. Patiently, he scanned his army's position across the water, waiting for the signal. That slime had better have earned his money. He breathed deeply as the blue and white check flag waved furiously as he ordered. Adjusting his sword-belt and checking one last time, he stepped onto the boat. "Let's get underway, gentlemen."

Seamlessly, two dozen oars were raised, and the light attack vessel glided smoothly across the water. Antonis clenched his jaw in anticipation as they made the swift crossing unnoticed towards the looming sea wall. To their left, the Christian fleet was engaged with the rest of the Ottoman ship. They would slip by unnoticed.

The captain urged his crew to full speed, telling them of untold rewards that awaited them within the Red Apple. He was glad to have been given the honour by 'The General' as Antonis was known to the troops, for he was sure they would be able to get in there and secure booty, whilst the others fought down the Horn, spilling blood without the hope of gold at the end.

The boat moved so rapidly that before long, it beached smoothly on the small pebbled shore. The four Anatolian archers paired off and fired left and right, hitting their targets on the wall. Wordlessly, the men jumped out of the boat and ran towards the sea walls. Goran, with a large crossbow, fitted an anchor and rope bolt into it. Taking aim, he fired it perfectly over the ramparts, pulling it taught as one of them swiftly clambered up.

"Hurry, before we are discovered," hissed Antonis, nervously thumbing his sword hilt as they nimbly shimmied up, while the others kept a keen lookout for any further defenders. He grunted satisfaction, it seemed the spies had given good intelligence.

Within a few moments, the Thracian tied the knotted rope around the crenulations and dropped it over the wall, and the others climbed up to join him.

"Captain, your men are free to climb once we have dropped into the city. Your first task is to open the gate. After that you can plunder what you like."

"Yes, General," he responded jubilantly.

Waiting until all his men were up, and the spot secured, Antonis then looked around one more time before climbing the knotted rope. As soon as he reached the top, he gazed over the city. The spot they had chosen was quiet and one of the more salubrious districts, but he gave it no more thought until his feet reached the ground on the other side, imbibing the smell of the City. It was almost five years since he last set foot here and he shuddered as he recalled that fateful day. Now, he would exact his revenge.

The squad moved silently. Each of them having had the map drilled into them until able to recite the route by heart, keen not to bump into any of the reserve force they knew were stationed near their objective. He hoped they had already been called into action but was leaving nothing to chance.

THANOS' head was still throbbing, and his shoulder ached. He knew he was lucky to have tripped as that, most likely saved his life. Passing along the wall, the noise of battle grew ever louder. He could clearly see the imposing figure of Giustiniani orchestrating the defence. The line of Christians seemed so pitifully frail from his vantage point yet somehow it held the thick mass charging it. A volley of fire came from the Turk. The Genoese crumpled slightly and one of his men helped him back. A gesticulating conversation ensued with the Emperor and the Italian was then escorted to the locked gate.

The line flexed as the Italians followed their commander and the Greeks closed ranks to save it. To his horror, he saw the pure mass of onrushing Turks break through. A huge Janissary ran up on the top of the wall and planted a flag. He was soon surrounded and cut down by the Greeks but the line had been broken and they swarmed in pushing the defenders back into the ditch where they had excavated the earth to shore up their outer wall.

Standing frozen, Thanos searched for the Emperor and saw him charge into the oncoming Turks. Within moments, the surging white caps broke into the city and began to fan out amongst the buildings. Knowing he could be of no help now, he turned away, and made his way to the prearranged evacuation point.

THE LOUD BANGING at the door made Katerina jump.

Agatha looked at her mistress in unspoken understanding and went to the window facing the street. "Who is it?" she shouted.

"It's me."

The maid relaxed at the familiar voice and made her way down the stairs. Hastily unbolting the latch, she let her master enter with the bloody sword in his hand.

"Quickly, lock the door. The city has fallen, we must put out the flag," he said, more to remind himself than as an order.

Hurriedly, Agatha obeyed, quelling all desire to panic and scream.

Planedes climbed the stairs and ventured onto the balcony that overlooked the street. Taking the rolled fabric, which he had hidden there, he unfurled the sash and hung it over the lip. Checking it was firmly secured, he finally let out a breath of relief and waited to hear the sound of advancing Turks through the city. He let out a little chuckle, confident that his daughter's beauty would compel Antonis to honour the pact.

Being father-in-law to the second most powerful man in the Turkish Empire would not be without its advantages. Idly, he dreamt of the riches he had craved all his life. A gust of wind blew the few remaining strands of hair off his scalp and he busily flattened them again, before making his way down to prepare his family.

He calmly strode into the salon to see his frightened wife and daughter sitting on the sofa clutching the wide-eyed child between themselves. "Sophia, why do you waste your energy with that boy?"

"Oh, do be quiet, Spiros, he is just a baby."

Katerina glared at her mother to prevent her saying anything further. Though they had never spoken of it she knew Sophia had become aware of the child's heritage.

The politician sniffed. "Whatever makes you happy. To more important matters. The city has fallen and as such we shall remain within the house, with a flag of surrender hanging outside. I suggest however, that you make yourselves presentable in preparation for any visitors." The last part was directed at his daughter.

The words disquieted her, but it was the calmness of his tone that unnerved. "What have you done, papa?"

"What?"

"You heard what I said."

"I did what I had to do to keep my family safe. Now, get ready, we don't have much time."

"No."

Planedes hummed in exasperation and turned away, ordering the petrified servant to bring him some wine. Before long he was firmly ensconced with his goblet, patiently waiting for his deliverer.

NICOLA REFORMED his Laconians in preparation of the message from Thanos when the sounds of panic began to filter towards the Blachernae. Even at this distance there was no mistaking the Ottoman standards flying on the ramparts. Momentarily, his shoulders slumped in despair, before his sense of duty took hold. "Themis, take what is left of the brigade and make your way to where the Cretans are stationed at the Horia Gate, the ships are waiting. Stick close to the sea wall, there will fewer enemy there."

"But, sir..."

"Three hundred and fifty Laconians cannot stem this tide. We must live to fight another day."

"What about you, sir?"

"There is something I need to do personally."

Reluctantly, the sergeant nodded and carried out his commander's wishes.

Nicola urged his men to retreat with much speed in ordered discipline, calling each member by name and giving an encouraging pat on the shoulder, repeating their destination and route they should take to each one as they filed past him and to follow Themis as he led the retreat. He waited until the last of his men had left the position before he silently stole away into the city. A sense of urgency overcame him once he entered the void, his pace quickening from a walk to a trot.

. . .

Entering the wide avenue, Antonis and his men fanned out along the edges, maintaining their brisk pace until they reached the house with the blue and white banner. Wasting no time, he rapped loudly at the door. Hearing a shuffle inside, he instinctively clutched his sword as the bolts slid open.

Hastily, he pushed the door open, and strode in past the terrified servant. "Where is your master?"

The mute servant nervously raised his eyes skywards before he could muster the courage to speak.

Antonis smiled humourlessly and climbed the stairs with Goran and three of his Thracians. "Secure the street and make sure no one enters," he ordered.

Silently, the remaining men obeyed and fanned out to cover the front entrance.

He deliberately thumped his boots on each step as he ascended, enjoying the sound of his echo as he went through the open door.

The unctuous Planedes smiled profusely as he saw the lithe figure enter the room. "Welcome to my home, my Lord."

Antonis checked half a pace when he noticed Katerina's shocked face sitting on the sofa with her mother. Agatha, the maid, stood aside, holding the toddler in her arms. A cruel smile broke across his face as he walked towards the chubby politician, and raised his hand in greeting.

Planedes leapt inside for joy as he saw his future son-in-law smile, knowing the pact had been sealed, and strode forward to greet him. "My boy," he exclaimed as he opened his arms wide then let out a quiet grunt, his body crumpling in the embrace. His legs gave way, falling heavily to the floor.

"At least I am an honest traitor. You are a coward and so receive a coward's reward." Casually, Antonis pulled out a cloth, wiped the blood from his sfakion, and turned to the horrified women. Slowly, he inspected the mother, then the daughter, before resting his eyes on Agatha. "That's a nice boy. Is it yours?"

The blandness of his tone terrified the maid, as she nodded her confused reply. The Greek moved towards her and instinctively she shied away, clutching the child but let out a squeal when his vice-like grip twisted her arm open and the boy fell into his waiting hand.

"There is no need to be afraid, Agatha, I'm not going to hurt you or your son."

Katerina felt a viscous choking in the back of her throat.

Antonis scooped the boy in the air and lifted his shirt with the tip of his blade, exposing the birthmark on his kidney. His thin lips curled, exposing his teeth, as his eyes rested on Katerina.

She was struck with horrified understanding.

"Your father betrayed this city. He even offered me your hand in marriage in our deal for his safety. Didn't work out very well for him, did it?" he said.

Katerina looked at the crumpled figure and felt pity for him, that after all his machinations for power, this was his reward. Fear for her child blended into anger and she glared back at him in defiance.

"There, there, my dear, we have lots to discuss. Will you have any further visitors, I wonder?" He sat down on the chair while stroking the wide-eyed boy's hair.

THE PANICKED POPULACE had flooded the streets; mothers clutched their children whilst their men carried whatever possessions they could. Nicola slowed his pace as he approached, unsure whether Katerina was inside. He stopped behind the last corner to the house and waited.

A matronly woman waddled past him and he heard her pleas to

come inside before a deep voice told her to go away. He inched his head around to see four heavily armed men guarding the entrance to Planedes' house and the Thracians' banner hanging over the balcony. He gulped as he remembered the last time he was this close to that banner. Silently, he prayed that history would not repeat itself. Outnumbered, he decided to find another way into the house. He paused at the sound of heavy footsteps and drew his sword, waiting for them to make an appearance. He broke into a relieved smile as he saw Thanasi with another Cretan approach and stuck out his hand for them to stop then put his finger to his lips once. "There are Turks already at the house," he whispered.

Thanasi pursed his lips in self rebuke.

"Where is your brother?"

"My father kept him as he was worried he would charge the Turks single-handedly."

He smiled, "Well, that's Costa."

"This is Petros."

Nicola nodded a greeting, "Good to see you have your bows."

Then quickly, he went over his plan of attack with them. The boys nodded their understanding and drew a bead on two of the Turks at the entrance. Finishing his count to fifty, Nicola strode purposefully towards the door in plain sight of the men guarding it. Before they could even let out a shout, two were felled by the Cretan arrows and he leapt the last few paces to silence the other pair. His swiftness was unwarranted, as Thanasi and Petros dispatched the other two with arrows to their heads, killing them instantly.

Grateful the door had been left ajar, he entered silently. The atrium was devoid of servants, the sound of voices filtered from above; resisting the urge to charge up the stairs, he took a moment to get his bearings. A noise brought him to, and he dashed into the shadows preparing for another Turk to appear. The tip of a sword poked through and he waited a split second more until a hand appeared, before gripping it. Off-balance, the man clattered to the floor and raised his arms in a final act of protection.

"What are you doing here?"

"Came to see if you needed help."

"Thank God I didn't have blood-lust, otherwise you were a dead man."

"Yes," said a visibly relieved Thanos and held out his hand for his friend to help him up.

"How did you get in? Weren't the Cretans standing guard at the door?"

"I came in through the side entrance."

"Hmm, it seems they are all upstairs and I don't know how many, but probably no more than five."

Thanos scratched his head in thought. "Five to two is high odds in this situation. I think we should take one of the boys with us."

"Agreed," Nicola called over and Petros joined them.

The three men crept silently toward the double fronted doors of the Salon.

Nicola paused, looked at his men then nodded to attack. With a loud crash, the huge Greek kicked the doors wide open and charged in upon the startled people in the room. Seeing a surprised Turk, he quickly dispatched him, before turning to see his brother spring up while clutching a young child with a dagger to his throat.

They began to circle each other.

"Holding the child won't save you."

Antonis hissed as he quickly scanned the room. Goran was locked in a brutal struggle with Thanos. He snorted in confidence at the outcome, but the older man ducked under a vicious swing and stabbed his blade into the chest of the tall Croat, then took a knee to recover his breath. Knowing he had to act fast before he was trapped, Antonis fixed his steel blue gaze on Nicola and bared his teeth in a madman's smile. "Say goodbye to your future, Brother." He whipped the sfakion across the young child's throat and threw the body towards Nicola whilst at the same time lunging at him.

Katerina screamed.

Nicola swung wildly and beat away the stabbing dagger whilst managing to break the fall of the stricken child.

Antonis attacked with unbridled ferocity and he withered under the repeated blows. Finally, he managed to find sure footing and there began a vicious bout of thrust and parry between them, with neither giving ground.

Katerina ran over to her wounded son and cradled him in her arms, her hands quivering as she vainly tried to stem the blood spurting from his neck.

Thanos looked on in horror at the scene before him and tried to stand to help his friend, only to fall sharply. A quick glance confirmed the Croat's dagger had managed to cut his hamstring whilst in his death throes. He cursed out loud at his absent-mindedness and knew he could be of no help. Spying his weapon on the floor, he picked it up, and threw it as hard as he could towards the back of Antonis' head.

The younger brother's legs buckled, and Nicola seized the good fortune to kick him down, the sword clattering away. Antonis backed up against the wall and Nicola held the tip of his blade at his throat.

"Go on, finish it," Antonis snarled.

"I can't kill my brother."

"We are not brothers."

Nicola pursed his lips and his eyes saddened. "But we are. Our father had a love affair before he married your mother, and I was the product. She died in childbirth and he had me adopted by Zenon."

Antonis gazed into his brother's eyes, looking for the lie, but found none. Then glancing around the room, he saw Katerina cradling her dead child, and the crumpled body of her father.

Thanos had managed to stand and was watching him, while the noises of the Turk beginning to ransack Constantinople filtered through the windows. Realisation dawned of what he had done. The reverberations of the death of his city that he had been instrumental in, splintering through him like cut glass. His eyes rested again on Nicola and the tip of his blade and his mind began spinning.

"Kill him," screamed Katerina.

"I cannot."

"Why not? Kill him!"

"He is my brother."

"Well, your brother killed your son."

Nicola paused and turned to face Katerina, whose green eyes were tear-filled.

She stared at him in angry guilt, "Yes, your son. I was going to tell you when this was over."

His shoulders slumped and his eyes widened as he fixed his gaze on the limp body she cradled. A sharp breath exhaled as if he had been winded and the tip of his blade dropped.

Sensing his moment, Antonis kicked at the sword tip that rested on the floor and leapt up as fast as he could to escape past his brother and to safety.

Instinctively, Nicola pulled out his sfakion whilst turning towards his charging brother.

Antonis felt the searing pain of the blade enter the base of his ribcage as he attempted to shove his brother out of the way. His hands tensed on Nicola's shoulders and his legs buckled.

"Forgive me, brother," Antonis said as he collapsed to the floor with the dagger still in his belly.

"Kill him! Finish him off," shouted Katerina.

"No need, it's to the liver and a mortal wound, he will die slowly," said Thanos.

She shook in pained anger, hissing, "It is better than you deserve and I hope it's painful."

The three stood over the prone body as Antonis' eyes glazed over and the dark red liquid seeped rivulets across the polished floor. The moment was broken when Thanasi ran into the room and announced the Turks were nearing the house.

"We must leave," said Nicola.

Hurriedly, Thanasi helped the shocked Sophia Planedes to her feet even as Katerina gathered up her child and swaddled him in a large cloth.

Nicola picked up his sword and turned one last time to look at his brother. Thinking better of pulling out the sfakion, he just stared sadly at him. "More is the pity it came to this," he said.

Antonis, merely turned away, preparing for his death.

Five adults and a swaddled child made their way into the city streets, thronged with the panicked populace fleeing the advancing Turk.

Nicola decided on the route closest to the sea wall, reasoning it would be the least crowded and quickly led the small band towards the relative safety of the Cretans at the Horia Gate. He breathed a sigh of relief when they found the back streets practically empty, and wasted no time urging the group towards their goal.

Two thousand paces became an eternity and on entering the Venetian quarter, crowds had gathered, as the Italian merchants began to flee to their ships in the Horn. Soon, their pace slowed to a crawl as the panicked people plodded together through the sea wall gates. The looming towers of the Horia Gate appeared. Perceiving the futility of fighting the panicked herd, Nicola led his weary group onto the sea wall.

Reaching the top step, he shouted out that it was he who had arrived and waited a moment before hearing the familiar Cretan accent of one of the guards.

"General, we have been waiting for you. The remnants of your Laconians have been filing past for some time."

Nicola felt relieved; at least his men had made it. He ushered the group past him and soon they were joined by guards, who helped the bedraggled survivors to the safety of the tower.

The youthful Cretan showed his pleasure at the appearance of Thanasi but was saddened as he learned of Petros' fate. Nicola felt for the young man; Petros was a cousin on his mother's side. "We knew the risks before we came. Come, let us take care of the living," added Thanasi.

Nicola shrugged at the young man's wisdom and quickly glanced around the wall before following him towards the Horia Towers.

MOTHER SUPERIOR SAT at her desk and waited calmly as the outside screams mingled with the roars of blood-lusted soldiers filtered through the peaceful calm of the convent. Gently, she rested her hands in her lap and stared at the yellowed letters she had placed there. She hoped the other nuns had heeded her advice and fled to safety on one of the boats at the water's edge near the Eleutheran harbour. They had diligently hidden and saved all the treasured texts and scrolls that her order had protected these last twelve hundred years. The sounds of splintering wood brought her back to the awful present, the screams of the nuns confirming they had not obeyed her command. The diminutive woman let out a long sigh and focused once more on the aged paper, her face breaking into a warm smile as she cradled the bundle.

"Soon, my darling, we shall be together for eternity." Absorbed in her own world, she did not hear the rampaging Ottoman soldiers as they broke into her study and cut her down where she sat.

MEHMET NODDED his pleasure as he saw the resistance crumble. His back straightened, and his shoulders squared as a sense of destined calm coursed through him. A flurry of messengers flocked to him to repeat the good news they had broken through. His mind went to Antonis and he wondered how they fared farther up the wall. He sent couriers and runners to find news of him and to tell the navy to blockade any fleeing vessels. Satisfied he had covered all options, he prepared himself to enter the city, deliberately slowing his actions to savour the moment of his lifelong ambition. In a short while, he was prepared and along with a guard of fifty Janissary, he rode towards the Military Gate, which had been flung open by his conquering troops.

Ever aware of symbolism, he had the standard bearer of the House of Osman beside him as they made their way into the Red Apple. His pulse quickened as the walls came closer and drew a sharp breath as he saw how forbidding they seemed even in their shattered state. As the army made its way through the outer wall, excitement overtook him. To the left he saw the devastated stockade and outer wall and the piles of dead and dying, noticing the white caps of the Janissary lying on the ground next to the Latin and Greek armoured bodies. "Find me the Emperor's body," he ordered.

Dawn had broken and now they were entering a new day. The sun in the cloudless sky radiated its heat onto the slowly moving group as it made its way through the gate.

"Allah Akbar. I take this city in the name of Mehmet, son of the House of Osman," he cried.

"Fateh," shouted the gathered men in unison.

For the first time, he smiled as his soldiers lauded him the all-conquering hero. He had finally won their love. Nothing could stop him now, he thought fervently. Entering the city, he saw its dilapidated state and vowed to rebuild this queen of cities to be more beautiful than it had ever been before. Suddenly, his pragmatism took over and he ordered the

Chavushes to fan out amongst the city with strict orders to kill any soldiers who were destroying buildings.

Soon they were on the Mese, going towards the heart of the city and Justinian's Column stuck out straight into the air. He was amazed at how little resistance there was and realised how few had truly defended Constantinople. He bowed his head in grudging respect.

Within an hour, they made their way to the square that faced Aghia Sophia and he dismounted to enter this most holy and ethereal places of Christendom. He was awestruck by its beauty and proclaimed the building sacred and not to be touched.

The populace that had sought refuge inside its ancient walls cowered in the presence of their conqueror and the patriarch stood to the front as Mehmet approached them.

"Who are you?"

"I am an orthodox Christian," he replied.

"Now, you belong to me."

"No, we belong to God."

Mehmet nodded and placed his hand on the priest's shoulder. "These people are to be spared," he ordered then turned around to survey the rest of his capital.

His men set up a camp in the Forum of Constantine under the shadow of Justinian's Column. Irritated by it, he vowed that it would be the first to go as soon as the city was fully secured. Messengers arrived with reports of events in other parts of the city. He heard the good news of his uncle's death, yet, still there was no news of the Emperor's body. The messengers informed him that Constantine had charged in at the moment of collapse in a final act of heroic bravery, they were sure he perished, but it would take time to locate the body.

The smiling relieved faces were broken by the arrival of one frantic-faced runner. "Your Majesty, we cannot seem to break into the Horia Gate. A group of Cretans under the command of

Skordilis refuses to surrender and says we have to kill them all or die trying."

Mehmet let out a smile, recalling the three ships that had run the blockade. It would be Antonis' people that would be the most stubborn. "I have my city. Offer them a truce and say they may leave on their ships with their banner and weapons intact. They have an hour to respond."

The astonished messenger nodded in obedience and scurried out to deliver his master's terms.

GIOVANNI FELT the strain in his narrow shoulders as he urged his crew to hurry to the other side of the Horn. He had deliberately taken down the Cross of St George, not wanting to implicate his father's colony on Galata, but he had vowed to come to Katerina's rescue and that was not something he would break.

Confusion reigned as ships began to flee the shore whilst the Turks dithered in the distance. Soon, his fustae landed on the harbour's edge and hastily, he rushed on shore towards the centre of the Cretan stronghold. He was amazed to find the hill men mingled with Laconians as they defended their castle within the city with ruthless efficiency.

Yiannis Skordilis was calmly discussing their options with Nicola and Thanos.

"It seems, my boy, we get to live to fight another day. I don't like it but there is no way we can defeat them. This is the best choice we have."

Thanos sighed relieved, as he thought the old hawk may just have fought it out to the last, just for the hell of it.

"Very well, let's get them on these boats in an orderly fashion and beware, the Mohammedans may double-cross us once we are underway."

"I have brought a boat too," piped up Giovanni as he approached.

Nicola smiled at his old Pandekterion friend. "Very good, let's get underway."

THE SULTAN WAS good to his word, the Cretans and the few remaining Laconians were allowed to freely board their vessels, and before long, had made their way clear through the chain and out into the Bosphorus, leaving the Ottoman fleet in their wake. Their sails billowed and soon, they were onto clear open sea heading towards safety.

EPILOGUE
LATER THAT DAY

Fatima sat in her tent beside herself waiting for news of her lover. She had sent scouts out, to locate him and news filtered back that Antonis had crossed the Horn with a dozen men on one of his fustae before dawn. She fought back the tears as panic welled up that he had not heeded her advice. Fearing the worst, that his desire for revenge had got the better of him, she redoubled her efforts, after tracking down the captain who had transported them. Extra scouts were sent amongst the buildings of the Phanar district, reasoning that he had his reasons to be there. She sat back and waited with bated breath for any news. Her maids scurried around her, tending to her every whim.

It was late in the day when one of the Thracians returned with a sombre face. "What is it?" she asked.

"We have found the General, Hanimefendi."

"Where is he? Is he alive?"

"He is alive, but barely. The wound appears to be mortal."

"Take me to him instantly," she ordered.

"But, my Lady, the city is still not fully secure."

"I don't give a damn. Have the best surgeons in his army

attend now," she replied and quickly ordered two of her maids to join her.

Her chest was tight with fear as she boarded the boat that rapidly carried her across the Horn. Once beached, she raced directly into the city, ignoring the acts of savage depravity that were happening around her. Her escort of two dozen of Antonis' Thracians let her focus on her unknown destination. They soon arrived at a house surrounded by his troops and she was led to where he lay.

She walked into the tent with trepidation, clutching a crumpled piece of paper tightly in her left hand, feeling the clamminess in her palms through the parchment. The first thing that struck her was the pungent smell that rested in the heavy airless space, involuntarily making her gag. Gasping as she saw the prone figure of her beloved, she rushed to his side and gazed over the body.

His usual glow had been replaced with a grey pallor and his eye-sockets were a vortex of shadow. Fear gripped her as she gingerly reached out to touch his forehead. The coldness of his skin shot though her and it took all the self-control she could muster not to recoil from the sensation. Slowly, her fingertips became accustomed to the feeling and regaining her inner composure, began to will her life force into him through her touch. Throwing the paper on the floor, she carefully added her other hand to his head and closed her eyes as she shuffled to the top of the stretcher in an effort to impart more of her energies into his being.

"My love, I am here, and you will be fine soon. I will not let you slip away from me. We have so much life yet to live. The city is yours and you are the power that created that. I will be here for you forever, my Antonis." She whispered into his ear.

Antonis' shallow breath remained weak but constant. Recognising her voice, he let out the faintest of groans. For a moment, his face softened, as he acknowledged his love. His eyes blazed as he gazed upon her, before they drooped, and his grip relaxed.

Looking down, she noticed the dagger still sticking in his belly. Fatima's primeval scream enveloped the City as she knew her soothsayer had been morbidly correct before she promptly passed out.

THE DAY AFTER

THE CHILL of the morning air sent shivers through the slight frame of Halil Pasha as he awaited his fate. He had elected to wear his finest blue coat threaded with silver, if he was to be put to death, at least he would meet his fate well dressed.

Though what he had done was for the good of his empire, he knew he had condemned himself to oblivion as he looked across at his conquering ruler perched triumphantly on his throne. The acrid stench of freshly burnt buildings still swirled in the air as the burial crews had begun their grisly task of cremating the dead to prevent the spread of disease.

Mehmet looked at his old Vizier and waved his hand in judgement. Without ceremony, he was dragged away to the waiting hangman's noose.

Halil felt no remorse for his actions because he was pure of heart in his decision, though, he took small comfort from the news that Zaganos Pasha was missing, presumed dead. He let out a wry grin as the noose tightened and felt the rope being pulled taught across his throat. The last thing he saw was the imposing red walls of Aghia Sophia. There could be worse places to die than in that glorious building's shadow.

TWO WEEKS Later

. . .

GIUSTINIANI LAY on his bed in his house in Chios as the surgeon tended to his wounds. "Leave me alone," he said.

"But if I don't tend to these, you will die," replied the surgeon.

"I am as good as dead, leave me alone, so I can meet my Maker." He waved weakly.

The surgeon thought better of arguing. "Very well, but I will come back this evening to finish my dressings."

The huge Genoese looked out across the Aegean and his heart was heavy with guilt, for he knew it was his action of opening the gate that had lost the city. Instinctively, he knew deep inside that the first consecrated Christian city had been lost for eternity to the followers of Mohammed. All his good deeds were for naught as in that final act, they were cancelled out. This will be my everlasting legacy.

"Forgive me, Constantine, for it is I, in a moment of weakness, who lost us the jewel of Christendom," he muttered to himself. Turning his head back to the calm sea, he languidly waited to join his Greek brother-in-arms.

NICOLA HELD Katerina tightly around her waist as they sailed into the harbour at Chania. The last few days had been tumultuous. To discover he had a son and the first act as a Father was to witness his murder, had been a pain he never thought he could endure. Katerina was beside herself with grief and guilt. He consoled her and forgave her omission, understanding why she had kept it secret. They had spent the time on board together, talking of all that had transpired, and he knew it would be some time before she could be healed, though, she would forever be scarred. During those moments he vowed, to all that he held sacred, to rebuild his family. The estate, combined with Thanos' wealth, assured their security. He spared a thought for his brother and the look in his eyes as he fell to the floor in Planedes' house and wondered if he meant those final words. An answer he would never know. Sighing, he drew Katerina tighter as they both gazed onto the welcoming Cretan shore.

Thanos joined them on the deck of the carrack. "Well, my boy, looks like you are finally going home," he said.

"Yes, it does, my friend."

"Never thought of Crete as somewhere to live but who knows, perhaps I can settle down amongst your wild hill people."

"If they don't kill you first, for leeching after their women."

"Me? I would never do such a thing," he exclaimed in feigned innocence.

Nicola laughed and turned to face his friend, "We shall see, Thanos, we shall see."

The End

GLOSSARY

Kri kri Breed of goat native only to Crete

Strategos Greek General

Lochias Staff sergeant

Topoteretes Lieutenant

Allaghia Platoon

Tagmata Regiment

Agoge Training ground

Fustae Small naval vessel

Dromon Fast Naval vessel

Carrack Transport Ship

Laconians Greek Elite Soldiers

Janissary Ottoman Elite Soldiers

Condottiore Mercenary

Sipahis Ottoman Soldiers

Rumelian Anatolian Soldiers

Arquebus Early handheld Firearm

Sfakion Cretan dagger

Pandakterion University of Constantinople

Kankileos Keeper of the imperial inkstand, *de facto* chief minister of the Empire.

Protospatharios First Spear holder awarded to military commanders

Despot Heir to the Byzantine throne as well as a title for ruler of a province.

Serbokrastor Title showing a close relationship with the Emperor

Blachernae Byzantine Emperors Palace

Bey Ottoman lord

Pasha Ottoman General

Hanim Lady/noblewoman

Gardas Friend

Yar Lover

Stadion Unit of distance equivalent to 150m

Bezant Byzantine unit of currency

Florin Florentine unit of currency

Studion Main thoroughfare through Constantinople

Red Apple The Islamic name used for Constantinople

ABOUT THE AUTHOR

Of Greek descent Zack grew up in London. After studying Marine Biology at University he spent a number of years in the field of renewable energy and conservation before turning his hand at writing novels.

Inspired by his Grandfather and uncle who had regaled him of tales from his family's past when he was young, he decided to humanize a crucial period of history into a novel.

Drawing from both his family history and in-depth research into the period. Currently he divides his time between Crete, Los Angeles and the Philippines.

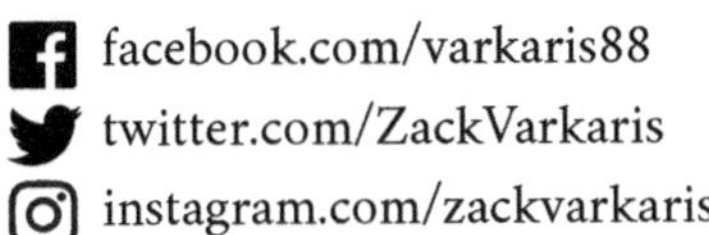

THE RUINS

Fatima entered the tent in trepidation while clutching a clammy and crumpled piece of parchment tightly in her left hand. The pungent smell resting in the heavy airless room struck her instantly and made her gag involuntarily. Gasping as she saw the prone figure of her beloved, she rushed to his side and gazed over the body. His usual glow had been replaced with a grey pallor and his eye sockets were a vortex of shadow.

Fear gripped her as she gingerly reached out to touch his forehead. The coldness of his skin shot though her and it took all the self-control she could muster not to recoil from the sensation. Slowly her fingertips became accustomed to the feeling and regaining her inner composure began to will her life force into him through her touch. Throwing the paper on the floor, she carefully added her other hand to his head and closed her eyes as she shuffled to the top of the stretcher, trying to impart more of her energies into his being. "My love, I am here and you will be fine soon. I will not let you slip away from me." She whispered into his ear.

Antonis' shallow breath remained weak but constant not recognizing her voice.

Looking down she saw the dagger still sticking in his belly and a sense of fury overwhelmed her as to why this had not been dealt with. His torso had been wrapped in white linen gauze that had been soaked dark with seeping blood. Instinctively, she reached forward to pull the dagger.

"Leave that alone!" Came an order.

She jumped, shrinking away from her intentions.

"Pull out that blade and he dies."

Fatima turned to see the Thracian's surgeon standing in the entrance to the tent as four helpers fanned either side of him bringing bowls of water and bandages.

The fastidious-looking man eyed up this lady amidst the chaos and quickly made his assessment. "We need to have everything prepared before we can operate."

Regaining her composure, she looked at the middle-aged surgeon. "Will he live?"

The surgeon nodded matter of fact. "He should already be dead from a wound such as this. But if anyone can make him live, I can."

"If he survives I will reward you with untold riches."

"Hanim, I do this not for riches but for the sanctity of life. Now, please, you must leave as we have work to do."

Helpers had set up bowls of steaming water and lined up sharpened shiny bronze instruments on a linen cloth covered table alongside rolls of bandages and a few earthenware pots of salves so pungent they broke through the stench that resided within the tent.

"I will stay, what can I do to help?"

The surgeon looked at Fatima, and thought better of denying her, and let out an exasperated sigh. "Very well, make sure we have a steady supply of hot water."

Fatima nodded and one of the assistants showed her where to go as he went out to fetch another bowl.

"Wash your hands before you come back." Shouted the

surgeon as he moved towards his patient lying on the table. Giving her no more thought, he cast a professional eye over his wounded general. "Allah, please give me strength to help my stricken pasha." He muttered before pointing to the bronze knife on the table.

Fatima shuddered as she exited the field surgery and followed the assistant towards the large fires that heated a water-filled cauldron that rested atop of them. The afternoon sun had begun its descent and for the first time she noticed the bodies of the dead and dying men arrayed before her. But their pain meant nothing to her, all that was important was that her beloved lived through this ordeal. Fear gripped her as she contemplated life without him; bereft of his touch and absent of his love. Quickly, she pushed the thought aside and focused on helping the nurse ladle water into smaller bowls.

He barked orders that the pot was to be kept full and boiling at all times while holding a bowl of steaming water, which he placed on the ground. "Wash your hands in this." He said and handed her a bar of scented soap along with a clean cloth.

Fatima duly obeyed and squatting down began to soak her hands to wash them thoroughly. All the while fuming inside that her hands were probably cleaner than anyone else's in this smouldering city. Finally satisfied with her ablutions, she stood up and grabbing the bronze bowl followed the surgeon's assistant back to the tent.

The air remained thick but the pungent odour of the salve pots had begun to overpower the stench of battle. The surgeon was already at his task and had cut the bandages and clothing loose from around the entrance to the knife wound. She stood frozen as the assistants scurried around the surgeon in precise deliberate movements. One had bandages all folded up, the other with water-soaked cloths, and the third by the instrument table awaiting instructions.

"Put the bowl down here." Said the last assistant.

Broken from her trance she obeyed then hovered in the background as the team went to work. First, the bandages were cut away and removed slowly then the assistant with the folded bandages began to stuff them in the space between Antonis' body and the surgeon's table. The nurse who had accompanied Fatima stirred all three of the salve pots one after the other in preparation. Dolloping a lump onto a cloth and rubbing it in he then placed it over the mouth and nose of Antonis for a few seconds before removing it.

Thinking better of asking what the last action was in aid of as they were engrossed in saving her love's life she held her peace.

Finally, satisfied after assessing the situation and that all was in place, the surgeon lightly shook his hands before rubbing them together and interlocking his fingers. He glanced at all his nurses and nodded to them. "Ready?" he said.

"Yes," all replied in unison.